HARD-BOILED CHRISTMAS STORIES

10 TALES *of*
YULETIDE HOMICIDE

featuring A BRAND NEW CASE *for*
DAN TURNER
HOLLYWOOD DETECTIVE

REVERSE KARMA PRESS

Published by Reverse Karma Press
Box 133, Foyil, OK 74031 USA
www.reversekarmapress.com

HARD-BOILED CHRISTMAS STORIES

Nowhere is the old saw about scratching a cynic and finding a romantic better illustrated than in one of the very few truly American art forms, the hard-boiled detective story. It all began in the early 1920s, when the pulp magazine *Black Mask* introduced its readers to a new kind of cynical, sometimes violent, crime-solver who would eventually squeeze the polite ratiocinators from its pages. The heyday of the hard-boiled dicks ("dicks," we should point out, was slang for "detectives") mostly ended in the latter part of the '40s, when an ex-comic-book writer named Mickey Spillane introduced a brutish protagonist with all the sentimentality leached from his soul, and Mike Hammer became the prototype for a new generation of ultra-violent, heartless investigators, both private and public.

During those in-between years, though, hundreds of hard-boiled detectives fought their way across thousands of pages and into millions of hearts. They were usually men, often loners, and almost always suckers for a sad story, a lost cause, or a hopeless quest. One of the genre's stellar writers, Raymond Chandler, not only penned great tales but also wrote with commendable insight about the genre itself. To the British-educated Chandler, his Philip Marlowe was nothing less than a modern knight errant. Despite the fact that he was a hardscrabble commoner working the dark underbelly of the city for a few bucks a day plus expenses, the hard-boiled detective also had to be, as Chandler famously noted in his essay "The Simple Art of Murder," "the best man in his world and a good enough man for any world."

Like the knights, the classic hard-boiled detectives knew well how the world worked, that it was too often an ugly, unfair and brutal place that buried gentle virtues and kind gestures under spadefuls of smothering darkness. Unlike their medieval brethren, however, these guys masked their chivalry with sour quips and copious slugs from the always-handy bottles in their desk drawers. They understood that they were trying to make a decent living in an often indecent business, but it was more than that. Deep down, they wanted to help humanity, wanted to restore compassion and kindness to the world – wanted, say, for themselves and others to be able to enjoy Christmas like a kid.

We've collected plenty of examples in this volume. There's "Nothing for Christmas," for instance, in which the hardest cop on Broadway turns into a soft-hearted sap, cutting the cons and crooks on his beat a day's worth of Yuletide slack. And "Big Mike's Christmas Carol" gives us a hard-bitten loser whose life transforms after he slips on a Santa suit. The characters in *Hard-Boiled Christmas Stories* are often violent and desperate, but they're also susceptible to the cleansing power of innocence.

Not given to talking about themselves and their feelings, most of the hard-boiled detectives would've snickered – or worse – if someone had referred to them as "romantic naturalists." But that's what they were. The term comes from one of America's greatest novelists, who, while he worked different turf than the detective-story writers, crafted classic tales full of noble struggles against corruption, suffering, and maliciousness. "I consider myself a romantic naturalist," John Steinbeck once wrote. "I believe I can't really change things very much, but that in no way absolves me of the responsibility of trying."

The message is clear: Despite all the evidence to the contrary, you believe – or you want to. You want to believe things you know are goofy and unreasonable and wildly sentimental. You want to believe that justice will always triumph, that good will banish evil, that virtue will be rewarded. You want to believe the old department-store drunk with the line of kids in front of him is really Santa Claus, that the raggedy boy with his nose pressed to the glowing display window will get that electric train he yearns for, that the consumptive young woman with the brave smile will sell all her bows and wrapping paper and have enough money for a wonderful holiday dinner for her and her widowed mother. You want to believe in peace on earth and good will to all; you want to soak up the messages in the carols even as the rational part of your brain is telling you it's all hooey.

That's why hard-boiled detectives drink so much. That's why they crack so wise, so often. And that's why we thought a collection of hard-boiled Christmas tales would be a dandy idea.

* * * *

While some of you who find yourself reading this are, like us, longtime fans of the vintage escapist literature known as "pulps," we realize others aren't. Even though the term "pulp fiction" has become ingrained in our popular culture, we figure most of America doesn't really know what a pulp is – or was.

So here's a quick rundown:

Pulp magazines – so named because of their low-grade rough-paper pages – were popular all-fiction publications, featuring slick lurid covers, whose sole purpose was to entertain the masses. Although they first came along well before the '20s, and didn't really die out until the '50s, their years of greatest success came in the three decades we refer to in the first paragraph of this introduction. In that time, the '20s through the '40s, hundreds of different pulps blossomed on newsstands and drugstore magazine racks across the country, promising nothing but thrills to the potential reader with a dime or fifteen cents, the price of admission, in his or her pocket.

They weren't all, or even mostly, about detectives. There were general-interest adventure pulps like *Argosy* and *Blue Book,* but most of these magazines dealt with specific genres. Besides detective and mystery fiction, other categories included western, sports, romance, horror, air war, and hero, super- or otherwise. Some, like *Ranch Romances,* blended genres; others, including the short-running *Zeppelin Stories,* whittled its subject matter down to a nub. They were all alike, however, in that they presented unapologetically escapist fiction, offering readers nothing more than a few hours of respite from the stresses of home and work and life in general. Although good arguments can be made in favor of treating the hard-boiled detective stories as real literature – especially the ones crafted by the twin giants of the genre, the poetic and evocative Raymond Chandler and the tersely elegant Dashiell Hammett – their primary purpose was simply to entertain folks who liked a good story, well told.

With one exception, the tales you'll find here are taken from original detective pulps, all published between the 1920s and 1940s. Most, if not all, of these stories are appearing here in book form for the first time, and many represent some of the best work done by a group of writers whose talent and output combined to elevate them to a plateau just below the rarefied, Olympian stratosphere inhabited by Chandler and Hammett.

The exception is coming right up, as we present thumbnail sketches of the writers whose work comprises *Hard-Boiled Christmas Stories,* in order of their appearance:

– Robert Leslie Bellem (imitated here by **John Wooley**) was an incredibly prolific wordsmith who created one of the pulps' wackiest heroes, Dan Turner, Hollywood Detective, along with many other characters and one-off (non-series) stories. A Philadelphia native (born in 1905) with a railroad dick for a father, Bellem – like many pulpsters of his generation – started as a newspaperman and worked his way into fiction. While he became prolific in many genres, it was the Dan Turner canon that made his reputation. Told in an outrageously slangy first-person style, the Turner stories first appeared in 1934 and didn't go away until 1950, showing up regularly in a rather disreputable line of pulps that boasted titles like *Spicy Detective, Speed Detective,* and *Hollywood Detective.* When the pulps died, Bellem bounced right into television, where he earned a good living as a scriptwriter until his 1968 death.

Bellem knocked out hundreds of Dan Turner stories, but we were unable to find even one with a Christmas theme. So we wrote our own, intentionally aping the style RLB used in the Turner tales. We know this is a cheeky move, but (a) we really wanted Dan – one of our favorite hard-boiled dicks – in the book, and (b) Wooley has been associated with Bellem and the Turner character for some 30 years, having edited the first-ever book of Dan Turner stories (*Robert Leslie Bellem's Dan Turner – Hollywood Detective,* Bowling Green University Popular Press, 1983), adapted four Turner stories for an Eternity Comics series in the 1990s, and written a radio play based on the Bellem story "Homicide Highball." The latter became the basis for the 1990 made-for-TV movie *Dan Turner, Hollywood Detective* (aka The Raven Red Kiss-Off) – which Wooley also scripted – featuring Marc Singer as Dan and Nicholas Worth as his cohort, Lieutenant Dave Donaldson. In 2003, Wooley collected and introduced 13 Turner stories for Adventure House's *Roscoes in the Night.*

– John K. Butler was one of those top-drawer pulp scribes we alluded to earlier, a writer whose carefully crafted stories shone like gems in the pages of a number of the better detective pulps, including *Dime Detective, Double Detective, Detective Fiction Weekly,* and *Black Mask.* Adept at both plotting and characterization, Butler may be best known

for his tales of Steve Midnight, the hard-luck L.A. cabbie, whose fares always seemed to be dragging him into homicidal jams. All nine Midnight tales first appeared in the pulp *Dime Detective, Black Mask's* only real rival when it came to quality; the Midnights were reprinted by Adventure House in the 1998 book *At the Stroke of Midnight,* edited and introduced by Wooley.

Born in San Francisco, Butler grew up in Auburn, California, a town located in the Sierra Nevada Mountains. He apparently began working with Hollywood studios in the silent days, penning and editing scenarios, although his name has yet to be found on any screenplays from that era. Perhaps frustrated with the movie biz, he cracked the pulps in the mid-'30s with the hard-boiled series characters Tricky Enright and Rex Lonergan, the latter character based in the city of Butler's birth and known as Lonergan of Frisco.

Through 1941 Butler was a popular and prolific pulpster. But by 1943 he'd left the field for good in favor of a second go-round in Tinsletown. From 1943 through 1958, he wrote dozens of movies, mostly for Republic Studios, which specialized in westerns and other action fare. In the late 1950s, like Robert Leslie Bellem and other pulp veterans, he did scripts for episodic TV as well.

There may be nobody better than Butler at delineating that blend of toughness and sentimentality that colored the classic hard-boiled genre, and there may not be a better illustration of it than the Butler-scripted Republic film *The Streets of San Francisco* (1949), in which a dour, world-weary cop (played by Robert Armstrong) adopts a gangster's kid (Gary Gray) after gunning down his pop. Butler's story in this collection, the aforementioned "Big Mike's Christmas Carol," is also a prime example of the hard heart with a soft center, something this writer explored often and well.

Butler died suddenly, at the age of 57, in 1964, following a round of horseback riding.

– Among other achievements, **Steve Fisher** penned one of the most harrowing detective novels ever, 1941's *I Wake up Screaming*. The book was turned into a hit A-picture for 20th Century-Fox, starring Betty Grable, Victor Mature, Carole Landis, and Laird Creager. Undoubtedly boosted by the success of that adaptation, Fisher soon was earning screenwriting credits himself, notably for 1944's *Destination Tokyo*, which earned him an Oscar nomination.

The Michigan native had begun his writing career while in the Navy, selling fiction to service magazines like, appropriately enough, *Our Navy*. According to the *Encyclopedia of Pulp Fiction Writers* by Lee Server (Checkmark Books, 2002), once Fisher rejoined the civilian ranks, "he came to New York City at 21 with a duffel bag, a banged-up typewriter, and five dollars." At the time, the Great Depression had settled over America like a shroud, and Fisher struggled mightily for a long period before he began selling to the lower-end pulp houses and book publishers. By the late '30s, however, he was regularly featured in top detective pulps like *Black Mask* and *Detective Fiction Weekly*. We've chosen one from the latter publication, a grim, first-person narrative about a murder along Hollywood's temporary ode to the season, Santa Claus Lane. (It's also the setting for our final tale in this collection, William G. Bogart's "Murder on Santa Claus Lane.")

The movie studios paid a lot more than the pulp houses, so Fisher's pulp days were over by the early '40s. Interestingly, his film work includes scripting a pair of 1947 movies based on works by the two leading lights of the hard-boiled genre: *Lady in the Lake*, based on the Raymond Chandler novel and starring Robert Montgomery as Philip Marlowe, and *Song of the Thin Man*, featuring characters from Dashiell Hammett's classic book *The Thin Man*.

In 1980, Fisher died in Canoga Park, California. At the time of his death, he was 67 and a writer for the long-running TV series *Fantasy Island*.

– While many of the authors represented in these pages had some colorful experiences and unusual jobs outside of writing, none but **Henry Leverage** – as far as we know – spent time as a resident of the notorious Sing Sing prison. Leverage, in fact, was writing and selling stories to pulps and other publications while serving time in the crossbar Hilton for car theft, following three previous convictions. According to John Locke's bio of Leverage in *Gang Pulp* (Off-Trail Publications, 2008), Leverage was also the editor of *The Star of Hope*, Sing Sing's official publication, during his incarceration.

Born in London and raised in the States, Leverage lived a relatively short life, dying at the age of 46 in 1931 – just as the pulp era was undergoing a momentary lull before shifting into high gear. He made the most of his time on earth, however, knocking out hundreds of stories. One of them, a detective tale called "Whispering Wires," appeared in the prestigious non-pulp *Saturday Evening Post* before becoming the basis for a play and then a 1926 movie from the Fox Film Corporation.

As is the case with our John K. Butler's story, Leverage's contribution to *Hard-Boiled Christmas Stories*, "Crooked Charity," involves a con, kids, and a Santa Claus suit, and while the old wax-museum gag may strain the credulity a bit, the author's copious, if slightly messy, storytelling gifts keep it all moving at a brisk and satisfying clip.

– Most of what we know about **Lt. John Hopper** could well be bogus. Often, the pulps would ask one of their writers to supply a bit of biographical information that could be shared with the readers. Not quite as often, especially when the author was someone who hadn't really done very much of anything but write, the info would be embellished or cut out of whole cloth.

With that caveat, we present the biography, changing nothing but some eccentric paragraphing and a quotation mark or two, that originally accompanied our Hopper holiday tale. The bio and story – a saga of redemption, death, and reprieve on the night before Christmas – come from the Dec. 24, 1933 issue of *Detective Fiction Weekly*.

"Lieut. John Hopper, who wrote "Big City Christmas," is a West Pointer, an Army man, and one who has traveled far over the face of the globe. But he likes best the big city, where he can see and feel the drama that moves among crowded streets and crowded homes. It is in New York City that he is living now.

"He gets a nostalgia every once in a while for the far-away places, and the report of an uprising in South America is a red rag before this warrior at rest. His impulse is to take the next fruit boat going south to the hot countries. If it were not for his wife, he probably would...

"Lieut. Hopper was born in 1903, just too late to take a hand in the World War, though he tried and would have succeeded if his parents hadn't overtaken him. He went to West Point instead, and blossomed out a handsome shavetail in 1927. He resigned his commission in the Army later to devote his attention to writing. And he has been doing that ever since, between globe-trotting and dreaming of a general's job in a South American revolution."

About all we can add is that his pulp career appears to have lasted a little over a decade, from 1928 through early 1939. The last Hopper pulp story we can find is a hockey novelette, "Puck Shy," in the Feb. '39 issue of *Popular Sports*.

– Many pulp writers moved into fiction from newspapering, which goes a long way toward explaining the cynicism, world-weariness, and hard drinking that became

hallmarks of the hard-boiled detective genre. If there was anyone in the '30s more cynical than a pulp detective, it was a reporter – both often dealt with humanity at its worst and most brutal, often resorting to the quick fix of alcohol to pull the curtain on both the images and the realization that nothing they could do would ever change things very much.

Jack Kofoed was unusual in that he apparently never left his newspaper career to write pulp fiction full-time, instead balancing both pursuits for several decades. He must've been a man with a lot of energy. A December 28, 1979 obit, written by William Tucker for the *Miami* (Fla.) *News,* called him a "salty journalist" and noted that he had been a newspaperman for 67 years, beginning early at the *Philadelphia Public Ledger.*

Later, Kofoed became a sports columnist in New York, where, according to Tucker, "he rubbed elbows with such giants as Damon Runyon, Mark Hellinger and Heywood Broun." (Here, his two-character play "A Broadway Christmas Carol" owes as much to O. Henry as it does to Runyon.)

The *News* obituary gives short shrift to Kofoed's work as a pulpster, noting only that "he wrote an estimated 17,000 columns in his career, countless pulp novels and sports pieces for magazines" before retiring from the *Miami Herald* a few months prior to his death at age 85. But Kofoed appeared in the pulpwood pages many times, selling to everything from *Exciting Love* to *Popular Sports*. His character Baldy Simmons, a Broadway habitué who appeared in more than 30 stories in both sports and detective pulps, came squarely out of the mold originated to great acclaim by his old acquaintance Runyon, right down to the Great White Way milieu, colorful nicknames, and present-tense narration. Then again, there was a lot of that going around in the pulps of the '20s and

'30s, when readers couldn't seem to get enough of the actual Runyon short stories and their eccentric but lovable characters.

– A favorite of hard-boiled-pulp aficionados, **D.L. Champion** created three of the most memorable continuing characters in the genre, even though all three were so unusual – not to say *weird* – that their stories are told by their aides, who provide a kind of welder's mask to cut down the glare of their bosses' personalities. The one you'll meet in this collection, Inspector Allhoff, is probably the most outrageous of the trio, which is something to say, considering that the other two are Rex Sackler, dubbed the Parsimonious Prince of Penny-Pinchers – a private investigator whose stinginess knows no bounds – and Mariano Mercado, the Germ-Free Dick, an obsessive-compulsive detective who preceded TV's Monk by about 70 years. The world of the legless, bitter, coffee drunkard Allhoff is a dark one, and never bleaker than in "A Corpse for Christmas," which finds him on a vengeful quest for a murderer when his aides just want to be home for the holidays.

Born in Melbourne, Australia, in 1902, D'Arcy Lyndon Champion moved to San Francisco with his family as an infant. By 1920, he was in New York, and in final year of that decade, he began selling stories to the pulps. He'd keep going for more than 20 years, until the very end of the pulp era, ending up with hundred of stories to his credit. Most, but not all, fit into the detective genre and exhibit a uniquely skewed sense of humor.

Champion died in New York in 1968. His ashes are interred next to those of his wife, the newspaper journalist Eleanor Moorehead Champion – who outlived him by 17 years – in Columbus, Ohio's Green Lawn Cemetery. Columbus was Eleanor's hometown; coincidentally, it's the site of the annual pulp-magazine convention,

PulpFest.

In 2001, Adventure House published a full book of Allhoff stories, *Footprints on A Brain,* edited by Alfred Jan and Bill Blackbeard.

– **John Lawrence** is another name that belongs in the upper echelon of hard-boiled writers; his stories of the Broadway Squad, published in both *Dime Detective* and *Black Mask,* are tough little gems featuring no-nonsense protagonists not above bending the law to suit their own purposes. The hardest man in the whole outfit is its leader, Lt. Marty Marquis – known as the Marquis of Broadway – who's featured here, as mentioned earlier, in "Nothing for Christmas," a story that finds even a hop-headed stool pigeon sharing in the holiday cheer.

A native of Windsor, Ontario, (b. 1907) Lawrence moved with his divorced mother from Canada to New York City in the latter part of the '20s, where he found work on Wall Street. According to Francis M. Nevins, who includes an excellent and detailed biography of Lawrence in his book *Cornucopia of Crime* (Ramble House, 2010), young Lawrence, "in those feverish late 1920s, made a great deal of money in a very short time."

Then came the 1929 crash, which, according to Nevins, soured Lawrence on the world of business so much that he turned his back on the Street and focused his energies on trying to write for a living.

By the early '30s, Lawrence was seeing print in the pulps, and he continued to knock out stories through the late '40s, with time off for service during World War II as an officer in the Royal Canadian Air Force. After the war, with the pulps starting their long tailspin into oblivion, Lawrence found work in advertising and public relations in his home country. Suffering from both lung cancer and emphysema, he died in Toronto in 1970.

— Given his fame as the creator of one of our great pop-culture icons, it's easy to overlook the fact that **Johnston McCulley** created stories and characters in all sorts of pulp genres, including detective and mystery, using many settings beyond the 19th Century California inhabited by his immensely popular character Zorro (who first appeared in a pulp, *All-Story Weekly,* in 1919). Over the next couple of decades, while keeping the Zorro fans satisfied, McCulley wrote lots of stand-alone pulp tales, like "Quiet Christmas Morning," included here. It's an ironically titled yarn in which the protagonist, a longtime beat cop, receives a Yuletide surprise.

McCulley also created other continuing characters. While none came close to matching Zorro's impact, several were intriguing, and one – Thubway Tham, a lisping pickpocket whose stories traded on the Damon Runyon formula (see our Jack Kofoed entry) – is both outrageous and annoying, in approximately equal measure.

Born in Ottawa, Illinois in 1883, McCulley came to pulp writing from the true-crime publications; several sources indicate he worked for the *Police Gazette,* the hotcha national tabloid that was a staple of barbershops and poolrooms for most of the 20th Century. During World War I, McCulley served as a public affairs officer with the U.S. Army; the year after Armistice was declared, Zorro made his first appearance.

It's very likely that Zorro, and the film versions of the character's adventures, was one of the reasons McCulley moved to Los Angeles. Even as he continued to craft tales for the pulps, he began doing original stories for crime and action movies. McCulley died in L.A. in 1958, a year after Walt Disney Productions introduced McCulley's creation to the baby-boomer generation via the ABC-TV series *Zorro.*

— Serious pulp fans may know **William G. Bogart** (b. 1903) best for authoring more than a dozen of the novel-length adventures of *Doc Savage,* one of the most enduring of the pulpwood heroes, under the house name of Kenneth Robeson. But Bogart was also a dependable hard-boiled writer, not only in the pulps, but also in three novels about a private investigator named Johnny Saxon, (Altus Press reprinted the trio in a 2010 volume titled *Hell on Friday,* with an introduction by Doc Savage's current author, Will Murray.) As delineated by Bogart, Saxon had been a p.i. who wanted to write, and when he made his first sale – to the pulps, of course – he walked away from the detective racket. A few years later, he had hit a wall. Trapped in the pulps and unable to graduate to the so-called "slicks" (like *Saturday Evening Post* and *Liberty,* whose pages were made of higher quality paper than the pulps, slick instead of rough), which paid better and offered more prestige, he burned out and went back to detecting.

Bogart's time not only as a writer but also as an editor (for Street & Smith, publishers of *Doc Savage* and *The Shadow,* another famed hero pulp, along with many other titles) prior to his writing career, gave his Saxon backstory the ring of authenticity. Not only were his descriptions of the various permutations of the writing business right on the money; he also accurately described the mindset of the typical pulp author, who hoped to move into the slick magazines, the movies, or novels after paying his dues and learning his craft as a penny-a-word pulpster.

Bogart, whose Saxon books broke him into the hardcover market, continued to write for the pulps, mostly short stories, even as his novels were hitting the stands. His last book appears to be 1947's *Singapore,* an adaptation of the Universal-International movie starring Fred MacMurray and Ava Gardner, and his final few pulp stories also appeared in the late '40s. We've chosen one from 1943, "Murder on Santa Claus

Lane," a tale of a rookie cop, Scrooge-like villains, and sweet redemption on Christmas Day.

Bogart lived for three more decades after the publication of *Singapore,* passing away in 1977.

— We also want to acknowledge, with deep gratitude, the contributions of **David Saunders,** the wonderful artist who did our cover and the interior illustrations for "Santa's Slay Ride," along with designing our title and logo. Just as Wooley wrote "Santa's Slay Ride" using Robert Leslie Bellem's approach and language, David painted the cover in the style of H.J. Ward, whose outstanding girlie cover art attracted tons of customers to newsstand pulps — including many that featured Bellem stories. David comes by his talent naturally; his father, Norman Saunders, was one of the greats, whose contributions to our popular culture range from memorable pulp-cover paintings to classic trading cards like *Mars Attacks* and *Wacky Packages.* We highly recommend David's lavishly illustrated book about his father, *Norman Saunders* (The Illustrated Press, Inc., 2009).

With *Hard-Boiled Christmas Stories* representing the maiden voyage of Reverse Karma Press as a solo publisher, we were blessed and grateful to have the veteran pulp-oriented publishers **Neil Mechem** and **Leigh Mechem** on board to guide us through the waters and away from the rocks. They were professional, empathetic, and first-class in every way, and we appreciate their willingness to participate in this venture. Check out their lines of pulp reprints and other top-flight material at www.girasolcollectables.com

For other services rendered, advice given, and research assisted, we thank **Mike Chomko, Doug Ellis, Joel Frieman, John Gunnison, Alfred Jan, John Locke, Jeff Martin, Will Murray, Phil Nelson, Michael H. Price, Tom**

Roberts, Frank Robinson, and **Robert Weinberg.**

And, in addition to the sources already mentioned in the text, these books and websites helped us craft the biographies of our contributors to *Hard-Boiled Christmas Stories:*

BOOKS: *The Adventure House Guide to the Pulps* by Doug Ellis, John Locke, and John Gunnison (Adventure House, 2000); *The Black Mask Boys* by William F. Nolan (William Morrow & Co., 1985); *City of Numbered Men,* edited by John Locke (Off-Trail Press, 2010); *A Comprehensive Index to Black Mask,* 1920-1951 by E. R. Hagemann (Bowling Green University Popular Press, 1982); *Dime Detective Companion* by James L. Traylor (Altus Press, 2011); *The Dime Detectives* by Ron Goulart (The Mysterious Press, 1988); *Encyclopedia of Pulp Fiction Writers* by Lee Server (Checkmark Books, 2002); *Ghost Stories: The Magazine and Its Makers* (Off-Trail Press, 2010); *The TV Encyclopedia* by David Inman (Perigee Books, 1991)

WEBSITES: *Galactic Central* (www.philsp.com), *Hidalgo Trading Company* (docsavage.org), *The Internet Movie Database* (www.imdb.com), *The Nostalgia League* (thenostalgialeague.com), *The Thrilling Detective Website* (www.thrillingdetective.com), *What When How* (what-when-how.com), and, of course, *Wikipedia* (www.wikipedia.org)

— All that's left to say is thanks to you, for acquiring and reading this collection and thereby helping the hard-boiled detective to continue his two-fisted fight for literary survival in an often cold and indifferent world. We hope you don't mind if we convey our gratitude with wisecracks on our lips, shot glasses in our hands, and, despite ourselves, the spirit of the season in our hearts.

HARD-BOILED CHRISTMAS STORIES

SANTA'S SLAY RIDE

by John Wooley
(after Robert Leslie Bellem)

Illustrations by David Saunders

CHAPTER I
Dan Goes to a Party

SANTA HAD ME in his sights, his roscoe poised to perforate my giblets.

Technically, that's not quite correct. I was the party about to be drilled to ell-hay, all right. Not by *his* gat, though.

By *mine*.

They say when you're about to be croaked, your whole life zips before your eyes like a triple-feature's worth of flying tintypes. But the scenes pinwheeling through my noggin as I waited for the *ka-chee* that would mark my exit from this mortal coil didn't start at the beginning. Instead, my cranial cinema was flashing events from just a few hours ago, when I'd started on the path that ended me up here, ferninst a killer in a red suit and long white beard, whose ho-ho stood for ho-ho-*ho*micide...

THERE'S PLENTY of tinsel in Tinseltown year-round, but they lay it on with a trowel when it comes to the holidays. Every Yuletide season, nothing will do but for every nook and cranny from the high hills to Hollywood & Vine to be stuffed and smothered with angels and mistletoe and gingerbread gents, store windows lit up like noontime on the Gobi and stuffed with all manner of big-geetus geegaws designed to part people from their greenbacks. I'd seen it all, and now that I'd seen it, I was back home in my wikiup, a turned-down radio whispering songs of good cheer.

It wasn't that I didn't have any Christmas spirit. In fact, I'd already had a good helping of spirits, thanks to the pair of snifters of Vat 69 I'd quaffed before the sun could get over the yardarm. Why the hell not? I asked myself. The studios were all shuttered, so Dan Turner, Hollywood snoop, wouldn't be called in to trip through the backlots for at least two more days. And if I wanted to get good and sloshed, why, I'd just tab that a Yuletide present to myself.

So, I settled back in my sofa and reached for my jorum of skee, turning the radio up a little when a hot combo started swinging "Good King Wenceslas." I'd no more than corked the bottle when the phone on the end table jangled a discordant note.

It was Bernie Ballantyne, the corpulent head mukluk at Paravox Studios.

"Hey, Philo," he said. "You're needed."

"Says you," I snorted. "I'm on vacation. Or didn't you hear about the great big star and three sheep wranglers and all that happy hoo-hah?"

He didn't seem to hear me. "Lynda Lannon's throwing a big Christmas party for her kid," he barked, "and you're invited. You'll be hip-deep in moppets, but the nice check I'm giving you will make it all worth it."

"Moppets? Nix on that, chum."

"C'm'on, now. They're nice little Paravox kiddies. Why, even Sally Sunshine's showing up at the soiree."

I winced. Sally Sunshine may have only been ten years old, but she reminded me less of the wholesome little star Bernie's studio made her out to be, and more of one of the witches in *Macbeth*.

"Isn't it the wrong holiday for Little Miss Sunshine?" I asked. "Halloween was a couple of months ago."

"Very funny, Sherlock. Har de har. *Angel of the Alley*'s already grossed a couple million frogskins for us, and it's still clicking the turnstiles. You might even say she's paying your salary."

"Yeah, and Hitler took Poland. So what?" I lit a gasper, inhaled.

"Anyway, Solly's got a photographer headed that way, and he tells me Lousie Loganofsky promised to show up and do a story. I'm even going to play Santa."

"Sounds jolly," I said. "What's it all got to do with me, Bernie?"

"Just this. I heard from Solly a few minutes ago. Lynda just told him she'd been getting phone calls from Sidney. Bad calls. Then they stopped. She's worried that he's going to try to sneak in and see their kid — maybe even try to snatch him. And Tex is packing a gun. You know what might happen. Even if we could keep Loganofsky from writing about a dustup, it might hit the papers — especially if someone got hurt. That kind of publicity would send Solly off a bridge. I might join him."

I took a last long drag, snubbed the remains of the coffin nail into an ashtray. "And so, you want me—"

"To go out there and keep an eye on things," he finished for me. "Make sure Sidney doesn't crash the party. Don't let Tex's six-guns leave their holsters. Keep the peace. You know."

I paused, drained the glass of firewater in one burning gulp. "Sure," I shot back. "I'm a regular Gandhi. Except my diapers aren't back from the dry cleaner's."

"With the check you're getting, you can buy some new ones – and a box of 24-karat-gold safety pins to go with 'em," he said. "Ronnie'll be over with the car in a few minutes. I'm not quite ready, but she can haul you over and come back for me. I'd like for you to be there as soon as possible."

"All right, Bernie," I said.

"Thanks, Hawkshaw."

I nodded, wistfully eyeing the bottle on the end table. "Sure Bernie. And happy damned holidays to you, too."

As I STOOD by the window waiting for Ronnie Armstrong to blow in with a studio chariot, I mentally shuffled through the players I'd be meeting up with anon.

Paravox star Lynda Lannon was a brunette cutie with a figure that would stop a loaded trolley, and a pretty good egg, from what I knew. Her divorce from Sidney Snaith, the radio comedian known for his impersonations of famous folks, had been a real knock-down, drag-out affair. One of the casualties had been Lynda's aunt Loretta, a silent star who'd gone a little balmy in the crumpet even before her recent stroke, which people figured had been brought on by the rancorous split between Sidney and her niece. Rumor had it that Loretta hadn't been a big fan of the Federal Reserve System during the Depression, so a lot of her fortune supposedly reposed somewhere underneath the grounds of the estate she had shared with Lynda and her family.

No one knew for sure, except maybe the old lady herself. And she wasn't talking. Especially now, as she wheezed through her days and nights in a private sanitarium.

Tex Allison, a Gower Gulch cowpoke who'd made it big in the shoot-'em-ups, had replaced Sidney in Lynda's affections. It probably rankled the rotund radio comic even more to know that nine-year-old Rod-ney, the fruit of his loins, idolized the lanky Okie sagebrush star. And why not? Tex's oaters, cranked out one after another by a Gower Gulch outfit, packed junior wranglers like Rodney into Saturday matinees from Maine to Mexicali.

Then there was Solly Wise – or "So Solly," as he was known around the studios. A reedy little gink who didn't look like he'd push a baby duck in the water, he always seemed to be apologizing for something. But it was all an act. So Solly was one of the smartest press agents in the biz; he'd figured out that bowing and scraping could get him what he wanted a lot faster than playing the hard guy. He seemed meek, but he would've croaked his own grandma with an axe handle for a big fan-mag spread on one of his flock.

A horn honked outside my wigwam. It was the Paravox buggy. And at the wheel, a redheaded wren who had the oomph to be a moom-pitcher star instead of what she was – Bernie Ballantyne's latest "assistant," and, by the bye, a former squeeze of one Dan Turner, Hollywood gumshoe.

CHAPTER II
Season's Bleedings

RONNIE ARMSTRONG sat behind the wheel of the purring roadster, a cap perched jauntily on her head. Even in chauffeur's livery, she had more curves than a scenic railway, and the 100-kilowatt smile she offered me showed a row of choppers white as polished ivory. I reached automatically for the back-door handle.

"I'm supposed to do that for you, Sherlock," she said as she hopped out of the expensive flivver and wrenched the door open. "I'd rather have you up front with *me*, though."

Suddenly, she grabbed the front of my shirt, fed me an osculation that sent hot coals tumbling down my gozzle. Her firm tiddlywinks pushed invitingly against my chest. It lasted just a couple of seconds, but I was dizzy as a waltzing mouse when she let me go.

"Whew, beautiful," I said, reaching for her. "How about best two out of three?"

"Nix," she grinned. "One more, and we may never get there. This is a professional visit, you know. And I've got to fetch His Highness as soon as I drop you off. He doesn't like to be kept waiting."

I folded my six-foot-plus, 190-lb. frame into the back seat. "All right," I said. "But I sure enjoyed our little voyage down Memory Lane."

For the past several months, Ronnie had been Bernie's exclusive property, the newest quail in his flock. Bernie's "assistants" were usually beauteous young she-males like her, the kinds of gals who'd be pageant winners back in their hometowns but were two-bits a dozen in Tinsletown. So, sure, they played up to Bernie. It beat slinging hash. And in return, he gave them jobs, plenty of geetus, and, every once in a while, a supporting part in a Paravox picture.

Bernie was funny about his women, though. As long as they were his "assistants," he demanded complete fidelity. If he caught – or even heard about – one of his harem going out on him, her heels'd be clicking on the bricks outside the Paravox gate before the next morning's sun peeped over the soundstages.

So when Bernie had recruited the Armstrong jane, I'd crossed out her name in my little black book. Bernie didn't scare me, but there was no sense upsetting the applecart. She wasn't the only one cashing Ballantyne's checks.

We made small chatter until she pulled up in the circular driveway of Lynda Lannon's tony igloo, winked goodbye, and left me standing there breathing exhaust.

The shindig was already underway on the grounds; in the setting sun, I lamped the figure of Little Miss Sally Sunshine, bullying the rest of the kids into playing some game or other. Her stage mother, who was built like a longneck squash, hovered nearby, making sure the other kiddies did whatever her darling little meal-ticket wanted.

Solly Wise, standing off a few paces from the crowd of tykes with a photographer by his side, was the first to spot me. He came scurrying over, grabbed my hand in his flaccid one, shook it like he was trying to prime a pump.

"Dan, Dan, thank you for coming out," he bleated. "And I've got to beg your forgiveness for bringing you here on Christmas Eve. I tipped Bernie after Lynda told me about Sidney's threatening calls, and how they'd stopped a couple of days ago. She's scared, I just couldn't stand the thought of something happening, especially with Vultur – er, Louise Loganofsky, on her way–"

"So you're the ginzo responsible for putting the quietus on my holiday cheer," I began, balling my hand up into a fist. "Why, I oughta..."

He took a couple of steps back, sudden fear in his glims. "Y-you're just kidding, right?" he asked. "You – you wouldn't really–"

He never got his answer, because just then I felt a cool hand on my shoulder, sniffed the fragrance of exotic perfume. I turned to see Lynda Lannon and her beau, Tex Allison, sauntering up behind her.

"Hello, Mr. Turner," she said, bussing me a sisterly one on the cheek. "Merry Christmas. Thank you for coming."

Tex nodded at me, stuck out his big lunch hook. He'd traded his ten-gallon chapeau for a red-and-white Santa hat, but the waist-high bulge under his coat told me he hadn't left his shootin' iron back at the ranch.

"Mr. Turner, I'm pleased to make your acquaintance," he drawled. "Would you like to come in and have a drink?"

I said that sounded like a right smart idea.

LYNDA'S BUTLER, a ginzo named Bunter, was on hand to dole out the giggle water. A cross-eyed gent who reminded you of Ben Turpin, he'd been around since the silent days, butling for Loretta Lannon, Lynda's aunt, for as long as anyone could remember. That didn't stop people from wondering about his Hun heritage, though, since there seemed to be a Nazi under every bed these days; whispers around town tabbed him as a Fifth Columnist.

Ratzi or not, he poured a first-rate drink.

We sat around all cozy while the Lannon twist spilled the goods on her ex. "He wanted to – to take Rodney away for a couple of days. Said he wanted to go fishing at Catalina with his son, think about his future. He says the network's talking about canceling his show.

"I can sympathize a little, even though Sidney's a snake in many ways. But I didn't feel it was... wise to let him have Rodney right now," she added, her blue glims flashing to her cowpoke for support. He reached out and covered up her hand with his own big paw.

"He – he's unpredictable, Sidney is – especially now that his program might not be renewed. So I kept putting him off. He was calling every day – and then the calls stopped. Not hearing from him, I think, is worse than hearing from him."

"When's the last time he dialed you up?" I asked.

"A couple of days ago. I happened to mention it to Solly today – the fact Sidney hadn't called, I mean. I told him I was worried. Well, you know Solly."

"Sure," I returned, motioning to the cross-eyed pantryman for another serving of skee. "Solly doesn't like trouble. So he dials up Bernie, Bernie jerks me out of my holiday reverie, and I have to ankle my nice cozy hogan on Christmas Eve."

She got up then and gave my shoulder a pat. The toilet water she sported did things to my smeller. "Thank you," she said.

"Don't give it a thought, toots," I returned.

It was getting dark outside, so she and her waddie excused themselves and headed out to corral the kiddies. I held up my empty snifter again, shook it. But the butler was already by my side. He'd taken on a furtive look.

"You – you're a detective," he whispered, looking around to make sure he wasn't being overheard.

"That's me. Dan Turner, private snoop."

"Do – do you know much about the law, Mr. Turner?"

"I try to stay away from it as much as I can," I said.

He looked uncertain, then motioned me toward the kitchen. "I – I think I can trust you," he whispered, a trace of the Old Country in his voice. His off-kilter orbs seemed to be revolving as he led me back toward the ample pantry and up the back stairs toward a room that I immediately tabbed as his own crib. He pushed open the door, hit a switch, and light spilled onto an immaculately clean room that was just about big enough to turn around in. Reaching in his front pocket, he came up with a folded slip of paper, held it out.

"I'd like to get your professional opinion about – this," he hissed, his eyes going every which way as he reached behind me to close the door.

Suddenly, he froze. Then a mountain fell on my head. I crumpled up like a ball of newsprint, swayed, felt hands under my coat. In a twinkling, a roscoe sneezed *ka-chow!* right beside my noggin. The last thing I saw was the liveried flunky grabbing his perforated midsection, catsup squirting over his digits – and an arm with a red sleeve grabbing the paper from his hand.

He hit the floor a second before I did. And even as I drifted to dreamland, I knew the Bunter blister was as dead as last year's Christmas tree.

CHAPTER III
Hide and Go Shriek

I AWOKE to a caterwauling that could've rattled a skeleton, accompanied by something hard poking repeatedly at my schnozzle. Trying to bring my glims into focus, I lamped young Sally Sunshine's distorted face above me, frozen in a scream. That didn't stop her from taking a few more good whacks at my smeller with the toe of her patent-leather shoe.

"Nix," I said, grabbing her foot as it made for my map again.

"Eeeeeeeeek! Helllllpppp!" she yodeled, looking from me to the defunct butler and back again. "Murrrrderrrr!"

"Shhh! Easy now, sis." I pushed myself up to a sitting position, felt the lump on the back of my conk. Someone had walloped me a good one, all right. I blinked, saw a few more kids, including little Rodney, huddled up behind her, looking at me like I was made of ectoplasm.

I still held Sally Sunshine's foot, and when she opened her mouth to scream again I gave it a little twist and hissed "shhhhhhhh!' again. This time, she piped down, looked at me like she'd stepped on a frog.

Releasing her, I started to ask her what was going on, but that was the exact time her gourd-shaped mama chose to rush into the room, take in the scene, and let out a wail herself. This started Sally going again, and I jumped up with as much haste as I could and whammed the door behind them both. On the way back, I realized my roscoe was AWOL. Whoever bopped me had snatched it, which suddenly explained the hands I'd felt on my person as I hit the deck.

"Hold on!" I shouted to the big-eyed assembly. "No more noise."

"Are you going to kill us?" asked Rodney.

"Not if you behave," I said.

"Is – is that man d-dead?" gulped Mother Sunshine, pointing in the general direction of the heap on the floor with one hand and clutching at her daughter with the other.

"Unless he sleeps with his eyes open, lady. But getting loud about the situation isn't doing anyone any good." I took in the quavering kids with one gaze. "So how come you tykes chose *this* room to invade?"

A few seconds ticked off before Rodney spoke up. "We – we were playing hide and seek. Sally was it – of course." A dark look passed over his young face. "She came looking in this room, and – and..."

"I saw *you!*" finished Sally Sunshine, pointing her rigid little digit at me. "Right there next to that stiff!"

I'd started to tell the little she-devil that she'd been taking in too many detective pictures when Ronnie and So Solly burst into the room. When they lamped the unmoving butler and the red-stained front of his shirt, both of them let out a gasp. So Solly ran quickly to the door and looked out of it as though he were being chased by a platoon of gyrenes. When he turned back around, his face was white as tapioca. He snicked the lock.

"Vultura just arrived," he hissed. "That big nose of hers can sniff out a scandal a mile away. Quick! We've got to hide the body!"

He grabbed the stiffening hands of the defunct butler as though the body were a sack of chicken feed, started dragging it toward a bed several feet away, in the corner of the room. The movement left a corpuscular smear on the floor.

So Solly had a lot of energy for a little guy. Before you could say Jack Robinson, he'd shoved the corpus delicti under the bedframe and kicked a throw rug over the bloodstains. Then, he addressed the kids, who stood as still as statues – even Miss Sunshine had zipped her yap.

"Now look, kids," he said in a syrupy voice. "There's been an accident here. That's all you need to know. Right now, it's just a secret between you and Uncle Solly, okay?"

The Sunshine moppet found her voice. "What about these?" she asked in a hard-boiled way, indicating Ronnie and me. "You gonna bump *them* off, too? Or did *this* guy – " She shook blond curls at me. "– do the deed? Maybe you're *both* in on it."

So Solly looked like he'd be delighted to wrap his thumbs around her windpipe and squeeze until the sun peeped up, but since she was Paravox's biggest little draw and he was the studio's press agent, he gulped down his pique and bent his knees until he was face to face with her.

"Now, Sally," he said, "your Uncle Sol didn't bump anybody off. Neither did your Uncle Dan. We'll find out what happened later, but right now –"

"What *happened?*" she interrupted. "Hell's bells, mister – can't you see he was *croaked?*"

So help me, I was starting to like the little dame. She'd sure gotten over her case of the quivering pips in a hurry. Now, she was playing it hard as an eight-minute egg.

"You shouldn't swear, dear," said her mother, whose lamps kept flickering toward the bed and the unseen lump underneath.

"Hell," returned Sally, "it scared the _____ out of me. What would *you* do?"

The scene was interrupted by a thump against the locked door. It sounded like someone had dropped a bag of rocks from four stories up.

"It's her," hissed So Solly. Stretching to his full height, which wasn't all that impressive, he took in the room with one glance. Keeping his voice low, he said, "Now, kids. You're all good little actors and actresses – and here's your scene. Nothing happened here, you were up in this room because... because..."

"We were playing hide and seek, like Rodney said," offered a rawboned boy in a flannel shirt. "That's really the truth, Mr. Wise."

"Okay. Okay," he said. "You were playing hide and seek. Sally found you and let out a scream. Perfect. Places, everyone."

The door danced from the pounding it was taking.

"One more thing," he whispered. "If you stick to the script, and you don't tell any of the other kids, or anyone else, about the – unfortunate thing that happened here, Santa will be extra nice to you. Get it?" He gave Sally's mother a glance. "That includes you, Mrs. Shifferdecker. And you know how deep the jolly old elf's bag can be."

She gulped and nodded, along with a few of the kids. Solly winked broadly and went to the door, flinging it open. "Well, Miss Loganofsky – what a wonderful surprise," he enthused.

The doorframe darkened with the bulk of gossip columnist Louise Loganofsky, known behind her back as Vultura. A big hefty dame, she wore a flowing dress that could've been designed by Omar the tent-maker, with her trademark orchid pinned atop her ample bosom. It was so big it looked like it might jump out and suck your face off if you got close enough to her.

Which no one in the room wanted to do. Everyone except me and Little Sally Sunshine stepped back a pace when the over-stuffed twist heaved her tonnage through the portal.

She took in the scene, let her malevolent eye fall on Solly Wise. "Well, well, well," she clucked. "What's going on in here, Solly?"

"Just an innocent childish game of hide and seek, played by some of Paravox's brightest young stars," he said. "Right, kids?"

They all mumbled and nodded, except for Little Sally, who looked like she'd been sucking alum. Ronnie shot a glance at me that said, *Think the old bird's buying it?* I shrugged, pulled my hat down over the back of my head to cover the lump.

Vultura Loganofsky took a couple of

steps, peered at the surroundings as though she had x-ray vision. It could've been my imagination, but she seemed to fix her focus a little too long on the bed that covered the remains of the perforated pantryman.

Quickly, So Solly stepped in front of her. "All right, kids," he said with forced frivolity. "Let's get downstairs and see if old Santa's ready to dole out the goodies." The moppets and Sally's mother, stuck to her papoose like mucilage, obediently began filing out of the door. Only a couple of them looked back with trepidation in their glims.

Solly stage-whispered to the big Loganofsky bim, "It's Bernie himself handing out the presents, Vul – er, Louise. Heartwarming story, eh? Big studio head takes time from his busy Christmas Eve schedule to play Santa? Make a great spread, wouldn't it?"

She harrumphed once or twice, and then allowed So Solly to take her ample arm and guide her out of the room. As they exited, he turned back to look at us, rolling his eyes like Mantan Moreland. Sally Sunshine looked back too, still wearing her screwed-up pan.

As soon as that door clicked shut, I felt my knees turn to gelatin. I didn't care if there were a dozen corpses, a regiment of storm troopers, and Beelzebub himself under that bed, I was headed there. I needed to lay my conk on a pillow for a few minutes and go over things – and try not to think about the gremlins hammering on the back of my skull from the inside.

CHAPTER IV
Santa Comes Early

I SANK into the deceased butler's mattress, closed my eyes, tried to picture what had happened in the room just before I'd taken the knee-bending whack to my melon. The cross-eyed gazabo had wanted to show me something, some piece of paper. He'd been mighty secretive about it,

too. What could it have been? And who could have taken it?

I don't know how long I'd been stretched out, trying to dope things out, when Ronnie's mellifluous tones cut through my reverie. I'd forgotten she was there.

"Dan?" her voice tinkled.

"Yeah, hon," I muttered.

"Are – are you hurt bad?"

I kept my eyes shut as I answered. "I'll probably live. Luckily, they hit me in the head."

"That's good. What are you going to do about – all this?"

"Right now," I said, still not moving a muscle, "I'm going to lie here a while. Then, I'm going to get up and call Dave Donaldson down at homicide."

"Oh."

She was silent for a little bit. When I heard her voice the next time, it was right above me.

"Dan?" she said again. "Dan? Are you asleep?"

I blinked, opened my peepers. Her face swam above me. It took a minute before I realized she was holding a sprig of mistletoe.

"When I saw you this morning," she said huskily, "I knew it couldn't ever be over between us. K-kiss me, Dan."

Throwing her chauffeur's cap aside, she let her titian tresses fall free as she leaned down and fed me a smacker that slithered all the way down to my toes.

Sure, I was about half-conscious and there was a defunct guy under the bed. But I wasn't the one who was croaked – and anyway, Ronnie's osculations could've made the dead get up and dance a jig.

"C'm'on, Dan," she whispered, feeding me another jolt of current. "Kiss me like you mean it."

I did, and I'll tell the world I meant it. After all, it was the season for giving, and she had mistletoe, and – and after all, what the hell...?

LATER, I stood over her, lighting gaspers for both of us. She lay back on the bed, as contented as a pussycat.

"Do – do you have to go *now?*" she asked teasingly.

"Yeah, toots. It's been swell and all that, but I've got work to do."

She took my hand. "All work and no play – "

"– makes Dan a wad of lettuce," I finished.

"Are you going to call that policeman now?"

"In a couple of shakes. First, I've got to take Lynda Lannon aside, give her the scoop. Unless So Solly broke the news to her, she's still in the dark."

"Can't it wait?" she purred.

I lamped her there, stretched out like a siren on the rocks, a come-hither look in her glims. Then I remembered the late Bunter who lay a few feet underneath her.

"Rain check, baby," I said. "But not here. In fact, you'd better get up and out before the Cossacks come."

She pouted. On her it looked good.

Flashing her a grin, I ankled the room, hotfooted it downstairs, where Santa was already doling out brightly wrapped packages to the Paravox kiddies. A couple of them cast worried glances at me as I approached. Sally Sunshine didn't notice; she was busy ripping the ribbons off a box as big as she was, standing just on the other side of a huge evergreen with lights that twinkled like stars and made a canopy over Old Saint Nick and the line of youngsters.

So Solly, even more nervous than usual, hovered around the proceedings like a hummingbird on helium, making sure the Logan gossipmonger had a good view of the proceedings and plenty of food and drink to toss down her ample gozzle. He gulped when he saw me, turned back quickly and fussed some more with the corpulent columnist.

I approached Lynda and her tall cowpoke, who both stood watching the proceedings. There was a worried look on her beautiful pan.

"I can't find him anywhere," she was whispering to Tex Allison. "I just don't understand it."

"Aw, don't worry, Lynda. He'll turn up."

I eased into the conversation. "Would you happen to be talking about your butler, sis?"

"Oh – why, yes, Mr. Turner," said the beauteous she-male. "Have you seen him?"

"I'm afraid so," I whispered, motioning them both outside. After we'd ambled out onto the patio and stood under the clear quiet night sky, I said, "Your man is serving spirits to spirits now."

"What?" Lynda asked, looking from me to Tex.

"He's defunct, hon. Croaked. Dead as Tojo's conscience."

"Oh, n-no." She put a hand to her kissable piehole. "Wh-what happened?"

I related the events of the past hour, told her we'd have to call in the gendarmes.

"I don't want to wreck the party," I said, "but maybe I can get Dave Donaldson to soft-pedal it a little, at least until old Vultura Loganofsky has flown the coop." I didn't know what the chances were of Dave cooperating – usually, he charged into killery like a bull after a picador – but we were chums, and he might be persuaded to see things my way.

"Incidentally," I said to the Allison blister, "any sign of Lynda's ex?"

"Nope. I been keeping both eyes open, too."

"Y-you don't think – no, Sidney *couldn't* have done it," the Lannon frail murmured. "He *liked* Bunter."

I shrugged. "We'd better get back to the party before Vultura's big smeller starts twitching our way. Point me toward a phone, and I'll put in the call."

A minute or so later, I was dialing up headquarters. I got Dave on the second ring.

"Donaldson. Homicide," he growled.

"Turner talking," I said. "Hoist your didies up to Lynda Lannon's domicile, and bring a meat wagon. There's a punctured cadaver here with your monicker on it."

Donaldson grunted. "How do you manage to keep turning up stiffs, anyway? Everywhere you go, somebody croaks."

"It's a gift, Dave. And look – can you be a little subtle? There's a kiddie Christmas get-together going on, with Santa and everything. You wouldn't want to upset a houseful of little angels, would you?"

"With a freshly iced stiff cooling on the premises, you're worried about ruining a party for the kids? I'm touched."

"They don't know about the bumpee," I lied. "And Louise Loganofsky's here. If she finds out, *everyone's* going to know about it."

Dave muttered something and hung up, but not before I heard a *click* on the line. That phone must've been connected to others in the house, and someone had listened in.

But who?

I SLIPPED BACK into the spacious living room, headed toward Lynda Lannon, who was standing there by herself, watching old Santa and the kiddies. Before I could ask her where her tall drink o'water had hied to, he came tromping down the balustraded staircase, his hand on the gun-bulge in his shirt.

"I thought I heard something," he said.

I nodded and turned to watch the moppets, all queued up like midget tramps in a soup line. Kris Kringle, aka Bernie Ballantyne, sat in a big throne-like chair by the big twinkling tree, his face covered with the best whiskers the Paravox makeup department could produce, ho-hoing to beat hell. As the kids came by, he asked if they'd been good, and then reached behind him and shoved a package or two into their waiting mitts, with a studio photog snapping

pics as fast as he could change flashbulbs.

I took a couple of steps toward the scene, keeping an eye out. Santa saw me coming, looked up and winked –

And that's when everything went black.

CHAPTER V
Lights Out, Everybody

VULTURA screamed like a crow cawing, and someone else shouted. There was the patter of running feet, the rustle of clothing. It took me a sec to glom onto the fact that some citizen had shut down every light in the place.

"Hey, Keller," I yelled at the studio photog. "Start flashing those bulbs."

The studio snapper obliged, illuminating the scene for just a second. In that instant, I lamped huddled kids, a shocked-looking Lynda Lannon – and an empty chair where Santa had been. In two shakes, Keller had shoved another bulb in, ignited it again. This time, I glimmed a movement at the window and then heard breaking glass – some ginzo was trying to exit the premises the hard way.

I beat it for that spot, my hip pockets scraping carpet. Scramming to the window, I heard a *thump* outside, felt the cool air from the broken pane. I dove out.

There was enough of a moon to show me the scurrying shadow ahead. I automatically reached for my roscoe, not realizing for a moment that it had gone astray. Then my foot hit something hard and I sailed glutei over teakettle, my smeller plowing up freshly cut lawn.

"D-Dan?"

I turned, hoisted myself up. The Armstrong chickadee lay on the ground, holding her ankle.

"What are *you* doing here, sis?" I bleated.

"When the l-lights went out, someone grabbed me – dragged me out the window," she gasped.

"You get a look at him?"

"N-no. It was dark, and his head was turned. I b-bit him and he dropped me, kept running."

She looked delectable, lying there under the stars. But I shook it off.

"Okay, Don't go anywhere. I'll be back to check on you in a minute."

I turned to resume the chase, but she grabbed at my brogan.

"P-please, Dan. Stay with me a little while. I – I'm hurt. I think my ankle's bleeding."

My ticker went out to her, but I had a suspicious bozo to catch. Gently shaking her off, I pattered off in the direction of the window-jumper, shouting back, "Keep cool, toots! Help's on the way."

It was quiet in the Hollywood Hills that night, so I didn't have much trouble hearing the rustle of my quarry in front of me. Cursing myself for not having a gat, I ankled along as noiselessly as I could.

Still in a hurry, he changed directions, headed toward the big circular driveway in front of the Lannon domicile. I caught the sound of a car door being thrown open.

Whizzing around the side of the house, I lamped a bulk climbing into the Paravox buggy – the same one that had hauled me to this clambake. I covered the distance in a jiffy, wrestled the door open.

Two things happened then. All the lights in the house flashed on, and I saw Santa twisted around behind the jalopy's wheel, my .38 nestled in his mitt.

And that brings the story right up to date.

"SAY GOODNIGHT, snoop," sneered Saint Nick, his finger tightening on the trigger.

"Santa," I yeeped, playing for time, "what the hell's gotten into you?"

Suddenly, the scene was shattered by the sound of a chariot, screeching up the long drive on two wheels. Santa's eyes flickered toward the noise just long enough – I

whammed him a good one on the beezer, snapping his scalp back against the dash, and he rolled from the car like a sack of wet cement.

Dave Donaldson climbed out of his wagon, roscoe at the ready. Behind him, an ambulance came churning up the drive, rigged to haul away any remains that might be cluttering up the premises.

"Thanks, Dave," I said as he drew up ferninst my bulk.

He looked sourly at me, then at the inert citizen in the red suit, catching a few winks on the pavement.

"Santa Claus?" he said unbelievingly. "What the hell *is* this, Turner?"

Suddenly, there was a dull thumping that seemed to come from somewhere inside the studio carriage.

"And what the hell was *that?*" he bellowed.

"All will be revealed in good time, chum. Right now, send your corpse collectors out back, have 'em pick up a wren that's lying on the lawn. Her ankle's been perforated."

As Dave gave the appropriate orders to his minions, the partygoers began pouring from the Lannon abode. Big Tex was the first one to arrive.

"Someone threw the switch on the fuse box," he said breathlessly. "Knocked out all the electricity in the house."

"You knew where to find it though," I shot back. "Right?"

"Sure, it's in Lynda's garage. I threw it back on." His glims narrowed. "What –" he began.

"Never mind," I said.

In a moment, the whole houseful – absent the defunct butler – was on deck. The grownups crowded up front, the kids stayed in the background – even Sally Sunshine, who stood looking defiantly down at the conked Saint Nick.

"You ice another one?" she asked, fixing me with a suspicious optic.

"Nix, kid," I said.

"*Another* one?" Donaldson erupted. "What's she mean by that?"

"I'll tell you in a minute," I stalled, watching as the two ambulance cops arrived back at the scene, hoisting Ronnie between them. One of them dropped down, started feeling around on her gam.

When everyone was gathered, I held up a hand, started in.

"You all thought Santa here was actually Bernie Ballantyne," I began. "So did I. But, as the man says, looks are deceiving."

Bending down with a flourish, I swept the whiskers off St. Nick's pan. The Lannon quail was the first to recognize the snoozing figure of her ex.

"It's – it's Sidney!" said Lynda Lannon.

"Yep." I nodded. "I never thought much of his radio portrayals, but it turns out he's a damn good mimic. Being about the same size as Bernie, he found it easy to take his place – especially under a mess of fake white fuzz."

"But – where's Bernie?" Lynda persisted.

As if in answer, another frantic knocking came from the car. I stepped around to the back, turned the handle on the trunk, and out popped the Paravox bigwig like a Jack-in-the-box, gagged and trussed up like a bulldogged heifer, clad only in his underwear. It took just a second to pull the blindfold from his glims and the bandana from around his yap – which led to an eruption like Vesuvius.

"What? What the hell?" he sputtered, looking around. "Where in blazes am I?"

"Right now, you're in the trunk of one of your cars, Bernie," I shot back. "You've been hauled to Lynda Lannon's teepee. Who did it?"

He fastened his optics on Ronnie Armstrong. He was tied up and couldn't point, but he fingered her nonetheless: "You – !" he began.

"*Hold it right there!*"

Suddenly, Ronnie Armstrong's ankle was fine as frog hair. She was in such good shape that she'd been able to snatch a roscoe from the ambulance cop who'd been examining her. Now, she waved it around.

"Drop those rods!" she shouted at Dave and the other cop. "Step back!"

"Now listen, sister –" Dave began.

"I've already killed one man tonight – I can make it two!" she yelled.

Dave's gat plunked to the concrete, followed by his fellow cop's revolver.

She wavered a little then. "I – I didn't mean to kill him, though. It's just that he started making a fuss when Sidney grabbed the map from him. He could've ruined everything." She turned to me, the roscoe's muzzle still leveled at the cops. "So – so I grabbed your gat, Dan, and plugged him. Then Sidney took it, hid it in his Santa suit."

"I figured that much," I said. "And you and Sidney are sweeties?"

"F-for a long time now." She seemed to see the red-and-white lump on the driveway for the first time. "Is he – is he – ?"

"Nope," I said. "Just drifted off for a while."

I lamped Dave, watching her like an eagle, looking for his chance. So I tried to keep her talking.

"You craved what the Bunter blister had," I said. "Unless I miss my guess, it's a map that told you the location of the Lannon loot – buried by Lynda's aunt Loretta years ago."

"Y-yes," she said. "Loretta was still fond of Sidney, he visited her often. Then, last night, when he went by to see her in the sanitarium, Bunter was there. He didn't see Sidney, so Sidney eavesdropped, heard Loretta give Bunter the map. I don't know what he promised her he'd do with it; I imagine he's been trying to get it for a while. They say he's a fifth columnist, you know – maybe he wanted to give it all to Hitler."

"If he did, you deserve a medal, baby," I

returned. "So why don't you just give the rod back to the cops and – "

"No!" She drew it up again, waved it menacingly. "This wouldn't have happened if you hadn't been here! We knew Sidney couldn't just walk right in by himself, so we got the idea to have him impersonate Ballantyne –"

"What?" yeeped the trussed tycoon.

"Shut up!" she shouted back. "Sidney's a great impersonator, and we knew he could pull it off. It was easy. Sidney hid in the back seat when I went to pick up His Highness. Bernie never knew what hit him. Sidney got in the suit, and that was that. We hoisted him in the back so no one would find him; we intended to let him go later. I had a story all ready about being hijacked."

She shot another gaze toward Bernie Ballantyne. "The idea was to grab the map, take off as soon as we could, and come back later to dig up the money. With Sidney's show going off the air, we needed that cash."

She leveled her blue glims at me, her mouth a tight line. "But then *you* had to come along. I tried to... detain you as long as I could. But when I heard you call the cops, I knew we had to scram. I found the fuse box in the garage, and we made our escape. But then – *you* had to chase us! And I had to play hurt, try to give Sidney some time!"

There was a wild look in the Armstrong cookie's eyes now as she surveyed the situation. Then she turned back to me. *"You _____ !"* she hollered, and her roscoe sneezed *ka-chee!*

A lead pill split the ozone beside me, furrowed a shallow crimson ditch across Bernie Ballantyne's noggin, His toupee jumped off like a tarantula, leaving his bisected dome as naked as a baby's tender bottom.

I swiveled around to see why she had missed me at such close range, glimmed her wavering woozily on her pins, Dave

and his two hirelings had her firmly in hand, the roscoe plucked from her mitt. Behind her stood Sally Sunshine, waving a baseball bat, threatening to whack the Armstrong cupcake again.

I grinned, "Say, little miss, you pack quite a wallop."

"We have a box out at Gilmore Field," she said, still eying the half-conscious bim she'd bopped. "I like to root for the Hollywood Stars."

"And here I thought there was a doll in that box Santa gave you."

"Nope," she said proudly. "Baseball stuff. I'm gonna learn to hit like Babe Herman."

I looked at her Ma standing beside her. "I like the cut of her jib, lady." Then, to the moppet, "If you're still around Tinsletown in a few years, look me up, huh? I'd like to show you the town."

She winked like a gal twice her age before we were suddenly interrupted by a squawking from the Paravox buggy. So Solly and Tex were trying to untie Bernie Ballantyne, A couple of drops of hemoglobin from the grazing had wandered down his forehead, and he was screaming bloody murder. Maybe it was because of the noise, but down at my feet, the Snaith character was coming to with a groan. I bent over, plucked my purloined rod from his limp mitt.

"You'll live, Bernie," I muttered out of the side of my yap. "So will this gink."

A FEW SHAKES later, Dave was snapping nippers on the fins of Ronnie and Snaith, neither of whom seemed fully conscious. The kids and grownups were gathered around, all yakking at once, and Vultura was clucking about what a wonderful tale all of this was going to make, what with Sally Sunshine's heroics and all. You couldn't have made So Solly Wise any happier if you'd told him the war was over.

"One thing, though," Dave said. "How'd you glom onto the notion it was Snaith behind those whiskers?"

"It was just before the lights went out," I told him. "I was watching old Saint Nick distribute the booty, and I knew something was wrong. It took me a minute, but then I figured it. He was reaching for the gifts and handing them out with his right hand – and Bernie Ballantyne is *left-handed*."

A FTER the blowoff. Dave and I stopped off at a little bistro on Sunset for a couple of Yuletide jolts, and then we wished each other Happy Holidays and said sayonara. When I crossed the threshold of my hogan, the season's music was still playing low and soft on the radio I'd forgotten to turn off.

Uncorking the Vat 69, I decanted myself three fingers and settled in. There was a nice check in my pocket, I had a fifth of skee at my side, and I was somehow taking comfort from the thought of there being one less partridge in Bernie's pear tree.

The clock on the mantel bonged twelve, Christmas Eve was over for another year, and, in the Turner household, there was peace on earth, and good will toward every damned gazabo on the planet.

THE END

IN *GUN IN CHEEK* (Coward, McCann & Geoghegan, 1982), his excellent book about what he dubbed "alternative crime-fiction," the noted mystery author Bill Pronzini wrote, "Anyone whose sense of humor leans toward the ribald, the outrageous, the utterly absurd is liable to find himself convulsed by the antics and colloquialisms of Dan Turner... The list of Bellem admirers is long and distinguished and includes humorist S.J. Perelman, who in an essay called "Somewhere A Roscoe..." called Turner the "apotheosis of all private detectives," and said he was 'out of Ma Barker by Dashiell Hammett's Sam Spade.' Heady praise indeed."

(In the early 1980s, Wooley was denied permission by the Perelman estate to reprint the "Somewhere A Roscoe... " essay in his *Robert Leslie Bellem's Dan Turner – Hollywood Detective* collection; those who'd like to read the whole thing – and it's certainly worth it – can find it in *Crazy Like A Fox*, published by Random House in 1944 and later reprinted by Garden City Publishing Company, or in the more recent *Most of the Most of S.J. Perelman*, another Random House volume published in 2000.)

As is the case with many of Perelman's essays, he sang Dan's praises with an air of sardonic bemusement. But his and Pronzini's words go a long way toward summing up the enduring appeal of the wackiest private snoop to ever set foot in the genre: The Dan Turner stories are, simply, great goofy fun.

The fun began in June of 1934, when author Robert Leslie Bellem launched his most famous creation in the pages of a pulp called *Spicy Detective*. A little over 16 years – and hundreds of stories – later, Dan made his final appearance with three tales in the October 1950 number of *Hollywood Detective* magazine, which then expired.

The story you've just read, "Santa's Slay Ride," is the first new Dan Turner adventure to be published in well over 60 years.

Big Mike's Christmas Carol

Mike got into that outfit without wasting any time—but he enjoyed every second of it

A Most Unusual Novelette

By John K. Butler

Author of "Defender of the Doomed," etc.

One last haul, and then he'd retire—but the yegg from
Brooklyn didn't count on being fingered by St. Nick

CHAPTER I

Recruit for Crime

ONE night in January, after Rusty and me been out of stir about three months—just long enough for our hair to grow back—we squat ourselves in a Frisco beer joint and discuss what we can do to turn an honest dollar. It's no cinch problem; don't kid yourself. Here we are, Rusty and me, a couple of ex-cons, and between us we done time in Leavenworth, Sing Sing, Nebraska State Reformatory, San Quentin, and the United States Navy. With a stack of records like that you can't just walk into a bank and ask for a job as cashier. Somehow they don't trust you.

Well, we squat there, talking it over, and crying into our beer suds about how hard it is for an ex-con to get going again, and I've figured out several angles which I now tell to Rusty. I tell him we might crack a few slot machines, or snatch ladies' purses in the movie theaters, or roll drunks on Howard Street. All this goes over Rusty's head. By the expression on his pan I can tell he thinks I'm talking small potatoes, like getting a job on the WPA., and I can tell his mind is working in

16

larger figures. Rusty has a good head for business, and he don't bother much with small potatoes.

Finally he says to me: "Look, Danny. You're on the right track but you caught the wrong train. Our problem is we got to have money. And like you say, money is in slot machines, and ladies' purses, and drunks' pockets. But that's all small stuff. Suppose a guy wants some real money? Where does he go?"

I take a pull of beer, not answering, and finally Rusty answers his own question. "A guy that wants real money goes to a bank. A bank is where money is. He goes there and shows his pass-book and draws out some money."

"That's all fine," I says, "except it's been a long time since I owned a pass-book, and I don't own one now."

Rusty grins at me and winks. "I got a pass-book," he says. "I got it right here."

With that he pulls back his coat and gives me a flash of a forty-five Colt that he's wearing in a shoulder harness.

He says: "I got a pass-book for you too," and he nudges me under the table, and the first thing I know I'm holding a Luger automatic.

Well, I'm a little taken by surprise for him to go hand me a rod like that, in a beer joint, since it's very much against the law for an ex-con to go around heeled. I give the room a once-over to make sure nobody is watching me, and then I slip the Luger into my pants pocket and pull my coat over it.

I says to Rusty: "Yesterday you was just as broke as me. Where did you get the dough to buy these pass-books?"

"I didn't buy them," he says. "My mother give them to me."

I think that remark is supposed to be a laugh, but it ain't. It seems that Rusty's mother lives in Frisco, and the rods belong to Rusty's brother, Bert. However, Bert won't need them at present, so Rusty's mother thoughtfully loans them to Rusty.

"Look," Rusty says. "My brother had a bank all cased in San Clemente. It's a tin-can bank in a hick town. My mother says she can steal us a car, and she says it's a cinch for us to knock the bank over. The only trouble is we got to get another guy. One to drive the car—that's you. Two to go into the bank. I'm one that'll go in, but we need another."

I think that over, and finally I ask him: "Why don't we get Bert on the job with us?"

Rusty sort of hangs his head and stares sadly into his beer glass. "Bert can't go," he says. "Bert has this bank all cased, but in the meantime the cops nabbed him for rubbing out a pawnbroker up north. They give Bert the rope up there. He springs through the trap at six A.M. tomorrow morning. So that's why he can't go."

AFTER this night in the beer joint, I don't see Rusty Nelson for two days. The first day I know that him and his mother have to go to church in order to pray for Bert, who walks to the gallows right on time—like a train—promptly at six A.M. And on the second day I know that Rusty and his mother are busy trying to steal us a car, and trying to find us a guy to go into the tin-can bank with Rusty.

When I see Rusty again everything is all set. He says him and his mother don't have no trouble mooching a car and putting on it some license plates that won't be hot. In fact, the license problem is a cinch. This is the first part of January, and last year's license plates are still good. So after the car is mooched, Rusty's mother nips a set of plates from her next door neighbor. It seems the neighbor has bought himself plates for the New Year and has tossed his old plates onto a junk pile behind his garage. So Mrs. Nelson sneaks out and swipes the cast-off plates from the rubbish and puts them on the stolen sedan. These plates won't be hot, and are still good till the fifteenth of January, and the cops won't be able to check the stolen sedan.

So that fixes us up swell on the bank

job in San Clemente. We got pass-books, and a car with phony plates, and everything is swell except we don't have a third party to work with us.

In that regard Rusty says: "My mother wanted to go with us herself, but I told her a woman's place is in the home."

"Who's going, then?" I ask.

"I'm not sure yet," he tells me, "but I think we can fix it. Did you ever hear of Big Mike Williams?"

I tell him: "Sure, I met Big Mike myself when we was both in Leavenworth, though that was over ten years ago, and I ain't seen him since."

Now Rusty Nelson tells me: "Look. Big Mike is living on a ranch near San Clemente. He got paroled from Leavenworth five years ago, and he's living with some dame down there. I guess the dame has tried to reform him, but my mother thinks we can get Big Mike on the job with us."

"I used to know Big Mike," I says.

"Sure. I heard you speak of him. That makes it a cinch. We'll go down and talk to him. Tell him how my brother has the bank all cased."

I says: "It's too bad about your brother, Rusty."

Rusty shakes his head sadly.

"Yeah. He was a smart guy. You could always count on Bert to know the—"

"Ropes?" I ask.

Rusty looks at me very sore. "Don't talk like that," he says. "Bert sprung through the trap at six A.M."

WELL, the weather is very bad that day when Rusty and me drive down from Frisco. It's the seventh of January, and there's lots of rain. The rain washes the highway, drips down from the trees, but Rusty and me are very snug in the sedan which Rusty's mother mooched for us, and when we pass a few motorcycle cops we can give them the laugh, because our license plates ain't hot.

We get into San Clemente about noon. It's a hick town all right. Just a few stores and gas stations, and Rusty and me ain't looking for stores and gas stations, we're looking for the bank.

We take a look at it, and it's a cinch, just like Rusty's brother has said. It's such a cinch that I feel sorry Rusty's brother had to spring through the old mouse-trap before he got a crack at it. It's the kind of bank you could knock over with a kid's water-pistol and a couple of firecrackers.

So after Rusty and me take our gander at it, we drive out a muddy road for a lot of miles through the sticks, and finally we come to a farm house that has *M. S. Williams* written on the mail box. We figure that this here place is where Big Mike lives, and it's a very nice place compared with Leavenworth, Sing Sing, and the other places where Big Mike has lived.

There it is, a nice little wooden house, painted white, sitting among a lot of trees. There's an orchard, a barn, some chicken coops, and it all looks very nice and snug in the rain. I can see smoke coming from the chimney and I can imagine that Big Mike is squatting in there with his shoes off taking life soft.

So I says to Rusty: "It looks like Big Mike has gone soft. This here dame has reformed him."

Rusty parks the sedan and gives a laugh. "Once a hood, always a hood," he says. "You go in and talk to him. Tell him about the bank in the town. Tell him we want to knock it over before three P.M. Tell him how my brother says it's a cinch."

"Shall I tell him your brother is dead?"

Rusty gives me a nasty look. "Why do you always have to bring *that* up?"

ANYWAY, I go up to the house and knock on the door. Rusty squats out in the sedan, smoking, and the rain comes down like hell. I wait at the door, and pretty soon it opens, and I see Big Mike standing there with his shoes off.

"Hello," he says.

I can see right away that he don't remember me, so I tell him my name. He nods, like he knew it all the time, and I walk in past him into a big living room.

It's a nice place, all right. The chairs are soft, covered with cloth that has colored flowers stamped in it, and there's a log burning in the fireplace. There's also a Christmas tree with fancy ornaments on it, and kids' toys around the floor.

Big Mike sits down in a chair, toasts his feet at the fire, and says: "The kids don't want me to take the tree down. You can't blame them. I'm their Santy Claus, and they had a fine time at Christmas."

Well, it turns out that Big Mike has four kids. That's doing a lot in three years of marriage, but it ain't so bad as it sounds when Big Mike explains that two of his kids are twins, being born at the same time. So that fixes everything up.

Big Mike calls in his wife to meet me. She is a nifty little woman, and I figure Big Mike has done fine for himself since he got paroled from Leavenworth.

"This is an old friend of mine," Big Mike says to the dame. "Let's give him a cup of tea."

Naturally, I figure that this is supposed to be a gag, about fixing me with tea, and I expect to get a Scotch highball, or at least a slug of gin.

But Big Mike's wife comes back with something steaming in a cup, and, sure enough, it's nothing but tea. Then she goes away and leaves Mike and me alone.

Well, after we chew the fat for a while I spring the big news on him about knocking over the local bank, and he don't go for the idea at all. He says he keeps money there himself. I think he means he has some hot loot ditched in one of the safe deposit boxes, but it seems he don't mean that at all. He takes a little book from his pocket and shows it to me. Him and his woman got seven hundred dollars, in figures, in the bank. They made the dough off the farm, which they got as a present from the doll's father when she ups and marries Big Mike. And they're saving up this here money so when the kids grow up they can go to regular colleges, and

not the kind of colleges Big Mike himself has gone to, such as Sing Sing and Leavenworth.

So I see there is no use trying to do business with Big Mike. He has certainly become a reformed character, and as I start to go out I tell him I guess it's his wife that done it to him.

He shakes his head, gives me a funny look. "No, he says, "it ain't really Josephine that made me see the light. It happened four years ago at Christmas. You sit down again and have another cup of tea and I'll tell you how it was."

Well, I can see by his pan that he has something on his mind that he's just sizzling to tell about, so I forget about Rusty Nelson squatting outside in the mooched sedan, and I park my torso in the chair again, and listen while he tells me the damndest thing I ever did hear.

CHAPTER II

Casing a Job

IT SEEMS that up to Christmas of four years ago Big Mike admits to being a very nasty character.

Around Brooklyn, New York, where he growed up, he was the kind of kid nobody liked to be stern with. He always played hookey from school, and when he was twelve years old he was making twenty bucks a week shooting craps with the gas-house gang. In his spare time, mostly evenings, he picked up a little extra dough rolling drunks and breaking into pawnshops. When he was sixteen he had gone to reform school twice and run away twice. When he was seventeen he stood six foot one in his socks, though he seldom owned a pair of socks, and he weighed two hundred and ten. He never got enough fights to satisfy him, even though he went around picking them.

One time, when he was still seventeen, a cop tried to put the pinch on him for mooching groceries, and Big Mike rasseled him, and yanked the cop's pants off, and hung the cop's pants on top of a telephone pole. This, of course, made the cop very sore, running around without his pants, and he phoned for the wagon, and three other cops—it took four of them— cuffed Mike around, and worked him over, and finally got him tucked safely into the wagon.

So Mike was always getting in scrapes like that, and his favorite sport, when not in the hoosegow, was walking up to some cop, rasseling him, and pulling the cop's pants off and hanging them on telephone poles.

It only took a few years of this sport to give Big Mike a very bad reputation in Brooklyn, and finally things got so bad for Big Mike that he had to skip out.

So he moved around the country, picking up odd jobs here and there. He would pick up a bank job in Cleveland—maybe take it for around a thousand bucks—and then he'd move to Philly and knock over some stores. Being a hard-boiled character, many guys of the same nature got to like him, and they would cut him in on larger jobs, so Mike finally got in with some New York hijackers. That didn't turn out so good, and he had to serve a stretch at Sing-Sing-on-the-Hudson.

Well, all in all, Big Mike's career went on for years, and when he was thirty-five he got to thinking that things wasn't so hot. He was serving a seven-year rap in Leavenworth at the time, so he had lots of days and nights to think it over. He finally figured that he'd spent half his life in hoosegows here and there, and that it wasn't much of a paying proposition.

So after he got paroled from Leavenworth, five years back, he keeps on the level for his probation, and then he slides down to Los Angeles, which is a city in California where a hood can often pick up odd jobs.

In L.A. he teams up with a guy named Ace O'Brien, and it seems that Ace, like Big Mike, figures that there's no percentage in spending half your life in hoosegows. So Ace and Big Mike figure on going straight, but first they want to knock off one little job that will give them capital to start in some honest business, like bookmaking, or selling lottery tickets around Alviso Street.

WELL, it's the twenty-third of December, just before Christmas, when Ace O'Brien gives birth to an idea. He takes Big Mike by the arm and leads him through the downtown shopping district. The streets are jammed with people buying stuff for Christmas presents. Women elbow each other along, loaded with packages, and there's squalling brats, and every corner has a Salvation Army guy dressed up like Santy Claus and ringing a bell, and trying to collect pennies for the poor.

When Big Mike sees these crowds he thinks of all the purses he might snatch, but he don't snatch any, because it's Christmas season and Big Mike has enough character that he don't want to steal money from people that are buying presents and trying to make their families happy. Big Mike has a very soft heart in matters like this.

Well, Ace O'Brien leads Big Mike into the Seventh Street Department Store. This is a big swank store, twelve floors high, and the building uses up a whole square block. Inside, it is jammed with people buying Christmas presents, and when Big Mike thinks of all the dough the management is collecting, he begins to feel that it would be a swell thing to own a department store himself, especially around the Christmas season.

Ace and Mike ride a crowded elevator to the top floor, where the toy shop is, and Big Mike has never seen so many toys in his life. Electric trains, bicycles, toy bears, Indian suits, rocking horses, doll houses, roller skates—all the kind of stuff that the squirts go for.

The floor is crowded with kids running around yelling, and getting their mitts on things, and the mothers are having a hard time, what with carrying packages and trying to keep their kids from tearing the store apart.

Over in one corner is a fat guy dressed

up like Santy Claus. He wears a red suit and cap, and black boots, and phony white whiskers, and a pillow stuffed in his pants to make him look fatter. His suit is doodadded up with white fur, and it don't seem to Big Mike that the disguise would fool even a blind man, but the kids go for this fake Santy Claus in a big way. They think he's the real goods.

Well, Big Mike stands and watches this Santy Claus for a few minutes, to see what his racket is. It seems the big bum is hired by the store. He sits on a throne covered with fake snow, and the kids stand in line and wait to sit on his lap for a few minutes.

When a kid sits on the bum's lap, he thinks he is sitting on the lap of Santy Claus, who is a very important guy that the kids all believe in. They believe that all they got to do is tell Santy Claus what they want for Christmas, in the line of presents, and they will receive the stuff on Christmas morning.

Of course, Big Mike knows that the Santy Claus business is just a racket meant for the kids, and that some hard-working John will have to buy the bicycles and skates and hide them under the Christmas tree for his kids. Big Mike knows for sure that this here bum hired by the store ain't going to go out Christmas and give away presents. The bum will probably be sitting in some beer joint, getting drunk, and the store will send a bill to Honest John on the first of the month, and he will have to pay for the presents the kids think they got from Santy Claus.

Well, Big Mike stands there and sees how the racket works. Each time a kid goes up and sits on the knee of this phony Santy Claus, at the same time the kid's mother comes up and parks nearby.

This heel that is supposed to be Santy Claus says to the kid, very friendly—like he is giving things away free: "What would you like for Christmas, young man?"

And the kid says, for instance: "I want a bicycle with red wheels, and a headlight, and a horn."

So Santy Claus says: "What is your name and where do you live?"

The kid is a sucker, of course, and gives him the information. Santy Claus writes this down in a notebook so that the store will know where to deliver the bicycle and where to send the bill.

Well, Big Mike watches this racket and thinks it's a very lousy trick for the store to pull, because maybe some of these kids have an Old Man, some Honest John, who can't pay a bill, even for a toy for his kid.

So Big Mike is kind of sore.

In the meantime, Ace O'Brien is tugging on Big Mike's sleeve, and Ace says: "I didn't bring you up here to look at the toys, you big goof."

"Then what did you bring me up here for?" Big Mike asks. So Ace tells him.

IT SEEMS that while this whole floor seems to have nothing but toys and the Santy Claus racket, there is also a section which is the business office for the store. Behind some glass partitions the bookkeepers are at work chalking up the gravy, and the money all comes up here from the other floors and is put in a safe.

Ace explains the layout to Big Mike. "Look," he says. "This is a cinch to knock over. I been watching it careful, and I figure they handle about twenty and thirty grand in cash through this business office. The rest is charge accounts, and the Old Man don't get his bill till after Christmas. We don't care about the charge accounts. If we knock this over about four o'clock tomorrow afternoon, we can walk away with about ten grand. When the big money comes up, they put it in a safe. But about ten grand is always wandering around the office in the late afternoon, while they fix the books. So me and you stick it up, and then we lose ourselves in the crowds. There's always so damned many people in the store, the cops won't know where to look. We can slip downstairs in the elevator, or the escalator, and then we're free and we got about ten grand to start an honest business."

CHAPTER III

Santy Claus Racket

WELL, this proposition sounds fine to Big Mike, and together they work it out careful. They study the floor till they know exactly how they can work it, and the next afternoon they hang around the toy shop, waiting for a chance.

Both of them are all rodded up. Big Mike has a Colt .44 stuffed down his belt, under his coat, and he carries a Smith and Wesson revolver loaded with tear-gas cartridges in the overcoat that is carefully folded over his arm. Ace O'Brien has a sawed-off shotgun concealed under his overcoat, which he is wearing, and he has an old Iver Johnson in the pocket of his pants.

They hang around there for an hour, pretending to be buying toys for kids which neither of them has got, and all the time they keep a slant on the business office.

Finally, they lamp a punk with a canvas bag in his hand. Right away they know it is more dough from the other departments in the store.

So Big Mike gives Ace the nod, and they both push into the business office. Big Mike pulls his tear-gas gun and lets fly. Ace O'Brien yanks out his sawed-off shotgun, conks the punk over the head with it, and then he points the gun at a dozen other employees in the room.

Ace is very calm, and he says: "All right, folks, this is a stick-up."

Big Mike's tear-gas takes out four of the opposition, crying into their hands, and the rest of them put their mitts up over their heads—all except one.

The one that is tough is a dame. She is about twenty years old, and she's got a build on her like a strip-teaser in the Follies. At first Big Mike thinks she is just some little tramp with a lot of nerve, but when he looks into her eyes he knows she is a nice girl.

It so happens she is powdering her nose when the two hoods barge in, and she throws the box of powder into Ace O'Brien's pan. This blinds Ace more than the tear-gas blinds some of the others. Ace can't see a damned thing. He backs up, rubbing his eyes, and he falls over a chair, and his gun roars like a cannon and brings plaster down from the ceiling.

Big Mike steps over and jabs his Colt .44 at the little dame. "Don't get tough, sister," he says, "or I'll whittle you down!"

That don't scare her a bit. She stands right up to him while he presses the Colt into her tummy, and she has red hair and green eyes, and the gun don't worry her.

"Go ahead and shoot, you rotten thing!" she tells him.

Naturally, Big Mike don't shoot. He's never shot anybody in his life, even though always a bad hombre, and certainly he has never shot a woman, and certainly he won't shoot a nice little twist like this one.

It seems she is a stenographer in the office, getting fourteen bucks a week for working like hell, day after day. She's the kind of dame that could make fifty a week doing a strip-tease, or more than that in other ways, but she is not that kind of dame. She would rather make just the fourteen bucks and make it honest.

Well, one of the employees, who is scared to death at the sight of the rods yells: "Josephine! Look out! Be careful!"

And Josephine says very calm: "Be careful of what?"

She slaps Big Mike in the puss and says to him: "I'm not afraid of you, you rotten thing! You think because you've got a gun in your hand that you're a hero. It would take more than a gun to make a hero out of *your material*. We work hard in this office, and we work for salary. The money that comes in here pays salaries to employees and profits to the men who own the store. If you think we're going to give it up just because you have a gun in your hand—"

With that she slaps Big Mike in the puss again, and tries to rassel the Colt away from him. Naturally, all this is very embarrassing to Big Mike. And to make it all worse, Ace O'Brien has got scared and taken it on the lam into the toy shop.

So there is Mike, with a gun in his hand, and eleven people who are scared of him, and a young dame who is not. She kicks him in the shins, keeps slapping his puss, and the whole time she is doing that none of the others come to help her. They are all scared of Big Mike.

Well, the dame starts to scream for help, all the time kicking and slapping Big Mike, and Big Mike begins to think that under different circumstances he wouldn't mind having a sweet little dame like this work him over. But right now he has to think of his career, and getting the hell out of here before the cops come, so he says: "Sorry, sister," and socks her on the jaw.

That puts her on the floor for a count, and Big Mike ducks out and runs across the toy shop.

H E DON'T see Ace O'Brien, so he figures that Ace got away. All he sees is a lot of women and kids, and a couple of private dicks barging out of the elevator.

So he sneaks down a hallway that has a sign: FOR EMPLOYEES ONLY, and he smacks through a door marked: MEN. There he is in the washroom, and the only other guy there is this fake Santy Claus that works in the toy shop.

The fake Santy Claus has taken his beard off and is smoking a cigar. He don't know nothing about the excitement in the business office, since he has been in here sneaking a smoke, and he is a natural victim when Big Mike conks him over the head with the barrel of the Colt. All Santy Claus can do is give a sigh and fall to the marble floor, conked.

What Big Mike does then, he does fast. Of course, Big Mike has had lots of experience when he used to de-pants policemen as a sport, and now Big Mike yanks the pants off Santy Claus—also pulls off his coat, cap, and boots.

In a very short time Big Mike has dressed himself in the red clothes and white fur that Santy Claus wore, and Mike even puts on the false beard. He tucks the pillow down over his stomach, and that pads him out, and when Big Mike looks at himself in the mirror, he finds that he has now become Santy Claus.

This bum who used to be Santy Claus is in his underwear, listening to the birdies sing, and Big Mike ties his wrists and legs, gags him with a shirt, and tosses him into one of the booths.

Then Big Mike, Colt under his belt, walks out into the hallway. Everything is going fine again, except that Ace has scrammed and they didn't get that ten grand from the business office, because of the spunky little dame in there.

Well, as Big Mike steps into the hallway, a couple of house detectives come running along with rods in their mitts.

One of them says to Big Mike: "There was a stick-up in the business office. Did you see anybody come this way?"

Big Mike strokes his fake white beard, and says: "I seen a man run down here and go out the fire escape. I thought he was a janitor."

So the two dicks climb out a window to look at the fire escape. They are looking for Big Mike, and they have no idea they have just talked to him in person, because Big Mike, in the red suit and cap, and the long white whiskers, makes a very fine Santa Claus.

Now as Big Mike strolls back into the toy shop he sees several of the employees which him and Ace stuck up in the business office, and these guys are all wandering around, some of them rubbing tear gas out of their eyes, and they have a couple of harness cops with them, and they are all hunting around for Big Mike and Ace.

Big Mike strolls right past them, and they don't give him a tumble because they are so sure he is the fake Santa Claus who works in the store. Well, Big Mike figures that in this disguise he can walk right out of the store, even if the cops are watching the doors downstairs, and once he is on the street he won't attract no attention because there are so many of those Salvation Army Santy Clauses ringing bells on the corners.

Well, Big Mike starts over to the elevators to make his exit, but he is suddenly stopped. He is stopped, not by cops, but by a whole gang of kids. They crowd around him, and rub their sticky mitts on him, and jump up and down, and all talk at once, like a lot of parrots yelling at him.

It seems they are fooled, just like everybody else, and they want to tell Big Mike what they desire for Christmas. Big Mike tries to shake them off, but a guy comes along and says very nasty to Big Mike: "What's the idea of trying to leave? You're not through work till five."

Big Mike realizes right away that this guy is floor manager, and he knows he will have to pretend to be Santy Claus in the toy shop till five o'clock.

This worries Big Mike a lot, because it is only four-forty right now, and in twenty minutes the cops might find that bum tied up in the washroom. If they find him, then they'll come right after Big Mike and the disguise will be worse than no disguise at all.

But there is nothing Big Mike can do about it. He has to take the chance. This manager is pushing him along, and the brats are pushing him, and Big Mike is pushed right over to the throne covered with fake snow, and Big Mike has to sit down on it, and pretend to be the store Santy Claus.

RIGHT away a kid jumps up on Big Mike's knee and begins to tell Big Mike what she wants for Christmas. She is a little female, about six years old, and she is quite a little gold-digger, because for Christmas she wants five dolls like the Dionne quints, and she wants a doll house, a dog, a pair of roller skates, a toy automobile, and many other things.

"That's okay with *me*," Big Mike tells her generously, and over her shoulder he winks at the kid's mother.

Well, the next brat to jump on Big Mike's lap is a little red-headed squirt, and the first thing he says to Santy Claus is: "Where is your book and pencil?"

"What book and pencil?" Big Mike asks him.

"You got to write down what I want," the kid says, "because last Christmas I asked you for a coaster with rubber tires and you forgot it. All you brought me was a new pair of shoes."

Well, Big Mike starts to tell the kid that maybe his Old Man is poor and couldn't buy the coaster, and had to settle for shoes that the brat could go to school in, but Big Mike catches himself when he figures the kid is dumb on the subject of Santy Claus and won't understand the real lowdown.

So Big Mike says: "I'll give you a coaster this year. Where do you live?"

The kid tells him, and Big Mike writes it in a book which he finds beside the throne. This is the book the store uses for sending out merchandise and bills.

One kid after another lands on Big Mike's lap, telling him what him or her wants for Christmas, and Big Mike begins to think there must be lots of fathers in the world who wish to hell there *was* a Santy Claus. It's a shame, Big Mike thinks, how all the fathers got to dish out gifts to their kids and not get any credit for it, because the kids think it comes free from Santa Claus.

Well, Big Mike goes on sitting there, and pretending to be Santy Claus for the kids, and all the time he is very worried about his exit from the store. The cops are hoofing around through the toy shop, and that smart little red-headed dame from the business office is going around with them. Big Mike looks at a clock on the wall and sees he has fourteen minutes to go yet.

A kid is now sitting in Big Mike's lap, and Big Mike says to him: "All right, young man. What do you want for Christmas?"

The kid looks sore and says: "Nothing from *you*. Come out from behind them fake whiskers—you don't fool *me!*"

Big Mike is scared for a second, because he thinks maybe this brat has spotted the disguise and will maybe squeal to the cops. Big Mike has half a notion to haul off and sock this fresh kid in the kisser, but he checks himself. He realizes that the kid is just some little punk that don't believe in Santy Claus, so Big Mike shoves him off his lap and tells him to scram.

Right away, another kid lands on his lap. This is a male squirt, about five years old, who says to Big Mike: "Have you ever seen a policeman?"

Well, of course Big Mike has seen lots of policemen in his time. In fact, Big Mike has seen more policemen than he cares for, so it is a hell of a question for the kid to ask Big Mike.

The kid goes on talking, and he says: "I want a policeman suit for Christmas, Mr. Santy Claus. But I don't want one like you brought me last year. That one didn't look real. I want one just like the big policemen wear."

"I'll bring you one," Big Mike promises.

"Do you know the kind I mean?"

Well, as soon as the kid pops that question, a city cop is walking by, glancing around the toy department in search of any man that might look like Big Mike or Ace O'Brien. This kid yells: "Hey! and grabs the cop by the sleeve. "I want to show Santy Claus your suit, Mr. Policeman," the kid says.

THIS is embarrassing to Big Mike, especially when the cop stops within a foot of the Santy Claus throne and looks very hard at Big Mike.

Big Mike says: "The kid wants a suit like yours for Christmas. He wants to show me what it looks like."

Well, the cop is nice to the kid, and pinches him in a friendly way under the chin, and says to Big Mike, who he thinks is the store Santy Claus: "You see that this little fellow gets a uniform like mine, or I'll personally come after you."

The cop laughs, thinking it is a fine joke, and Big Mike says: "I certainly don't want you to come after me."

Well, the cop walks away and Big Mike writes the kid's name and address in his book. It is Jimmy Johnson, 1717 West Fifth Street. Big Mike makes a note: "Cop suit."

The kid don't want to leave Big Mike's lap, on account of he thinks he is sitting on the lap of Santy Claus, and, to a kid, this is supposed to be a great honor.

Well, it seems that while Big Mike is sitting there his pillow has worked up over his stomach and the butt of his Colt .44 sticks out. The kid spots it and hauls the gun loose, and fondles it.

"This is the best cap pistol I've ever seen!" the kid squeals in joy. "Or is it a water pistol?"

With that, the kid starts to pull the trigger, to see if the rod is a cap pistol or a water pistol, and Big Mike's heart jumps up in his throat. If the kid pulls that trigger he may assassinate several people in the store, and Big Mike would hate like hell to see a five-year-old kid get the rope.

So Big Mike manages to rassel the rod away from the kid, to ditch it, and Big Mike is very glad to find out that the cop wasn't looking and that nobody except the kids saw the rod. However, Big Mike is not taking any more chances and he pushes Jimmy Johnson off his lap and tells him to scram.

Well, at this time a person steps up to Big Mike, and it is not a kid. It is a woman about forty years old, and she is not much to look at. Her coat is all shiny at the elbows, and she carries a battered leather purse that probably don't have no more than carfare in it.

She leans over close to Big Mike and whispers in his ear: "Will you help me?"

Big Mike says he will, thinking she wants to touch him for a dime or so, but it turns out that that ain't what she wants.

She says: "I've brought my children to see you. I have five of them and they just had to see Santy Claus. They have their poor little hearts set on bicycles for Christmas, but my husband lost his job and we just can't afford it. I don't want to disappoint them about the bicycles, so I thought you might persuade them toward something else. My two youngest are only six and seven, and they're too young to have bicycles anyway. The others are old enough to have them, but we just can't afford it."

"I see," says Big Mike. "You want me to steer them off on something else besides bicycles. That's okay with me. How about me telling them they ought to have policeman suits?"

"You don't understand," she tells Big Mike. "My husband and I have been going without necessities for the past six months—longer than that. The most we can afford to spend is two dollars on each of the children. If you can persuade them they'd like something that costs two dollars, you can be sure I'll get it for them, and I'll pay my bill right after Christmas. I promise to pay the bill."

Well, Big Mike feels sorry for her and he is about to tell her she don't have to pay the bill at all, when it occurs to him that he don't work for the store, that he is only a hood who tried to stick up the business office, and that he has only seventy-four cents on him. But he tells her he will do his best with the kids.

Well, she brings her kids up to him, all five of them, and the last two are too big to sit on his lap. In fact, the last two are such big kids that Big Mike wonders why they still believe in Santa Claus. When Big Mike was the age of these biggest kids, about twelve or thirteen, he was shooting craps in Brooklyn, stealing groceries, rolling drunks, and otherwise earning a living.

Anyway, Big Mike talks to the kids very confidential and tells them they ought to have a shirt for Christmas, or maybe some underwear, or some new pants. Mike figures that their father and mother can afford this sort of stuff and it will be a good investment, since the kids have to have clothes anyway.

But the kids won't listen to reason. They want bicycles for Christmas, and they don't know that the Old Man can't

afford to pay the bill. In fact, they don't even know their Old Man has to pay. They think the bicycles will come from Santy Claus—free.

Well, Big Mike works himself into a sweat, but he can't seem to sell the kids on shirts and underwear instead of bicycles.

So finally he says: "Okay, I'll bring you bicycles."

At that time, of course, Big Mike is speaking for Santy Claus, not for himself. His only idea is to get rid of the kids, because it is now five o'clock by the clock on the wall, and Big Mike wants to slip by the cops and make his exit.

Well, the kids go away happy, thinking they'll get bicycles for Christmas, but the woman hangs back near the Santy Claus throne. Her eyes have tears in them, and this embarrasses Big Mike. She rubs her hands together, rough red hands that she probably uses to take in washing and make enough dough to feed the kids.

The tears start to roll down her cheeks and she says to Mike: "I wish you hadn't done that."

"Done what?" Big Mike hardly knows what he has done. He is busy watching the clock and thinking about ducking out of the store.

"You doublecrossed me."

Well, Big Mike feels very bad when she accuses him of that, because he has never doublecrossed anybody in his life. Even when he was up in Sing Sing, doing a nine year rap, he kept his mouth shut when seven cons planned a getaway. Nobody could ever accuse Big Mike of being a doublecrosser.

But that's what the woman calls him, and she goes away before he can say anything more to her.

IN THE next few minutes, Big Mike makes his way out of the store. He gets downstairs in an elevator and gets out on the street. He sees several cops standing around out there, but he slips past them and boards a trolley, and after that it's a cinch.

When he arrives home—home being a six-bit flop in a boarding house on South Spring—Ace O'Brien is waiting for him.

"Hello," says Big Mike.

"What the devil you doing dressed up like that?"

So Big Mike tells him.

Ordinarily, Big Mike would be very sore at his partner for running out on him during the stick-up. In fact, ordinarily, in a case like this, Big Mike would grab Ace O'Brien by the collor with his left hand, and with his right fist he would knock Ace's teeth down his throat. But right now Big Mike is feeling too sad to sock anybody.

Big Mike sits down on the bed, pulls off the Santy Claus beard, pulls off the red coat, the fur, and takes the pillow pad off his belly. He finds the notebook that has all the names and addresses of the kids who want things, and he knows that many of them will not get these things. It makes him feel awful sad, and for a while he wishes there really was such a guy as Santy Claus, and that Santy Claus would take the kids the stuff they got their hearts set on. However, Big Mike has to conclude there ain't any Santy Claus and the whole thing is a tough proposition for the kids.

He thinks back how he had those kids sitting on his lap, and how they told him what they wanted, and how he won't really bring it to them. It's a doublecross all along the line, and Big Mike hates like hell to be a doublecrosser, especially to kids.

All of a sudden Big Mike jumps up from the bed and snaps his fingers. He says to Ace: "I got a job for us. Go steal a car."

"Steal a car?" Ace asks. "What for?"

"I got a job for us."

"Where?"

"The Seventh Street Department Store."

Ace shakes his head. "It went sour on us once. I don't want it again. Not today."

"But this is a cinch," Big Mike says. "We can bust in at night when it's closed up except for the janitors."

"That's no good," Ace tells him. "At night the money is all locked in the safe."

"The hell with it," Big Mike says. "The hell with the money in the safe."

CHAPTER IV

—In the Worst of Us

WELL, it seems that on the night before Christmas, while all the young squirts are asleep in their beds and waiting for Santy Claus, two guys break through a window in the basement of the Seventh Street Department store, and these two guys are Big Mike Williams and Ace O'Brien. They sap a night watchman and tie him up. They push guns into the kissers of a crew of janitors who are cleaning up, and they scare and fight their way to the toy department upstairs.

Up there, they steal a lot of stuff that has not been sold for Christmas. They get twenty-three bicycles, fourteen Indian suits, a pile of dolls, doll houses, tin soldiers, baseball bats, catcher's gloves, teddy bears, electric trains, and many such items.

They cart this stuff downstairs and load it in the stolen car and manage to drive away just as the burglar alarms are ringing through the streets.

Ace O'Brien says: "I've hocked a lot of loot in my time, but it's the first time I ever hocked teddy bears. You ain't crazy by any chance?"

"No," says Big Mike, busy driving the car.

"Where you intend to peddle it?"

"I don't intend to peddle it," Big Mike says.

He's got that notebook in his pocket, the one that shows the names of the kids, and where they live, and what they want. He drives to one of these houses after another, and leaves some presents on the front porch.

He drives to the place where the woman lives, with the five kids. It's a dirty old shack near the river bed, on a muddy road. Big Mike himself carries up five bicycles and dumps them on the porch, and then he throws a rock at the front door, so somebody'll come out and find what he's left.

From inside he hears a kid's voice yell: "Mama! Mama! I heard him! It's Santy Claus! I told you he'd come! I told you! Didn't I tell you?"

The woman's voice says: "Go back to sleep, darling. I think Santy will leave you a nice toy in the morning."

"Bicycle!" the kid yells. "He'll leave me a bicycle! You just wait and see!"

Well, Big Mike is back in the stolen car again and driving to another address. He and Ace O'Brien visit about sixty places, always leaving something, always throwing a rock at the front door, or some way attracting attention.

After they vi 't these sixty houses, Big Mike says: "Hell, I forgot something!"

Ace O'Brien says: "We still got seven more teddy bears, nine baseball bats, and a pair of roller skates."

"Ain't we got a policeman suit?"

"No," says Ace. "But we got a cowboy suit."

"That's no good," says Big Mike. "There s a kid at 1717 West Fifth Street and he wants a policeman suit."

Ace O'Brien is tired out, and he says: "If you think I'm gonna knock over any more toy stores, you're crazy."

"We won't," says Big Mike. "But we got to get a cop suit. The real goods. This kid Jimmy Johnson wants the real goods."

Well, at just that time Big Mike happens to see a police officer walking along the sidewalk, so he pulls the car over to the curb and says: "Merry Christmas, officer."

"Merry Christmas to you," says the cop, very friendly.

Big Mike gets out and socks him on the jaw, knocking him colder than a dead oyster. And with that, Big Mike goes back to his old sport, the sport he had when he was a punk in Brooklyn. He pulls the pants off the cop, and he also removes the cop's coat and badge, his belt and gun, his whistle and handcuffs.

With all this stuff over his arm, Big Mike climbs back into the car. "Well," he says, "Jimmy Johnson wants the real goods, and he's gonna get the real goods."

So at 1717 West Fifth street the doorbell rings, and a man comes to the door. There is nobody on the porch. There is just a car going away down the street. But on the front steps there is a policeman's uniform—pants, coat, badge, belt, gun, cap, even a policeman's underwear.

The chances are that this stuff is much too large for Jimmy Johnson to wear on Christmas morning, but anyway, it's the real goods, and nobody can doubt that.

BIG MIKE and Ace O'Brien work till midnight when they run out of toys. Then they go back to the rooming house to sleep, and the first thing they know they are pinched.

It seems the cops have showed their mugg-book to that smart little red-headed dame in the Department store, and she has put the finger on a couple of photographs which are fine likenesses of Ace O'Brien and Big Mike Williams. "Those are the men," she says.

So the cops pick up Ace and Big Mike at the rooming house, and bring both guys into court before Judge Hutchinson.

The judge gives Ace nine years in Folsom for a rap he broke away from.

And the judge says to Big Mike: "I sentence you to Folsom Prison for nine years for attempted robbery of the business office of the Seventh Street Department Store, for armed robbery of the toy department, for stealing an automobile, for smashing a window when you delivered toys on Christmas Eve, for your past bad record, for assaulting an officer and stripping him of his uniform. Nine years, Mr. Williams. But at the same time I suspend sentence."

Big Mike's jaw hangs open. "You what?"

"I suspend sentence and put you on good behavior, Mr. Williams. I do this because several parents of children have come to me and told me that you played

Santy Claus on the night before Christmas, and that they will personally vouch for your character in the future. So I'm going to let you go. But if you revert to the bad character you were some years ago you will be doublecrossing people who trust you, and worse than that, you'll be doublecrossing children."

"I never doublecrossed anybody in my life," Big Mike says.

The judge smiles. "And see that you never do. Go out and get yourself an honest job and pay back to the department store all money that you owe them for stolen toys."

SO THAT'S exactly what Big Mike goes out and does. It so happens that he gets married, and the girl's Old Man gives him a ranch near San Clemente, and Big Mike becomes a farmer and grows fruit, such as peaches, apricots, oranges and lemons; also grows chickens and eggs. Out of the profits he pays back the store, and he also puts away money for his own kids to go to college. Every Christmas he has a lot of fun playing Santa Claus for his own kids, and he also plays Santy Claus for the poor kids on the ranches. He is now a completely reformed character, and he wouldn't think of going back to his old way of chiseling dough, and he has even given up his favorite sport of pulling pants off cops. In fact, a cop is now one of Big Mike's best friends, and every Christmas, Big Mike comes into the cop's house dressed up like Santy Claus

and leaves some presents for the cop's kids.

So you can see that Big Mike is very soft.

I know as soon as he tells me about this, that there is no use trying to get him to stick up the bank with Rusty and me.

And furthermore, he says to me: "If you try to stick up that bank I'll go down there and kick your teeth in. It's a nice little bank where the farmers put their money."

"I don't want to stick it up," I says. "It's Rusty Nelson that wants to." In that way I pass the buck to Rusty.

"Tell Rusty to behave himself," Big Mike says. "There's nothing in the world like settling down and raising your own kids." He points at the Christmas tree and the toys on the floor. "If you and Rusty want to work for a living, I'll give you a job down here, plowing and irrigating, and taking care of the chickens."

"I'll speak to Rusty about the proposition," I says.

So I start out the door, into the rain, on account of I want to tell Rusty that Big Mike won't go on the bank job with us. And I also want to tell Rusty I don't figure to go myself; not today, anyhow.

And just as I'm going out the door, I turn to Big Mike, and I ask him: "What ever happened to that red-headed dame in the department store—the one that fouled you on the stick-up and turned you over to the cops?"

Big Mike sort of grins. "That's the girl I married," he says. "That's Josephine."

IF THE TALES here are all "hard-boiled," then what, exactly, does the term imply?

Before the 1920s, tales of murder and mystery were generally rather polite affairs, with a gentlemen detective (and they were, indeed, mostly men) solving a heinous crime through analysis and study, as though he were the baron of some manor, sitting in his library piecing together a challenging jigsaw puzzle over a snifter of fine old brandy.

The pulps changed all that. The protagonists who first began appearing in *Black Mask* during the '20s were just as liable to fight and shoot their way to conclusions as they were to piece together clues, and they weren't exactly upper-crust characters, either. These tough and very American creations, whose pulp heyday came in the '30s and early '40s, came to be known as hard-boiled — as distinguished from gentlemanly, polite, and restrained.

If Christmas Comes—

By Steve Fisher

Author of "Murder At Malibu," etc.

Joyeux Noël, Fröhliche Weihnacht, Felices Navidades—but there is no Merry Christmas when Tony Key is on your trail . . .

THERE are a lot of things we like about Hollywood that the people outside don't know about, could not know about, because they are just the small every day things of living. They are things bigger than glamor and glory and money, that never make the publicity columns, and yet are the things that bring flesh and blood and breath to we who are idolized, symbolized, fictionized, and looked upon as immortal beings. In the days when I had to struggle to keep body and soul together, I used to think that money and fame would make a difference, but I know now that it doesn't; it makes it easier, but that is all. There is never anything different. So the little things, the elements around us that we see day in and day out are the things that count. They are the things that make us laugh and weep.

Things like the sunshine, and the careless freedom of Hollywood Boulevard, and the parade of girls in slacks, and the blondes who wait on corners and aren't afraid to be picked up if you wear a white sweater and have a Packard roadster. The little barbecue stands where you drive in, after a show, and have food brought to your car, and sit there and eat it and laugh far into the night. Like the beaches which are ordinary beaches but can be gone to either winter or summer. Like the mountains and resorts, and places to dance like the Grove, and places to eat like Musso-Franks where even Garbo will sit at the counter to eat her dinner. Things like open air markets that spray floodlights across heaven to advertise oranges ten cents a dozen; or the little movie house that has a surprize preview picture given to them an hour before the second show goes on.

Little things like those, intangibles all, count up, and mean something, and make Hollywood the best place to live and earn your bread in the whole world. The sentiment and the laughter, things too small to mention, things I cannot even remember—and then the very best of all these things. The day that makes the whole year worth living. Christmas Day in Hollywood.

If you ever went away, Tony, could you *ever* forget Christmas? There is no snow. There is only California grass and trees and flowers and the weather at its worst, but when you walk along Hollywood Boulevard you see Christmas different than you ever did before. In the first place it isn't Hollywood Boulevard then, it is Santa Claus Lane. All of the street signs are changed to that (remember?) and on each electric lamp for the entire length of the boulevard there is a color picture of a different star. You *are* a star when your picture is in the gallery along Santa Claus Lane because you're with the best this town ever turned out. You're with Marie Dressler and Jean Harlow and Rudolph Valentino and Lillian Tashman—all of those great ones of today too. Mickey Mouse and Lionel Barrymore and Mae West and Clark Gable and Luise Rainer and all the others. You can see them all on Santa Claus Lane and you can see the ones who aren't posted and who are big. The producers and writers and directors and screen editors. You can see them in open roadsters. In the lobbies of hotels. In the doorways of apartments. Sitting in Henri's, or standing at the Brass Rail, or looking in at the Vine Street Derby for turkey like they never get at home. You can see success and failure and people drinking whiskey which a director said was the "curse of a nation."

IT WAS like that when I came on the boulevard at seven o'clock, which may be early in New York but isn't in Hollywood. You had called me, remember? I left the hotel as soon as I could get dressed. The drug store from where you had called was on the corner of Highland, but I thought I would walk. I would walk because it was Christmas and I wanted to see the shops dressed up, and the people who were also walking, but for a different reason than I. They were trying to walk off a hangover.

I remember now that I thought it was queer that you should call me because I thought of you only as an agent. A pretty good motion picture agent, I will admit, but no more than that. It was not until later when you started the investigation that I learned your agency was just a blind and that in reality you were a special studio detective. Rather, that your job was to put a heavy foot on the Hollywood crime wave in picture circles; and that made you the world's highest paid detective.

I came into the drug store and you

were standing there over the corpse. You were wearing flannels and white shoes, a white sweater and a black coat which is, I guess, the way you always dress, except that your patent leather hair wasn't so patent leather as usual, and I thought I saw trouble in your green eyes, or on your smooth-skinned face.

"Hello, Ben," you said. "Merry Christmas."

"Hello, Tony," I answered. "Merry Christmas to you."

"And Merry Christmas to a corpse," someone said, and I looked up and saw that it was Betty Gale who said that. Betty, your pretty platinum blonde secretary who has curves in the right places. "Hi, Ben," she went on, "how is Hollywood's most prolific scenario writer?"

"I am fine," I said, "who is dead?"

And then we all concentrated our attention on the corpse. It was that of a man, a little man whose hair was sandy and whose blue eyes—which were still open—stared glassily up and past us at some Christmas tinsel on the ceiling. I noticed he was lying there doubled up, and I said:

"How did he get it?"

"Poison," you told me. "He came here for an antidote."

"Yeah," said Betty Gale. "The poor dope was only about half conscious. Must have been whacky drunk. You know. When the store opened he wobbled in and asked the clerk how you could tell when you've been poisoned. He wanted to know how you could tell whether it was poison or appendicitis or indigestion."

"Then he dropped where you see him now," you said, "and he hasn't moved since. The druggist tried to work with him but couldn't. There'll be a wagon pretty soon to take him away."

I nodded, still trying to figure out why all of this should interest you; and why you had called me. I saw a bamtam-weight guy with gray hair wandering around the store and you introduced him as Mickey Ryan of the Homicide Squad, but that wasn't until later.

"I suppose you wonder why we sent for you?" you said, and I noticed you were looking at your fingernails.

"Yeah," I said, "I *am* a little curious. Just a little though. It's a nice morning to be out."

"Don't you know the corpse?" you asked. I didn't like the sharp edge in your tone.

"No I don't, Tony."

Betty Gale shrugged. "Well, you can't always be right, Tony, my lover. You said Ben Thompson would know

the stiff and he doesn't. So what? Do we pay his walking expenses back to the hotel?"

You looked at Betty and said to me: "Isn't it a shame? She's so pretty when she's quiet, too. You would never think she was crazy to look at her, would you?" You lit a cigarette. "Ben," you went on, "I did think you might know the guy, but that wasn't the real reason I asked to see you. Though Betty may claim that it was. The real reason is that I know you are sweet on a girl named Stella Mathews. That's right. You are sweet on her, aren't you?"

"Sure," I said, "plenty."

"Well," you replied, and I noticed a flicker in your green eyes, "it may surprise you to know this, but that guy on the floor was her husband."

I opened and closed my mouth. I was struck dumb with what you had told me. I honestly hadn't known a thing about it until you said it then. I stared down at the corpse and I still couldn't believe it. Stella was so young and naive; so sweet and—oh hell—you know all the words, and I know them, I've written them into enough movies to know them by rote.

YOU went on: "Yeah, he was an assistant film cutter at Parmet, that's all. I got his name from his wallet. William Blake. Betty scooted back to my office and looked up the data on him. She's a good girl in ways like that." Then as though you had let something out, you added: "We have a file something like they have at Central Casting Bureau, only we list *every* studio job, not just the actors. We have the registered history of everybody here. Sometimes it comes in handy." You didn't say why it came in handy, and I thought at the time it was to help you place talent in the right places, which, as an agent, you were supposed to do.

"So Blake was her—her—"

"Her husband," you said. "I want you to tell us all you can about her."

"There isn't much to tell," I replied, "if you know what love is."

Betty said: "Tony Key never knows what love is at this time in the morning."

"I met Stella at the studio," I continued, as you arched one eyebrow at Betty. "She was just a little extra kid. I'm sure she was straight. If she had been married to Blake it must have been off with them, because I took her home once. She lived in a little twenty-five-dollar-a-month apartment on Kingsley Drive. One of those places that has a nice front, and inside, a fold-in-the-wall bed. Sometimes she didn't have enough to eat and I'd help her out. Gradually, as time went on, I fell in love with her. I don't know why or how. A writer who has been earning close to two thousand a week in Hollywood for five years has a pretty wide choice of women. But there was something about the kid that seemed straight and honest to me and .. ."

"And the bug bit you," said Betty.

"Precisely," I agreed.

You yawned and said: "Betty's right, this is one sweet time of the morning to be talking about love. But let's go over and see Stella." You turned to the bantam-weight Homicide detective. "See you in court, funny face," you said. "I'm going to walk around town a little on this case this morning, then I'm going to bed. Don't glut yourself on Christmas turkey."

"Don't worry about me," Mickey Ryan told you, "I do all right."

You and Betty and I left the drug store.

We drove over to Kingsley Drive.

Stella was in red pajamas when she opened the door and I will say she looked neat. She had been in bed so that she hadn't a chance to wash her face, but it was the prettiest face for that time of morning I have ever seen. Her hair was gold on her shoulder and her eyes were as big as quarters, and bluer than the kind of sky they talk about in western pictures. She was a beautiful little tike. And I was very much in love with her.

"Ben," she said, looking at me in amazement. "What is this? It's not Xmas Eve anymore, and anyhow, I'm *not* having a party."

"Honey," I told her, "this is Tony Key. He has something to talk to you about. Tony is a big agent and if you treat him right you can't tell what he might do for you."

"No," Betty Gale came in, "you certainly can't. You can't *ever* tell about Tony."

There wasn't much more Stella could say and we all came into the apartment. It was a mess, all right, with the bed covers all wrinkled, and a man's pipe on the divan, a bottle of whiskey—half empty—on the kitchen table. She had a little half-pint Christmas tree in the window and there were a couple of presents tied up in red paper and green ribbons lying underneath it.

Stella stood looking at us, and you told her right away: "William Blake is dead. Poison."

She went dead-white. Her hand went to her throat. "He—he—"

"Don't know," you said, "maybe he drank it accidently, maybe it was suicide. He was pretty drunk when the end came. But from the way he was talking I think it was murder."

"Murder?" she echoed.

"That's right," chirped Betty.

"Something they hang people for in this state."

You asked her: "You were married to him, Stella."

"Yes," she answered frankly, "but—but we had separated. We didn't see each other anymore. It was something in the past that I thought I could bury and forget." I noticed there were tears in her eyes.

YOU moved across the room like a cat then, Tony, in your flannels, your coat, that sweater. I could tell that you had gotten an idea when she said that. You picked up the two presents from under the little tree. "For Bill," you read, then the other: "For Ben."

"For me?" I asked, and I gulped down a lump of pain that was in my throat. I didn't know that she was going to buy me anything, and it affected me quite a lot.

"Yeah, for you," you said, and handed me the package which turned out to be a green smoking jacket. I kissed Stella for it right there because she was already so nervous that she was sitting on the bad crying.

"Look," you went on, talking to her. "You've got to answer some questions."

That was when I interrupted and told you she had had enough for one morning. I asked you who you thought you were to take such authority. I guess I got tough with you. But you told me. You told me off then, and Betty added you were not only a detective, but the world's highest paid one. After that you went on with the questions.

"This present marked 'For Bill', Stella. For Bill Blake, isn't it? William Blake?"

"I—ah—"

"It is," you said, "I know it is. Why did you tell me you never saw him anymore?"

"Well—on Christmas."

You were nasty: "I catch. You don't see each other all year, but on Christmas you exchange presents."

"Well—yes."

"Tripe," you said, "plain tripe." Then you turned and picked up the pipe from the divan.

"Pipe," said Betty Gale, "plain pipe." Then to Stella: "Honey, he's going to ask you to whom the plain pipe belongs. Have a good answer ready or he'll catch you up."

"It belongs to Roger West," Stella whispered, "his initials are on the bowl of it."

I guess we all looked up then. Roger West, like Clark Gable, was one of the really big stars. I thought she must have stolen it from the studio for its sentimental value, but she went on:

"I don't want to lie to you about anything, Mr. Key. Roger West was here last night. We had a few drinks together."

You put the pipe in your pocket, and said: "You get around, don't you, Stella?"

I was so shocked that I couldn't speak. She had never spoken of knowing West and though there was really no reason that she should have, I felt as though I had been cheated. I felt in my pockets for a cigarette. I knew Stella didn't smoke and finally bummed one from Betty. You were in the kitchen sniffing at the whiskey bottle. It sat among a lot of dirty dishes and wet cigarette butts that had turned brown, the color of the tobacco.

"Well," you said at last, "it's a cinch somebody poisoned Blake, and when we have the autopsy report we'll know what kind of poison. Meanwhile, Betty, my sweet, it looks as though we spend Christmas Day barking in blind alleys. Let's go visit Roger West." You looked at me. "Want to go, Ben? Or do you want to stay here with Stella?"

"I'll go with you," I said. "Stella's in no condition for company."

I just said that in front of her, but when I got outside I told you: "Listen, finding out what I have about Stella has made me pretty sick." This was the truest thing I ever said. "I want to walk it off or something. You don't mind, do you? The murder doesn't mean anything to me, but Stella does— or did. I'm all in a turmoil about her."

You patted my shoulder. "Okay, Ben, but if you want to go, don't think you'll be in the way."

"It isn't that," I said. "It's that I'm tired, and all confused. I want to walk —walk a lot. Then go home and take a cold shower and drink coffee. You know, when you called I rushed out without even changing my shirt—and well, I guess I'm pretty filthy. But I'd appreciate it though, on account of Stella, if you'd drop by and let me know how things turn out. Or Betty could phone me."

"Nah," you said, "we'll come over. Just have a good Christmas drink ready is all."

I WANDERED around for awhile, just as I told you I was going to, then I went back to my hotel. I was pretty blue. I wished that none of it had happened. I had been happy with Stella and now, knowing what I did, I didn't think I could ever be so much in love with her again. I smoked a lot of cigarettes and paced around. When it came two o'clock I tuned in Bing Crosby and heard him sing *Silent Night,* which he sings every Christmas. It's broadcast from coast to coast and

across to England, of course, but that too somehow seems like Hollywood tradition.

I had changed my trousers and was wearing the green smoking robe Stella had given me, when you came in with Betty Gale. You looked pretty glum and flopped down in a chair, crossing your legs, and putting a cigarette in your mouth and lighting it.

"Roger West admits loving Stella," said Betty, "which would be swell copy for Winchell except that Tony is paid to keep down publicity like that as well as to solve murders."

She didn't make me feel any better, saying that, and I phoned down for Tom and Jerrys to be sent up.

You said moodily: "Out side of that, West was a fizzle. Couldn't get anything out of him."

"Yeah," said Betty, "I thought he was a He-Man, even though he's as handsome as seven hundred dollars. But he wears lavendar pajamas, and doesn't smoke or chew, and eats oysters for breakfast."

We sat around, not saying much, then the drinks came up. They warmed us, the foam slopping over a little, and you perked up and said: "You know, Mickey Ryan, that little Homicide detective, has a lead, and I would not be surprised but what he was on the right trail this time. The only trouble is that Mickey can't figure a thing about the murder and doesn't know how to prove what he thinks. Well, we're all in the same boat. But Mickey has another film cutter—Wilt Davis— who everybody knows has hated Blake for years. Mickey and the rest of the cops have been questioning Davis. Just a little while ago they let him go."

"Since when," said Betty, "do you go around scavenging discarded police suspects?"

You wriggled your finger at her. "Tush, sweetheart. Cops have discarded killers before."

You got up, walked up and down the room. You stopped at my dresser and stood biting your thumb, though I don't think you saw the mess of junk on the dresser or anything else in the room. You were thinking. At last you turned.

"Well, I can't sit around and drink when there's murder doing. Up and going, Betty. We'll take a look in at this brother film cutter who they say had hatred in his heart that was like rattles on a rattlesnake. He worked right with Blake—Davis did, and—well, come on."

I was nervous and restless, and terribly blue. I thought anything would be better than staying in the room. I asked: "Can I go along?"

"Sure, Ben," you said.

So I put on my coat and shoes and followed along with you and Betty. I was beginning to admire the way you worked and I had taken a liking to Betty.

You remember what Wilt Davis' apartment looked like. It was pretty ritzy for an assistant film cutter, and the pretty brown-haired maid who answered the door didn't seem to fit the surroundings either.

"I'm beginning to see why these guys like their jobs," said Betty. "This is the next thing to elegant. And elegant is a special word with me."

When Davis came out you would have thought he was a producer instead of a film cutter. He was short, and heavy, and I remember how his eyes shone beneath the heavy black brows that were so prominent on his fat face. He was smoking a cigar; and his radio was playing a popular song: *I Get That Old Feeling.*

"Yes, I disliked Bill Blake," he said, "that isn't news."

"Any particular reason?" you asked.

"Several," said Davis, who was in an ugly mood, "but I see no reason for going into those particular reasons."

"Where were you last night?" you asked.

"Drunk," said Davis. "I was on a round of Christmas Eve parties and I got stinko. I don't remember what I did after midnight."

You went after him for more details, but he stuck to that story, and at last you said we might as well leave. When we were outside walking—the three of us—Betty remarked:

"I can see how the police failed to get anywhere."

YOU didn't say anything, and we drove in your roadster back to Hollywood Boulevard. You parked in front of the drug store where Blake's corpse had been. We got out and went in. You stepped into the telephone booth for a moment. When you came out you looked at Betty, and told her:

"Cyanide."

"You poor fellow. What you want is a Bromo. Not cyanide. Imagine! So wacky he asks for cyanide!"

"Listen, my stupid platinum assistant," you growled, "cyanide is what they found in Blake's system. I just called the morgue."

"Oh," she said, "oh—that's different."

You lit another cigarette, and then we went out on the boulevard. We walked along without speaking and I was looking at the light posts and the pictures of stars on them and glancing about to see if I could spot any of them in the flesh. Then suddenly I noticed you had stopped. Betty and I hadn't noticed and were a few feet ahead. We stopped and came back. You were in front of a cafeteria.

"Let's go in for coffee."

"Coffee?" echoed Betty. "At this time of day? In *there?*"

"Lamb," you said, speaking to her, "because I give you eighty-five dollars a week and pin money on the side, is no reason you should spurn a perfectly respectable cafeteria."

So we went in, though she didn't feel like coffee and neither did I. This was an all night place, and at four in the afternoon—which it was now—it wasn't in any too good condition. A few sidewalk cowboy extras were having their turkey hash, but outside of that the place was empty. You drank two cups of coffee and kept looking around you, and I saw that same troubled look in your green eyes.

At last you said: "You two excuse me for a moment, please." You walked off.

"I knew two cups of that java would do that to him," Betty told me, and we laughed about it.

We laughed, but we were both nervous because we knew that you were up to something and we didn't know what it was. It must have had something to do with the murder. It seemed to me that you had been acting queerly since leaving Davis' place. Twenty minutes passed before you came back and then if we looked into your face for some sign of expression, we were discouraged because you showed no concern. You sat down. You put a cigarette between your lips and lit it.

"Just take it easy, Ben," you said, "and sit here like nothing has happened, and pretty soon Mickey Ryan is going to come in and get you. I phoned him."

"What do you mean?" I said.

"I mean you brought Bill Blake here under the pretext that you were going to sober him up. You got coffee for him and put cyanide in it. Then, because you didn't want the doorman to see you leave you went into the men's room and out that window. When you come in this place you take a check from an automatic machine. The only time you are seen is when you go out and pay for the stuff they punch on your check. So you went out the window in the men's room figuring Blake would die right then and there and that that would be all there was to it."

"You're crazy," I snapped, "you're just crazy as hell, Tony! You can't prove that!"

"Listen," you said. "When you went out that window you jumped into the dirt down below. There's foot marks that'll fit your shoe."

"But a lot of men wear shoes my size!"

"Sure. But very few men have a check from this cafeteria up on their dresser, like you have. You must have dumped it there when you emptied your pockets to change your pants. If you had paid for your food you would not have had the check because they take them from you. And so you can't steal a check and come in and eat a big meal on a check that's punched for maybe a nickle. They have them marked by the day. A different color for every day. I spotted that on your dresser a little while ago. I took you along with me to Davis' because I wanted to throw the net around you slowly. I didn't want you to be suspicious. I didn't want you to have a chance to get out."

"What net?" I demanded.

"Murder net," you said, "can't you see that I have the set-up right now? You were jealous of Stella's husband and figured you had to get him out of the way. You and he and Stella were at her apartment drinking after Roger West left. West doesn't smoke and neither does Stella, but the kitchen is littered with whiskey-soaked cigarette butts and I put the rest together. The presents under the tree for both you and Blake. It all fits into a perfect picture."

I was gasping, trying to speak.

"I was first suspicious though," you went on, "when you made the break you did after leaving Stella's apartment this morning. I was first suspicious then and that's why Betty and I came back—*not* to drink your Tom and Jerrys. You said you were filthy, that your shirt was dirty because you hadn't had time to *change* it. You You meant to say put on a clean one. But your tongue slipped. But the fact was clear: when I called you had just gotten in from the street and were still dressed. You were dressed, because an hour previous to that you had put the cyanide in Blake's coffee and had jumped out the window of this cafeteria."

Betty Gale was smiling. "And if you don't think that's a murder case, Ben, try getting out of it when they put the noose around your neck."

"It's a murder case," I breathed, "it's that all right. From such clues you trace my movements which covered hours. Oh, you've got something there. There's no getting around that." I straightened up and I guess my face was pretty pale, but I said: "Can't we go out and have a drink on it? One last good Christmas drink before that Homicide man gets here?"

SO I'M here in San Quentin now, writing this, Tony. Writing this and watching the hours tick past me. They say it'll never come, that they all

hope the same thing, but I'm hoping for a reprieve. Hour after hour I keep waiting for it.

I have written this because it was on my mind and I had to write it, and because also it may be the last writing I will ever do. I was paid two thousand dollars a week for writing, and I guess the habit was too great to break. So maybe it was that. Maybe it was the writer in me that made me put this down on paper, although when I started out, I remember I had something to tell you. It was something I thought you should know, though it really makes no difference.

It was—oh yes—it was that a certain song I heard only once has been buzzing through my mind. The only words I know are those in the title, but they keep coming back. The title is *The Lady Is a Tramp,* and that's what I wanted to tell you. I didn't know Stella was really married to Bill Blake. She told me only that he was someone who had something on her and she hinted that she could never be happy until he had "gone away somewhere." It wasn't until I got up here that I saw the truth. I was obsessed with my love for her, and as Blake seemed to have some mysterious power over her that could make her do what he wanted, and because she cried about this, and because I thought he stood in the way of my love, I killed him. I didn't tell her I was going to, so she is no way an accomplice, but I knew that that was what she wanted me to do.

It wasn't until I went around with you that I saw what it was. She was married to him and they were operating a little blackmail game of their own. He would do the dirty work and she would make up to big-money people like Roger West and myself and they would share the proceeds. But she was getting tired of splitting the money and tired of Blake, and seeing how nuts I was about her she worked on me to kill him. Subtly, of course. You couldn't pin anything on her in a million years. But she wanted Blake out of the way and that was her method. I was the sap. The fall guy. I did it for her. I killed him. But she was the instrument behind me.

I did that because I loved her, Tony, but she hasn't been around to see me, she hasn't even sent me a card; and I keep thinking of how sweet she was, then that song comes into my head. It keeps coming back all the time. That song: *The Lady Is a Tramp* . . .

Well, Tony, I guess that's all—only I keep thinking of Hollywood, and the little things that made life there, like the Barbecue stands and Musso-Franks and the markets that spray the heaven with lights to advertise oranges at ten cents a dozen—and of Christmas. It's so lonely here. Maybe I'll get pardoned. Maybe they won't hang me. But, Tony, if—if Christmas comes to Hollywood again and I'm not there . . . If I'm not there, take a walk down Santa Claus Lane for me, will you?

"Crooked Charity"

By HENRY LEVERAGE

When Santa Claus started handing out the little Christmas presents, Big-scar Guffman, Convict No. 27, stood in line for a queer one. What's this got to do with a museum? Read and find out!

WHEN BIG-SCAR GUFFMAN left a dummy in his cell and squeezed into the line of silent men who were making their way to the chapel for the Christmas entertainment, he figured upon an escape from a penitentiary that was pronounced unbeatable.

The dummy had been so lifelike that he chuckled to himself as the convicts twisted and squirmed their way through the cell block and upstairs to the chapel. Big-scar closed his eyes and tried to imagine just what a guard would see who would peer through the bars of cell 27.

Apparently a convict lay there, with legs crossed and a newspaper over his face, as if he had fallen asleep in the act of reading. The yegg had practised the part for over two months. The guards had grown tired of tapping the bars and waking him up. They were reasonably sure to count him "in" that night.

Big-scar had made further plans. Getting out of the cell was the first step in a ladder to freedom. The other steps of this ladder were a matter of luck and nerve. He had sworn to be out of the prison by Christmas.

The yegg sat through the prison movietone entertainment like a man in a trance. He failed to applaud when the warden announced, before the final reel, that turkey would be served for the Christmas dinner.

The movietone drew to a close. Big-scar began planning a second step in the escape. He waited as the long line of men started to file through a doorway. He paused at a platform upon which the warden and guests were standing. He edged to one side where there was a space behind the movie screen.

No one noticed him. He squeezed along a wall and then vanished behind the platform. The space there was sufficient for him to lie down with his head in his arms. He breathed slowly, as the feet of his fellow prisoners shuffled away in the distance.

Their number seemed endless. The warden and his guests stepped down. The lights were turned out, one by one. A door clanged at the foot of the steps. A gong sounded.

"I win round one," Big-scar grinned to himself.

The stroke of the gong was followed by another. Then, after a grim wait, Big-scar heard the jingle of the "count" signal. The guards had counted the dummy in 27. The principal keeper had phoned for the sentries to come off the wall. The prison was in darkness.

The yegg crawled out, listened with head cocked sidewise, then rose and tiptoed to a barred window. Through this he saw the white sheen of the ice in a river. Beyond this ice was a far-off shore.

He reached down, pulled a hacksaw blade from his shoe, wrapped its end in a handkerchief and went to work on the central bar.

The tempered steel bit into the soft iron, like a knife cutting cheese. In ten minutes he felt the blade pass through. He waited then. No sound came to him of discovery.

The yegg climbed on the sill. He braced his feet against the window's edge, and pulled the sawed bar until it left an opening through which he could crawl. He stood upon the coping, breathed into his palms and gained a narrow ledge that ran around the building below the chapel windows. Along the ledge he worked, holding his hands close to the wall. He came to a drain pipe and lowered himself till he stood shivering within the shadow of the building.

The prison yard was deserted save for a lantern that bobbed up and down at the end furthest from Big-scar. He crouched as he crossed the open expanse. He shinned an iron fence, and crawled upon his stomach till he reached the ice. There he waited, glancing back. There was no sign or sound of discovery.

Big-scar frowned. Danger would come at midnight when the hallkeeper would flash a light into his cell. The newspaper and the dressed dummy would probably be discovered. The siren would blow. The constables would be notified. He resolved to place as many miles between himself and the prison as running would permit.

He hurried over the ice of the river till he had passed below the southern wall. Then he edged inshore, scrambled up the bank, and ran down a railroad track.

A crossing led him where he found himself between snow-covered hedges of estates that stretched back from the road in long vistas of contentment and rest.

Big-scar went on. It was Christmas Eve and all the world was at peace, except himself and the Law.

THE STARS that spangled the heavens were like powdered diamonds in a black velvet band. Snow and ice crunched and crinkled under foot.

Once he gained a cheerful thought. He was on his way to a city whose arms would reach and close him in their grip. He could hide with gangsters until the pursuit was over. Then he could come out and mooch to other cities.

The yegg liked the thought of being lost among a million people. He had little fear of being captured, providing he would stay away from his old haunts.

He plodded on through the snow with one thought in his mind: he must reach a racketeer's dive before the police were notified.

Costella and the whole Central-Office force could search until they grew tired. Costella and O'Morpha had made the pinch from which the yegg was escaping.

Both dicks were hard-boiled eggs. It was just like them to spoil a Christmas day.

He made progress through the silent estates of the rich. He held before him the glow in the sky that marked the city. It was like some aurora of wealth and security. It lured him on to greater effort.

Big-scar glared over his shoulder now and then. No sound or echo of the escape disturbed the attenuated air. He concluded the hall captain had flashed a light into cell 27 and then gone on satisfied.

The yegg's prison clothes were dark gray. They might be mistaken for a workman's garb. His cap worried him. It was round, with a small vizor that would give him away to anyone who had visited the prison.

Big-scar searched to right and left for a house in course of construction. There would be another cap or hat in such a place. Painters or plasterers always left them. Also, he could pick up a paint-pot or a tool and walk into the city like a laborer. The police would hardly suspect or question him in such a guise.

The road he followed widened into a square whereon was a gasoline station. The yegg paused before it and studied the windows. There was nothing inside the station except oil in cans.

He had taken a step away when there rose the low rumble of a far-off siren. It swelled, then died to an echo. It rose again. It filled the air with its menace. It spoke of gunguards, white faces in the cells, a country-wide pursuit wherein it would be unsafe to move. It indicated a Christmas eve air of broadcasting his description.

Big-scar ran as he had never run before. He charged along a road as if all the furies in the world were after him. He covered a mile in fast time when he brought up standing and blowing before the arbor gate of a snug estate.

He held his burning sides as he crouched under a hedge.

"Somethin's comin'," he said through gritty teeth.

There sounded footsteps in the lane that led down from the country home. The steps came closer. Big-scar braced himself and waited for almost certain discovery. He felt that he would have to bean somebody.

Out through the snow-draped boxwood came the figure of Santa Claus. It was such a Santa Claus as the yegg had read about in prison tracts. White whiskers draped over great horn buttons. Merry eyes and a scarlet nose peered through these whiskers. The cap on Santa's head was cocked and debonair. In the pack on the back of the apparition was a pile of toys, hobby-horses, dolls, whips, with bells upon their ends.

The yegg clicked his frozen lashes as Santa Claus swung at the arbor, whistled a tipsy tune, and went up the road without glancing back. Big-scar scratched his head. His face grew dark as he heard the sound of the prison siren to the north and toward the river. Its notes were insistent. It seemed to say:

"Prisoner has escaped! Prisoner has escaped! Fifty dollars reward!"

Swinging, the yegg watched the burly form of the man who had come out of the estate. He was evidently going somewhere with presents to hang upon a Christmas tree. Big-scar remembered the days when he had believed in Santa Claus. That was when he was about three years old.

He dashed after the figure in the road.

The footprints of the Santa Claus had not run in a straight line. They zig-zagged across the road in the manner of one who had imbibed too much.

The approaching yegg noted that the Santa Claus was about his size and general weight. He determined to possess himself of the Kris Kringle outfit, pack and all. It would be a disguise in a million. In it he could go anywhere and grin at the police.

BIG-SCAR slowed his steps as he tailed the staggering figure ahead. He glanced back now and then and listened. The siren was sending its warning blares out over the country. They bore no resemblance to holiday cheer.

The escaping yegg's chance came when the tipsy Santa Claus stopped by the side of the road, rested his pack upon a snow-covered stone, and sat down heavily. Big-scar drew the hack-saw blade from his pocket and advanced with all the noise he could make.

"Put up y'ur mitts!" he commanded.

The Kris Kringle whiskers quivered as two pudgy hands shot into the frosty air.

"Look out, or I'll shoot," menaced Big-scar, standing at a safe distance and brandishing the saw. "I'll shoot at th' first move. Y'u greaseball!"

"Spare me! Spare me!" came from Santa Claus.

"Take off that outfit y'u!"

One hand came down, then jerked upward again as Big-scar stepped forward.

"Get 'em off! Take off 'em whiskers an' things! All off or I'll plug y'u!"

The man rose, swaying from side to side, and began to unpeel his coat. The trousers followed. The whiskers and cap and nose dropped to the snow.

"Beat it!" growled Big-scar. "Beat it while th' goin's good. I'm goin' tu fire in three seconds. One, t'u—"

The yegg had a glimpse of a thoroughly frightened householder leaping over hedges, bushes, and fences in the manner of a jackrabbit.

He pocketed the saw as he heard a crash of glass where the man had stepped through a low greenhouse. He held his sides as he roared with glee. It was the first time he had laughed in years.

The figure that hurried down the snow-covered road five minutes later, was a different one from the convict who had climbed out of the great prison and escaped. Big-scar carried the Santa Claus pack. The wig he wore, allowed free vent for his mouth and eyes. It concealed the tell-tale scar on his right cheek.

A nose which was of papier-mache and colored like a ripe strawberry was almost the original hue of the yegg's nasal appendage before it had been whitened by prison life and lack of booze. He felt no cold, although the temperature was almost zero and falling. He reasoned that it was between twelve and one on Christmas morning.

Lights shone ahead. Big-scar trudged along until a suburban town opened up before him with its close-nested homes mantled in security like hens at roost. He found the pavement hard and clear under foot. He passed citizens who waved at him and answered his cheery "Merry Christmas."

A motor-bus stood waiting, as if for him, at the junction of two streets. He entered it, fished deep within his inner prison-suit pocket, and brought forth a silver dime. He had other money secreted from prison guards. The yegg caught a glimpse of himself in a window. No one of the gun-guards who were combing the county would have suspected in him the object of their search. The paper nose, the white whiskers, the pack crammed with toys, were his passport to the gates of the city he was now entering. He seemed the personification of the day and the season.

The bus stopped under the shelter of a structure which would lead to the subway. Big-scar climbed out, followed by the sleepy passengers. He had not long to wait for an early morning train that would take him into the heart of the city.

He parted with a nickel at the turnstile and entered the rear car. His heart jumped. He recognized two Central-Office detectives who were sitting at the front end of the car. They eyed him, then fell to talking.

Big-scar breathed a sigh of relief.

They had not recognized him in his guise. It was as if he possessed a mantle of invisibility. He leered at them.

The click of the car wheels on the rails became music to Big-scar. He longed to take off the gigantic red nose and breath more freely. He looked around to see if he could possibly roll a drunk for a bottle.

The yegg saw moving pictures of stations crowded with well garbed merry-makers, white walls that blazed with familiar advertisements, and displays of food posters that made his mouth water.

HE CROUCHED closer into his seat and glanced about the car. It was empty except for the two Central-Office men who were in the further end. One of these men had a turkey under his arm. Big-scar tightened his belt.

He lifted his Kris Kringle pack and examined its contents. There were toys enough in it to stock a nursery or to grace a large Christmas tree. At its bottom the yegg felt boxes of dates and candy and twisted paper things that would explode when they were drawn apart. He crammed them deeper within the pack, swung it upon his shoulder, and waited.

The Central-Office dicks rose at a station. They braced themselves as the train came to a grinding halt, then hurried out on the platform. They had not suspected him. He stood erect as the train gained speed. The next station would be the one he wanted to get off at. He stood in the vestibule with cool nerve. The train drew up, he stepped to the platform, and hurried up a stairway to the familiar street.

Down this he walked briskly, his eyes glinting. He was free! He was disguised to perfection. He felt like one of the wise men of the East bringing gifts to the Magi.

The yegg recognized the landmarks

as he passed into another and meaner street. There was O'Connor's speakeasy. Its front door was closed. He could see the long shining bar with the frosted mirror behind, and underneath this a row of black bottles.

A bartender came from the rear. A light shone there. A crowd sat at the tables drinking beer and whiskey.

A pal or two might be celebrating there.

He hesitated as he passed the saloon. He was of a mind to try the side entrance, stalk in on the gang and surprise them. Possibly they were talking of his escape at that very moment. He mooched on. He feared a stool pigeon.

Suddenly near a hiding place where he wanted to secrete himself, he saw two lurking forms. He felt the grip of a nameless something at his heart. He steeled himself as he had often done in days gone by. The two forms were fly-mugs. He felt sure that they were waiting for him. He went boldly by them and recognized Costella and his side-partner O'Morpha. They had made the pinch at the bank. They knew of his escape.

"Can't be him," Costella said cautiously.

"I ain't so sure; he's about due."

"In that outfit? Why that's some mission stiff with a pack of toys. Take another gap at him, O'Morpha."

AN ALLEY behind the Huber Museum, was a familiar getaway for the yegg. He had once or twice taken that route when dodging the coppers. He remembered a barred window, high up, through which an agile man might break into the Museum. Once before he had considered doing so. He had given up that plan, realizing that wax and plaster and paste jewels, worn by some of the effigies, were not negotiable with fences.

He reached the spot beneath the window. No one was in the alley. It was too early for anyone, save festive souls, to be stirring. The sun had not yet struck across the roofs or broken through the nipping mist.

The yegg sprang for the window's sill, secured a grip, drew himself on the ledge, braced a knee and yanked at the center bar of the window. It was of rusty iron; it gave where lead had been poured into the stone. Again he braced his knees, adjusted the Santa Claus pack, and bent the bar out of the way. Then he jerked at the sash, which came up, with a shower of dust and cobwebs. Big-scar peered inside the Museum. He saw a storeroom's walls, canvas frames, crates of excelsior and barrels of plaster-of-Paris.

A door lead from the storeroom to the Museum proper. This door was slightly ajar.

"A nifty hiding place!" the yegg said as he dropped to the floor and drew down the sash, after straightening the iron bar. "Here's where I smash those fly-mugs if they are still trailing me."

He realized that there was a watchman or two within the Museum; there also might be a charwoman at work, scrubbing floors. Big-scar's mind was made up; he wanted one more try at freedom.

He opened the door that led from the storeroom and crouched like an ape, ready to spring on someone. His shaggy brows worked up and down as he squinted uncertainly in his efforts to pierce the gloom of the Chamber of Horrors. His papier-mache nose came loose.

A uniformed guard stood, leaning against a display case almost in the center of the Museum. The sight of the gold-braided uniform roused the yegg's anger like a sudden slap in the face. He ground his teeth and made ready for a leaping spring. Prison screws and coppers were the yegg's particular meat.

He covered the distance like a tiger. The blow he struck, the watchman would have slain a giant. Big-scar's fist went through a wire frame and plaster. The watchman was an image, designed to confuse visitors. This image crumpled to the floor and lay prone.

The yegg stared around and saw a hundred wax faces making mock of him. Marie Antoinette, Danton, Napoleon, Josephine, Jesse James, Jack the Ripper and Chapman were enjoying the occasion. Between two booths, filled with effigies, the yegg discerned himself—a Santa Claus with a pack of toys.

He set about his task of destroying the effigy. He crushed the figure's head, stamping at the powder beneath his prison-made shoes. The noise he made was slight. He pressed the exhibit into an unrecognizable mass. He examined the suit on the figure. The proprietor of the Museum, always a stickler for detail, had clothed the effigy in a woolen suit, big buttons, gaudy tie and flashing shirt. This outfit was a ringer for the one Big-scar wore. He sat down and listened for sounds while he donned a pair of real leather shoes.

There came a sudden sound at the front of the Museum that indicated guards were unlocking doors. A whistle shrilled through the building. Another sound came from the rear near the store-room.

"CAUGHT!" thought Big-scar "I'm surrounded. Maybe they heard me. Maybe them coppers tipped me off to th' guards."

He got up and looked about him. He realized that it would be well to conceal the evidence of destruction. There was an imitation showcase alongside Santa Claus' form. Small toys filled the case, to lend realism to the exhibit.

The yegg began shoving the broken plaster beneath the showcase. His foot moved while he watched a giant

door swing inward.

They were opening the Museum for the day, though it was still quite early. The proprietor of the place was known for his long hours and industrious habits.

The drowsy guards had not yet detected the fugitive's presence. Big-scar glared at them through his false whiskers.

A group of patrons, led by an old man with a guide book, entered the building. A girl screamed when she collided with a horror in the shape of a plaster-of-Paris pickpocket.

"I gotta pose fer Santa Claus," concluded the yegg. "I can't make a get-away without stirrin' up a lot of gumshoe guards."

He climbed a pedestal and sat down when the group, headed by the old man, strolled by. He heard the guide explain:

"This 'ere old Kris Kringle, or Santa Claus. He was brought here especially for the Holidays. He's almost alive."

" 'E is, is'e?" thought the yegg with inward glee when the group strolled toward Jack the Ripper's booth.

Workmen came out of the storeroom. They started hammering at a new exhibit, at the back of the Museum.

Attendants approached at the head of more visitors.

"I wonder if I have to sit like this all day?" the yegg queried to himself. "It's an outrage—me dyin' fer somethin' to eat an' drink."

At ten o'clock a commotion started at the entrance. The yegg straightened himself and stared over the top of the showcase. The aisles were dotted with patrons. Among them he discerned the uniforms of a brace of cops. Behind the cops loomed familiar forms—those of Costella and O'Morpha.

The menaces from Headquarters

were darting glances to left and right. Near them walked the Museum's proprietor.

"Somebody tipped 'em off," sighed the yegg. "They're goin' tu make a search of th' Museum."

The detectives paused at the crushed figure of the sham guard which Big-scar had smashed with his fists. The proprietor bent over the figure while the two dicks looked around knowingly. Both had heavy overcoats on. O'Morpha's pocket bulged with a quart bottle.

Big-scar smacked his lips. His nose itched.

"I hope they don't connect me with beaning th' guard," he grinned.

His hopes were set at rest; the two detectives shook their heads. It wasn't likely that the yegg would leave such evidence of his presence in the Museum.

By roundabout aisles Costella and O'Morpha approached the yegg. The bloodhounds from Headquarters were making a thorough search of the Museum. They sized up everybody, questioned guards and workmen, looked behind gruesomely painted curtains. They neared Santa's booth, followed by the Museum's proprietor.

"This," explained the manager, "is for the kids. See, he's loaded with toys. We'll give them away tomorrow, or maybe this afternoon if the crowd is thick enough."

A cold feeling went up and down Big-scar's spine. He held himself in position with a mighty effort. He felt Costella's sharp eyes on his back. O'Morpha remarked dryly:

"It's a rotten imitation of Santa Claus. Eh, Costella? It don't look life-like."

Costella replied: "No resemblance. When they do these things, why don't they do them proper? Why don't they make the effigies true to nature?"

The dicks moved on.

COLD sweat stood out on Big-scar's brow. It had been a close touch-and-go between him and liberty. He was afraid to turn his head and watch the two detectives.

A diversion came at noon when a group of children, led by a teacher, filed into the Museum. The children all carried boxes or baskets. One boy perched himself near the Santa Claus booth and opened his box. He devoured most of the contents, finally taking out a piece of pie. The yegg, who had eaten nothing since escaping, glared at the pie. He leaned toward it—then hesitated.

The boy laid half the pie on top of the lunch box and went for a glass of water. Big-scar selected a present from his pack and rose from his chair.

Temptation and hunger steeled the yegg's nerve. The sight of his favorite pie made the risk seem small.

He got the portion and thrust it into his mouth. He rubbed his soiled whiskers and resumed his position in the chair.

A cry went through the aisles of the Museum when the boy returned and missed the pie. The present did not appease him. He ran toward the teacher and explained what had happened. Scholars were accused. They denied the theft in loud terms.

"That's a bad rumble tu make over a piece ov pie," thought Big-scar. "What would they do if I copped a whole one? Maybe they'd hang me fer it."

He cast an anxious eye about for escape. The workmen at the back of the Museum had ceased their labors at noon. Perhaps a getaway could be made in that direction. There was the bent bar in the storeroom through which he could squeeze. The yegg started out of the booth. He tiptoed a few cautious steps when voices caused him to halt stiff in his tracks.

Other children were approaching. He was caught. He advanced to them and unloaded his pack, giving each a present.

"Merry Christmas," he said through his beard. "Wish I had more presents, kids. "Now beat it away. I'm goin' tu be a wax image again. Beat it, kids."

He resumed his rigid position on the dais until nightfall.

When the doors were closing, he heard Costella's voice saying: "We'll plant in here tonight. Every clue leads to this Museum."

"Aw, Big-scar couldn't be here!" O'Morpha protested.

"Someone got in here. There's a twisted bar."

The yegg sat like a steel spring, ready to pounce on the two sleuths as they sauntered around, flashing spotlights into every booth. They stopped finally and sat down at a little gold-painted table drawn from the Marie Antoinette Exhibition.

"It'll be a tough night watchin' this dump," declared Costella. "But it's chief's orders. Guffman, alias Big-scar used to live near this Museum. Give me a drink, O'Morpha."

Costella's side-kick produced a bottle of Holiday booze. He upended the bottle before offering it to Costella. Big-scar whose nose was almost white from keeping temperate, sniffed the alcohol. It brought tears to his eyes.

The papier-mache mask and beard fell around his gigantic neck. He waited, leaning forward toward the sleuthes. They drowsed, each groggy from drinking.

Over the intervening distance the yegg reached his arm and gained the bottle. He clutched it in his cotton-covered fingers. The remaining half portion almost vanished down his throat. He set the bottle nearer Costella than O'Morpha, and staggered to his chair. He waited.

STRATEGY might succeed where force would fail. O'Morpha awoke and reached blindly for the bottle. His hand strayed over the table. He blinked his eyes, then, as he grabbed the remaining drop, he cursed his partner drunkenly. Costella awoke. The yegg-heard an argument, hot and heavy between the dicks.

"You're a hell of a guy, takin' it all!" Costella accused.

They drowsed, after almost drawing guns on each other.

A second inspiration came to the yegg. He shifted the pack from his shoulders, got down and tiptoed toward the sleeping sleuths. His hand touched the little gold-painted table. He gripped the bottle, swung it overhead, and brought it crashing through O'Morpha's slouch hat. Big-scar ducked around a booth and started crawling like a grizzly toward the rear of the Museum.

The diversion of O'Morpha recovering from the staggering blow and lunging at Costella was time enough, to throw both detectives off guard. Over went the little table. Blows were exchanged. Arms swung. The brace of fly-mugs crashed together into the Marie Antoinette booth, O'Morpha cursing:

"Take that an' that, yu hit me with th' bottle!"

"You copped th' booze!"

"Nifty," remarked Big-scar shedding the whiskers and mask from his neck. He threw a knee over the window-sill where the twisted bar was.

Behind him he heard sounds of struggling; ahead in the nipping air was freedom.

"It ain't been such a bad Christmas after all," he grinned. "An' them poor kids got toys they w'uldn't ov got, if I hadn't played Santa Claus."

While the taxi was traveling at full speed, he dropped off

Big City Christmas

A Novelette

By Lieut. John Hopper

*The Actors in This Gripping Drama Faced Death, Disgrace, Starvation,
the Triumph of a Career All between Dark and Dawn of Christmas Day*

CHAPTER I

The Bum

JAMES WILSON stood on the corner of Thirty-Fourth Street and Broadway watching the last minute shoppers swirl past him, their arms filled with packages, jostling and being jostled. It was eight o'clock, Christmas Eve. The jammed, weary department stores closed at nine.

Jim Wilson wasn't doing any Christmas shopping this year. His frayed pants pockets contained forty-five cents —all the money he had in the world. He pushed the upturned collar of his thin coat closer to his neck. He was cold—chilled to the bone.

The gusty wind twirled the front page of an evening newspaper through the legs of the sidewalk throng. It finally came to rest at Wilson's feet. The headlines caught his eye, and he picked it up. As he read, his ungloved hands were blue with cold. *Merry Xmas to All* across the top. Below:

COVELLI GETS CHAIR CHRISTMAS MORN

Governor Refuses Reprieve

Wilson caught the irony of the headlines, and snorted aloud. *Merry Xmas to All!* Especially to Covelli, who—

ever he was and whatever he had done, shivering in the condemned cell, waiting fearfully until the break of the Christmas dawn, when he would stagger forth to receive his present from society—death.

Wilson crumpled the paper and tossed it into the street. He felt a surge of bitterness against society, that condemned a human being to die on Christmas morning.

Or go hungry—and cold. Especially a man who lived right and wanted only the chance to earn his bread.

A year and a half ago, Wilson had a job—repair man for a telephone company. But they had let him go that fall, not because he wasn't a good man, but simply because they had to cut down overhead. Wilson had remained in New York until after the New Year, trying his best to get a job. But it seemed that there wasn't an opening in the whole, big city for a good electrician; even for a man willing to use his two hands at anything.

Then he had heard that unemployment wasn't as bad on the West Coast. It had taken the little money he had left to reach San Francisco. Jim Wilson was not a man to take a licking from Fate lying down, or to exist by charity—especially when there was a girl whom he hoped to marry.

Luella Kennedy was the girl. At the time, she had been social secretary to the wife of a prominent lawyer, Jackson Towner—that was before Towner became district attorney.

San Francisco had been no better than New York. Wilson returned through the West and the Middle-West, occasionally working a day, or two. But the work had always run out, and he had drifted gradually Eastward.

Luella was drawing him back. He was hungry for sight of her, hungrier than he was for good food. He had not heard from her in over three months. He had supposed that it had been impossible for her letters to keep up with him. The places he had rested his head didn't forward mail.

Two days before Christmas, he had hit New York.

From the cold, clanging, freight yard, he had gone directly to a speakeasy off of Eighth Avenue, near Columbus Circle. It was owned and operated by his wartime buddy, Terry O'Toole, a lean Irishman with dark, curly hair and brown, friendly, humorous eyes. Terry slept in the back room of his speakeasy. He agreed to let Jim do likewise. As for money, Terry had said, without being asked, that he hadn't any. Business was terrible.

Jim Wilson started looking for Luella Kennedy. She had vanished without trace. A telephone call to the district attorney's apartment on Park Avenue had given him the disturbing information that she had lost her job about three months ago, and that no one in the district attorney's family knew her present whereabouts. Jim had gone to the walk-up apartment house on Twelfth Street, near Fifth Avenue, where she and another girl had shared a small apartment. The apartment was vacant, and the unsympathetic janitor didn't know where the occupants had moved to.

That was why Jim Wilson was standing on the corner, scanning the belated, bundle-laden, Christmas shoppers. He hoped to see Luella. Just a year ago, he had been one of a similar crowd of last minute shoppers, with Luella clinging tightly to his arm. Luella said she loved to do her Christmas shopping in the last minute. Christmas Eve, the big stores jammed, the streets crowded with people and packages. It gave her a delicious, excited, Christmasy feeling.

THE huge department store on the corner was her favorite shopping place. Ever since five o'clock, Wilson had been on guard before its doors, which swung continuously, creaking with the frost. It was a forlorn hope, he admitted to himself, that Luella would appear in the crowds. But it was his only hope, and he was going to remain until it faded completely with the closing of the store.

He stared bleakly into its brilliant windows. His mind would take up the same, unanswerable question: where was Luella? Perhaps, he winced mentally, she had given up her job to marry. His memory of her love and loyalty rose immediately to deny this. She had said that she would wait for him.

He stamped his feet and clapped his hands together to drive out the cold. There had been a flurry of snow that afternoon, and the pavements were still wet and glistening from it. A Salvation Army Santa Claus stood on the corner ringing a handbell.

Suddenly Wilson's heart bumped, and then stood still. He saw her— Luella! She was emerging from the department store, loaded with packages. He stared.

He was about to call her joyfully, when he noticed that she was smiling at a man beside her. He was short, fat, and dark, sleek and prosperous looking. His hand held Luella's arm possessively.

He steered her through the sidewalk throngs to a taxi beside the curb. Wilson watched them get in. He saw the smile which she gave the man as he sank down beside her.

Wilson's icy fists clenched savagely, and his lean, hard jaw tightened. It was a shock, a tougher blow than the cruel knocks he had received during those long, weary months when he had found courage to keep his head up with pride, and fight, because of her.

The taxi swung away from the curb and slipped into the traffic bound downtown, but it was held at Thirty-Fourth Street by a red light.

Wilson came to a sudden decision.

He hailed a taxi cruising down the street, and indicated the car he wanted to follow. The driver eyed him narrowly, estimating whether or not his poorly dressed customer would have the fare. He finally decided to take the chance.

The two taxis proceeded down Broadway to Thirty-Second Street, where they turned east and traveled across town to Lexington Avenue. They turned right on Lexington, and Luella's taxi drew up before an imposing apartment building. Wilson sat in the darkness of his cab, watched a doorman hasten to assist Luella and her escort with their packages. The trio vanished into the brightly lighted foyer.

Wilson descended from his taxi. The fare was forty cents. He hesitated a moment, and finally, with a shrug, gave the driver the entire forty-five cents. The man accepted the nickel tip, and touched his cap cynically.

" Merry Christmas!" he said, shifting his gears.

" Same to you."

Wilson thrust his hands deep into his empty pockets. He hunched his shoulders against the cold. He wandered closer to the doorway of the building, and could see through its revolving door that the foyer was furnished luxuriously with carpets and polished furniture. A tiny Christmas tree stood in one corner beyond the elevators. Luella and the man were not to be seen. Evidently they had already gone up in one of the elevators.

Wilson swallowed hard. He supposed she had married. She certainly had married well, he concluded bitterly.

He jammed his cold hands deeper into his pockets and shivered. He stared upward at the tall, broad face of the building. He saw many lighted windows. In some there was the steady glow of a candle to light the way of the Christ child.

He wondered which window belonged to Luella.

His thin lips parted in a small, bitter smile. Ah, but it was cold! He had never been as cold as this except once— fifteen years ago, in France. But he had been a hero then, and it had been his duty to suffer cold—and death— and anything else that might have happened to him—while the muzzle flashes of the cannon lighted the way for the Christ child.

And now he was a bum. The fat-necked doorkeeper of the place where she lived had told him so.

CHAPTER II

The Big Boss

ABOUT a hundred feet vertically from the sidewalk where Jim Wilson stood, Guito Bono sat behind a huge, flat-topped, mahogany desk.

Very few people knew that Guito Bono owned this building. He held it in the name of a dummy corporation, as he did all his other financially juicy properties in Manhattan. And no one, outside of a half dozen persons closest to him, like Paul Jaffin, his secretary; Tony Carlova, his collector of moneys;

and Al Rocchi, boss of his muscle and rod men, knew that he sometimes used the tenth floor, furnished, for business. It was always kept vacant for him.

As Guito sat at the big desk, which gleamed somberly in the soft, shaded lamps of the room, he looked more like a banker, or a solid, responsible business man. He was neither tall nor unduly short; neither nervously thin nor visibly stout; he was just the solidly built, executive type American of perhaps Latin extraction, in a smooth, tailored sack suit. There were streaks of silver in his coal black hair. But his beady, ferret-like, black eyes and his cruel, sensual mouth gave him away; they mutely spoke of ruthless murders, double-crossings, bribery, and dealings in the dark.

Now the stubby, powerful fingers of his right hand were drumming a nervous tattoo on the polished top of the desk. He was frowning unpleasantly.

Beside the windows, gazing down into the street, stood Jaffin, Guito's secretary. Jaffin was smooth looking, slender, blond, and hard. No one knew his real name except, possibly, Guito. Gossip had it that he had been someone in middle Western society— before he had written too many checks which he couldn't make good. No one knew where Guito had got hold of him; it was quite a few years back.

Guito struck the desk with a heavy fist.

"Damn!" he exploded. "Why don't Al come back with that woman?"

Jaffin turned his back to the windows.

"Give them time. The stores must be packed with last minute shoppers— especially the toy departments."

His greenish eyes fell soberly upon Guito.

"Why don't you give up this nasty

business, Guito? I've gone through a lot with you, and murder was the worst I thought I'd see. But when it comes to stealing a kid—on Christmas Eve, too, by heaven—that's—"

"Shut up!" ordered Guito savagely. "It's the only way. The district attorney knows that Covelli won't take the chair tomorrow morning with his mouth shut. Covelli'll squeal, and that's the finish for all of us. We got to save Covelli from the hot squat."

Jaffin selected a cigarette from a slim, silver case.

"It's hell," he sighed, "when these D. A.'s decide they're going to run for governor, and start in to clean up the town to make a noise for themselves."

Guito Bono rose from his desk and began to pace the carpet. Guito, whose hand was felt in every racket, whose ill will was enough to make prominent officials worry, and whose ire had sent men to their deaths, was worried.

Guito Bono had realized the limit of his ambition. He was acknowledged ruler of the liquor traffic, and the chief beneficiary of its enormous revenues. This height—or depth—he had attained in fifteen years.

He thought of those fifteen years as he walked to the windows and stood beside Jaffin, to stare moodily down upon the street. Raising his eyes to the apartment building across the way, he saw a small, lighted Christmas tree on a table behind a window.

Christmas Eve! It is peculiar how people's thoughts turn back to what they were doing on Christmas Eve a year ago, two years ago . . . fifteen years ago.

Guito remembered the one fifteen years ago. It was in 1917 during the war. He remembered it because it was the last Christmas he had been poor. He had been so wretchedly poor, a lean, cold, half-starved youth hanging around Bowery saloons and poolrooms, hoping to find a Christmas reveler too drunk to know that his pockets were being robbed. Before the next Christmas, Prohibition had come into force, and Guito knew how it felt to have a full stomach, and to wear clothes that were not hand-me-downs.

Now his fortune was in the multiple millions, and his name stood for power. And yet, before the end of Christmas Day, he was likely to be standing behind prison bars, in the shadow of the electric chair.

GUITO winced at the thought. Jaffin gave him a sidelong glance.

"How did you get onto this woman, this Luella Kennedy, anyway?"

"I know everything that happens in Towner's home—as well as in his office," replied Guito surlily.

"Yes, I know," soothed Jaffin. "Through Mears, the butler. But Luella Kennedy?"

"She used to be Mrs. Towner's secretary. They fired her about three months ago. When I thought of taking Towner's kid, I knew she was the one who could put it over for me. I had a hard time locating her. She thinks I'm a big butter-and-egg man, or something, from the Middle West. A friend of Towner's. In fact, I told her that Towner himself recommended her to me. I'm supposed to be in town for a few days on business, and I need a secretary. My name's Marcosson—Joseph Marcosson. None of this stuff bothers you. I'll handle everything. You just keep your mouth shut."

Jaffin grinned.

"Okay, Guito! But who is Al Rocchi supposed to be?"

" My valet," Bono answered shortly. Jaffin laughed cynically.

" That bloodthirsty devil anybody's valet !"

A buzzer sounded in the apartment. Guito nodded at Jaffin, who quickly crossed the room and opened the door.

With her arms filled with bundles, Luella Kennedy came into the room, followed by Al Rocchi, sleek, fat, and enigmatical. He was laden with packages, too.

Luella faced Guito Bono with a smile.

" The stores were crowded," she said breathlessly, " but I think I got all you wanted."

Jaffin studied her covertly as he tapped another cigarette upon his silver case. She had soft brown eyes and a marvelously clear skin. Tendrils of silky brown hair escaped from under her small black hat. Her winter coat was plain, with a cheap fur collar.

" I haven't had so much fun in a long time," she gasped. " I'm glad you let me do your Christmas shopping, Mr. Marcosson. But so many toys !"

Guito Bono spread his hands helplessly. " I don't know what I would have done without you! I am glad that Mr. Towner told me about you. There is one more favor that you could do me. Are you sure," he broke off to ask anxiously, " that you have nothing else to do? I know everybody likes to be home on Christmas Eve."

Shadows appeared in her eyes. She thought of Jim Wilson—wherever he was.

" No," she smiled. " It's—it's all right. There's no one waiting for me."

" Well, Miss Kennedy," said Guito, " I'd like to have you deliver a present for me—if you don't mind. A present for Mr. Towner's little boy."

" Donald !"

" Yes. Of course you knew him if you worked for Mrs. Towner. Pick out the nicest toy you bought. It's just something to show my appreciation to Mr. Towner for his favors to me."

Luella hesitated. Guito added sharply:

" What's the matter?"

" Oh, nothing," she smiled. " I was just thinking—I mean I wish I had known I was going to see Donald to-night. I would have taken him a present from me."

" Take anything you like from the rest of the presents. There'll be plenty left for those nephews of mine."

" Oh, thank you so much! I can pay you for whatever I take."

" Oh, no! Not at all. There's some Christmas wrapping paper and ribbon and stuff in the room down the hall. Al—Alfred will show you where. I'm going to send him uptown with you. I could have sent him by himself with the present, but I thought you'd like to see the Towners again. And I don't think I'll be seeing you until the day after Christmas, Miss Kennedy. Thank you for doing my Christmas shopping for me. It's something that only a woman can do—right." He smiled at her. " Good night. And Merry Christmas !"

Al Rocchi followed her to the door, and when she was out of sight in the hall, turned, and looked at Guito with a wink.

CHAPTER III

Santa Claus

WHEN the door closed, Jaffin strolled back to the windows to look down into the street. He saw a man with shoulders hunched against the cold, standing on the sidewalk in front of the building. Guito sat down to his desk.

"Go out and get me a bum off the street," he said to Jaffin. "Any bum that wants to earn five bucks playing Santa Claus for a while tonight."

Jaffin stared.

"Say, Guito, what's the matter with you? Is this business of Covelli driving you nuts?"

Guito's beady eyes glittered.

"Yeah, it's driving me crazy—like a fox! What do you think I dug up that jane for? To send a Christmas present to Towner's brat? Hell, without her Al wouldn't have a chance to get within a mile of the place. Towner's got dicks watching his place. He knows something might pop, with Covelli due to take the juice tomorrow. But there ain't nothing wrong with his wife's old secretary dropping in with her boy friend to leave a Christmas present for the kid, is there? Al knows what he's suppose to do once he gets inside the joint—and so does the butler."

"But the bum, Guito? What the devil—"

"You know Judge Gorham? Every Christmas he sends a guy dressed up as Santa Claus to the Orphans' Home with a bagful of toys for the kids. It always makes the newspapers. Gorham is a friend of Towner's, see? To this bum, I'm Judge Gorham. The bum won't know any different. Now go ahead out and grab one. He's going to be the fall guy."

Jaffin frowned and shook his head doubtfully.

"Damned if I understand what you're up to, Guito, but if you really mean it, there's a bum standing down on the sidewalk now."

"Okay. Go down and bring him up. Make it snappy."

Two minutes later Jaffin led Jim Wilson into Guito's presence.

"This man says he'll be your Santa Claus—Judge Gorham."

Guito Bono scowled across his desk.

"Ah, yes! Thank you . . . uh . . . Smith," he said to Jaffin.

Jaffin smiled cynically. Yet he was actually admiring Guito. Jaffin was forced to admire him. No one closely associated with Guito Bono could deny that he was a remarkable man. He had virtually lifted himself to the top by his own bootstraps—by his cuteness, his callous ruthlessness, and his astonishing ability to find a solution to every problem and to play any part in that solution.

New York's liquor traffic was big business, and no ordinary man could hope to control it. It required better than average brains and ability to climb to the top of any big business.

And Jaffin knew that Guito Bono was fighting with every ounce of his ability for his business—and for his very life.

If Covelli, sleeplessly pacing his cell in Sing Sing, should lose hope before dawn, and squeal what he knew, Guito Bono was through.

GUITO BONO and Jim Wilson looked at each other. Guito saw a bum whose chief ambition was probably the price of a drink. If Guito had not been so worried about his own affairs, he might have noticed certain marks of character. The hat Jim Wilson held in his two hands was old and shapeless, but not dirty. His suit was unpressed and threadbare, but it was clean. His bright, shining, red hair needed cutting badly, but it had been carefully combed that afternoon. His shirt was woolen, but there was no greasy rim where the collar met the lean, bronzed neck. His tie was slightly frayed, but unspotted.

Jim Wilson saw a man called Judge Gorham. He looked near enough to anybody's conception of a judge—prosperous, able, with an air of authority.

Certainly this place he lived in was suitable enough for a judge. Jim wondered if Luella's apartment was as luxurious as this.

It would have astonished him considerably if he had known that Luella was, at that very moment, in a room down the hall wrapping toys while the man he supposed to be her husband watched her through heavily lidded eyes in a face inelegantly known as a " dead pan."

" I—uh—have some presents I'd like to have delivered tonight." Black eyes focused on eyes of light blue. " They're toys for—uh—children, children of some friends of mine. I thought it would be a nice idea to send them around by somebody dressed as Santa Claus. The kids," Guito smiled, " will like that.

" I have a suit in the next room," he continued. " The toys, are packed in a bag. It won't be much trouble. Take you about an hour, or so. My chauffeur will drive you in the car. He has a list of the places where you're to go. I'll give you five dollars."

Jim Wilson did not take long to consider the offer. With five bucks he could eat a decent Christmas dinner himself!

" I'll do it."

Guito rose from the desk and threw open the door of an adjoining room. When the door had closed behind Wilson, he picked up the French telephone on his desk.

" Send for my car right away. Have the chauffeur come up here."

Then he turned and faced Jaffin. He was smiling.

" Like taking candy from a baby. Nobody but me would have thought of it."

" What?" asked Jaffin.

Guito raised his hand. " Wait and see."

The chauffeur came into the living room before Wilson reappeared. There was nothing unusual about the man. In his neat, gray uniform and black-visored cap, he would have been accepted anywhere at face value. Perhaps he was more powerfully built, and his face was a little grimmer than one usually sees behind the wheel of a town car, but then, some people like strong, silent, austere chauffeurs.

Guito stepped beside him quickly, and said in low tones:

" Remember, go up to Towner's right away. You have to get there before Al and the woman. Don't let the dicks worry you. They don't know you, and you don't know them. You're just Judge Gorham's chauffeur."

The chauffeur lifted a black-gauntleted hand and cast a warning look toward the doorway of the adjoining room. There stood Santa Claus. Jim Wilson's blue eyes gleamed over a long, white beard, which completely hid the lower half of his face. His red hair was covered by a tasseled red cap. A huge bag bulging with toys stood beside him. It reached practically to his chest.

Guito's beady eyes sparkled, and his heavy lips smiled.

" The suit's a perfect fit! All right. you can go along now." He nodded at the chauffeur.

When the door closed behind them, Bono turned to Jaffin triumphantly.

" In the bag, Jaffin," he growled. " In the bag. The bum goes in, but he don't come out. The kid does—in the bag."

Jaffin's eyes widened.

" I couldn't use one of the boys for the job," continued Guito. " The dicks would pound him, and he might crack. But the bum can't—because he don't know nothing."

" By heaven, Guito," breathed his secretary, " you're smart!"

" Never mind that stuff, Jaffin. Go out and give Al the high sign that it's time he was leaving with the woman. They'll take a taxi."

Bono sat down at the desk and began twisting his fingers in evident agitation.

" It's make or break for us tonight, Jaffin. Fifteen years from the slums," he concluded tensely, " and damned if I'm going to let any district attorney break me!"

Jaffin went out, and shut the door softly behind him.

CHAPTER IV

The District Attorney

JACKSON TOWNER lived on Park Avenue, approximately twenty-five blocks north of Guito Bono's apartment building on Lexington. The district attorney's home consisted of the fifth floor of a quiet, exclusive building, which was noted not only for its high rentals, but also for the social standing of its tenants.

Towner's small family his wife and young son, did not require such a large apartment, but his official position and his political aspirations demanded it. Besides there were several servants to be cared for, including the butler, Mears.

Towner was in his study. In an arm chair opposite his desk sat Tom Mahoney, commissioner of police,

silently smoking a thick cigar. Towner was at the telephone.

" Get me the warden at Sing Sing Prison," he was saying.

He was a large, big-boned man, with straight, iron-gray hair. His age was approximately forty-five. He wore rimless glasses over a pair of penetrating grayish-green eyes. His long, hard face was marked by two deep furrows, which began beside his high-bridged nose and ended at the corners of his thin, straight mouth. It was the face of a man who had evidently worked hard to obtain what he had, who was proud of his standing with his fellow-men, who had ambitions, and who never made compromises with either his duty or his ambitions. It was not a kind face. Men admitted that Towner was just, but they also said that his share of the milk of human kindness must have been skimmed.

While he waited for his connection he glanced at a clock on his desk. Almost nine o'clock! He frowned impatiently into the mouthpiece. Donald was being allowed to remain up until nine because it was Christmas Eve, and his father had promised to tell him a story about Santa Claus. Confound Sing Sing! Why didn't they answer?

He finally heard the warden's voice.

" Covelli hasn't talked yet, Mr. Towner. He's sure his friends will put a stop to the execution."

" All right, Warden. Thanks. He'll talk before dawn," Towner added grimly. " Call me just as soon as he does."

Towner replaced the hand instrument in its saddle, while Tom Mahoney flicked the ash of his cigar to the carpet.

" The newspapers are riding us," began the portly police commissioner uneasily, " because we're killing Covelli on Christmas morning. They claim it's inhuman."

Towner tightened his thin lips.

"When the cheap newspapers stop making heroes out of live gangsters, and martyrs out of condemned ones," he replied, "we'll have fewer recruits to the underworld. It isn't inhuman to execute a wanton murderer—a human rat—at any time."

The district attorney extended a fist across the top of the desk.

"If Covelli talks, Tom, we've got Guito Bono." Towner's voice vibrated with excitement. "We've never been able to get anything on him before that would stick. With Covelli on the witness stand, I'll send Guito Bono to the chair. And that will go a long way toward breaking up New York's underworld."

The police commissioner shifted his heavy body uneasily in the chair, and ran his stubby fingers, still holding the cigar, through his yellowish white hair.

"If Covelli squeals," he muttered. "But I'm not so sure he's that yellow."

Towner sat back in his chair and adjusted his glasses on his nose.

"I think he'll tell," he said decisively. "That was one reason I had the execution set for Christmas morning. An experiment in psychology, Commissioner. Of all the times to die, I think most people would pick Christmas as the worst. Even in prison, it's Christmas Eve tonight. I'm counting on it to affect Covelli. And he knows that his sentence of execution will be commuted to a comparatively short term of imprisonment if he'll talk about Bono."

The telephone on Towner's desk rang sharply.

"Yes?" he answered. "From Judge Gorham? Oh, yes, it's all right. Tell him to come up, please."

The police commissioner arose to his feet and adjusted his fur-lined overcoat around his thick, sloping shoulders.

"Santa Claus is paying us a visit," explained Towner smiling, as he replaced the telephone. "Judge Gorham sent him. A nice thought—and a picturesque way of sending presents. One of your men stopped him in the lobby. I told him it was all right."

THE police commissioner relighted his cigar.

"The judge sends one to the Orphans' Home every Christmas, too." Mahoney's plump, red cheeks blew out a cloud of smoke. "Well, I can't stay any longer, Jackson. I was on my way home, and I thought I'd drop in to see what you'd heard from Sing Sing.

"I see," he added, "that my men are on duty downstairs." He gave the district attorney a significant look. "I'm going to keep them there until after this Covelli execution blows over. You never can tell what some of Bono's hopheads might attempt to pull."

Towner rose behind his desk and took off his glasses.

"Thanks, Tom. I appreciate it. But I feel that they are hardly necessary, and it seems a pity that they should have to stay here on Christmas Eve on my account."

"We'll leave them here just the same," returned the commissioner bluntly. "People who come into this building tonight have got to say where they are going. One of the men rides up in the elevator with them to see that they go where they said. No one can get to your floor without your okay first."

"The rest of the tenants won't be on speaking terms with me after this, Tom," Towner laughed.

The two men shook hands.

"Good night, Tom—and a Merry Christmas to you," said Towner.

"The same to you, Jackson—many of 'em. And call me at once, if Covelli cracks. I'll give the orders for the round up."

He paused at the door.

"If Covelli doesn't break by dawn, why don't you have the Governor reprieve the execution for a day or so? After all, Jackson, it's a helluva note to hand a man the chair for a Christmas present."

Towner smiled, but his eyes were as cold as pieces of ice.

"This is not a time for sentiment. Covelli might not break until they're strapping him into the chair. If we give him one reprieve, he'll never break."

The commissioner thought of the newspapers and s i g h e d. Jackson Towner was a hard man. Some day he would be governor, all right. If he succeeded, in sending Guito Bono to the chair, he would be a long way on the road in the favor of the people.

After the door closed upon Mahoney's broad back, Towner returned to his desk, where he sat down and rested his head upon his elbow. He was tired . . . tired . . . tired. Nothing but work. He couldn't even let up on Christmas Eve!

Ambition is a slave driver. Jackson Towner was surely a slave to his ambition. He intended getting some place— a high place in life—higher even than where he was now.

Tonight, this Christmas Eve, was likely to bring him the governorship of the State. It depended upon one man—in the cell of the condemned.

The telephone at Towner's elbow shrilled, banishing his reverie. He took it up with eager fingers. Perhaps Sing Sing was calling. But the voice of one of Mahoney's men in the lobby came to his ear.

"There's a lady down here, Mr. Towner, by the name of Miss Luella Kennedy. She says she used to work for your wife. She has a present for your son. She's got a boy friend with her."

Towner frowned with disappointment. He remembered Miss Kennedy, who used to be his wife's secretary. It had been Towner's idea to let her go. Joan, his wife, didn't really need a secretary.

Towner also remembered that Luella had been fond of Donald. It was nice of her to call with a present on Christmas Eve.

"It's all right," he told the detective in the lobby. "Have them come up, please."

By the time Towner replaced the telephone, his mind was already off on other things. He pulled some papers from a drawer, settled his glasses more firmly on his nose, and leaned forward to read.

————

CHAPTER V

In the Bag

THE butler led Jim Wilson into the reception room, where Wilson rested his big bag of packages in the middle of the floor.

"I've got a Christmas present here," he said, "for Donald Towner. It's from Judge Gorham."

Wilson had been astonished when the chauffeur had told him that their first call was at the district attorney's home. That was where Luella had worked. Remembering that Gorham was a judge, and therefore undoubtedly a friend of the district attorney, Wilson had dismissed it from his mind as a natural coincidence.

For a moment, Mears silently studied the red and white figure in front of him. Mears was the type of butler that could immediately take the part in a motion picture story of society. That was why Jackson Towner had hired him—without a very careful scrutiny of his references. The top of Mears' head was bald. He had side-burns, and a lean, phlegmatic face. His forehead was craggy above his impassive, dark eyes. His nose was pinched over his tight mouth.

"I'll inform Mr. Towner," Mears replied suavely. "Wait here, please."

He strode silently from the room, carefully closing the twin, curtained, glass doors behind him.

Alone, Jim Wilson let his gaze wander around the luxuriously furnished room. It was warm, quiet, and dim. Several, silk-shaded lights cast their golden glow only in an immediate circle, bringing out the gleam of a polished table, illuminating the satin brocade of a chair, or a sofa. In a fireplace, a small fire of coals glared redly. A holly wreath, with a large, red bow, hung on the mantel.

A quiet ache spread in Wilson's breast. He thought of the cold street from which he had come, and shivered. His blue eyes narrowed with momentary bitterness. It did not seem fair that some people should have the comforts of the world, while others had none.

The minutes passed, and he began to wonder what had happened to the butler, and why no one came to accept the present.

At that moment, the double doors swung back, and Mears walked in, followed by Luella and Al Rocchi.

"If you'll wait," Mears bowed to Luella, "I'll inform Mrs. Towner that you are here."

"Wouldn't you like to see the—the boy?" interposed Rocchi suddenly.

Luella smiled at the butler.

"Oh, yes!" she said eagerly. "If he hasn't gone to bed yet—and **Mrs.** Towner doesn't mind."

The butler bowed silently and closed the double doors behind him.

Jim Wilson had been staring at Luella. His heart was pounding furiously.

Luella turned with Al Rocchi, and surveyed the man dressed as Santa Claus. She smiled at the costume; Rocchi was heavily-lidded, apathetic.

Wilson took a step forward.

"Luella!" he said hoarsely.

The girl's smile faded, and she stared. The blue eyes, above the white whiskers, seemed vaguely familiar. Rocchi suddenly became alert, eying Santa Claus and the woman narrowly. The silence in the room took on a tenseness, and the w a r m t h and shadows became alive with impending drama.

"Luella—it's me—Jim."

He had forgotten the man with her.

Suddenly Luella gave a cry and ran across the room to throw her arms around Wilson's neck.

"Jim!" she cried brokenly. "Is it really you?"

Rocchi's heavy lids dropped lower, and his hand darted into his overcoat pocket.

"Hey!" he snarled. "What's this?"

BEFORE either Wilson or Luella could answer, the double doors opened again and a slim, fair-haired woman entered, guiding before her a small boy with golden, curly hair. His gaze was on Santa Claus, and he stood as one wonder-struck.

"Oh, mummy!" he finally breathed in awe. "*Santa Claus!*"

Mears was closing the double doors, which shut off the room from the rest of the apartment. He stepped into the shadow of a long drape. His impassive eyes began to glisten beneath their heavy brows.

Joan Towner smiled.

"How have you been, Luella?" she asked, in a soft, friendly voice. "It's so nice of you to call tonight. Donald has asked for you many times since you left."

She noticed suddenly that Luella was crying. She took a step forward anxiously.

"My dear! What's the matter?"

Luella Kennedy smiled through her tears. Her hands were nervously twisting her tiny handkerchief. Her thoughts were whirling from the surprise of meeting Jim.

Al Rocchi took his hand from his overcoat pocket and stepped into the center of the room. The dim light gleamed on the ugly, blue-black barrel of an automatic.

"Never mind that stuff!" he ordered harshly. "One peep out of you two dames, and I'll plug the kid. That goes!"

Mrs. Towner recoiled in horror, her face deathly white. Suddenly she kneeled and drew Donald tightly to her.

Luella Kennedy stared at Rocchi with amazement.

Jim Wilson acted—immediately and instinctively. He hurled himself at Rocchi. At that instant, the butler stepped swiftly from beside the drape. His upraised arm came down in a crushing blow. In his fist was the barrel end of a gun. Wilson sagged suddenly to the carpet.

Luella let out a short scream and dashed for the closed double doors. But Mears slipped his gun into his hip pocket and stepped in front of her. One big hand clutched her face. The other arm passed around her, holding her in a powerful grip.

Mrs. Towner remained absolutely still. The mother remembered what Rocchi had said about the child.

Holding the gun upon the pair, Rocchi kicked over the bag of toys. They spilled across the floor. Among them were pieces of stout cord and small wads of cloth. Rocchi snatched up one of these wads and jammed it into Luella's mouth. And while Rocchi continued to guard Mrs. Towner, Mears trussed Luella thoroughly. That done, he laid Luella upon a sofa and approached the wife of the district attorney. She shrank back. As he seized her, she decided in desperation to shriek. But Mears was too quick for her. Before a sound came out, he had thrust a gag between her teeth.

Crying, the child ran for the doors. Rocchi caught him, and held him while Mears bound his mother and placed her in a sitting position against the wall.

Mears was breathing heavily, and there was a triumphant glitter in his eyes.

"The walls of this place are thick," he said. "Nobody heard a sound."

"Come on! Get busy," snarled Rocchi, "before somebody walks in on us."

Mears stood over Wilson, and looked down upon the unconscious man.

"He's good for a while," he said to Rocchi. "No use wasting time in tying him up."

Working speedily, Mears stripped the Santa Claus suit from Wilson's unresisting body. He donned it himself, pulling the tasseled cap over his bald head, adjusting the false beard over his face.

"How do I look?"

"Okay," grunted Rocchi. "The dicks downstairs'll never know you ain't the same Santa Claus that walked in a few minutes ago. Now, tie up the kid gently and put a cloth over his mouth. And don't hurt him."

Mears did as he was told. He put the child in the bag in an upright position, and stuffed toys and packages around his small body.

Rocchi crossed to the sofa where Luella lay helpless. He bent down to speak in her ear.

"We're borrowing the kid for a little while. We ain't going to hurt him, but his old man has got to do us a favor before we bring him back. You want to go along and take care of him? He'll feel better if you're with him. We ain't going to hurt you either, sister."

Luella was frightened, but she managed to think. She thought of the helpless, defenseless child.

She nodded to indicate that she would go.

"You won't try to pull any funny stuff, sister?" demanded Rocchi, narrowing his eyes upon her. "No breaks when we pass through the lobby. Act natural, like you did coming in. If you don't—it'll be all up with you and the kid. Get me?"

Luella nodded her head again, Rocchi unbound her and took the gag from her mouth.

"Let's blow," he said briefly to Mears.

The butler, dressed as Santa Claus, swung the bag across his shoulder. Luella stared at Jim, lying lifelessly on the floor. Her heart was twisted by his lean face and his shabby, inadequate clothing. Then she raised her eyes to Mrs. Towner's face, and saw in the gaze of the district attorney's wife a mute appeal to watch out for her child. Luella nodded her head in silent promise.

"Come on!" ordered Rocchi gruffly. He had opened the double doors and was waiting for Luella to precede him.

Fifteen minutes later, the telephone in Jackson Towner's office broke the stillness. Again Towner lifted the receiver eagerly. Perhaps Covelli had broken at last!

An unfamiliar, guttural voice came to his ear.

"Listen, Towner. If Covelli dies, you'll never see your kid again."

Silence followed this amazing information out of a clear sky.

At first, Towner did not understand the significance of what he had heard.

"What? What?" he cried into the mouthpiece. He jiggled the connector impatiently, and finally heard an operator's impersonal voice, "Number, please?"

"I was talking to someone!" cried the district attorney.

"I'm sorry, sir. There's no one on your line now."

Suddenly a blinding flash of illumination swept through Towner's brain. A great fear filled his being. He tore himself from behind the desk, ran across the room and flung open the door.

"Joan! Joan!" he cried. "Donald!"

———

CHAPTER VI

Christmas Bullets

THE ceiling lights of the reception room had been turned on, and the room was bright under their glare. The fire on the hearth had died to red-veined ashes.

Jim Wilson sat in a chair directly under the lights. His red hair was disheveled, and beads of perspiration stood out on his forehead.

"I tell you I don't know anything about it!" he cried.

Three men were grouped around him. They were solid, powerful, iron-jawed men with grim faces. Earlier in the evening, they had been on guard in the lobby.

One of them now brought the flat of his hand against Wilson's face.

"Come on, now! Where did they go with the kid?"

Wilson was beginning to think that he was going mad. He seemed to be living in a nightmare. What was happening to him couldn't be real! He had told the truth—about Luella and everything.

But still they didn't believe him. They had been torturing him for what seemed an eternity. Questions and blows. And they wouldn't tell him anything about Luella.

"I tell you, I don't—"

At that moment, the double doors opened, and the district attorney e n t e r e d, accompanied by Tom Mahoney.

Towner glared at Wilson with murderous hatred. The commissioner was smoking a cigar. The ceiling lights gleamed brightly on his yellowish white hair. The blue eyes studied Wilson soberly.

"It's Bono's work, all right," he was saying to the district attorney. "Nobody but Bono could think up such a scheme. The girl was in on it, of course. Pretty smart—sending in a Santa Claus, and then the girl and the man! Naturally my men didn't think anything of it when they saw the same Santa Claus go out with the girl and her friend."

He turned to one of the men standing beside Wilson.

"Nobody in that Lexington Avenue apartment. Manager says it was hired by a man named Marcosson, from Chicago. He cleared out a couple of hours ago."

The commissioner jerked his head at Wilson.

"Take him down to Headquarters," he ordered shortly.

The three men seized Wilson, and hustled him across the room. Wilson struggled in their grip, and twisted to face the commissioner.

"Let me go!" he pleaded. "I don't know anything about this, I swear I don't!"

The commissioner remained silent. Towner tightened his hard face and clenched his fists. Wilson was dragged from sight.

The police commissioner shook his head.

"His story sounds straight to me, Jackson."

"Nonsense!" exploded the district attorney. "He's one of them all right. He got hurt in the scuffle, and couldn't make his getaway."

"That isn't what your wife says," reminded Tom Mahoney gently.

"Joan was beside herself," replied Towner sharply. "She doesn't know what really did happen."

The police commissioner watched Towner pace the room agitatedly.

"Well, what are we to do?" he asked finally, quietly.

"Do! Do!" Towner turned on him savagely. "Search every inch of the city. Hunt down that fiend Bono."

Mahoney gazed solemnly at the end of his cigar.

"It isn't going to be so easy—to find Bono—before dawn."

Towner whirled.

" What do you mean ?" he rasped.

" Just this. Bono has a lot of hide-outs, and most of them the police don't know. And here's another thing that perhaps you haven't thought of. Even if we're lucky and find where he has the child hidden, he might . . . he might . . . He knows what it'll mean to him if you keep your intention of sending Covelli to the chair."

Towner let himself down into a chair, where he sat slumped, staring at the far wall. He saw his ambitions crashing about him. His only chance to get Bono—clean up New York—through Covelli. Success, of which he had been so confident earlier in the evening, would make him his party's natural choice for governor in the next election.

It was gall and wormwood to Jackson Towner's prideful soul to admit defeat in anything. Now he was faced with defeat at the very hands of the man he had set out to destroy.

" Can't—can't your men do something?" he implored the police commissioner.

Tom Mahoney was silent.

" It—it isn't dawn yet," continued Towner.

P o l i c e Commissioner Mahoney stared curiously at the district attorney, but Towner had covered his eyes with his hand.

O N the way down from the fifth floor in the elevator, Jim Wilson was thinking desperately. He knew where they were taking him. To a police station—which meant more hell.

It was not the thought of imprisonment, or even the excellent possibility of a third degree, which caused the torment within him. It was his dreadful anxiety about Luella.

They had said upstairs that she was in with that gang. Jim Wilson knew it was not true. Luella had been duped, as he had been.

But where was she now? That was the question that burned in Wilson's brain. He could only imagine her in terrible danger. Men ruthless enough to kidnap children, would do anything.

As the elevator silently dropped to the street floor, Wilson became panic-stricken by the dreadful hopelessness of the situation and his utter helplessness. He felt that if he were only free, he could do something. The thought of being caged, doing nothing and knowing nothing, maddened him. He knew that he wouldn't be able to stand it. He had to escape it somehow.

The wondering, awed operator of the elevator pulled open the doors, and the three detectives pushed Wilson into the lobby.

A police car was waiting at the curb. The chauffeur saw them approaching and bent forward to switch on the ignition.

Although it was only eleven o'clock, Park Avenue was almost destitute of p e d e s t r i a n s. Occasionally figures hurried by, their coats around their ears. Automobiles swept along the double roadway. People were anxious to get home.

Crossing the sidewalk, Jim Wilson decided to make a bid for escape. An instant before, he had been dazed, spiritless in the hands of the detectives. Now, with a sudden wrench he freed his wrists from the grips of the men beside him. The next instant he was racing down the street at top speed, the cold air sharp in his nostrils.

Three spurts of red, and three brittle cracks in the quiet of Park Avenue Christmas Eve.

The three bullets missed their mark. One chipped the corner of a building as Wilson rounded the block, and drove a tiny piece of stone stinging into his face. He clapped his hand to his cheek instinctively, and his fingers came away wet with warm, sticky liquid. His heart pounded.

Behind him he heard the wail of a police siren. The detectives had leaped upon the running board of the police car, and its driver was now swinging the long machine around the corner, its tires squealing.

Wilson reached the end of that block yards ahead of the police car. Along the avenue, which was at right angles to the street down which he had fled, appeared, a cruising taxi, its driver unaware of the cause of the commotion. Wilson made a flying leap for its running board, and held on by his finger nails. The startled driver stared at his bloody face, in which his blue eyes were burning fiercely.

" Keep on!" Wilson ordered savagely. " Drive like hell!"

Whether it was Wilson's macabre appearance, or the tone of his voice, the driver pushed his foot down on the gas pedal.

Down the avenue sped the taxi, outdistancing other cars. The police car rocked after it. Through one red light —and another.

Jim Wilson, looking back, saw that the police car was gaining rapidly. Then he looked ahead, and saw the blue and white globes of a subway entrance. Without a word to the driver, and while the taxi was traveling at full speed, he dropped off the running board. He struck the pavement with terrific force, pitched forward on his hands and knees.

He scrambled to his feet, not even knowing that his hands were raw, and

that his bloody knees were showing through his torn trousers. Two leaps carried him to the sidewalk. The next instant he was dashing down the subway stairs, taking the steps three and four at a time.

He vaulted over the turnstile, taking it in his stride.

The best luck of the evening awaited him. Along the platform, a downtown train was just closing its doors. He managed to squeeze through into a car, where he took a position in the gloom of the vestibule, mopping the blood from his face. The train started.

CHAPTER VII

Veterans' Conference

IT is a mistake to believe that all New York speakeasies do a rushing business. Some of them do little, or none.

Terry O'Toole's speakeasy was in the dreary basement of an old brownstone house off Eighth Avenue, near Columbus Circle. There was a long, narrow room, with an ancient, scarred, mahogany bar running nearly its length. On the wall beyond the bar were some stained, cracked mirrors, and a cash register, little used. Over the top of the mirrors was a wreath of holly. Below it, written on the mirrors with soap were the legends, " Merry Christmas," and " Happy New Year."

Beyond the barroom, and connected to it by a narrow door, was a dingy, dark, back room. Here were two cots, covered with army blankets, a couple of chairs, a cheap dresser, a trunk, and miscellaneous baggage. The cots belonged to Terry and his wartime buddy, Jim Wilson.

Terry was not running a speakeasy because he liked it. But a man must eat, and have a place to sleep, he had figured philosophically, when he had lost his job, and a friend of his, who had owned the place formerly, had offered to sell it to him for a small cash payment down.

Terry had found that the friend had grossly overstated the remunerativeness of the place. The friend had never returned for the balance of the payments, and Terry had retained ownership, mostly because it was a cheap place to sleep. Occasionally someone wandered into it by mistake and spent a dollar or two for beer before being overwhelmed by lonesomeness.

Although it was Christmas Eve, and better business might have been expected, Terry was asleep stretched out on top of the bar when the buzzer whined several times impatiently. Terry slept on top of the bar in order not to miss any customers, and because it afforded a change from sleeping in his cot.

He opened his brown eyes, raised himself to a sitting position, ran a hand through his dark, curly hair, and yawned. He then jumped to the floor and stood up in his lean, hard, six feet two length.

He crossed to the street door and slid back the cover for the peephole. His face fell.

"Oh, it's you, is it?" he said, as he unbolted the door and swung it open. "I thought it was a customer."

Jim Wilson slid inside and closed the door behind him hurriedly. Terry walked back to the bar, yawning and stretching.

"Gosh, what a Christmas Eve!" he remarked. "Deader 'n a stuffed fish."

"Terry! The cops are after me!"

Terry O'Toole instantly became all alive. For the first time he noticed Wilson's appearance in the dingy, yellow light of the place, the frayed trousers at the knees, the cut in the face, the dirty, lividly raw hands.

"My gosh, feller! What you done?"

Jim told him about the men in the apartment building on Lexington Avenue, Luella, the kidnaping of Towner's child, and his escape from the police.

Terry's eyes narrowed, his prominent, Irish jaw tightened, and his sinewy fists clenched.

"The rats!" he muttered savagely, "The damned, dirty rats! Stealing a kid—on Christmas Eve, too!"

Wilson walked the length of the long room, endlessly back and forth, his fists clenched at his sides, his mouth a tight line of suffering. Terry sat on the bar, his long legs hanging over, and watched his friend with honest compassion. The two men had been friends in the war, had met for the first time at the front. Their friendship had been cemented in blood and fire. Terry had seen Jim Wilson up against some pretty tough situations, badly wounded during the war, after it—broke, and down-and-out.

Wilson raised his clenched hands above his red hair.

"They'll murder her, Terry! They'll murder her and the boy as sure as death. I know it! But what can I do?" he demanded crazily. "The whole police force of New York must be looking for me by this time. If I stick my face out on the streets they'll get me, Terry."

Terry O'Toole looked vastly perturbed.

"You can't go out, Jim. The police would maul you to pieces—especially after you beat it out on them."

His face suddenly lighted.

"Listen, Jim! I know a couple of guys who can get you out of this, if anybody can. They were soldiers, the same as us during the big scrap. But they made good when they got back. Now their word counts for something around this town. They're big shots up at the Legion, too. Good guys."

Terry slid off the bar.

"I'm going up to the Legion and see where I can get ahold of them," he continued with determination. "They ought to be home on Christmas Eve anyway.

"You stay here, and don't let nobody in while I'm gone. When I get back I'll give you a signal—three long buzzes and three low knocks on the door. Get me?"

He placed an arm around Wilson's shoulders.

"Take it easy, Jim. Don't do anything foolish now. And don't worry about the cops. You know New York cops never bother a speakeasy."

IT was after midnight when Terry returned. He was accompanied by two, silent, sober-faced men, citizens of substantial standing. Both men were solidly built, but not fleshy. Their firm faces and clear skin showed that they remembered the value of exercise, learned in the army fifteen years ago.

"Here are the men I told you about, Jim."

Terry's glance turned to the taller of the two.

"This is George Vickers. He was adjutant of Company F, of the old 569th."

Vickers' serious eyes studied Jim's face as they shook hands.

"Dick Brent, Jim."

Brent's smile illuminated a freckled face.

Vickers cleared his throat uneasily.

"Terry phoned me," he said to Wilson. "I thought I'd better come over and bring Dick with me. This is," he added soberly, "pretty serious business."

"It's a crying shame," exploded Brent, "when a man's home isn't safe from thugs and gangsters even on Christmas Eve, in a big city like this! Something should be done about Bono. I wish," he concluded grimly, "that the job would be given to some ex-service men I know. There's only one way to handle skunks like him, not by law and courts—by bullets! The yellow rats can't dodge lead like they can jail."

George Vickers compressed his lips. He agreed with his former first sergeant on this, as well as on nearly everything else.

"Perhaps Dick and I had better go and see the police commissioner," he frowned at Wilson. "I know old Tom Mahoney. He's no fool, and I think he'll listen to reason."

Wilson's former agitation had quieted to one persistently driving thought.

"The police are no good," he said bitterly. "Keep them off of me, and I'll find Luella—somehow."

Terry O'Toole wagged his head solemnly.

"And to think," he grimaced, "I buy beer from Bono. I have to," he added significantly, "or else—"

"Bono!"

Wilson stared at Terry.

"Yeah. The old—"

Thoughts were racing pell-mell through Wilson's brain. A tiny spark had lighted a conflagration of possibilities and wild plans. A desperate man grasps at any hope or scheme.

"You deal with Bono's men?" he interrupted O'Toole. "Can you get one of them in here? We could make him tell where Bono is."

Vickers shook his head.

"I doubt," he said, "that it would work. In the first place, how would you get one of Bono's men to come here at this hour? In the second, we couldn't make him talk. In the third place, he probably wouldn't know where Bono had taken the girl and the child."

But Terry O'Toole had caught Wilson's idea.

"I can get Tony Carlova himself down here," he said eagerly. "He's the guy who makes the collection for Guito. If any of Bono's men know where Guito is, Tony will.

"Listen! I'll call up and order some beer, but they'll turn me down. I know, because they did it yesterday. I thought I'd get in a fresh supply for Christmas. I owe them money, see? And they won't deliver until I pay. I'll say I've got the money now, and to send Tony over to collect it. He'll come. He always does. Catch that gang not being around when there's any money to be got!"

"This collector doesn't travel alone, does he?" asked Vickers.

Terry shook his head.

"No," he confessed. "He travels with a bodyguard and they usually have a chauffeur to drive them around. But the chauffeur never comes in. He waits outside in the machine."

Wilson's eyes were glittering.

"What of it?" he cried. "There're four of us."

"But they are undoubtedly armed," Vickers reminded him.

"I've got a gun," interposed Terry. "It was the one I had when I was in the army. I bought it, and brought it home for a souvenir. But," he confessed, "I ain't got any bullets for it."

Dick Brent's hazel eyes were shining.

"Let's do it!" he urged. "We can get away with it. It seems like old times, George. Remember the night we

crawled out into No Man's Land and grabbed off a Heinie listening post?" He drew in a deep breath. "Gosh, this seems like the first time I've been really alive since the war ended! Funny how alive you feel when there's danger around!"

Vickers was thoughtful, but the beginning of a gleam was showing in the depths of his eyes. He was thinking of his family and Dick's, whom they had left in the happiness and security of Christmas Eve. In answering Terry O'Toole's appeal for help for a comrade he had not expected to be pitting himself against gangsters. An intense, curious thrill rippled down his spine. He remembered that he had led men over the top.

"It's worth a try," he said to the intent, waiting faces of the men around him. His jaw tightened, and his eyes narrowed. Now that he had made his decision he was once more the officer whom men had followed over the top in blind faith.

"I think," he continued grimly, "we had better question this Tony Carlova ourselves, instead of handing him over to the police. After all," he concluded significantly, "the police only dare go so far, but I remember a few army methods of getting information out of a prisoner."

CHAPTER VIII

An Empty Gun and Water

APPROXIMATELY half an hour later three men stood at Terry O'Toole's bar, each with a glass of beer in front of him, each with a foot on the brass rail. In the center of the bar, George Vickers and Dick Brent were conversing in low tones. Jim Wilson was at the end nearer the door. Terry himself was at the other end, polishing an army .45 with an oily piece of cloth, and regretting that he had no ammunition.

The hearts of the four ex-service men were beating rapidly. Terry had telephoned the headquarters which kept him supplied with "goods," and had been told that Tony Carlova would be over in about thirty minutes to collect the money already due.

The buzzer whined. The hand of George Vickers, holding a glass, trembled. Terry swiftly thrust his gun out of sight on a shelf under the bar and went to the door to peer through the peephole. He gave his companions a significant nod, and then threw open the door.

Tony Carlova stepped into the room, followed closely by his bodyguard. Guito Bono's collector of accounts, general treasurer, and disburser, was diminutive in form, and elegantly dressed. His appearance belied his temper and disposition, which more than one man had found to his astonishment and regret. Tony Carlova was a dangerous man, especially with a knife.

His bodyguard was big and hulking. He belonged to Al Rocchi's division of muscle and rod men.

Carlova took in the three men at the bar with a lightning glance, and then walked directly to Terry, who had resumed his position behind the bar. The bodyguard remained in the center of the room, one hand in his coat pocket, eying the room with suspicion.

Terry O'Toole's smile was hearty and guileless.

"Merry Christmas, Tony! Have a drink on me?"

He knew that Tony Carlova never drank, nevertheless he set a glass and a quart bottle of Bono's liquor in front of him.

Carlova's pearl-gray fedora made a slight, negative gesture.

Terry picked up the bottle and glass, passed along the bar, and put them down in front of the bodyguard.

"Better have a drink! It's Christmas."

The bodyguard glanced for permission at Carlova, who nodded his head. Approaching the bar, the guard placed his foot on the rail and poured himself a drink.

"Let me have a shot of that!" grinned Vickers amiably.

"Sure!" said Terry genially. "Help yourself, will you? I've got a little business to attend to."

To reach the bottle, Vickers had to move down the bar, next to the bodyguard. Dick Brent moved with him.

Terry returned to the upper end of the bar, where Carlova was waiting. Out of the corner of his eye, he saw that Wilson had wandered in front of the street door as if to go out. Wilson was to protect the door.

"How's business?" asked Carlova perfunctorily.

"Oh, not so good, Tony," replied Terry. Glancing at the men at the bar, he added, "Christmas helps, though. That's why I need the extra barrel tonight, Tony. I've got your money here."

Reaching under the bar, he took a firm grip on the unloaded .45. The next instant, Carlova was staring blankly into its menacing muzzle.

The mirrors revealed to Tony's bodyguard what was happening. He smashed his glass on the bar with a curse, the liquid spilling across the mahogany. His right hand dived for the pocket of his coat.

At that moment, Vickers was in the act of pouring a drink. Swiftly changing his grip to the neck of the bottle, he brought it down on the head of the bodyguard, who clutched at the bar futilely, and then slid to a senseless heap on the floor.

"Say! What's the big—" snarled Carlova.

Vickers and Brent seized him and searched for weapons. In a holster under his armpit they found an automatic; in a hip pocket, a large, ugly looking claspknife.

"All right," said Vickers grimly. "Into the back room with him!"

JIM WILSON found the pistol in the coat pocket of Carlova's bodyguard. Terry O'Toole shook his head and handed him a wooden bung starter.

Wilson took a position beside the street door, while Terry drew the bolt and opened it. Beyond the low flight of dark steps and the sidewalk was a powerful looking enclosed car waiting at the curb. A dark, solid figure sat patiently behind its steering wheel.

"Hey!" called Terry. "Come in and have a drink!"

The driver turned his face toward the lighted doorway, but hesitated doubtfully.

"It's okay," assured Terry heartily. "Tony says you can have one, being it's Christmas."

The chauffeur descended to the sidewalk and clapped his gloved hands together.

"Br-r-r-r, it's cold!" He was coming down the steps. "I need a drink."

Not until he had passed through the door did he see the crumpled body of the guard on the floor. His eyes widened with alarm.

"Where's Tony?" he cried. "What—"

He never knew what hit him. Stepping silently and swiftly from behind the door, Wilson swung the heavy mallet against the chauffeur's ear, knocking him halfway into the room, where he collapsed on the floor.

Terry O'Toole grinned and rubbed his hands together.

"Like clockwork!" he gloated. "Easy as pie!"

The door of the back room opened and Dick Brent thrust out his head. His hazel eyes danced as he noted the still forms on the floor.

"Good work!" he approved enthusiastically. "Terry, have you a piece of hose around here?"

"What do you want the hose for?"

"To make the little guy talk."

Wilson crossed the barroom with grim, purposeful strides.

"I'll make him talk! I'll—"

Brent barred the doorway.

"Not your way, Jim! I don't blame you, but his kind would take a beating to death before they'd open their mouths. Vickers has a better way. It'll produce results."

After rummaging behind the bar, Terry finally brought to light a length of rubber tubing, which he used to siphon beer.

"Just the thing!" approved Brent, his eyes gleaming.

He held the tube before Wilson's grim face.

"The old water treatment! The army used it in the Philippine Insurrection to make stubborn natives talk. It doesn't hurt them, but they can't stand the steady drip-drip of water on their foreheads. They always talk."

He disappeared into the back room.

"Come on, Jim!" invited Terry. "Tie up these bozoes so they can't start anything when they come to."

Some time later the door of the back room opened again and George Vickers and Brent appeared.

"He talked—finally," Vickers announced cryptically.

Wilson's eyes glittered.

"Where did he say—"

"Uptown," cut in Vickers. "West 225th Street. We've got the number."

"That's way uptown!" exclaimed Terry. "Maybe Carlova's lying?"

Vickers shook his head grimly.

"It's the right address. They don't lie—under the water treatment. They might try—at first—but we kept it up long enough to make sure.

"We'd better turn over our information to the police," he said soberly.

"I'm going up there—now!" cried Wilson.

Terry O'Toole caught his arm.

"Wait, Jim! No use in going off half-cocked! You can't do anything alone!"

Wilson swung around with blazing eyes.

"I'll do plenty! And I'm not going to wait for the police. Every minute —every second—might mean the difference between life and death for Luella and that—that boy. *Let me go, I tell you!*"

Vickers, Brent, and Terry stared at one another. Vickers' jaw tightened.

"Time does count," he said slowly.

Brent's eyes were glowing again, and his freckled face was eager.

"Bono's men will be watching for riot squads and those damnable sirens. That stuff would give them time to make a getaway, or—or bump off the girl and the youngster. But they don't know us. In fact," he added excitedly, "we could use that car outside. It's one of theirs."

Vickers smiled at his onetime first sergeant.

"This is some Christmas, Dick!"

"Ain't it great?" grinned Brent. "Like old times!"

"It'll be a grand Christmas present for the city if we bag Bono," said Terry.

"For Towner—and for Jim," added Brent.

"Come on!" demanded Wilson, with savage impatience.

"Gosh!" grinned Terry O'Toole. "You can't beat the old doughboys! We held 'em up with an empty pistol, and now we're going up in their car to clean out the big boss with the guns of his own men!"

CHAPTER IX

Dawn

G UITO BONO and Jaffin, his secretary, sat in the living room of the upstairs suite in an old graystone two-story house on West 225th Street, in the section of the city known as Marble Hill. In the front room downstairs, Al Rocchi and Mears, the Towner's butler, were talking together over a pint of whiskey. Outside, in the deep shadow cast by the house, two men with their overcoat turned up to their ears, leaned against the high porch, and silently kept watch on the street.

The neighborhood belonged to the solid, respectable middle class. It was the last place where one would expect to find gangsters and racketeers, who are supposed to adhere to the very high or the very low.

The hour was late. No person nor automobile had passed along the street in over two hours. The apartment building across the way was dark, save for three or four windows where an illuminated holly wreath or an electric candle glowed through the silent night.

The living room upstairs was furnished far less luxuriously than Bono's private apartment in the Lexington Avenue building. Here there was a cheap oak library table, with a couple of armchairs and two straight back chairs to match. A floor lamp stood beside a silent radio in a corner. The rug was an inexpensive domestic.

Guito Bono sat in a rocking chair beside the table. The light from the table lamp glinted on the streaks of silver in his black hair, and fell upon his exposed neck. He had loosened his necktie and collar.

Guito poured himself a drink from a bottle that stood under the lamp. Tossing the liquid down with a gulp, he stared through the doorway into the next room. He could see the district attorney's child on the bed sleeping peacefully. Luella Kennedy sat in a chair beside the bed, her hat off, her face white and strained.

Jaffin, in a chair across the room from Bono, opened his thin silver cigarette case, and finding it empty, shrugged his shoulders.

For the thousandth time, Bono looked at his watch, which was attached to his vest by a thin platinum chain. Then he stared at the window, where darkness still showed below the three-quarters drawn shade.

"It'll be dawn pretty soon," he muttered, more to himself.

"Yes," Jaffin agreed wearily. "It'll be Christmas Day."

Bono twisted his fingers.

"Damn Christmas! I wonder what's happening to Covelli?"

"You'll know as soon as anything important happens, Guito. Our man at Sing Sing is on the job. He'll call if anything happens to Covelli."

Guito Bono glared savagely into the next room.

"If Towner wants to see his kid again, he'd better lay off Covelli."

He relapsed into brooding silence.

The hushed minutes of early Christmas morning dragged by. Jaffin looked at the window. The darkness seemed less dense—or was it his imagination?

Suddenly the crack of a pistol shot shattered the stillness outside the house. It was followed by three more shots in rapid succession. Bono had been about to pour another drink. Now he sat as one frozen, the bottle poised over the glass.

Jaffin leaped from his chair, flung himself across the room, and tore open the door leading into the hall. Down the stairs he saw Rocchi and Mears hurrying to the front door. At the same instant, he heard a crash of glass. It sounded as if the big, porch window of the front room had been kicked in.

Jaffin darted back into the living room, slamming the door behind him.

"It must be the cops, Guito!" he cried. "What are we going to do?"

Receiving no reply, he whirled to face the room. His eyes widened. Guito Bono, with a maniacal glitter in his black, beady eyes, was advancing upon the doorway to the bedroom. In his hand was a pistol.

"Guito! What're you going to do?"

Bono curled his lips, baring his teeth, but he did not look toward his secretary.

"I'm going to kill that kid," he snarled, "like I said I'd do! I'll show Towner that he can't do this to me!"

Luella's scream followed his words. Then a child's startled, frightened cry. From downstairs came the shouts and curses of men, punctuated by scattered pistol shots.

Jaffin hurled himself across the room and seized the wrist that held the gun.

"Don't, Guito! We're not baby killers!"

Snarling savagely, Bono fought to

regain control of his gun. Jaffin held on desperately. Suddenly there was a muffled report, and Jaffin stiffened. In front of Bono's gleaming eyes, he spun half around, and then wilted to the carpet. Bono looked down in triumphant hatred at the back of Jaffin's blond head.

"Try to stop me, will you?"

He was turning when the hall door burst open, revealing Jim Wilson in the doorway. Guito's eyes widened.

"You—you—the bum!" he cried incredulously.

That instant of surprise and astonishment cost Guito Bono his opportunity to shoot for his life. Wilson whipped up his pistol and fired once, twice. Guito Bono caved in the middle, and pitched across the body of Jaffin, his secretary.

IN the office in his home on Park Avenue, the district attorney sat on the black leather couch, with his face buried in his hands. Tom Mahoney, the police commissioner, was behind the desk. His yellowish-white hair was rumpled, and his red face was strained. A stubby cigar stuck in the corner of his grim mouth.

"You've got to call off that execution, Towner! It's almost dawn—and my men haven't been able to locate a trace of Bono."

"Call it off, Tom! Telephone Sing Sing that I order a reprieve. They know the governor left it in my hands. Hurry!

"Oh, Lord!" he groaned, as Mahoney grabbed for the desk telephone. "I don't know why I've been so stubborn and selfish! I wanted to wait until the last minute, in the hope —in the hope that I could get Donald back without—without losing anything myself. I—I thought the police could

do it. I depended on them. Surely they would recover *my* child."

The police commissioner silently cursed the operator for her delay.

"Dawn!" the district attorney raved wildly. "If it's too late, how can I ever forgive myself, or face my wife again? What have I done, with my ambitions and schemings? Oh, Lord, if you'll return Donald to me unharmed, I promise—"

"Get me Sing Sing immediately!" said Tom Mahoney furiously to the operator, who had answered at last.

There was a knock on the door, and two of Mahoney's men, who were on guard in the building, entered. They stood aside for Luella Kennedy and Jim Wilson, who was carrying a tired, golden-haired boy. In the hall behind were Terry, Vickers, and Brent.

Jackson Towner sprang from the couch and rushed across the room to take the child in his arms.

A few minutes later, connection with Sing Sing was established. The police commissioner looked at Towner.

"How about Covelli?" Mahoney asked slowly. "They want to know whether or not to go ahead with the execution."

"Tell them no, Tom. Today is Christmas." He looked at Jim Wilson.

"I don't know—I don't know how to thank you," he said chokingly.

Old Tom Mahoney, commissioner of police, put his hands on the shoulders of Jim Wilson and Terry O'Toole.

"I'm offering them jobs with me," he said. "We need men like them on the force."

Jim Wilson glanced at Luella, and his heart beat faster.

Dawn was spreading across the harbor, over the skyscrapers, the apartment buildings, and the park. It was Christmas in the big city.

A Broadway Christmas Carol

The man's hand slid under his coat to the butt of a gun

Two Damaged Souls Are Thrown Together on a Festive Night and Exchange Yuletide Gifts—of Justice!

By JACK KOFOED

Author of "Patrolman Peterson," "The Affair of the Necklace," etc.

A WHITE - SHOULDERED gale howled and shuddered and piled feather pillows of snow through the cross-town length of Fifty-second Street.

The Coq d'Or, one of the brightest ornaments of the thoroughfare, is usually gay with a swing band, a blues singer and girls who dance the way you expect girls in a Fifty-second Street night club to dance. This night it was not gay. A Christmas tree, gaudy with colored lights, stood in a corner near the bar, and the ceiling was festooned with holly, but they had, somehow, an air of withered flowers after a funeral.

The waiters yawned over empty tables. The band played occasionally, without spirit, selections like "God Rest You, Merry Gentlemen," and "Holy Night." There was no one to dance even if they had trumpeted and blared the latest hit. Every employee was thinking of a family or sweetheart or someone he wanted to be with. No one goes to places like the Coq d'Or on Christmas Eve if he can find a home whose doors are open to him.

In that beautiful and expensive room, the only customer aside from a man and woman at the bar, was a sleepy and depressed salesman.

The man at the bar wore costly English tweeds and a flat brimmed felt hat pulled well down over his forehead. His mouth looked as though it had been chipped out of defective marble with a dull chisel. His sharp nose seemed crowded between eyes that were like dark gimlet holes. But apparently he was the only man in New York satisfied to be a night club ornament at that particular moment. In spite of his grimness there was a furtive air of happiness about him, like the glow of a fire seen over tree tops.

The waiters and bartenders did not recognize him, but they knew the type. He was a right gee, as the mobsters say—a man who would be at home in any kind of lawlessness, perhaps a killer imported from another city. When he ordered a drink his voice had the whispering hoarseness so common to his breed, and his eyes smouldered when there was the faintest delay in serving him.

QUITE obviously the woman was not with him. A high chair of chromium and red leather stood between them. At first the man had not noticed her, being concerned with his own secret pleasure. When she ordered a hot toddy he looked around. He was glad he had taken the trouble, for she was worth looking at. Her hair was blond—not the blond usually seen along Broadway, but with sunshine in it—and her eyes were as blue as the sky over Capri. The man had been in Capri once, when the district-attorney's office was trying to serve a warrant on him for grand larceny, and he remembered the blueness. He no-

ticed, too, that her legs were slim and firm in flesh-colored stockings, and her high heeled slippers were hooked in the rungs of the chair. It was not hard to see she was unhappy.

There was normally no sentiment in the man who lounged against the bar, but it did not seem to him that any girl as good looking as this one should be unhappy on Christmas Eve. His curiosity was aroused, and he moved into the empty chair between them.

Usually he let women severely alone. They had never done men in his business any good. If John Dillinger and Baby Face Nelson could have come out of their graves to speak they would have so testified. But this was a little different. He wanted to talk to somebody—and it might as well be a pretty girl.

"You look kinda lonesome, sister," he said. "That ain't no way to feel tonight."

Her blue eyes met his gimlet ones. "What's there to be happy about?" she asked.

"Well, Christmas for one thing," the man said. "No one can call me sappy, but I'd rather have this night than any other on the calendar."

"That's the reason I'm homesick, I guess," said the girl. "I'm sitting here when I want to be home in Poplar Falls. Right now they have trimmed the tree with shiny balls and tinsel and little colored lights. Cake and wine on the table and people coming in—everybody saying, 'Merry Christmas!' and meaning it, too. What have I got in place of those things? A hot toddy to remind me of Dad, who always drinks a couple on Christmas Eve."

The man called for a hot toddy himself, though he had been drinking a rum collins.

"I know how you feel," he said, "because that's the way I feel myself. That's the way practically everybody feels—kind of homey, I guess you'd call it. No matter how much they travel they're anxious to get back to their own neighborhoods. Dutch is fed up with Newburgh and

Malone and them jerk towns, and itches to get back to the Bronx—and how much do you think Mr. Capone would give to trade Alcatraz for a little flat in Chicago? Poplar Falls sounds like a whistle stop on the Grasshopper and Dungaree Railroad —but no doubt it means as much to you as the West Side does to me. Now, I know this is no part of my business—but why aren't you in Poplar Falls tonight?"

"I wonder just what pop and mom are doing at this moment," the girl murmured dreamily. She looked at her wrist watch. "It's seventeen minutes after eleven. They're probably helping Aunt Hattie into the car so Pete can drive her home." A tear twinkled like a black star on her mascara.

THE man took a drink of his toddy. He seemed to be considering something very carefully. The very nature of his business demanded that he be cautious in every move he made, for a false one might end in his being strapped in the electric chair up the river at Ossining.

"I'm the last person in the world," he said, "to fall for a hard luck story from a blonde. They're a dime a dozen to me—but after all, this is Christmas Eve, and I'm lousy with money. So, if you want to get back to Poplar Falls I'll buy you a plane ticket and stake you to taxi fare to Newark so you can be home for dinner tomorrow. Maybe I'm being a sap, because you may live in Brooklyn and just be taking me for a ride. So what? I feel just the way you been talking, even though I've got no pop or mom to greet me under the mistletoe."

The girl smiled. It was a wistful, unhappy smile; not the sort that should be seen on Christmas Eve, even in the Coq d'Or. But she was prettier than ever when she smiled.

"I'm not lying. I really do live in Poplar Falls. It's in Illinois—about sixty miles from Chicago."

The man took out a roll of bills, skinned off a few and put them in her hand.

"There's three hundred bucks," he said. "That'd get you home if you lived in Mexico."

The girl looked at the money, hesitantly, as though she did not quite understand. He noticed a slim band of platinum on the third finger of her left hand. Married, eh? Well, her romance was probably over or she wouldn't be wanting to go back to her folks. It didn't matter to him. Tonight he was just a Boy Scout, doing his good deed without hope of reward.

"It's awfully nice of you," the girl said, "considering that you don't even know me."

"You don't know me, either, so that makes it even."

"But I do."

The badly chiselled mouth drooped at the edges. The gimlet eyes became sinister. The voice that had been light with cheer suddenly rasped into a throaty snarl.

"Yeah?" he said. "A wise skirt! Who am I?"

"You're Bitsy Carpenter."

The man's hand slid under his coat to the butt of a gun slung in a holster under his arm-pit. The feel of it was comforting, for he had lived by that gun for a long while.

He was quite sure, too, that if anyone recognized him in New York he would have to use that gun. But the saw-bones who had given him that face lifting job swore his own mother wouldn't know who he was. How had this skirt tabbed him so easily?

"I gave you one Christmas present tonight so you could get back to Poplar Falls," he said. "Now I'll fix it so you can go in a coffin. Get up and walk out with me, and if you make a false move I'll blast the heart out of you."

The girl shook her head.

"Don't be like that, Bitsy," she said. "If I had wanted to turn you up do you think I'd tell you about it? I could have called Detective-sergeant Johnny Brodwell, and he would have walked in here and laid a blackjack across your skull, right where you part the hair. Then they would have had you, and you wouldn't have known I had anything to do with it."

His hand slipped away from the gun butt. What she had said was perfectly reasonable. If she had wanted to turn him up she could have done it with no danger to herself. The affair had him worried. Something was happening that was not visible to his gimlet eyes.

"Yeah, I guess that's right," he admitted. "But who are you? What's this all about anyway? Here I am, hiding out where Brodwell or nobody else can find me. I come to New York for Christmas because I'm homesick. I have my nose changed and grow a mustache. I don't look like me anymore—but you spot me in a minute. What's the low-down?"

"I'll tell you," the girl said, "but first I want to get something off my chest."

BITSY shot a swift, suspicious glance around the empty room. The shoe salesman had fallen asleep. The cigarette girl was juggling a red ball that had fallen off the tree. The band had gone out for a smoke.

"Okay," he said, "but give it to me straight."

"I was brought up in Poplar Falls," the girl told him. "It isn't much of a town—a Main Street town—but it's a nice place to live now that I look back on it."

"Broadway's good enough," Carpenter said, grinning thinly.

"I graduated from high school and got a job in the bank. Pop and mom were awful proud when I brought home my first week's pay—sixteen dollars."

"Sixteen bucks!" echoed the man. "That's just about as much as two rounds of drinks cost in this place. And you worked a week for it!"

"The girls are probably working for fourteen now," she said, "but that's not what I started to talk about. I met a boy. He was the handsomest thing I ever saw in my life — black eyes — curly hair — *you* know. You've seen the type in the movies. He was from New York,

and I fell for him like a brick from the top of Radio City."

"You don't need to say any more," the man said. "The scenario is as clear to me as though I read it only yesterday. The guy hands you the old raz ma taz. You fall for it, and he runs out on you. You're too ashamed to stay in Poplar Falls and too proud to go back to it.

The girl shook her blond head.

"You're right on the first count, Bitsy, but that's all. I *did* fall for him. But we went over to Harper's Run, and were married by Squire Hinchman. We came home, and the family was tickled pink. They didn't think anybody in Poplar Falls was good enough for me—and here was a sure enough big shot from New York taking me for his wife."

An old woman with a shawl and dirty finger nails came in selling papers. Any other night they would have thrown her out, but since it was Christmas Eve nobody said anything. Bitsy Carpenter gave her a ten dollar bill.

"I'm up a tree," he said. "You get happily married and the family loves it—and still you can't go home for Christmas. Maybe I'm nuts—but it's beyond me."

"It won't be in a minute," the girl said. "The next week my husband stuck up the bank, knocked it off for thirty thousand dollars. Nobody thought I had anything to do with it, which I hadn't. But they got a great kick out of it because they thought I had been high hatting the old town. I didn't care anything about that. I didn't care anything except for that boy of mine.

"When he let me know where he was I went to him. The cops never caught up with us—but in the six months I lived with him in New York, while he spent that dough, I learned a lot of thing I'd never heard of in Poplar Falls."

Carpenter nodded wisely.

"Let me tell you something, sister," he said. "Go back—and tell the neighbors to jump through hoops. You want to go home. Well, go. That's where you belong. Look at me. Eight months ago I killed Lush McMurray, and the dicks would give a month's pay to get me for it. But I can't stay away from New York at Christmas—here I am, risking my neck. You can't lose as much by going home."

There was a queer look in the girl's eyes. "Honest, Bitsy," she said earnestly, "I told you this, thinking you would get it right away. Didn't you ever hear of Poplar Falls?"

A VAGUE remembrance seemed to stir in him. His badly chiselled mouth twisted. Suddenly he looked up. His face was as cold as the snow in Fifty-second Street.

"Poplar Falls!" he cried. "By God! I get it now. That's where Lush McMurray knocked over his first bank. So you're his wife, eh?"

"His widow!" said the girl. "A couple of minutes ago you gave me a present, Bitsy—but it wasn't anything compared with the present you gave me when you turned a Tommygun on Lush McMurray. I told you I learned a lot during the time I lived with him—I learned about how rotten and selfish some men can be—"

Carpenter nodded and said harshly:

"He was a rat and a doublecrosser, and had it coming to him. It's not hard to see that a girl like you couldn't get along with him. In my day I've killed more guys than were in the Lost Battalion, but nothing gave me as much pleasure as wiping out this McMurray lug. He got it where he deserved it—right between the shoulder blades. It's never wise to give a sucker like that an even break. But what I'm anxious to find out is how you tailed me. Nobody even knows I'm in New York, and if that gumshoe Brodwell ever finds it out I'm a gone goose."

"Maybe some day I'll tell you that, Bitsy," said Mrs. McMurray. "It's kind of a secret—and I don't tell secrets any more than you do. I'll have another toddy with you, and then see if I can get a plane to Poplar Falls. I can smell mom's dinner already."

Carpenter took out his roll again.

"Better take a couple hundred more," he said. "You've made this a pleasant evening for me — money's the cheapest thing along Broadway. Any time you care to have a husband bumped off let me know."

They drank their toddies. Nora McMurray fixed her tricky hat, though it looked perfectly charming as it was.

"Merry Christmas, Bitsy," she said. "It's a good idea to make each one the best, for you never know when it will be the last."

He watched her walk out of the bar, admiring her ankles and the lateral motion of her slim hips. It occurred to him, though, that he had better leave New York when he was through with this Christmas Eve celebration. It was bad to be homesick for the sidewalks of New York — but it would be worse if somebody besides Nora found out he was there.

*   *   *   *   *

The girl walked into the Powder Room and dialed Spring 7-3100.

"Hello," she said in a low voice. "Police Department? Detective Bureau, please—Is Sergeant Brodwell there? Johnny—I've found Carpenter. Yes—I sat and talked with him, and told him I was glad he had killed Lush. I had to do it this way, because I want him to know who turned him up. He gave me five hundred dollars to get back to Poplar Falls. That's just about what he took out of my husband's pocket when Lush lay dying in the gutter. But I want you to do me a favor. Bitsy is having a swell Christmas Eve—his last one, though he doesn't know it. He'll be in the Coq d'Or for a couple of hours yet. Don't take him till he's ready to leave. Promise? Okay. And when you put the bracelets on him tell him those extra hours were my Christmas present to him."

She went out into Fifty-second Street, and told a taxi driver to take her to the Newark airport. There was a plane West at one o'clock. Her job was done—and she was going to eat Christmas dinner at Poplar Falls.

A CORPSE FOR CHRISTMAS

An Inspector Allhoff Novelette

By D. L. Champion

Author of "Dumb Dick," etc.

CHAPTER ONE

Lady Bountiful and the Beast

THE snow, ghostly confetti, swirled down Centre Street toward the Battery, hammered silently against the window, then turned to gray water as it trickled, discouraged, down the dirty pane. Across the street a scarlet Salvation Army Santa Claus stood huddled against the cold, ringing his bell dispiritedly. Ten feet above his head a billboard announced categorically that only two shopping days remained until Christmas.

I turned from the window, lit my pipe and looked around the unkempt room. A pair of Allhoff's pajamas hung, like an unwashed specter, from the hook over the sink where the frying pan should have been. The door of his bedroom was open and the bed was in its customary condition—unmade. A stack of dirty dishes stood like a greasy Tower of Pisa upon the stove, and I reflected that if the waste baskets weren't emptied soon we'd probably revert to that Central American custom of heaving the rubbish out the window into the street below.

The gurgle of the percolator broke the silence and Allhoff's little agate eyes lit up. He waited for a long interval while the pot performed its perverse alchemy of transmuting perfectly good coffee and water to unpotable tar. Then he snatched the pot up with a trembling hand and filled his cup. He drank gratefully and audibly.

I WAITED until he was well through the third pouring before I spoke. Then I cleared my throat and said: "Allhoff, do you know that in two days it'll be Christmas."

He replaced the cup in the saucer with

A day for saps and suckers—that's what the most-hated copper on the roster of the "Finest" thought of Christmas. He made only one concession to the Yuletide season. If someone wanted to hand him a corpse for an Xmas gift he was perfectly ready to reciprocate in kind and wrap up his own grave-meat with holly and a red ribbon to put on a killer's tree.

Allhoff sat close up against his desk, staring at the coffee percolator upon its electric base as if the heat of his angry eyes would expedite the boiling of the water. A chipped cup and saucer, colored cafeteria gray, stood before him. A cracked tumbler half filled with sugar was on his left. He rattled a battered tin spoon impatiently as he watched the coffee pot, much in the manner a hophead watches opium cook.

I smoked my pipe quietly and thought troubled thoughts. Yesterday afternoon, in a weak moment, I had promised Battersly a favor which entailed appealing to Allhoff's better nature. Now that the time for action had arrived I was beginning to regret it. However, I wasn't sucker enough to broach the matter until Allhoff had consumed at least two cups of the viscous fluid which he firmly believed was coffee.

a clatter that somehow sounded ominous. Before he answered he snatched up a pencil and scribbled furiously on a scratch pad. Then he screwed his bullet head around and stared at me with bitter narrowed eyes.

"If the conversation is taking an actuarial turn," he said unpleasantly, "I'll hold up my end by remarking that it's precisely one hundred and fifty-eight days till Decoration Day, and a hundred and ninety-three till the Fourth of July. I'll remark further—so what?"

He swung his head around again and buried his face in the coffee cup. I sighed and refilled my pipe. This was going to be every bit as difficult as I had expected. I waited while he loaded up the percolator and tried again.

"Listen," I said amiably, "I don't know if anyone ever called your attention to it, but Christmas is a period of good will and congeniality. Whole families gather for reunions. Enemies forget their hates and buy presents for each other. The world dedicates itself to joyfulness and cheer. It's a period of happiness, of gladness and unselfishness."

Allhoff swung around in his swivel chair. He stared at me over the rim of his coffee cup. There was an unholy expression in his yellow pupils.

"You've left out something," he said. "It's also a period when the storekeepers make a fortune by shilling the yokels into buying presents they can't afford. When a million morons get drunk and go home to beat their wives. Christmas is a merry period during which the Nazis will undoubtedly blow thousands of British into little pieces, and give the concentration-camp boys an extra ration of arsenic for breakfast. When a couple of million people are on relief and fifteen percent of the kids in Georgia have rickets.

"Christmas!" he concluded with a grating laugh. "I'm glad you told me about it."

After that speech it didn't take much intelligence to make me realize I wasn't making any headway. I was annoyed enough to forget discretion.

"Listen," I said. "Did you ever read Dickens?"

Allhoff regarded me suspiciously. "Why?"

"Once," I told him, "there was a guy called Scrooge. He was a louse—like you. But he met up with a ghost on Christmas Eve and it scared hell out of him. He was a pretty good guy after that."

Allhoff refilled his cup and laughed. "I don't believe in ghosts," he said shortly.

I puffed at my pipe, sighed, and searched for a fresh approach to the matter in hand. Before I found one, Allhoff, regarding me shrewdly, said: "Simmonds, I hardly believe you're handing out all this Christmas sweetness and light

for the good of my soul. Suppose you tell me in simple one-syllable words what the devil you're driving at?"

I took a deep breath and realized that was exactly what I should have done in the first place. "All right," I said. "It's about Battersly."

He scowled and his eyes blazed at the name.

"He wants to go home for Christmas," I went on hurriedly. "He hasn't seen his mother back in Indiana for a couple of years. He'd like to stay there for a week. Until after New Year's. With your permission, of course."

Allhoff's face was saffron fire. His lips twisted as he uttered a single obscene word. He was glaring at me but I knew the epithet applied to Battersly.

"So," he said bitterly, "in addition to his other charming characteristics, Battersly possesses the moral courage of a jackrabbit. Why didn't he ask me himself?"

"You know the answer to that."

"I also know the answer to the original question," snapped Allhoff. "It's no. The department grants Christmas leave to anyone not on actual duty. Battersly's entitled to it. He can have it. But he doesn't get another single hour. If he wants to go to Indiana let him do it in one day. He can fly. Better yet he can run there and back. He's got the legs for it, hasn't he? While I—"

I had been afraid of this. He was rushing up to his boiling point like hot mercury.

"Allhoff!" I said sharply.

His little eyes glazed insanely. He banged a fist on the desk like a rubber mallet. I sighed resignedly as he opened his mouth to curse me. Then, to my intense relief, the door opened.

BATTERSLY, handsome and erect in his patrolman's uniform, stood holding the doorknob. He indicated Allhoff with a wave of his hand and said: "This is the occupant of the apartment, ma'am."

I gasped at the breathtaking beauty of the girl who entered the room. She was tall, dark, and she walked with regal bearing. Her gaze was arrogant and her eyes were blue and distant as an Arctic sea. She wore a suit which even my untutored eye recognized as an exclusive model.

On her left arm she carried a magnificent diamond bracelet and a huge covered basket. She put the basket down on Allhoff's desk, offered him a dazzling smile which, nevertheless, held a marked degree of condescension, and said: "Will someone please tell me the time? I'm sure I'll never get through my rounds before luncheon."

I didn't quite understand what she meant by that, but I glanced down at my wrist watch and said: "It's exactly seven minutes past nine."

She thanked me distantly and politely. Then she looked around the room and wrinkled her patrician nose. She shook her head in obvious disapproval.

"I should think you'd keep the place clean," she observed, "no matter how reduced your circumstances."

ALLHOFF blinked, looked from the girl to the basket. Like myself, he waited perplexedly for her to explain what the hell it was all about. The girl smiled down at him again, and there was something in her manner that reminded me of the local gentry bestowing a Christmas call on the worthy peasantry.

"I am here," she announced to Allhoff, "on behalf of the Society League's Holiday Aid Organization. We are giving you this basket. Each year we supply everything needed for a real old-fashioned Christmas dinner to the worthy poor."

She whipped the cover off the basket. Fruit, vegetables and canned goods were piled neatly about a huge turkey that thrust its naked torso into Allhoff's face.

"So this," said the girl as if she were talking to an imbecile, "is for you, my good man."

My good man! That killed me. Battersly looked at her apprehensively. Allhoff's face grew slowly purple. For the moment he was absolutely speechless. I took the pipe from my mouth and grinned broadly. This, I decided, was one of the high spots of my routine life.

Because Allhoff chose to live in this sordid tenement slum, he had been listed as one of the worthy indigent entitled to draw a charity Christmas meal. I saw furious baffled rage well up in his eyes and I felt uplifted.

With a mighty effort he controlled his temper, assumed a degree of distant dignity as he spoke.

"Madam—" he began, but the girl waved a jeweled, deprecating hand and cut him short.

"Don't thank me," she said. "And there's no need to be embarrassed. It is the duty of the better classes to provide for the unfortunate. We—"

"Madam!" Allhoff was a roaring lion now. His cheeks were the color of crimson orchids in bloom. There was wild fury in his eyes. "I am neither indigent nor unfortunate. My salary is ample. My bank account is healthy. Therefor, I must ask you to remove this charity basket. Give it to someone who needs it."

The girl with the regal bearing was one of the few people I had ever seen who stood in no awe of Allhoff's roaring. She watched him with her cool eyes and when she spoke it was in the tone of an adult admonishing a recalcitrant child.

"Come now," she said. "Don't let foolish pride stand in the way of your enjoying a good meal. Perhaps your circumstances are not entirely your fault. But it really is silly to pretend you don't need this food."

She paused for a moment and smiled

a class-conscious smile. For the first time in my life I saw Allhoff utterly speechless. The indignity put upon him was too much for his larynx. He made an odd gurgling noise in his throat and stared at the poised beautiful creature before him with the dazed expression of a man watching water run uphill.

THE girl reached over and patted the fat drumstick of the turkey. She retained her patronizing air. "Look," she said, "you'll be glad I didn't take you at your word as you munch this drumstick on Christmas day. There's really nothing as good as a turkey leg. Fat and rich. You wouldn't want your foolish pride to deprive you of two fat legs, would you?"

My stomach turned over at that. I heard Battersly's swift intake of breath. Allhoff's face was as twisted as a Communist editorial. He slammed his hands down on the desk-top, pushed the swivel chair backwards halfway across the floor. He pointed down toward his thighs, to the pair of leather pads where his knees should have been and wriggled his stumps in a little macabre dance.

"Damn you!" he shrieked, and his voice soared close to hysteria. "I've already been deprived of two legs!" He jerked his gaze away from the girl who remained calm and elegant under this outburst and glared at Battersly. "You!" he yelled. "You brought this strumpet in here. You brought her in here to mock me. You—"

Pale and nervous, Battersly interrupted him. "I never saw her before, sir. I met her in the hall. She asked me who lived in this apartment. I—"

"You lie!" screamed Allhoff, still dancing a frenzied rigadoon with his stumps. "You brought her here to jeer at me. You didn't dare do it yourself. First, you rob me of my legs. Now, you bring this slut here to sneer, to insult me with her damnable charity. A Christmas basket! My God—"

I decided to cut in before he achieved an apoplectic coma.

"Allhoff!" I said sharply.

He switched his gaze to me long enough to curse me obscenely. I looked over at the girl. She remained completely aloof. There was faint contempt upon her face and her smile was icy, totally without humor.

Allhoff looked at her, too. There was murder, unholy and clear in his eyes. She met his gaze unflinchingly. I had never before seen anyone stand like a rock before the tidal wave of Allhoff's fury. She cleared her throat and said with contemptuous indifference: "What a horrible little man."

Then she swung around on a high French heel and strode with imperious dignity from the room. Furthermore she left the Christmas basket on the desk behind her. The door slammed and Allhoff stared after her, speechless. For that matter, so did I.

I had seen Allhoff indulge in a thousand hysterical outbursts. I had seen the victims of his wrath register fear, rage, sullen resentment. But heretofore no one had ever remained remote and indifferent. The girl with the basket had subtly conveyed the impression that Allhoff was some gray crawling form of life beneath her notice.

Battersly, with rare discretion for him, went quietly into the tiny bathroom and locked the door. Allhoff turned his head slowly until his gaze rested on the turkey. Then he found his tongue.

He cursed wildly, snatched up the fowl and hurled it to the floor. He scattered the vegetables with a frenzied hand. He called the girl a string of ugly names. He swore at Battersly with all the venom of his poisoned tongue. He kicked his stumps violently and spoke for a solid ten minutes. The words poured from his twisted mouth like oil from a gusher.

I refilled my pipe and made no effort

to stop him. This was one of those occasions when nothing short of a blackjack applied forcefully to the base of his skull could have accomplished that.

THE genesis of Allhoff's psychosis went back to a bloody night several years ago, when he had been leading a raid on a gangster stronghold on upper West End Avenue. Battersly, a raw recruit in those days, had been assigned to effect an entrance through the rear in order to disable the Tommy-gun operator who, it was expected, would be guarding the front door.

Battersly carried out the first half of his job well enough, then developed an understandable case of buck fever and didn't shoot in time. At the zero hour Allhoff came battering through the front door to be greeted by a hail of machine-gun bullets. A score of them almost cut off his legs. The Bellevue surgeons completed the job after gangrene had set in.

But Allhoff lost more than his legs in that foray. Something of his mind went, too. He became a bitter misanthrope. Hate and venom bubbled within him, a ceaseless hot spring.

Departmental rules forbid a legless inspector and he had resigned forthwith from the force. But the commissioner did not intend to lose his best man that easily. Devious bookkeeping in the comptroller's office arranged it so that he was paid his former salary. He had set himself up in this tenement flat in order to be near headquarters. And while he had no official standing, woe betide the rookie who didn't believe that Allhoff's orders took precedence over those of anyone else. The commissioner would back him to the hilt in anything he cared to do.

Allhoff's first act in the new régime was to demand that Battersly be assigned as his assistant. When that request had been granted he proceeded to exact his bitter and terrible revenge. I, who had come up with Allhoff had been given this thankless detail, too. Ostensibly, I was to take care of the paper work. Actually, I was supposed to pour oil on the troubled waters when Allhoff gave way to his flaming temper.

It was the most unpleasant assignment I'd ever had. But all my efforts at transfer were denied by the commissioner. He knew that while Allhoff was by no means fond of me, he probably disliked me a little less than anyone else. So here we were, the three of us—me, waiting patiently until I was eligible for my pension, Battersly and Allhoff, waiting for the latter's death to release each of them from the bitter thrall in which they were held.

CHAPTER TWO

Murder—Vice Versa

IT WAS a little after one o'clock when the Gerson case came up. For two hours Allhoff had been drinking coffee steadily and silently. Battersly busied himself with a sheaf of onion-skin reports. I sat by the window staring out into the snowy street.

A copper from headquarters came in, saluted Allhoff stiffly, laid a package and a large manila envelope on his desk.

"The commissioner wants you to look these over, Inspector," he said. "It's pretty cut and dried, but he'd like your corroborative opinion because of the prominence of the principals."

Allhoff, still in a savage mood, gave him the silent treatment. He sipped coffee and didn't look up. The copper stood there, red-faced and angry, for a moment. Then he swung round abruptly and strode from the room. Allhoff continued to devote his attention to his coffee so I got up, took the package and envelope from his desk and carried them back to my own.

For the next fifteen minutes I studied the reports and exhibits in the Gerson case. A casual examination convinced me that the homicide squad already had the correct answer. But when anything out of the ordinary occurred the commissioner always liked to have Allhoff's opinion on the record, too.

Eventually Allhoff, as crammed with coffee as an A & P warehouse deigned to turn his head and grunt in my direction: "What've we got?"

"Emile Gerson," I told him. "The gold-mine guy. Been sort of wacky ever since he made his fortune, according to the papers and the report here. Lived with his nephew in that gloomy dungeon overlooking the Sound at Whitestone. The nephew's a college professor—philologist. Apparently he was something of a screw-ball in his own right. Both drunks. They—"

"Listen," said Allhoff irritably, "I read all the papers every morning and I've got a memory like an elephant. The Gerson family's no good. Since they got money they all proceeded to drink themselves to death. Only a couple of them left. I know all about Emile Gerson. I know all about his nephew. Tell me something new."

"I will," I said. "They're dead."

There was a moment's silence. Battersly dropped his reports and swung around in his chair. Allhoff lifted his eyebrows and the coffee pot at the same time. He filled his cup with liquid ebony.

"All right," he said. "What happened?"

"Gerson and Harry Welch—that's the nephew—had one hell of a row yesterday. Welch threatened to kill Gerson, then kill himself. Witnesses testify that Welch claimed they'd both be better off dead. It was a real drunken brawl. Welch claimed money and booze had ruined them. This morning Welch carried out his threat."

Allhoff sipped coffee noisily. Then he put down the cup and grunted. "What's in that package?"

"Exhibits A to Z. Articles homicide took from the corpses' pockets. Random stuff they picked up."

Allhoff held out his hand. "Let me see it."

I handed him the cardboard container. He opened it and peered at the contents. "All right," he said. "Let's hear the report. Don't skip anything."

I looked at him in disgust. The report was long, detailed and deadly dull.

"Listen," I said. "This is sheer routine. The commisioner merely wants a corroborative opinion. Welch killed his uncle, then shot himself. Homicide's got the whole thing cleared up."

Allhoff took a wrist watch out of the cardboard box and examined it. "Homicide's been wrong before," he announced. "Now what's in that report?"

I SIGHED, picked up the single-spaced typewritten sheet and proceeded to itemize the details in a bored tone.

"At nine ten this morning, one William Leroy, the gardener, was in the greenhouse. He heard two shots, raced into the study. He found Gerson and Welch dead. Each had been shot through the head. The gun was in Welch's hand. There was a note—a suicide note written by Welch—in the roller of his portable typewriter."

Allhoff looked up from the wrist watch he still held. "Who else lives in that house?" he asked. "And where were they when the shots were fired?"

I consulted the second page of the report.

"One—" I said, "Jonas Kline, secretary to Gerson. He was at a barber shop over on Northern Boulevard. He was getting a shave, if you're going to insist on all the details. Two—Alicia Dale, second cousin to Welch, was here in Manhattan. The cook and the maid were in the laundry, some distance removed from the house. They heard the shots and rushed to the study. A W.P.A. road gang outside heard the firing, too. Homicide checked everyone. They had solid alibis all around."

Allhoff snorted contemptuously. "Homicide has a habit of finding out who didn't commit the crime," he said. "Why don't they ever find out who did?"

"They found out this time," I told him. "Harry Welch."

"All right," said Allhoff. "What else?"

"My God," I said impatiently, "what else do you want? Homicide's got it cleared up, I tell you. They even interviewed Gerson's lawyer and his doctor. I suppose you'd like the doctor's report?"

"Sure," said Allhoff blandly. "What is it?"

"It won't make any more sense to you than it does to me," I told him. "Gerson was anemic, dipsomaniac, given to brooding. A marked *M. Agitata* type."

Allhoff glanced up sharply. He took an official-looking piece of paper from the box on his desk.

"This came out of Gerson's pocket," he said and there was a little tremor of suppressed excitement in his tone. "It's a federal court summons returnable at nine o'clock this morning. Income-tax stuff. Did Gerson answer it?"

I thumbed through the report. "That's on page six," I told him. "I was coming to that. No. His lawyer was down there waiting for him. Gerson was supposed to be there. The federal people were about to issue a bench warrant for him. But what the hell's all that got to do with it?"

He didn't answer. There was a far-away expression in his little eyes. Battersly watched him apprehensively. He knew that expression of Allhoff's as well as I did. It boded no good for someone.

"What else've you got there?" he demanded.

"I shrugged my shoulders. "You've got it all. All except the suicide note left by Harry Welch."

Allhoff held his coffee cup an inch away from his lips and looked at me expectantly.

I detached the typewritten note from the report and began to read aloud—

"This family was rotten without money. With wealth we are even worse. We should all have been decimated years ago. I'm doing my part now.

"The signature — *H. W.* — is typed underneath."

Allhoff bent forward and snatched the paper out of my hand. He studied it for a moment and an unholy gleam came into his eyes. He put down his coffee cup and said: "Now what do you suppose that note means?"

Battersly answered before I could. "I guess," he volunteered, "he meant the Gerson family was a bunch of no-goods and after the old man made his pile they became a bunch of drunks. He meant they should be wiped out."

"Bright boy," said Allhoff in a tone which implied exactly the opposite. He turned to me. "What do you think it means?"

"Listen," I said wearily. "It's written in simple English, isn't it? It can only mean what Battersly has already said it means. Welch thought the family should be wiped out. He proceeded to set the example by killing his uncle and blowing out his own brains."

ALLHOFF smiled his prime, grade-A, unpleasant smile. He wore an air of superiority which nettled me. "Do you know what I think?" he asked loudly.

"Sure," I told him. "You think you're a combination of Sherlock Holmes, Charlie Chan and God Almighty. You think—"

"Damn you!" he yelled. "Do you know what I think about this Gerson case?"

"You tell me."

"I will," said Allhoff. "I'll tell the whole damned police department. Emile Gerson killed himself. Harry Welch was murdered."

"That's what everyone else thinks," I

told him. "Only you're getting it mixed up. You—" I broke off suddenly. Allhoff never got anything mixed up. "Say that again," I demanded.

He grinned unpleasantly. "I said," he repeated, "Gerson killed himself. Welch was murdered."

I stared at him. Then I looked back at the typewritten papers on my desk. Battersly screwed up his face and watched Allhoff perplexedly.

"Allhoff," I said, "this is a beautiful flight of fancy. Homicide has been on the scene, has checked everything. They claim Gerson was killed and Welch committed suicide. You, apparently using nothing but silent communication with the stars, brazenly announce that *Gerson* committed suicide, while *Welch* was murdered."

Allhoff poured some coffee before he spoke. Then slowly and insultingly he said: "There are times, Simmonds, when I think you are dumber than homicide. Then again there are occasions when I think homicide's dumber than you. It's a hairline decision."

I was getting sore now. But before I could speak Battersly's curiosity overcame his natural reluctance to direct conversation with Allhoff. "But, sir," he said, puzzled, "how can you tell? How can—"

"He can't tell," I cut in. "He's impressing us. He's going to impress the commissioner too—tell him how dumb homicide is. But, of course, Inspector Allhoff wasn't on the spot and by now homicide's obliterated all the hot clues. So the inspector can't prove his case."

Allhoff's howl of rage shook the fly-specked chandelier above our heads.

"Damn you!" he roared. "Shut up. You dumb copper, I've got all the evidence in the world. You and the whole damned homicide squad are muddy minded cretins. Don't tell me Harry Welch killed Gerson and then shot himself. He didn't. Gerson killed himself. Welch was murdered. And I'm going to prove it, too."

I realized he was serious enough. But if he'd dug up enough to prove his theory from the report I'd given him, I was willing to sign my pension over to the Burglar's Union. He was glaring at me now, his eyes flashing like neon signs.

"You still don't believe me, do you?"

"No," I said. "But what was all this loose talk about evidence?"

"First," said Allhoff, and his eyes glittered, his nostrils quivered like those of a bloodhound taking the trail. "First, consider old man Gerson's condition. He's anemic. He's given to brooding, and that *M. Agitata* which seems to baffle you, means *Melancholia Agitata.*"

"Which," I said, "in turn, means . . . ?"

"It means he's a manic-depressive type given to deep spells of melancholy, accompanied by a jittery nervous condition which accentuates the melancholy. Gerson was just the *sort* of guy who'd commit suicide."

I SCRATCHED my head and blinked at him. Allhoff had based a theory on some pretty slim stuff before this, but now it seemed he was going in for sheer guesswork.

"Second," he continued, "take that federal court summons. An income-tax rap is important. Gerson knew it was important. He'd told his lawyer he'd meet him in court. He was due there at nine o'clock this morning. He didn't go. Why?"

"I'm the straight man," I said. "Why?"

"If you intended to commit suicide within the hour, you wouldn't give a damn about a summons either."

"Nuts!" I said and ran my fingers through my hair.

Allhoff looked at me hotly. "You think it's thin, don't you?"

"Thin?" I echoed. "It's invisible."

"All right," said Allhoff. "There's more than that. Now let's take Harry Welch. Here's his wrist watch. It's got his initials on it. That watch was wound up this morning. As near as I can figure, some time around eight o'clock. If Welch intended to kill himself would he wind up his watch?"

"Allhoff," I said, "do you feel well? For sixty bucks a week you can go up to Bill Brown's health farm at Garrison. In a month your mind would be as good as ever. Why, I knew a guy once who—"

Allhoff called me a filthy name, then drank some more coffee and became calmer.

"The most important item of all," he said, "is that suicide note. Welch didn't write it."

I was getting very bored. "No?" I said politely.

"No," snapped Allhoff. "Welch was a college professor before he became a booze-fighter. He was a philologist of high reputation." He swung around in his chair and faced Battersly. "You," he said. "What does *decimate* mean?"

Battersly blinked, frowned for a moment, and said: "Why it means to wipe out, to annihilate."

"Ha," said Allhoff and waved a finger under my nose. "Now, you. What does *decimate* mean?"

"It means just what Battersly said it means," I answered wearily. "And now may I please go to lunch?"

"The guy that wrote that note," said Allhoff, ignoring my question, "was as dumb as you two. He also thought *decimate* means to wipe out." He hammered his fist on the desk and raised his voice. "But it doesn't! It means to reduce by a tenth. As, for example, when every tenth man in a mutinous regiment is shot by the military authorities. Nearly everyone uses the word incorrectly, believes it means to obliterate."

"So," I said, "granting you're a purist, Harry Welch was just another of us mugs who misuses a word."

"No!" yelled Allhoff. "He was a phil-

ologist, wasn't he? Words and their derivations, their meanings, were his business. He'd never make a mistake like that. Harry Welch never wrote that note. Besides—look here."

He picked up the suicide note and held it out to me. "Note that signature Note those initials, *H. W.* The typing there is somewhat lighter than the body of the note. Someone else typed those initials."

I took the paper from him. "My God!" I said. "Someone else wrote the note. Now a third party has typed the initials."

I STUDIED the paper and decided he might be right, and then again he might well be wrong. Perhaps there was an almost imperceptible difference in the shading of the note itself and the signature. But it was so slight as to be entirely negligible.

"Just supposing you're right," I said. "Harry Welch was murdered. A phony note was planted. Your Gerson suicide theory suffers from an acute case of the shakes. Why couldn't the person who wrote the note have killed them both?"

"It's barely possible," said Allhoff, with the air of making a munificent concession. "But my idea is that Gerson wrote that note before he killed himself. Then after Harry was murdered, someone switched it and signed those initials to make it appear that it was written by Welch."

I thought that over and decided that I still put my faith in the homicide squad.

"You've made four points," I said. "Gerson's mental condition, the summons, the wrist watch, and the definition of the word *decimate*. Each point is inconclusive."

"Each is indicative," snapped Allhoff. "Taken all together they make the whole case look screwy. Besides, there's another important point."

"Which is?"

"I feel I'm right," said Allhoff. "I sense it."

My God, he sensed it! In another week we'd be solving murder cases by fasting, prayer and astrology.

"In any event," said Allhoff, slipping from his chair and landing on his stumps with two dull thuds, "in any event, we're going out to Gerson's right now and look things over."

"Listen," I said in disgust, "can't we wait till after Christmas? The day after tomorrow's a holiday."

"Not if we're working on a case," said Allhoff virtuously. "A copper must be prepared to make personal sacrifices for the public good."

Which was a very noble speech coming from Allhoff. To him holidays and working days were exactly the same. He spent three hundred and sixty-five days a year drinking coffee in this slum, a fact which made it a hell of a sacrifice for him to give up Christmas. I said as much aloud but he took no notice of my sarcasm. Followed by Battersly, he was already clumping off in the direction of the stairway.

I sighed, stood up and went along. As I crossed the room my foot slipped on something soft and rubbery. I looked down to see the turkey which had been presented to Allhoff for Christmas. I kicked it viciously across the room and put on my coat.

As I walked down the rickety stairs I was hoping against hope that for once in his life Allhoff would take only forty-eight hours to admit he was wrong. Otherwise we'd all be eating hamburger sandwiches for Christmas dinner out at Whitestone Landing.

CHAPTER THREE

Alibi Allhoff

WE WENT out to Long Island in a police car with Battersly driving. Allhoff sat thoughtfully next to me in the rear seat and said nothing. I was seething with disgust and annoyance at being dragged out here on a fool's errand.

Gerson's home was an ancient brownstone structure built close to the water's edge on Long Island Sound. Secluded, it stood alone in the center of a couple of hundred acres, bleak and inhospitable.

I tugged at an old-fashioned bell-pull and a maid opened the door. She stared down at surprise in Allhoff, but he gave her no opportunity for questioning. He clumped right past her into the house. Battersly and I tagged along behind him.

Allhoff led the way through a large and empty living-room into a wide hall where we could hear the sound of voices. We paraded down the corridor in single file until Allhoff stopped before a door through which the voices sounded clearer. He jerked it open without knocking and waddled inside.

The room was obviously the study, quite probably the study in which Emile Gerson and his nephew had been found dead. Bookcases lined the walls. A broad mahogany desk stood at the far end of the oblong room like a pulpit. At the other end a vast fireplace yawned vacantly.

Two men stood up quickly as we entered. One of them, bald, ancient, and possessed of a quavering voice became indignant.

"What does this mean?" he demanded. "Who are you people? I—"

The second man interposed quickly. "Wait a minute, Kline." He looked thoughtfully at Allhoff. "This is Inspector Allhoff, I presume?"

Allhoff likes to be recognized. His mouth twisted in what he fondly believed was an ingratiating smile and he admitted his identity.

The other took a fat cigar from his lips and patted his rounded stomach. "Well, well," he said. "Glad to meet you, Inspector. Heard a lot of things about you. I'm Amberson, Emile Gerson's attorney. This"—he indicated the gray oldster at his side—"is Jonas Kline. He was Gerson's secretary."

Allhoff nodded to acknowledge the introduction. But he stood upon no further ceremony. He waddled the length of the room, climbed up on the chair behind the desk, seated himself like the presiding officer at a director's meeting.

"Now," he announced, "I want to see everyone in the house."

Jonas Kline appeared annoyed. "Good gracious!" he said. "We've had policemen here all morning. I thought everything was completed. I don't see why—"

Little Amberson interrupted him for a second time. "Now, Jonas," he said. "I'm sure the inspector knows what he's doing. Perhaps he doesn't know that headquarters is quite satisfied with its conclusions."

"I'm not satisfied," said Allhoff arrogantly. "And I still want to see everyone in the house."

Amberson hesitated for a moment. Apparently he knew of Allhoff's reputation for he turned to Kline and said: "All right, Jonas. Never obstruct justice. Get everyone down here to see the inspector."

Jonas Kline shrugged his shoulders and walked from the room without enthusiasm.

AMBERSON puffed on his cigar and regarded Allhoff curiously. Battersly and I exchanged a glance of mutual commiseration. We knew from Allhoff's manner that he was going to play the role of super-sleuth to the hilt this time. We'd be lucky if we got out of there within the week.

The maid came shuffling through the door followed by a large competent woman, quite evidently the cook. Both of them had answered several questions for homicide in the morning and by now were quite docile. Allhoff swiftly took them over the jumps.

They had been in the laundry at the time of the shooting. They'd heard the shots, run to the study to find Leroy, the gardner, standing on the threshold staring at the corpses.

Allhoff dismissed them with a wave of his hand. Then he stopped the cook in the doorway by saying darkly: "Wait a minute. There's one very important thing."

The cook looked at him inquiringly.

"Can you make good coffee?" he demanded. "Black, thick and strong?"

The cook was quite confident that she could.

"Then make it," said Allhoff. "At once!"

Jonas Kline hustled back into the room, followed by a handsome giant, with blond curly hair and unintelligent eyes.

"Leroy," announced Kline.

Allhoff nodded. "You heard two shots, didn't you? You found the bodies."

"Yes, sir."

Allhoff leaned over the desk and shook his forefinger. "So you're the one man in the house with no alibi."

That didn't disturb the blond at all. "And no motive," said Leroy.

Allhoff scowled. He was getting nowhere at a great rate. He turned to Kline. "At the time of the killing you were in a barber shop. Is that correct?"

Kline twisted his fingers together nervously. "Absolutely. Three barbers can testify to that. I—"

But Allhoff was addressing Amberson now. "I suppose you, too, can account for your movements at the time Gerson and Welch died."

Amberson regarded Allhoff with more amusement than anything else. "I hope you don't think I killed them, Inspector. Your own homicide squad has already ascertained that I was in federal court waiting for Mr. Gerson."

"Allhoff," I said, "we can still get back to town in time for lunch."

He ignored me. He scratched his head and appeared more worried than I had ever seen him before. For once a case wasn't opening wide at his magic touch. For once Allhoff's psychic prescience wasn't working.

"This Dale woman," he said to Amberson. "She was some sort of relative, wasn't she?"

Amberson nodded. "Second cousin to Harry Welch. Even more distantly related to Gerson."

Allhoff bit his lip and looked thoughtful.

Amberson shook his head. "No, Inspector," he said. "I know what you're thinking. And you're wrong. She—"

My nostrils caught a subtle odor of aphrodisiac perfume. My ear caught a rustle of silk. I saw Allhoff glaring toward the door like an enraged boar before I turned my head.

A voice said: "I'm Alicia Dale, Inspector. Did you want to see me?"

I gaped at her. It was the girl of Allhoff's charity basket!

SHE swept across the room toward the desk where Allhoff sat. She was every bit as calm and remote as she had been two hours ago. She smiled condescendingly down at Allhoff who looked like a bomb about to burst.

"So," he said in a thick strangled voice, "it's you."

"Yes," she said, still smiling. "I would have told you my name this morning, but when working among the unfortunate, I prefer strict anonymity."

Allhoff made a rattling sound in his throat and his eyes were yellow coals. I knew he would much rather pin a murder on Alicia Dale than on public enemies number one to ten, inclusive.

"I warn you," he said wrathfully, "you're under suspicion. I'll check everything you say. I'll do my damnedest to break down any story you tell."

Alicia Dale regarded him with sardonic mockery. "In that event," she said coolly, "you'd better begin by cross-examining

yourself, Inspector. You're my alibi."

I saw a bullfight once in Juarez. The bull with a dozen darts in its back had until this moment, always been the top in baffled rage to me. Now Allhoff moved into first place by several lengths.

Since he was beyond speech, Alicia Dale spoke again.

"Someone in your office was kind enough to tell me it was exactly seven minutes past nine. As I understand it, Leroy found the bodies three minutes later. That's my alibi, Inspector. Break it down."

As I saw it, and with considerable rejoicing, Allhoff was going to be thoroughly and completely wrong for the first time in his life. If he intended to pin a murder on Alicia Dale he must first impeach the evidence of his own eyes and senses. And from what I'd heard from the others it was going to be equally difficult to pin it on anyone else.

This time homicide was right and Allhoff was wrong and great would be the gloating in the precinct locker-rooms.

"Alibi or not," snarled Allhoff, "you're a relative of Gerson's. As far as I can ascertain, the only living relative. You'd be in line for Emile Gerson's money. You had motive."

In my opinion, Allhoff was so sore he was getting childish now. Considering the girl's conclusive alibi, this motive business was a pretty slim prop. Then, to my glee, Amberson swept even that prop away.

"You're wrong, Inspector," he said. "I was trying to tell you that before. Miss Dale doesn't get the Gerson estate."

Alicia Dale's derisive smile remained steady. "Of course not," she said.

Allhoff looked like something in a cage. "Who gets it?" he snapped.

"There's a son," said little Amberson. "A natural son of Gerson's. Illegitimate. Born some ten years ago of a girl whom Gerson loved very much. She died when the boy was a baby. Exacted a dying promise from Gerson that the child would never be brought up in the Gerson family. Should never know who his father was."

Allhoff drummed an angry spatulate forefinger on the desk.

"Where is this boy?"

"In Illinois. Being brought up by his uncle on his mother's side. Everything goes to that boy. Lock, stock and barrel. The uncle, Peter Lovelace, and myself are named as executors. Gerson kept the whole thing under cover. Very few people knew about it."

"That's right," said Alicia Dale. "Only Amby, here. Harry Welch and myself."

"Four alibis," I said gayly. "And not a single motive. If we go home now, Allhoff, we'll duck the traffic on the Queensborough Bridge."

"No," said Allhoff and his voice was a hoarse, enraged scream. "There's been murder here. I know it! I know it!"

I DECIDED to give him the works. "I've got an idea," I told him. "The kid out in Illinois had a fight with his uncle. The uncle wouldn't give him money for candy. So the kid hitch-hikes to New York, knocks off his father in order to inherit the estate. Then he can buy all the candy he wants. Oh, yes, and about Harry Welch. He—"

Allhoff let out a roar like a wounded lion and began an oath-filled diatribe.

Alicia Dale's cool voice cut in on him. "I can't stand noise and vulgarity," she said sweetly to me. "I'm going up to my room. If the inspector wants me when he gets over his tantrum I'll be there."

She turned and swept out of the room. Allhoff stared after her and if a look could kill she'd have withered in her tracks.

"Oh, by the way," said Amberson. "I've already wired Peter Lovelace. He's flying here immediately to consult with me about the estate. Arrives at Newark airport at eleven tonight. Can you pick him up in the car, Leroy?"

"Yes, sir."

"We'll put him in the south room," said Kline. "I'll probably be in bed when he arrives."

"Lovelace is blind, Leroy," said Amberson. "Take good care of him. Take him up to the room and tell him where everything is."

Allhoff looked up swiftly. "Blind?"

Amberson nodded. "Been blind all his life. That was one of the reasons that the boy's mother wanted him to live with the uncle. Figured the uncle would be better for the boy than the Gersons. And that the blind man would be greatly aided by the lad."

Allhoff grunted and closed his eyes as if in deep thought. But he wasn't kidding me.

"Allhoff," I said. "If we leave now—"

"Damn you," said Allhoff. "We're not leaving. We're staying here overnight. Kline, can you put us up?"

Kline admitted reluctantly that he could put us up. He left the room in order to consult with the maid. Leroy followed him. Amberson stood up and put on his coat.

"Well, Inspector," he said breezily. "Got to get back to the office. I'll be out here first thing in the morning to see Peter Lovelace and also to find out what you've picked up. 'Bye."

He strode cockily from the room, leaving Allhoff still registering profound cerebration. He still wasn't fooling me and judging from the expression on Battersly's face he wasn't fooling him either. We exchanged winks.

"You know," said Allhoff at last, "a woman like that Dale girl is capable of murder."

"That," I told him, "is sheer rationalization. You hate her guts, hence she's a murderess. Besides, you would look like an awful fool when she'd put you on the stand to testify for the defense. Old Alibi Allhoff. That's what the whole department'd be calling you after that."

He grunted. "Well," he said, "suppose she killed Welch before she left the house."

I laughed aloud at that. "So everyone's crazy," I said. "Two servants and a dozen W.P.A. guys all imagine two shots at the same time while Alicia Dale is standing in your office handing out a free turkey. No, Allhoff. For once one of your psychic hunches has collided with a fact. You're wrong as hell this time. You may as well admit it."

"Damn you," he said darkly. "I've never been wrong in my life."

The superb egotism of the guy got me. Hit him in the face with a fact and it made no difference. Allhoff had called it a murder and a suicide in reverse and that's what it would be until they laid him in a protesting grave.

CHAPTER FOUR

Blindman's Buff

JONAS KLINE showed us to three single rooms in the north wing. I stayed in mine, keeping away from Allhoff and everyone else, save for an appearance at a gloomy and conversationless dinner.

I went to bed early and prayed that Allhoff would come to his senses in time to let me get home for Christmas dinner. Since Battersly wasn't going to have an opportunity to go to Indiana, I decided I'd invite him along, too. Before midnight I was fast asleep.

The shot awakened me, and the scream that followed brought me back to complete consciousness. I sprang out of bed, pulled on my trousers, grabbed my gun and went racing down the corridor. As I gained the stair-head, I saw Allhoff skidding down the steps in front of me.

Behind me, I heard doors open and the sound of footsteps. There was a ten-watt light in the lower hall that apparently had been left burning. By its illumination I saw Allhoff careen down to the door of the study. His hand jerked out and touched a light-switch on the wall.

I looked down to see Allhoff prodding a man's body with the stump of his leg. Then he bent down and touched the fallen man's pulse. The prostrate figure had a thin sensitive face and deep fathomless eyes. There was an ugly red hole in the side of the head. Allhoff dropped an inert wrist and turned to me.

"Dead," he said over his shoulder, then added bitterly: "Do you figure it was suicide, Sergeant?"

cont'd next page

THE PEN & INK ILLUSTRATIONS from "A Corpse for Christmas" and the next story, "Nothing for Christmas," were the work of a prolific artist named **John Fleming Gould**, who was a mainstay of Popular Publications. As was the case with the writers, many pulpwood artists hoped to break through to the higher-paying general-interest "slicks," such as *The Saturday Evening Post*, *Collier's*, and *Redbook*. Gould was no exception – after spending part of the '20s and all of the '30s drawing interior illustrations for titles like *The Spider*, *G-8 and His Battle Aces*, and *Operator No. 5*, he made the jump to the slicks.

Among the other artists whose work is reprinted here are **Peter Costanza** ("Broadway Christmas Carol") and **Bob Jenney** ("Quiet Christmas Morning"). Jenney's work can be seen in many early comic books; he came to pulp illustration after serving in the Navy during World War II. Constanza was also a noted comic-book artist, notably with Fawcett Publications, where he worked with *Captain Marvel* creator C.C. Beck. Baby-boomer superhero fans remember him for his work with characters like Magicman and the venerable Jimmy Olsen, Superman's pal.

At the moment I didn't figure anything. Behind me up the hall padded Battersly and Jonas Kline. They came to a full stop at the side of the corpse.

"What's wrong?" asked Battersly.

Allhoff threw him a contemptuous glance. "What do you think's wrong?" he growled. "Arson?"

Jonas Kline literally wrung his hands. "Good Heavens," he murmured. "This house is cursed. Another one. Who—who is it, Inspector?"

"If you'll look through his pockets," said Allhoff to me, "you'll undoubtedly discover that it's Uncle Peter Lovelace from Illinois."

I looked in the pockets and found a bankbook that proved Allhoff was right. Allhoff was watching Kline who muttered apprehensively, and cracked his fingers.

"You," said Allhoff. "Go to bed."

"But—" said Kline.

"To bed," shouted Allhoff in his I'll-brook-no-nonsense tone.

Kline, still murmuring to himself shuffled off toward the stairway. Allhoff entered the study and switched on the light. The first thing I noticed was that one of the sections of bookcase had been pulled away from the wall, revealing a safe set in the paneling. The safe-door was open, and examination proved it empty. Allhoff ran a hand through his thinning hair and his eyes narrowed.

Battersly stood in the doorway, staring down at the corpse. "Gee," he said. "And the poor guy was blind. Now why would anyone want to kill a blind man?"

Allhoff did an about-turn like a Prussian Guard. "What's that?" he said sharply. "Say that again?"

Battersly looked at him oddly and repeated: "Why would anyone want to kill a blind man?"

"My God!" said Allhoff. "Out of the mouths of babes! You've actually put your finger on something. No one *would* want to kill a blind man."

"But they did," I pointed out reasonably.

"Shut up," said Allhoff. "I'm thinking. Things are slowly falling into place. Peter Lovelace. A concealed heir. Empty safe."

This was gibberish to me but I knew better than to interrupt. He turned suddenly to Battersly again.

"What room's next door to this one?" he said. "Look on both sides."

BATTERSLY went out into the corridor and returned a moment later. "There's a dining-room on the left," he reported. "And a lavatory on the other side. Why?"

"Stay right here, both of you," said Allhoff. "Neither of you talk."

He climbed up into a big armchair and bowed his head in his hands. Battersly and I stood there in silence, feeling like fools. Allhoff was deep in his heavy-concentration act. And when he put on one of these seances I never knew if he actually had something or whether he was merely acting as the moving pictures had taught him a big-shot sleuth ought to act.

It was a full five minutes before he came out of it. But when he lifted his head his little eyes gleamed and his voice was hoarse with excitement as he spoke.

"Battersly, you're going back to town."

Allhoff took a notebook and fountain pen from his pocket. He scribbled something on a page then tore it from the book. Next he dragged out his checkbook and scrawled in that. He handed the check, the note and a key to Battersly.

"You'll be at the Second National Bank the instant it opens," he said. "Give 'em that note and they'll let you into my safe-deposit box. That's the key there. You'll find a stack of bonds. Consolidated Motors fifties. Get 'em. Then cash that check. Get fifty twenties. Have the cashier wrap 'em up neatly with a rubber band. Be back here as soon as possible."

"What am I supposed to do?" I asked.

"You'll stand guard," he said. "You'll stay up, walk around this house and see that no one leaves it. In the meantime hand me that portable typewriter."

I picked up Harry Welch's typewriter —the one the suicide note had been written on—and carried it across the room to Allhoff. He placed it across his stumps and put a sheet of paper in the roller, began to peck at the keys as I left the room with Battersly.

Battersly went outside and drove off in the car. I strolled around the house and wondered who and what I was supposed to be guarding. Long after dawn I still heard Allhoff laboriously hammering away with two fingers. He didn't come out of the study till about half past six. But instead of going up the stairs to his room, he clumped across the hall toward the front door. I regarded him with sleepy eyes.

"What now?" I said. "Aren't we ever going to bed?"

He looked over at me and grinned unpleasantly. "I'm going out to the greenhouse," he announced. "I love to smell flowers in the early morning. It starts the day off right."

He went out into the dawn as I stared after him wondering if he was being satirical or if the millenium had actually arrived.

IT WAS early morning and we were gathered in the study awaiting a call to breakfast. Jonas Kline stood by the window staring out at the snow. Battersly was smoking a cigarette. I sat before the big open fire and chatted desultorily with Alicia Dale.

The study door pushed open suddenly and Allhoff waddled into the room. He nodded to us all, hoisted himself up into a Morris chair and yawned elaborately.

"Terrible night," he said. "Hardly closed an eye."

Alicia Dale commiserated with him. I could have sworn I detected a note of mockery in her voice, but Allhoff, usually more sensitive than I to these things, apparently did not notice it. He thanked her gravely for her interest, then looked around the room and said: "I'm sorry to have to delay this case, but we'll all be here a few days yet. I can't permit anyone to leave the house."

That was jolly news to me and, judging from the expressions of the others, to everyone else as well.

"I'd expected to break this case this morning," went on Allhoff, "but in order to clinch it I'll have to have this house, these grounds, thoroughly searched. There's some concealed evidence hidden away somewhere. This is a pretty big establishment and it'll take four or five men quite a few days to do a complete job. I'm sorry but there's no alternative."

The fact that he was apologizing should have aroused my suspicions, but the realization that I wasn't going to spend Christmas at home after all, had me too annoyed to start delving into Allhoff's private motivations. But his next sentence brought me up sharply.

"However," he was saying, "there's no point in inconveniencing anyone unnecessarily. For instance, I won't need you, Battersly. Simmonds tells me you wanted this week off, wanted to go home to Indiana. Well, go ahead. A plane leaves Newark in exactly two hours. You'll just have time for breakfast, to get home and pack."

I stared at him. Allhoff exuding the Christmas spirit was either a miracle or something exceedingly suspicious. But Battersly, overwhelmed with gratitude, took the offer at its face value. He came to his feet, beaming. "Thank you, sir," he said. "Thank you very much. I—"

Allhoff waved him to silence. "There's just one little favor I'd like to ask—"

"Sure," said Battersly. "Anything at all. I—"

"I've a few presents to send out. I'll wrap them up and leave them on the hall table for you. Pick them up on your way out and take them right out to the airport. They're all west-bound. I've let them go until the last minute and it'll save time."

Battersly kept grinning like a fool and yessing him. The rest of the assemblage was bored by the whole proceeding. But personally, if Allhoff were on the level, I was prepared to believe in fairies, Eddie Guest and the love-story magazines.

Allhoff sending Christmas presents! Reason tottered at the thought.

He turned to Kline, smiling with a cordial politeness as phony as a politician's handshake.

"I suppose I may borrow some wrapping paper and string from you?"

"I'll let you have some, Inspector," said Alicia Dale. "I've a lot of stuff left over from my own presents."

Allhoff thanked her profusely and slid down from his chair.

"I'm so sleepy I'll not bother about breakfast," he announced. "If you'll just send those wrappings up to my room, I'll get my presents ready and take a little nap. Battersly, I'll leave the stuff on the hall table for you. You can pick it up after you've eaten."

He waddled out of the room as I stared after him. And a moment later the maid announced breakfast.

I went in to the table lost in profound thought. Since my association with Allhoff, I had seen him do a number of peculiar things, but never before had he neglected his morning coffee.

CHAPTER FIVE

Without a Leg to Stand On

HALF an hour after Battersly had departed for town bearing Allhoff's surprising Christmas packages, Allhoff himself thumped down the stairs, locked himself in the drawing-room. Through the panels I heard the excited hum of his voice as he used the telephone.

Ten minutes later he reappeared, eyed me coldly, ordered me to assemble the household in the study.

When I had done so the room resembled an inquisition chamber, with Allhoff, seated behind the desk at the far end of the room, playing Torquemada. I stood at his right like the Palace Guard. Scattered about the vast gloomy room were the others.

Jonas Kline was obviously nervous. His fingers constantly twined about each other like living ivy. His ancient bones cracked like rattling dice. Little Amberson, who had arrived shortly after breakfast, sat by his side to provide an interesting study in contrast. He smoked an expensive cigar almost as fat as himself, and beamed expansively and impartially upon all of us. He was on the side of virtue, law and order and wasn't letting anyone forget it.

The maid and cook stood nervously beside the door. They had entered together bringing a pot of bitter coffee and a cup for Allhoff. Unaccustomed to mixing with the gentry, their manner was anything but easy. No one had remembered to ask them to sit down and they were too well aware of their places to do so.

Leroy, however, stood upon no such feudal ceremony. He lounged back in a leather chair beside Allhoff's desk, smoked a nonchalant cigarette and kept his vacuous eyes upon the svelte figure of Alicia Dale by the window.

The girl watched Allhoff with distant, derisive eyes, cold and blue as a polar sea. She remained completely self-possessed, regal, imperious. She was the only person I had ever known who was utterly indifferent to Allhoff's nasty personality.

I turned my head away from the group and glanced out the window. It was still snowing. Tomorrow would be Christmas, and I thought with anxiety of the fifteen-pound turkey in the icebox at home. If Allhoff didn't pull whatever he had out of the hat within twenty-four hours, he would claim it was a departmental emergency and cancel my leave.

My jaundiced reverie was broken by Alicia Dale's voice.

"Inspector," she said, and the contempt she got into the single word was amazing. She somehow made it sound like an oath. "I'm tired of being held in this house under police surveillance. Will you please solve this case immediately?"

Her tone was jeering, her manner impertinent. I fully expected Allhoff to blow up. But he didn't. True, his eyes flashed, his sallow face sucked up some color, but his tone was steady enough as he answered. "Of course," he said. "Before noon, Miss Dale."

Leroy took his eyes off Alicia and stared at Allhoff. It seemed to me that there was a flicker of anxiety on his handsome countenance.

"As I have announced before," said Allhoff gravely, "Emile Gerson killed himself. He wrote a suicide note and blew his own brains out. Upon hearing this shot, Harry Welch entered the study."

Little Amberson took his cigar from his lips and clucked impatiently.

"Indeed you did tell us all this before, Inspector," he said. "I—"

Alicia Dale interrupted him. "Let the inspector finish, Amby. He undoubtedly has elaborated on that theory by now. I'm beginning to see it myself. Uncle Emile, upon seeing Harry enter the room, realized that he had forgotten to kill Harry before he committed suicide. So he slid hastily back from the grave, shot Harry, put the gun in his hand and jumped back again to Gehenna. They're both there now, playing two-handed pinochle."

I LOOKED again at Allhoff. This was a brand of comedy he definitely did not like. The back of his neck looked like molten iron. Yet he held on to his temper with a strange tenacity, went on as if he'd never been interrupted.

"When Harry Welch entered the room, the wall-safe behind that section of bookcase was open. The bookcase was pulled out of place. In that safe were bonds and cash. As Harry Welch stood, dumfounded, staring at his uncle's corpse, someone else came into the study."

Amberson, who couldn't bear remaining out of the conversation for any length of time, came rushing in again.

"I get it," he said excitedly. "That third person saw the open safe, saw some valuables inside. He recalled the quarrel between Welch and Gerson and promptly turned it to his own advantage. He killed Welch, switched Gerson's suicide note so that it would appear Welch wrote it, planted the gun in Welch's hand and made off with the stuff in the safe."

Allhoff nodded at the lawyer like a school teacher showering approbation upon a bright pupil.

"Absolutely correct," he said. "That third person saw an opportunity to kill Welch and steal the bonds and money which were in the safe."

Bonds and money? That gave off an overwhelming piscatorial odor to me. Allhoff had sent Battersly back to town for a bagful of bonds and money and now it looked as if he were about to pin a made-to-order robbery on someone. It was very, very fishy. but I held my peace.

Jonas Kline coughed nervously behind his thin hand. "Who was this person, Inspector?" he asked. "Have you any idea who it was?"

"Certainly," said Allhoff. "It was you, Leroy. Wasn't it?"

His casual manner staggered me as much as the question itself staggered Leroy. After all, you don't ask for a confession in a murder case as offhandedly as a hostess inquiring if you take two lumps of sugar in your tea.

Leroy sat upright in his chair and stared at Allhoff. There was no guilt in his expression. Rather utter and complete surprise.

"You're crazy," he said at last. "I didn't do anything of the kind. You're crazy."

Alicia Dale smiled sweetly. "Check," she said.

When Allhoff failed to blow up this time, I decided we were approaching a world's record. Three times he had been insulted in the past five minutes. Three times he had ignored it. He was just a curly little lamb this morning and that made me very suspicious that an earthquake would break loose before long.

"Leroy," he said quietly, "you'll make it a lot easier on yourself if you'll sign a confession."

Leroy stood up and appealed to the lawyer. "Mr. Amberson, he's crazy. I didn't kill anyone. He can't make me sign nothing, can he?"

Amberson nodded judicially. "You certainly can't, Inspector," he said pompously. "Not unless you've got something more than you've shown us."

Now Allhoff threw off his mask of serenity and politeness. He leaned forward over the desk and glared at Leroy. When he spoke his voice came roaring up from his bowels.

"Leroy," he shouted, "you're guilty as hell and I can prove it! Here." He pulled open a drawer of the desk, groped inside for a moment, then slapped a package of blue-and-gold-engraved bonds on the desktop. He took a swift encore on the gesture and came up this time with a packet of currency. "There," he went on. "Bonds and money. Taken from the safe. Identified by the bank as having been drawn by Emile Gerson. Found in the bureau of your room. What do you say to that?"

LEROY didn't answer immediately, but had he asked me what *I* said to that I would have told him. The bonds, I observed, were Consolidated Motors fifties. The currency was twenty-dollar bills. My suspicions were verified. This was the money and the bonds that Battersly had gotten from Allhoff's bank this morning. So this was either desperate bluff or outrageous frame-up.

Allhoff continued to shout at Leroy. "I've enough evidence here to send you to the chair! A signed confession will make things easier on you."

Leroy's face was ashen. The usual emptiness of his eyes was occupied by fright. "Listen," he said rapidly. "You got it wrong, Inspector. Why, the murder wasn't even—"

Alicia Dale's voice sounded like a frozen bell. "Don't even bother answering him, Leroy," she said. "He's got nothing. If he had a case why would he be so eager for you to sign a confession. It's a frame."

Leroy looked at her doubtfully. Then he turned to Amberson again. "You're a lawyer," he said nervously. "Has he really got anything?"

Amberson tried very hard to look like Oliver Holmes. "If the inspector is prepared to prove that the bonds and money were in that safe, that they were later found in your room, he's got a damned good case. I wouldn't want to handle it."

Allhoff grinned unpleasantly. "Frame-up or not," he said, "it's a case. Iron-clad. Leroy here hasn't a single defense witness. I've got several for the prosecution."

If Allhoff had even one witness for the prosecution, I was prepared to perform a most humiliating action in Macy's window at high noon. But, undoubtedly, Leroy was impressed with his words.

"I suppose," he said desperately, "you're charging me with killing Peter Lovelace, too."

"What's the difference," said Allhoff callously. "I can only burn you once. However, if you'll sign a confession, it'll simplify things. I'll guarantee you don't get the chair."

Leroy was close to panic now. He bent over Allhoff's desk and his face was the color of the snow on the windowsill.

"No," he said vehemently. "No! No! I didn't do it! I won't sign. You—"

"Leroy," said Alicia Dale, "sit down and tell him to go to hell. If he's got a case let him give it to the D.A. He hasn't got a leg to stand on! Have you, Inspector?"

That last crack was a bombshell to me. I glanced quickly from Allhoff to the girl. She was smiling with diabolical ingenuousness and looking squarely at Allhoff. He glared back at her and there was a terrible threat in his eyes.

Allhoff took a deep breath and cleared his throat. Fearing the worst, I came rushing up to stem the tide.

"Allhoff," I said, "Miss Dale is a thoughtless young girl. I'm sure she meant nothing. Anyway you're solving a murder case." I figured he'd like that. "You can attend to her later."

To my surprise he nodded. Then he said a peculiar thing. "Of course," he murmured quietly. "Of course. That was my original intention."

He thrust his hand into his vest pocket and withdrew a typewritten sheet of paper. He unfolded it and handed it to Leroy.

"Here," he said. "A typed confession. All you have to do is sign it."

"No!" screamed Leroy, pounding the desk frantically, "I'll never sign it! It's a lousy frame-up. It's—"

Amberson said sententiously: "You can't use coercion, Inspector."

"Nor force," said Alicia Dale.

"Look," said Allhoff to Leroy. "I've got you dead to rights and you know it. You'll never get an acquittal with what I've got. All I ask is that you read this confession. If it's true sign it. If not, hand it back to me unsigned." He paused for a moment, then added something I didn't understand. "Remember, Leroy, you're not getting paid any more."

I WAS damned certain Leroy wasn't guilty. Aside from Allhoff's bond-and-money plant there was the matter of the shots. According to the evidence, those two reports had sounded within a very short time of each other. If Leroy had entered the study at the time of Gerson's suicide—always assuming it *was* a suicide —he must have thought fast and acted faster to have killed Welch and rifled the safe before the cook and maid arrived upon the scene. Of course Allhoff was framing Leroy cruelly. But Leroy was certainly convinced that he'd go through with it.

He took the paper from Allhoff like a man handling a rattlesnake. He sank back in the Morris chair and began to read. The rest of us stared at Allhoff. Personally, I thought he was a little wacky. Under any circumstances Leroy would be an utter fool to sign that confession. What optimistic idea convinced Allhoff that he might was beyond me.

Leroy reached the end of the page and laid the paper down on the desk. His face was deathly pale and he was breathing hard. He hesitated for a moment, then held out his hand.

"Inspector," he said in a voice that was scarcely audible, "give me a pen."

That staggered all of us. There was deadly silence as the nib of Allhoff's pen scratched across the paper. Allhoff picked it up and put it back in his pocket.

Leroy, speaking through livid lips said: "You promised I wouldn't burn, Inspector. You promised."

"You damn fool," said Alicia Dale evenly.

Amberson got out of his chair and sputtered excitedly. "You can't promise immunity on a first-degree murder case, Inspector. You—"

Jonas Kline cracked his knuckles in a frenzy. "Leroy," he said. "I can't believe it. I—"

I turned on Allhoff with bitterness and

astonishment. "You damned lucky copper. You were guessing. You ran a wild madman's bluff. You hadn't the slightest vestige of evidence that Leroy was the killer."

Allhoff twisted his head around and grinned crookedly at me. There was a grimace on his face I couldn't quite classify. "As a matter of fact," he said distinctly, "he isn't the killer at all."

"Goodness gracious," said Kline. "You accuse Leroy of murder. You get him to sign a confession. Now you say he isn't guilty. It's most irregular, Inspector."

"Allhoff," I said wearily, "what've you got up your sleeve? Let's hear it and we'll all go home."

"All except one of us," said Allhoff. "One of us is never going home again."

CHAPTER SIX

Cold-Turkey Christmas

THERE was utter silence in the room. I could hear Leroy's heavy breathing and that was all. Allhoff leaned over his desk and his face was a flaming lamp of triumph.

"Miss Dale," he said. "Yesterday morning you called on me. You very kindly brought me a turkey which I didn't want. I now have the opportunity of repaying you, by giving you something you don't want either."

Alicia Dale lit a cigarette. She looked bored.

"All right, Allhoff," I said. "And what doesn't Miss Dale want?"

"Death," said Allhoff melodramatically and the word rolled gloatingly off his tongue. "It is quite true, Miss Dale, that you were legitimately engaged in delivering food to the indigent. Further, it is quite true that your errands for sweet charity's sake brought you into the neighborhood in which I live. But your call on me was deliberate. Not accidental."

Alicia Dale watched him with her cold steady eyes. Not a muscle of her face moved.

"You have a perverse character," went on Allhoff grimly. "Perverse and ironic. You needed an alibi. Any one of your indigent families could have given it to you as well as I. But it amused you to have the best copper in the department to cover you up."

"What the devil are you talking about?" I asked him. "Whether you like it or not, she is covered up. If she was in our office at seven minutes past nine—and, by God, she was—she couldn't have shot Harry Welch at nine ten."

"No," said Allhoff. "She couldn't. That's why she killed him a half-hour earlier."

Alicia Dale studied her coral nails for a moment. Then she looked up and blew smoke from her patrician nostrils.

"Inspector," she said, "do you make a habit of drinking this early in the day?"

Across the room, Leroy uttered an odd choking sound and buried his head in his hands. I considered Allhoff's charge, decided he was talking through his hat and told him so.

"According to you," I said, "everyone else is nuts. You can't go behind the obvious testimony in this case."

"Can't I?" said Allhoff. "Now get this! Emile Gerson came down to the study early yesterday morning. He'd been brooding all night. He'd made up his mind to kill himself. He'd typed out a note on his nephew's typewriter, then proceeded to blow his brains out. At this time the servants, still in their living-quarters over the garage did not hear the shot. That W.P.A. gang hadn't come to work yet, so they didn't hear it either. Shortly afterwards Miss Dale came into that room. Maybe she heard the shot and came to investigate. Maybe Harry Welch found Gerson and called her. I don't know and it doesn't matter. It's enough that she and Harry Welch were in the study together. That no one else in the house knew of Gerson's suicide yet."

IF ALLHOFF were right, the girl was magnificent. She smoked a cigarette as calmly as if she were being accused of a misdemeanor by the local constable.

"Now," went on Allhoff, "Miss Dale who thinks swiftly and logically, saw a tremendous opportunity. She killed Harry Welch and went in search of Leroy."

Leroy's face was still in his hands. The Dale girl yawned and looked out the window.

"In my book," said Allhoff, "Leroy was more to Miss Dale than a gardener. He's probably nuts about her. She can wind him around her finger. She told him of her plan and he agreed."

"What plan?" I said impatiently. "For heaven's sake, Allhoff, come to the point."

"It was simple enough," said Allhoff. "All Leroy had to do was to give Miss Dale about twenty minutes to get to town. That twenty minutes would also be time enough for the maid and the cook to begin their laundry chores. It also permitted time enough for that W.P.A. road gang to get to work."

I watched him closely. From the hard twisted expression of his face I knew he wasn't bluffing this time.

"So in twenty minutes," he continued, "Leroy entered that study again. He fired two shots out the window. Those two shots were heard by the servants and the W.P.A. boys. They all came running along to investigate. Leroy—"

"Wait a minute," I said. "If Leroy fired two more shots there would have been four bullets fired from the gun in Harry Welch's hand. There were only two."

"You're a fool," said Allhoff quite amiably. "Leroy fired his two shots with another gun entirely. He had plenty of time to hide it, between the time of his notifying the police and their arrival."

"Of course, you've found that gun, Inspector," said Alicia Dale with heavy irony.

"Of course," said Allhoff. "I have it here in my pocket. Leroy, you know, has a rather obvious mind. It seemed logical to me that he'd hide the gun somewhere in the greenhouse. I found it early this morning, buried in a box of humus."

I recalled his sallying forth to bid a bright good-morning to the flowers and kept my mouth shut.

"Leroy," continued Allhoff, "took his own sweet time about calling the coppers with the result that the medical examiner arrived on the scene over an hour later. Of course, he couldn't ascertain the time of death within twenty minutes or so. So, Miss Dale had her alibi. Leroy needed none. He had no motive."

Alicia Dale smiled pleasantly at him. "I had no motive either, Inspector," she said. "You overlook that."

"The hell you didn't," said Allhoff. "You wanted to get your fingers on the Gerson estate."

"But listen," said Amberson. "The Gerson money goes to that illegitimate kid in Illinois."

"A little thing like that doesn't bother the inspector," said Alicia Dale. "I've already sent the kid a poisoned lollypop. The inspector's coming to that, aren't you, Inspector?"

"You never knew there was a kid in Illinois," said Allhoff. "Not until Amberson told you yesterday afternoon."

"But she said—" I began, when he interrupted me.

"I know what she said. I've already told you she thinks like a rattlesnake strikes. The fact of the money going to that kid was a body-blow to her. But she never showed it. She pretended at once that she'd known it all the time. The instant she lost the money, she pretended knowledge of the will and immediately lost the motive as well."

ALICIA Dale lit a second cigarette from the butt of the first one. Her hands were as steady as the West Wall before Gamelin began pecking at it.

"Let me finish that theory for you, Inspector," she said evenly. "Realizing I'd lost the estate I became very angry, so angry that I decided to kill Peter Lovelace just for spite. Is that it?"

"Partly," said Allhoff. "You killed Lovelace. But not for spite. You killed him through ignorance."

"My theories can't keep up with yours," she said. "You'd better explain that one."

"I will," said Allhoff. "When you realized you weren't going to get the Gerson money, you began to worry. One reason was that you'd be unable to keep your bargain with Leroy, pay him whatever you promised him. So you needed cash to get away before anyone could break him down."

"So I held up Uncle Peter?" she suggested brightly.

"No," said Allhoff. "You knew that there was money, valuables of some sort in that safe behind the bookcase. You didn't bother to take it yesterday because you were sure it would revert to you legally and legitimately when the will was probated. But when you found it didn't, you decided to take it yourself last night."

"What's that got to do with Lovelace?" asked Kline.

"Lovelace opened the study door as Miss Dale was rifling the safe. She realized at once that if there were a witness to what she was doing, I might well figure out why she was doing it. So she shot Lovelace, ran from the study, up the backstairs to her room."

"Allhoff," I said, "that won't do. Lovelace was no witness to what she was doing. He—"

"Sure," said Allhoff. "I know. But Miss Dale didn't. She was out of the room when Amberson told us about it yesterday. She doesn't even know it now."

"Know what?" asked Alicia Dale and now for the first time I caught some tension in her tone.

Leroy lifted his head from his hands and told her in an agonized voice. "He was blind, Alicia! He was blind. My God, he couldn't see what you were doing."

He groaned and replaced his head in his hands. I thought the girl had paled a little, but her bearing was that of Queen Mary.

"It sounds very good, Inspector," she said. "But I don't quite understand what a blind man was doing wandering about a strange house in the middle of the night."

"That had me worried for a little while," said Allhoff. "Then I remembered something. Leroy brought him into the house after the rest of us had gone to bed. Undoubtedly, he asked to use the lavatory, to clean up after his trip. Leroy showed him to the one next door to the study. During the night he wanted to use the lavatory again. The one downstairs was the only one he knew the location of. He tried to find his way there."

"And got the wrong door," said Amberson eagerly. "Opened the study door by mistake."

Alicia Dale crushed out her cigarette in a hammered-silver ash-tray. She looked Allhoff squarely in the eye and said in an even, low voice: "Are you quite sure of all this, Inspector?"

Allhoff's tone was soaring and triumphant. "I can prove it," he said. "Before a jury composed of the Skeptics Society and foremanned by Robert Ingersoll, I could prove it."

"Suppose you do?"

Allhoff leveled a forefinger at her. "Last night," he said, "you took from that safe exactly four thousand three hundred and eighty-five dollars in cash. Six thousand-dollar Arkansas Railroad Bonds, and a diamond necklace that had belonged to Gerson's family. Furthermore, you left fingerprints all over them."

IT STILL didn't seem right to me. Murderess or no, Alicia Dale wasn't dumb enough to hide the stuff in a place where Allhoff could have dug it up so soon.

"This is a big house," said Allhoff. "There's a lot of acreage surrounding it. That gave you the edge. It might have taken me weeks to find what you took from the safe. I didn't want to spend the time."

"Then," I demanded impatiently, "how do you know what the loot consisted of? How do you know Miss Dale's fingerprints are on it?"

Allhoff grinned unpleasantly. "Since I didn't want to search for the missing items," he said, "I gave Miss Dale an opportunity to produce them for me. Miss Dale has a habit of thinking quickly. She thought quickly enough to take advantage of that opportunity."

"Goodness gracious!" said Jonas Kline. "What are you talking about, Inspector?"

"Those Christmas presents of mine," said Allhoff. "The telephone book, the dirty sheet and the glass tumbler I so neatly wrapped up, addressed at random, and had Battersly take out with him."

"Allhoff." I said wearily. "Will you stop talking Choctaw."

"It's not Choctaw to Miss Dale," he said. "Is it?"

I looked at the girl. Though she still held on to her magnificent poise her face was pale and her lips compressed.

"You will remember," said Allhoff to the rest of us, "that I did not tell Battersly how many packages I would leave for him. You will note further that I announced I would be resting in my room at the time he picked them up. Those two facts offered a golden opportunity to Miss Dale. She took it."

At last I saw it. I said, grudgingly: "So Miss Dale, knowing the house would be searched and desiring to get that incriminating stuff out, wrapped it up as a Christmas package and put it with your stuff so Battersly would mail it for her?"

"Right," said Allhoff. "She addressed it to some place where she could pick it up at her convenience. But in the meantime, I called headquarters—the I-bureau. Told them to get hold of Battersly at his apartment. Told them to check the prints on the loot with the prints on a tumbler I'd sent in one of *my* packages. It was a tumbler Miss Dale had used while cleaning her teeth this morning."

"You've a lot of clues, Inspector," she said. "You've done a lot of ingenious reasoning. But it won't look any too strong on an indictment."

"Perhaps not," said Allhoff. "But I've provided for that." He leered at her. "I made Leroy believe I'd frame him for murder. I pointed out to him that since Miss Dale did not inherit the Gerson money she would be in no position to help him financially. Then, when I slapped a typewritten statement under his nose, detailing exactly how the crime had been committed, he cracked."

"Then that wasn't a confession of murder he signed?"

"No," said Allhoff. "Accessory after the fact. That's bad enough, but Leroy didn't know it. Leroy can turn state's evidence now. He can help send Miss Dale to the chair."

Up to this point, Allhoff had remained remarkably calm. Now he leaned far forward over his desk. He glared at Alicia Dale and his wicked little eyes burned.

"You came to my office," he said. "You insulted me. You mocked the loss of my legs. You jeered at me. You derided me. Well, you'll burn now. I hope you'll remember, when they strap you in the chair, that Inspector Allhoff sent you there! I hope you keep remembering while you burn in hell!"

His manner indicated that the State of New York was about to electrocute Alicia Dale for contempt of Allhoff rather than for first-degree murder.

IT WAS then the girl cracked. The garments of Boadicea fell from her like a chrysalis from a butterfly. Her lip quivered. Her eyes were suddenly moist. She moaned and fell back in her chair.

Allhoff regarded her with a horrible grin, then he snatched up the telephone from the desk, called the precinct house, and demanded a wagon. From the savage triumph in his little eyes, I knew he was having a very merry Christmas.

Then, as he hung up the receiver a horrible suspicion occurred to me.

"Allhoff," I said. "Did you send Battersly away from here merely to—"

"I sent Battersly out on departmental business," he snapped, glaring at me.

My suspicion became a crystallized fact. "You mean you're not granting him a week's leave? You mean—"

"We're in the police department," said Allhoff, "not a kindergarten. I told him he could go home to provide a logical excuse for his carrying those packages out of the house. I told headquarters to rescind that permission when they went to his apartment."

I felt physically sick at that. "Allhoff," I said bitterly, "how can you build the kid up like that and then let him down? Haven't you a single decent instinct. After all, it's—"

"It's Christmas," said Allhoff. "You don't have to tell me again. And once it was the thirteenth of May."

There was hate and bitterness in his gaze. May 13th was the date upon which his legs had been amputated. And all the words in the world would never assuage the wound that operation had opened in his soul. I was still looking at him, feeling utterly frustrated, when we heard the howl of a police siren outside.

Allhoff took his eyes from me and stared at Alicia Dale, who cowered in her chair.

"A merry Christmas, Miss Dale," he said, as the coppers pounded at the outside door. "A very Merry Christmas."

IN ADDITION TO STAND-ALONE STORIES, the hard-boiled pulps bulged with series characters, and *Dime Detective* gave the reading public some of its longest-lived and most outrageous. Along with Dan Turner (whose original exploits did not run in *Dime Detective,* but in several pulps from a different publisher), "Hard-Boiled Christmas Stories" presents two of the longest-running of those recurring crimefighters: John Lawrence's Marquis of Broadway, taking center stage in the following story, and D.L. Champion's incredible Inspector Allhoff, hero – if that word can be used under the circumstances – of "Nothing for Christmas."

The hard-boiled series characters usually had jobs that regularly thrust them into homicidal situations – private investigators, newspaper reporters, cops. Allhoff and Marty Marquis belong to the latter category, although neither is exactly a traditional law enforcement officer. Marquis and his Broadway Squad are some of the roughest, most unrelenting, rule-breaking protagonists in detective fiction, and Allhoff is, well, one of the most unusual.

Interestingly, both characters appeared in exactly 29 stories each, with Allhoff debuting in the pages of *Dime Detective* in 1938 and departing after '46, Marquis, on the other hand, began a year earlier and lasted two years longer than Allhoff. In tallying up the Marquis appearances, we included five tales of the Broadway Squad, which shone a spotlight on his supporting characters rather than him. One of those appeared in *Dime Detective,* the book that ran all the Marquis stories; the other four were in *Black Mask,* the pioneering pulp picked up by Popular Publications in 1940.

NOTHING FOR CHRISTMAS

A Marquis of Broadway Story
By John Lawrence

McGuire threw a whistling smash across the bar and caught Coy in the mouth.

Every year, come the yuletide season, the little czar of Manhattan's Main Stem was taken suddenly with a noxious flux in the form of an acute attack of the Xmas spirit. Even a crook deserves a break at such a time, the Marquis told his squad, so any packages they wanted to hand to hoodlums had to be plainly marked 'Not to be opened till after Christmas.' Murder of course was a different matter, and could be brought out from under wraps any time.

CHAPTER ONE

Blood on the Snow

THE VAST mezzanine of the hotel was deserted, illumined only by glow from the green-shaded dim lamps on the writing-desks. The little blonde hugged the wall, out of the radiance, as she fled around two sides of the huge balcony, her cheap, fur-collared coat tight around her lush little body.

She reached the west stairs, ran down four steps—and faltered. The interminable, subdued lobby below was, at ten minutes after midnight, not entirely deserted.

Vast areas of thick-piled carpet were as empty and silent as a stage, but there were loiterers—too many loiterers—here and there in club chairs and settees. Her bright, hatless blondness, her peach-fleshed rounded bare legs, her flamboyantly young little figure would draw a dozen pairs of eyes if she descended on them.

She had to shrink back, huddle there in the gloom, almost whimpering, her blue eyes strained and frightened in her pert, painted angel's face.

The lobby slumbered on. With shaky, unconscious fingers, she poked at her damp, corn-colored hair, wriggled her warm little body hastily, straightening her girdle with her free hand. Minutes passed. More minutes. She began to go into a glaze of fright—and then, mercifully, the revolving doors at the west side of the lobby suddenly rustled.

The chasseur, his uniformed shoulders snow-dotted, appeared momentarily and held up fingers toward the bell-boys' bench far across by the desk. Three boys rose up and came quickly over. They pushed out one revolving door at the same moment the other swirled round to debauch five rowdy college boys, one after another, noisy, stamping, singing.

Seconds later, the bell-boys filed in, laden with luggage, paraded in a momentary, conspicuous caravan across toward the desk in the wake of the youngsters.

The girl moaned, pressed the back of one hand to her mouth and slipped breathlessly down the stairs, tried to shrink into herself as she fled to the shelter of the broken row of potted rubber-plants, hurried toward the exit. Her peach-blond, grubby little face had high fever spots as she finally ran into the shelter of the revolving door. The chasseur outside, kicking his ankles together and blowing plumes of breath into the snow-swirling night air was an unavoidable peril. She summoned all her resolution, buried her chin in the fur collar and threw her weight at the revolving door. It spun her crackingly out—so quickly that she was turned away from the uniformed giant, her heels rattling her away down the sidewalk before he could turn and get out his hasty, "Cab, lady . . . ?"

She was sure that a dozen flashing little steps carried her into the invisibility of the black, snow-sifting street, beyond the reach of the marquee's lights.

ONLY two or three dull neon signs burned in the store windows of the narrow little side street as she hurried over the dark, deserted blocks toward Sixth Avenue. One or two vague forms passed her in the storm, but they were ghostly figures, instantly gone. Her heart pounded up till it was a hurt as she reached the corner and scampered around it.

A distant blue street lamp spotlighted the darker shadow at the curb ahead that was the coupé, and she almost sobbed with relief as she ran on toward it. Little wisps of vapor were around the car's exhaust, but it showed not a light. In the instant that she snatched for the door handle, the door drifted silently open and she scrambled hastily in. The man behind the wheel reached across to pull it quickly closed. His voice was a thick whisper.

"Did you get it?"

"Yes."

"Did you feed him the Mickey? Is he out?"

"Yes."

"Did anybody see you? What took you so long?"

She swallowed. "He—he wouldn't take a drink till—till after. Nobody saw me but the elevator boy and he didn't know—I took the elevator from the mezzanine and went to nineteen and walked down. Then I left the same way."

"You sure you got it?"

"Yes, Al."

His whisper became softer, gentler. "You're my baby." He let the clutch in silently and the car slid away from the curb, still lightless. They hugged the piled-up snow, crept four blocks south, then turned into a black slot of a street and went two more blocks, stopped again.

"Let's see it, baby."

She pushed a worn leather billfold into his hands in the dark. "What—what is it, Al?"

"How the hell do I know? You're the one that said he was blowing off about how much the stuff in it was worth. However, I've made a few inquiries and I think there's a Christmas present somewhere here for us."

The faint beam of a tiny flashlight, muffled in his gloved hand, shone on the worn pin-seal wallet on his lap. With one hand, he expertly rifled it of papers. He was suddenly quiet.

For a full minute, he was perfectly

silent, and then another. Then he snapped the light out. He said in a tight, choked voice: "Baby—you're there!"

She suddenly collapsed into great, racking sobs, her face in her hands. "Oh, Al—don't ever ask me to do anything like that again. I couldn't—I couldn't. Oh, please tell me everything's all right—that it's all over now and you won't make me go back to him, ever. Oh God, Al, if —if I didn't know how desperate you were and if I didn't love you, I—you know I love you now, Al, don't you?" And when he sat in motionless silence, "Don't you, Al?"

"Sure, baby. You did fine."

"Al—Al—everything's all right, isn't it?"

"Sure, baby. I was just wondering what he did with his money. Doesn't he carry any money in this thing?"

"Oh, I—there was some money in it, Al, but I took it out and left it on the dresser."

"You—did—what?"

"I left the money there. You—you wouldn't want me to—to steal it, Al? He—then he'd have the cops after us. This way, you said he—that we weren't doing anything the law would. . . ."

THE falling snow was a curtain outside, closing them into a little world of their own. After a minute, he said lazily: "You wouldn't be scared of a cop or two, would you, baby?"

She grabbed his arm and blurted hoarsely: "Oh, Al—Al—you swore. . . ."

"Don't get excited," he soothed, after a minute. "You're not going to have any law trouble. I was just wondering if you were really as scared of cops as all that."

She swallowed desperately and her eyes shone white in the darkness. "N-no, Al, I guess not." Her voice shook with strain. "No, of course I'm not. Certainly not. Al! No, I'm not!"

For a full minute or more, she felt his eyes looking down at her. She tried to control the little shaking in her stomach, but she could not restrain her blurted: Al—there isn't really—we're not really going to have the law after us . . . . Al, answer me! We're not, are we?"

He seemed finally to rouse himself. His voice was soft and reassuring. "Of course not, baby. I was only kidding. Everything will be jake." He hesitated again and then said: "I guess you know I'm for you now, baby."

"Oh, Al—and I'm for you."

He breathed softly through his nose. "I've been thinking about it, baby. I got to wondering—why don't we make it legal?"

She caught her breath. "Al! Oh, Al, you mean—but I—I thought you *were* married. . . ."

"Think nothing of it. I don't tell anybody much of the truth about myself— not even my real name, as you know— unless I get to think a lot of them. I— there's a little church down a piece from here that caught my eye yesterday." He sent the car away from the curb again, crept on west. "It's off by itself kind of, down among the warehouses, but it gets me, somehow. I thought maybe we could get it attended to there."

She cried breathlessly: "Oh, Al—do you really mean it?"

He turned south into the maze of Chelsea, drove for five minutes, in and around the narrower, darker streets. Mellow light glowed through the snow storm. He slid the car in again to the curb—or as close to it as the heaped-up snow would permit—and the mellow light was the open, arched vestry of a church. It was small, unpretentious, set back in a snow-lumped little yard.

He said: "I mean it baby. This is Sunday. A week from today is Christmas. Suppose we figure on Christmas Eve."

"Oh, Al!" She burst into tears, threw herself into his arms. He cupped her shoulder in his gloved hand, cradled it. He kissed her hot, wet mouth hard, forced her head back against the seat cushion.

He mumbled huskily, "My baby," and kissed her hard again. His hand, cradling her shoulder, crept up, played around the collar of her coat, pressed it down. He let his gloved fingers stroke her neck, her cheek, her chin—and then slid them suddenly in between his mouth and hers.

Light shimmered dazzlingly for the tenth part of a second as he brought his free hand from under his coat. Simultaneously, he wrenched her clamped head cruelly—and her coat fell open. She tried to scream as his hand drove poundingly at her chest, but his hand across her mouth smothered her effectually. All that came out was a sort of *"Mmmmm-mmmm!"*

She arched her body frantically, threshed in his grip. He jerked his hand back and hammered it up home again—and again. She kept making the sound, trying to twist. Sweat came out in beads on his forehead, as he hastily tried to watch the deserted sidewalk. He had to sit, clenching her to him for over a minute before her struggles began to weaken—and then her flailing hand slapped down on the door handle. The door burst open and she pitched out. He was almost dragged out with her, had to hastily release her, dropping the reddened knife as he caught himself desperately. She went head over heels into the snow-pile at the curb, flopped down, thuddingly, on the sidewalk beyond.

SHE was doubled up, like a jack-knife, her hands clutching her stomach as he dived frantically after her. Blood was leaking through her fingers, staining the snow under her. Her eyes were already glazing. He gave the street one blazing glance each way, snatched her up under knees and neck, stumbled back through the snow and threw her back into the car, slamming the door. He dragged a sleeve across his forehead as he ran back around the back of the car—and for the first time saw the spidery thing at the sidewalk's edge.

He swung back and his breath went out in a startled curse.

He jumped over and stared down at the thing—an old-fashioned iron pot, hung by chains from a tripod and covered by a wide steel mesh. There were a few coins lying in the bottom of the pot. He swung burning eyes in all directions, trying anywhere to make out a human figure—and then headlights cut through the falling snow—a car coming heavily up the street behind him, the glare catching him full.

He swayed, a stream of profanity chattering under his breath, ran on around to the driver's seat, heaved the slumped girl up and over into the corner, climbed hastily in. He held her upright with one hand against her breast, while he himself hunched down as low as he could. The glaring headlights came abreast, went on past him. He still stayed huddled down, out of sight. The heavy rear end of a truck was visible in his headlights as the vehicle puffed and strained along away from him.

It was not till it stopped, half a block ahead and two uniformed, muffled men dropped from the driver's cab and hurried across the street into an all-night Coffee Pot, that he realized what it was—a snow truck.

Only one second he hesitated, then goosed the coupé swiftly forward. He braked it sharply as he neared the rear of the truck, peered quickly across at the steamed-up window of the dingy little restaurant.

He ran the coupé directly alongside the truck, jumped from the driver's side and ran around. He took one more look at the street, at the restaurant—and then opened the door. He caught the girl in his arms as she slumped out, hastily mounted the running board and turned about. With a great heave, he tossed the body up onto the edge of the open truck, half filled with snow, toppled it over.

He was back in the driver's seat, bulleting the car up to the corner and across town, long before any other sign of human life appeared on the street. His lips moved as he kept repeating the number of the Department of Sanitation Truck, over and over.

CHAPTER TWO

Traffic Trouble

THE snow went on, through Monday, through Tuesday and Wednesday, mantling the city in white, creating an ephemeral fairyland, delighting a surprised New York. A white Christmas loomed.

Some time Thursday night the extended downfall ceased, but a bracing cold spell caught and held the sparkling white blanket intact, and the city did not dirty it up for twenty-four hours.

Even the sloppy Broadway district seemed reluctant to turn it into the customary sleazy gray mush. It was still high-piled, white and shining, on Friday, when the Marquis' nightly round brought him up to the corner of Fifty-fourth. As McGuire, the red-headed camera-eye of the Squad detached himself from a hotel pillar to join him, the Marquis turned and looked back down at the night-club and theater section. Even at two A. M. it was a kaleidoscopic fantasy—green red, and blue neons, blazing, flashing signs, glittering icicles trimming some of the low buildings.

"*It* even looks like Christmas," the Marquis said.

"Charlie Riskin is still around. I just saw him in Coy's joint. "

"Well, what the hell? If he wants to spend Christmas on Broadway in a quiet way . . . . "

The redhead's chubby face was pinched and troubled. "I wish I knew what gets into you every year at this time," he said bitterly. "All right. I know I might as well talk to a brick wall. You—the great Lieutenant Marquis—the wisest, hardest-boiled cop in the business. Yet wave a piece of holly under your nose and—nuts. You want the section quiet for Christmas, don't you?"

The Marquis' deep-sunk somber blue eyes traveled inimically over the red-head's belted camels'-hair topcoat, his brown pork-pie hat. "So I get sappy at Christmas."

"Of course you do," McGuire fretted. "Everybody on Broadway knows it. Riskin—a killer, a forger, a hold-up guy, a racketeer, dynamite, a potential one-man crime wave. He couldn't get into the section with a detachment of marines any other time."

The Marquis looked thoughtfully at the ground, touched his chin with one small, black-gloved finger. He looked over and halfway to Eighth Avenue, to where a perpendicular sign burned redly: *Coy's Bar and Grill.* "All right. If you're such a hell of a sleuth that you can't nose out what he's up to, I'll do it for you." He squirmed his blocky little body in his dapper black clothes, touched the tight black silk scarf in the throat of his neat Chesterfield. "You say he's over there?"

"He was, fifteen minutes ago." And, as they walked across, "What's your bright idea for reaming him?"

"Well, we might ask him."

McGuire made a frantic disgusted sound in his throat, plodded on in sullen silence.

They had crossed Seventh, were within a pace or two of the dim entrance to the grog-shop when Riskin came out. He was thin, wiry, with a pale-saffron bony face, pale-saffron eyes and pale-saffron hair. He stopped, his hands in the pockets of his green guard's coat, his eyes without any expression whatever.

"We were just wondering about you," the Marquis told him. "McGuire seems to think you're in town on business."

"McGuire ought to know better," the other's soft voice said, after a minute, "the way he's been nosing around me the last week. I'm here on a holiday, spending my good dough in your section, minding my own affairs and keeping my nose clean. Christmas isn't my idea of a time to work."

"I hope you mean that. This district is closed up tight till New Year's. I want it absolutely quiet and peaceful and I'll kick in the face of anybody who breaks loose."

"I heard you the first time," Riskin said wearily.

They watched him to the corner.

"So he isn't cooking a job," McGuire said bitterly. "You know because he told you so."

THE Marquis eyed him dully, stepped around him to the door of the saloon. Coy, the owner-bartender, was behind the bar, counting his cash. The door, under the Marquis' hand, proved locked, and he had to wait till the black-haired Irishman came out and opened it.

"We'll have a couple of drinks with you," the Marquis told him. The other walked stolidly round behind the bar. He had powerful shoulders, a tapering body. They ordered Scotch highballs and he set them on the bar, never once saying anything or looking directly at them, then humped himself on a stool with his back to them and returned to his accounts.

They sipped the drinks. "You know, Coy," the Marquis said, "I should think you'd smarten up. You're where you are today because you always played the grifters' side of the fence, instead of the cops'."

The aproned Coy suspended his figuring, looked wooden, but gave no other sign of having heard.

"Let's see," the Marquis continued. "You owned a big place in Chicago and one in Saratoga—the Golden Peacock, wasn't it? With name bands, games upstairs, the best floor show in town and a whale of a take. Then you had a swanky roadhouse in Detroit and a place in Montreal."

When the craggy, gaunt-faced Coy still said nothing, the Marquis finished: "And now you're down to a one-armed dump like this—because you did favors for grifters. Grifters like, say, Charlie Riskin, instead of right folks who could do you a turn now and then. Come here. It might be one of the greatest surprises of your life to know the birds running top spots on Broadway that play along with us."

Coy's wiry hair was black as the Marquis' own and his dark-blue eyes as deeply sunk in his craggy face. He stared dully at the Marquis' scarf. "Well? What am I supposed to say now?"

"Charlie Riskin has been hanging around here a lot, hasn't he?"

"No. He's been in once or twice—maybe four times."

"What's he in New York for?"

"I wouldn't know."

The Marquis nodded absently, drummed his fingers on the edge of the bar. "You aren't fool enough to think you could even keep this drum in action twenty-four hours if I decided otherwise?"

Coy stood like a rock.

"Maybe," the Marquis suggested, "you might run into some information about Riskin some time in the future? Say by tomorrow night."

The other's eyes were hollow, his muzzle pinched and white. "Listen, Marquis—before I'd turn into a lousy stool-pigeon . . . ."

McGuire erupted, "Aw, for God's sake," rose up on his bar stool and threw a whistling right-smash across the bar. He caught Coy full in the mouth, slammed him back against the cash register and four glasses fell off the pyramid on the shelf, exploded on the duckboards. McCoy bobbed back like a punching dummy, his fingers gripping the bar, his face doughy and a little trickle of blood down one corner of his chin.

McGuire started around the bar. "What this guy needs—"

The Marquis caught his arm. "Take it easy, Ace. Give Mr. Coy a chance to think the matter over." And to the motionless, white-faced Irishman: "Along about now is the time for you to get wise to yourself brother. We'll be around tomorrow night."

"*Mister* Coy!" McGuire raged when they were outside. "Gentle—! Why didn't you kiss him? Next we'll be taking our hats off . . . I'll take Big Johnny and give that surly ———— . . . ."

"Forget it," the Marquis said soothingly. "You're all excited over probably nothing at all. What the hell? Even Riskin can have a little Christmas sentiment, can't he?"

"Thank God it comes only once a year," McGuire said bitterly. "The way you soften up, we'd have a thieves' paradise here if it came twice."

THERE was a clear, cold, high-riding moon shining down on the snow-banked streets. They strolled together over the remaining parts of the section to the north, making one or two routine stops, finally reaching the northermost boundary of the district—Central Park South—just at three o'clock.

Then the weird little accident occurred.

The glittering hotel night-clubs along the south side of the wide avenue were just letting out their celebrating clients at the curfew hour. Cars were parked in moderate numbers across on the north side, along the edge of the Park. The trees that lined the curb solidly on that side were heavily laden with snow—heavily enough to cast a thick border of shadow all along the sidewalk that paralleled the low stone wall of the Park.

The Marquis and McGuire turned west, strolled on toward Seventh Avenue.

Screaming, wrenching metal—and then a thunderous crash, whirled them round in their tracks.

A single glance was enough to show exactly what had happened. A blue Packard convertible, attempting to park behind a Chevrolet full of exuberant revelers, had caught the lighter car just backing out. The Chevrolet had been pitched forward into the rear of a limousine. The force of the second impact had crumpled the radiator of the Chevrolet, and a frightened woman was screaming inside it, but it was obvious that no one was hurt.

For a moment, people all over the street—those just emerging from the closing night-clubs, some halfway across the street and some making their way in one direction or the other—all turned back to stare. Then they started to converge and the doors of cars not yet away from the curb popped open. The top-hatted driver of the Chevrolet wrenched his door open, half fell out, bawling maledictions at the driver of the blue Packard.

The Packard's door opened quickly and a tall man in a belted blue guard's coat and black Homburg hat got out.

In the moment that the crowd closed in, the Marquis and McGuire saw the tall, bony, Homburg-hatted man swiftly turn and go round the rear of his own car—and be swallowed by the shadows.

A sirening prowl car was already whining to the scene, coming across from Fifth Avenue, and, in moments, it was at rest beside the blue Packard, the two bluecoats going noisily and efficiently through the regular routine, and attempting to move the crowd along. The Marquis and McGuire stood watching dully from across the street.

Not till the greater portion of the crowd had been moved away and only a sprinkling of die-hards still loitered, could they see through to the scene around the Packard. The recorder, one foot on the running board of the Packard, his book open on his knee, was writing. The top-hatted driver of the Chevrolet and, apparently, one of his passengers, stood staring belligerently at the book. There was no sign of the Homburg-hatted driver of the Packard, but that did not immediately impinge on them. A trim, medium-sized youngish man of military erectness, in square-shouldered light-colored overcoat and rolled-brim gray hat, was handing a card from a card case to the scribbling bluecoat. As he turned a little, the moonlight made his features quite visible—a pleasant-looking, if slightly wooden, blond

face, with a clipped and pointed small blond mustache.

His words became audible, as he was telling the Chevrolet driver quickly, in a voice slightly slurred by an accent: "I accept full responsibility. If you will call me in the morning, I will take care of everything. Meanwhile, I beg you to let me send you home in a taxi and I will have a tow car take your car to a garage. Officer—if you will please make that phone call and satisfy yourself. . . ."

"Yeah. Tom here's the number." The recorder passed the card over to the driver of the prowl car, who walked quickly across the street to the nearest hotel and vanished within.

THE driver of the Chevrolet, evidently still a little drunk, muttered something unintelligible and the recorder turned soothing attention to him, finally herded his party into a cab and sent them spinning away—just as the other bluecoat re-emerged from the hotel.

"Yeah. It's O. K.," he said, when he reached the car's side again. "He says *he'll* stand responsible for the damage. And he wants *you*"—he nodded at the blond man—"to meet him at your office right away."

Not till the recorder said, "O. K., then, Mr. Hamlin, you wanta be more careful how you drive this time o' night. Lots of stews out. Hey—I still say you're foolish to pay him a dime. He was cock-eyed. . ." and the blond man had replied quickly and crisply, "That part of it's all right. Thank you, officer," and opened the driver's door of the undamaged blue Packard to climb quickly in, did the queer little discrepancy dawn.

McGuire gasped, "Hey—wait a minute. *That* isn't the guy who was driving that can when it hit . . ." just as the Packard backed, swung out—and was away, down the street. "Say, what the hell. . . ?"

The Marquis was already moving out into the street, his somber blue eyes curious on the vanishing tail-light of the Packard. The bluecoat driver of the prowl car was already back in his seat. He hastily ducked a glowing cigarette under cover as the Marquis rounded the car, saying to the recorder: "Let's see your book on that

accident just now, will you, Harry?"
"Huh? Oh, hello, Marty. Yeah sure. It wasn't anything."

The Marquis absorbed the information that the blue Packard belonged to E. L. Solloway, of Park Avenue, but was being driven by Donald Hamlin, of West 96th Street, Donald Hamlin was assistant manager of the Regal Motor Sales—on Broadway, just a few blocks below the street they were on.

He said curiously: "Solloway? That wouldn't be Solloway the Wall Street banker. . . ?"

"Yeah. That's him. Why? Hey, there's nothing wrong, is there? We just called Mr. Solloway at his home and he said—"

"Hell, no. Just curious, that's all," the Marquis said and handed back the book. "Thanks. See you around."

They walked aimlessly, casually, back till they were around the corner of Seventh and out of sight of the prowl car. Then they stopped and looked at each other muddily.

"The car belongs to Solloway, the private banker," the Marquis said. "You know—he's the father of that swell little redhead that pops up every once in a while in a Broadway show. But Solloway wasn't driving it, because he was at home. And this Hamlin wasn't driving it—but he jumps out of thin air, with all the papers, evidently, and claims he was. And Solloway covers him."

"Somebody's screwy," McGuire muttered.

"Maybe we better poke down past that Regal Motor Sales. I'd like to know. . . ."

They walked down Seventh Avenue, then across, so that they came to a stop in the shadow of the building directly apposite the Regal showroom.

THE Regal was a vast, corner establishment of plate glass, fronting on two streets. It was an old-established, well-known concern. The first thing they saw was the blue Packard, parked along the side street, presumably opposite the side entrance. No one was in it, nor, for a minute or two, did it seem that anyone was in the darkened, moon-shining motor showroom.

Then a match flared, just inside the front door, and they saw the blond man standing there, lighting a cigarette. The match died and left the glowing ember of the cigarette.

McGuire whispered: "Listen—whoever *was* driving that bus must have shot into that space at a hell of a speed, to knock the Chevvie. . . ."

"I thought of that."

"Well, are we just going to stand here?" McGuire husked after a minute.

"We—" the Marquis began and went silent as a taxi came racketing up Broadway with a broken tire chain flapping, came straight up and past them as they huddled there. They had one swift glance of a spare, tall man with fine, waving white hair, in the tonneau. He was sitting forward on the rumble seat and his sensitive, aristocratic face was strained and tense, his fine gray eyes on fire.

The taxi plowed to a stop, twenty feet beyond them, and the old man descended swiftly, threw the driver a bill, then stood there, shivering, till the hacker had pulled away around the next corner.

The Marquis said, "That's Solloway," just as the banker plowed quickly and with frenzied awkwardness, across through the piled snow, heading directly for the door of the showroom.

The door of the showroom opened to meet his approach, and, in the instant before it was closed again—with Solloway inside—the old man's hoarse, frantic voice blurted in a crazy whisper: "He—he called me, just before that policeman did. Dear heaven, Donald—what happened? You did as he bade?"

The closing door cut off the rest. After a minute, a light went on, somewhere behind partitions, deep in the heart of the showroom.

"Jumping hell," McGuire whispered. "What *is* it?"

Then the sudden, staggering possibility dawned in the Marquis' questioning mind. He shot out suddenly: "By God, I believe—it sounds as though. . ." and caught his breath.

The blood slowly surged into his face and his eyes momentarily glowed yellow. He strode out of concealment, his teeth tight. "By the living God, if it is—in my section—on Christmas—I'll tear some-body's heart out and feed it. . . . Go take a look at that car," he snapped as they mounted the opposite curb. "See if the other bird left anything around. This Hamlin hasn't had a chance to go over it thoroughly. Go on—move!"

He walked grimly himself to the front door of the showroom, stood there tight-jawed a moment with his hands in his pockets peering in. Then he tried the door, with silent caution. It was, as he half expected, unlocked.

A second later he was inside, in the overheated, dark showroom.

From the lighted office beyond parti-tions, he could hear quick, urgent short phrases of talk and his teeth clenched as he heard Hamlin's slightly slurred voice say desperately: ". . . exactly as he or-dered. He himself threw the whole thing into confusion by colliding with another car as he pulled in. Naturally, I was out of the sedan, fifty yards up the street. I—I saw him drive away in the sedan a mo-ment later and there—I couldn't think of anything to do but go down and claim the convertible and say I was driving. Any other way would cause an investiga-tion. . . ."

The broken voice of the old man blurted: "Of course, of course. You did the right thing, Donald—but what in God's name—he phoned me and told me furiously that it would cost more now. He told me to come here, and then hung up."

Hamlin's bitter, worried voice said, just as the Marquis reached the two-inch crack of the lighted office door: "It can't be that this made any difference. Obvi-ously, he was going to demand more any-way. . . ."

The Marquis opened the door and said through clenched teeth as he stepped in: "Who? Who's this son-of-a-witch? Just give me his name—that's all."

CHAPTER THREE

Switch-Car Pay-Off

THE two men—the blond, military-looking Hamlin, now with his crisp-curling hair uncovered, and the white-haired, ascetic Solloway jumped to their feet. In both the youth's bright blue eyes

and the old man's gray ones, there was fright.

Solloway choked hoarsely: "Who—what—in God's name, who are you? How did you get—"

"I'm a friend of your daughter, Bar-bara. I'm crazy about her and she's a friend of mine. I'm Lieutenant Marquis of the Broadway Squad."

The old man almost cried out. He seemed to shrink and his hand went to his mouth. "Please get out—go away, Lieu-tenant," he stammered hastily. "Please—you don't know—it's important that we—please go away—I'll explain tomor-row. . . ."

"Explain, hell," the Marquis clipped. "I don't need any explanation. I've been around long enough to know this pattern when I see it! Somebody's been snatched, haven't they? By God, is it your daughter, Barbara?"

They stared at him with fear-sick, stunned eyes.

The Marquis said: "Come on. It's my job. Apart from the fact that I'd go all out for your daughter any time, this —— chose my district for this attempt at a switch-car payoff. I won't take time to explain why that's a deliberate slap in the face for me, nor how I feel about any-body who would pull this at Christmas time. I know the gag. You had money in one car and drove around till another car signaled you behind, then parked and got out and walked away—far enough so you couldn't recognize him. Right? Then he switched from his car to yours and beat it?"

The blond Hamlin swallowed and nod-ded. His eyes were stark on the Marquis.

"How much money did he get?"

Hamlin choked out: "Fifty thousand dollars."

"You don't know who the kidnaper was —or do you?"

"No, no," the old man blurted broken-ly. "She—she came down here—to Broadway—yesterday, to see her theat-rical agent. From there she was supposed to drive out to Long Island. But she didn't get there. About eight o'clock, I got a call at my home, saying she was safe and to get the money together. He—he said he would instruct Hamlin how to deliver it—he had already called Hamlin here and told him he was to act as go-between."

"Why? Where does Mr. Hamlin come in?"

"He—he is a great friend of my daughter—a very dear friend. She was supposed to see him last night as soon as she returned. He . . ." The old man suddenly made a desperate sound like a sob in his throat. "Mr. Marquis, if you *are* a friend of Barbara—please, for God's sake, do nothing—go away—let us treat with this devil till we get her back. . . ."

"I'll handle that part of it," the Marquis clipped. "This payoff—I gather that he must have taken Barbara's car along with her? Then he drove it back tonight and switched to your own?"

"Yes, yes," the old man groaned, "that was how we were to know that he *did* have her. Donald was to drive around till he heard the signal on the horn and then park as soon as he recognized Barbara's car. Mr. Marquis—for the love of mercy, please leave this in our hands. He threatened that if I went to the police, or anybody, he—he'd send me Barbara's ear for —for Christmas. . . ."

The Marquis' round, ordinarily pink-cheeked little face was white. He said in a soft voice that shook: "This isn't the first kidnaping I've handled, Mr. Solloway. Trust me to take care of that angle. Can you give me any possible idea who the kidnaper might be? It could be some enemy of yours. . . ."

"No, no," the frantic old man moaned. "I have no enemies—except business rivals—not vicious ones. And he was— he sounded like a criminal—cold and vicious. . . ."

"You, Mr. Hamlin—didn't you catch even a slight look at him during the switch?"

THE blond man's face had frozen into a white, not unhandsome, stiff mask of desperation. He swallowed hard again. "I—" he started and stopped. "I can't be sure. It was only for a part of a second when the moon fell across his face but —I *think* I saw—I got the impression that he was Albino. His hair was even lighter than mine and his eyes seemed— well, reddish. . . ." He finished desperately: "But I could have mistaken every part of it—moonlight—just an instant's glance. . . ."

"You don't know anybody like that?" the Marquis shot at the old man.

Solloway shook his head.

"And she was in my district the last seen of her?" the Marquis insisted. "Where is this agent's office that she was visiting?"

"On Forty-sixth Street, just off Broadway."

"Give me the license number of the sedan—the one he drove away in. No, don't be afraid, I'm not going to broadcast any alarm. But I have private means of putting a net out for it."

The old man mumbled the license number huskily from memory and the Marquis scribbled it on a scrap of paper on the desk. He said, "Just a minute," and walked out again into the showroom, peered out to find McGuire in the vicinity of the blue Packard.

Then he saw the redhead around at the front door of the car, bent down, apparently trying to scrutinize a square card in the moon's rays. When the Marquis opened the door, the redhead looked up quickly, stepped over and handed him the card. "This was in the muck on the floor under the dashboard. What the hell is all this?"

"A snatch," the Marquis said savagely.

The redhead gasped. "Who?"

"Barbara Solloway—that sweet little redhead with the violet eyes—you know. Some —————— - ———— snatched her right on Broadway, apparently. And what we just saw was the payoff—or one payoff. Here—the rat drove away in a car with this license number. Get the word around quietly that I want that car spotted and phone the boys at the Agency that I want someone to get to it the minute it turns up—get to it and take a plant on it. Grab anybody who tries to get in. Or look for a tall Albino around it. Get that over fast. What's this?"

"Looks like it was stuck in the windshield, but fell down in the excitement."

"All right, get going."

The redhead trotted off, vanished around the corner. Not till then did the Marquis peer closely at the card he had in his hand. He walked back toward the office, got it in the light—and for a second, puzzlement held him frowning in the doorway.

The card was a picture. It was a picture of the head of Donald Hamlin, the blond assistant manager. But it was as though he were standing behind a huge white billboard that blotted out all the rest of the picture, leaving only his bare head and throat hanging there in the top center of the photo. Across the face of the picture had been typed: *My friend, I hope you are obeying instructions to the letter.*

He was about to hand it over to the two in the office, when thought of fingerprints on the glossy surface occurred to him. And another queer, rising feeling in his stomach that was absolutely without definiteness or clarity. He took another, closer look. The weird, senseless feeling of urgency grew stronger, without his being able to comprehend it in the least.

He looked over at the white-haired old man. "Mr. Solloway, I'd like to ask you a question or two in private," and when he had the old man out in the gloom of the salesroom, he groped: "How long have you known Hamlin? Who is he?"

THE old man faltered wonderingly: "Why, he—he's an Austrian. He was a titled man in his own country but he—he had to leave the country two years ago when the trouble happened over there. He—my daughter was on the committee to help the refugees—they all barely escaped and were penniless, without even passports when they reached here, most of them. She—well, she asked me to help get him a job and I did—here. In God's name, don't think there's anything wrong with Donald. In two years, he's become assistant manager here. The owner tells me he's one of the hardest-working men, and the most valuable, that he's ever had. And—between ourselves—I happen to know that he's more than fond of Barbara and she of him. I expected an announcement long since and she—well, she as much as said she did too. . . ."

"All right, that's what I wanted to. . . ."

Then light hit him like the kick of a mule. He said hoarsely, "By God—wait a minute," and swung back to the office.

As he strode in and closed the door behind him, he needed only one more glance at the picture to realize that it was not

exactly a picture, but a picture *of* a picture—with details blocked out by a white mask.

Hamlin was huddled at the far end of the room, his wooden face pale, his bright-blue eyes white-rimmed and hypnotized on the card.

"You whelp!" the Marquis said through clenched teeth. "I'm going to have you flayed alive. Austrian refugee, eh? You blasted stir-bug! What pen did you do time in?"

The other choked: "What? What are you talking ab . . . ?"

"Can it! Do you think I've looked at twenty million rogues'-gallery pictures without knowing one when I see it—even if most of it's blocked out. I'll give you just five seconds to tell me where the girl is!"

The starch seemed to go out of the other as though it were quicksilver. He was suddenly young, desperate, frantic. He dropped into a chair, ground the heels of his hand over his hair and his eyes were moist and soft with terror. "All right," he croaked desperately. "I am a stir-bug. I have done time—but I swear to God I don't know where she is. No—wait—" as the Marquis jerked a blackjack from his hip and started for him with murder in his eyes. "You can slug me all you want later. But let me talk first. It'll finish me —but it may save her. Listen—and get it fast. I'll have to tell you the whole thing so you'll believe me.

"I was manager of a branch of the Los Angeles Cement Company. Eighteen thousand dollars in cash disappeared from the safe overnight. I was the only one who knew the combination, except the owner. You can take it or leave it—but I didn't take that money. My boss, the owner, Arthur Boltby, insisted that I did. The loss put an awful crimp in the business. I wasn't bonded. He bore down on me and the evidence was enough to send me over. I swear to you that I am sure now Boltby took the money himself—he was hog-wild half the time on liquor and women and he couldn't have taken much more cash out of the firm otherwise without the creditors cracking down. Not that that occurred to me then—or for years afterwards, and it doesn't matter anyway.

"I served four years and got out on

parole. I couldn't get anything to do—oh, yes, pick-and-shovel jobs to keep soul and body together—but I'm not a pick-and-shovel man. About two years ago, I heard of an opening in Holland and I managed to get over here. But the situation was a frost. I couldn't catch on. I thought I'd rather starve here than over there so I shipped back—stowed away, if you must know.

"The joker was that the ship was crowded with Austrian refugees—people who had got out one way or another when Austria got swallowed up by Germany. The boat was a madhouse, overcrowded, undermanned. The passengers were herded like cows. Most of them had nothing, but almost all had been of importance at home.

"I—there was very ragged count kept of them and I managed to mix with them as soon as we were out to sea. I had one presentable outfit of clothing. And I swear that this and nothing else is what happened when I got off."

HE POUNDED the table with his closed knuckles and sweat ran down his face as he rattled it out. "There were a group of people with cars on the pier. One of them was Miss Solloway. She and the others were there simply and solely out of the goodness of their hearts to offer help to the refugees. They didn't ask me who I was, or if I were a refugee. They just assumed I was. All she asked me was if I had anywhere to go.

"I said I hadn't. All right, I knew I was grifting—but I had exactly ninety-eight cents in my pocket and nowhere to turn. I—well, I put a fancy *von* name on myself and they took me to a hotel, put me up. The next day she took me down to Wall Street to her father. He never questioned me—I didn't *have* to lie to him. He assumed everything about me that she had, knew I had no papers or money. It didn't even surprise him that I knew none of the other refugees. He was even relieved to find I could speak English to him. He offered to get me a job.

"He did—with this outfit. They took me on and I've been here two years now. I give you my word no man ever worked harder or more conscientiously than I have. At first I was afraid every moment

of exposure. Miss Solloway tried to provide a social life for me, but I ducked it, told her that for a while I wanted to do nothing but try to make good on the job. God knows it was the truth. I asked them to just forget about me for a few months, till I justified their faith in me. I—well, maybe I gave myself a little accent and used a few Austrian expressions, but I swear to you all I wanted was to hang on to this chance. I half intended to tell them all about myself some day, if I could.

"To make a long story short, Miss Solloway refused to abandon me. I saw her at least once a week and I—well, I fell in love with her. And, as far as a girl can go without ever having had her hand so much as held, I guess she did with me. You can believe that—I never so much as touched her. I knew it was impossible, but I couldn't tell her that. And I was on fire for her, but I—I bottled myself. I went along, hoping—or not hoping, or something—that she would meet somebody else, either in her theater jobs or in the course of everyday things—I don't know just what I thought—or if I thought. This is all I can tell you—it got to the point where I *couldn't* tell her the truth about myself, where the thought of her finding out what a shabby fraud I was, was the one thing I feared most in the whole world. So help me, I even thought of getting her to marry me and vanish with me someplace. I even thought of trying to make love to her and say I *had* a wife somewhere. Even that seemed less dishonorable than marrying her.

"And then Boltby suddenly caught up with me out of nowhere.

"I don't know yet how he spotted me or when, but he evidently didn't get in touch with me at once. By the time he did call me, he had apparently gotten a full line on me and not only that, but he had carefully gone through a legal process in California and managed to secure a civil judgment against me for the money I was supposed to have stolen years ago, and got it past the statute of limitations. Anyway, he phoned me a week ago and calmly informed me that he was here to collect the money.

"It was blackmail, and it wasn't. But it was the payoff for me. I tried to tell him I had no part of eighteen thousand dollars—twenty-odd, he claimed, with interest—but he had gotten the idea that I was going to marry Miss Solloway. He had gotten some of those blocked-out rogues'-gallery pictures made and ˙ he mailed me one, then called again and pointed out that, to effect a garnishee on my salary, he would have to yank me into court and prove that I was using an alias, that I was—well, who I was. He told me his business had petered out in California and he had practically nothing and that, as I owed him this, he wanted it.

"I stalled him. I had to and there was only one way I could do it. I pretended I *was* going to marry Miss Solloway, but that the announcement couldn't come till after Christmas was over and I promised that I could borrow the money then and give it to him. I gave him every cent I had in the bank in the meanwhile, a thousand-odd dollars."

H E HESITATED for breath, dragged a sleeve across his forehead and plunged on. "I think he had me followed around. A couple of times I thought someone was shadowing me, but I couldn't catch him at it. Anyway, I had till after Christmas—as I thought. I was simply going to pull out and vanish, but I—well, I wanted to spend Christmas—to wait till the last minute.

"And then something happened. I don't know what. Believe me, Boltby was a tricky, cunning rat but he hadn't the stomach for kidnaping, or for threatening murder. But someone called me last night and announced he had become Boltby's partner, that Boltby had decided he needed a little professional guidance in cashing in his claim. And get this, Marquis—that man is a killer. I spent enough time in prison to know, even by his voice. For God's sake, believe that—this situation is desperate.

"He calmly informed me that he had Miss Solloway. He told me he was holding her for fifty thousand dollars ransom, that he had picked her up as he went off the parkway on Long Island, and that he had managed so that she had not seen his face. That much I believe. God knows I did everything I could to make sure. He told me he was calling Mr. Solloway and outlined the arrangements and he—he

gave me that description—that Albino description. I was to give that to anybody who asked me. You get it, don't you? The perfect set-up—a clean job with me the only possible identification, either now or later—and me forced to give the false description. And I was to make damned sure the old man did as he was told. Otherwise it was no longer any question of simple exposure for me, you can see—he would kill her and I would probably end up taking the rap for it anyway.

"I swear to you, Marquis, that if you were any other cop on the force, I'd stand you off—if I had to murder you. But if anybody can save her, I think you can. You're supposed to know everybody on Broadway and every crook in the business. I can't conceive who he is—except that he's a professional. But maybe you can—and maybe you can figure how to handle Boltby. Boltby is the weak link." ˙

"Where is this alleged Boltby?"

"I had one of his calls traced to the Grauman Hotel, on Thirty-fourth Street, but there was nobody registered under that name there."

"What's he look like?"

"Like a fat little pudgy spider—black hair, heavy black eyebrows, a slack, soft face—he's dumpy, and short. At least that's how I remember him. But he had one pointed ear and that would be sure identification. If I had dared, I might have tracked him down, but there wasn't any point to it before—and since last night, I haven't dared make a move. You —I know you're not fool enough to let him get wise that you're in on this, but even so, for God's sake make your move fast. This new partner has a brain like a steel trap, he's already collected fifty thousand dollars and if he gets the idea he's in danger, he'll snuff her out like that and vanish. Why wouldn't he? Whatever additional money he's figuring on wouldn't be worth the risk. Can—for God's sake—can you do something?"

For a second, Marquis stood in an absolute frenzy of indecision. For once, he was almost completely swept away by the terrible, tumbling sincerity in the blond youth's voice.

He groaned out hoarsely: "You —— pup, if you're lying now, I'll have you killed by inches."

"I swear to God I've told you every word of the truth. For the love of Heaven, take a chance, Marquis. I don't care what you do to me afterwards—but do something. I'm not going to move. He told Mr. Solloway—just half an hour ago—to come here and wait with me for new instructions. Mr. Solloway is arranging to raise money tonight if we have to—but I don't—I can't trust them even to go through with the thing now." He almost sobbed. "Every minute may count, Marquis—"

The Marquis' teeth snapped. He said: "All right. But if you're out of line you'll wish you'd never been born. . . ." He strode hard-heeled out into the salesroom.

Hamlin hurried after him, rattling at the dim figure of Solloway outside: "Mr. Marquis is going to do something for us. Would it be all right if he took the convertible . . .?" and when the old man stammered assent, Hamlin pressed keys in the Marquis' hand and blurted: "If—if we get a call, what will I do?"

"Call McCreagh's Ticket Agency where my squad has its unofficial headquarters. Just leave word you called. I'm. . . ."

He did not finish it, went on swiftly outside, rounded to the blue coupé. McGuire came out of the shadows opposite, throwing away a cigarette, and the Marquis threw him the keys, "Get in and drive this crate to the Grauman Hotel—fast."

The redhead sprang to activity and they shot away. "What the hell?" he said as they whirled down Eighth, and when the Marquis had clipped the story with short, grim phrases on the way down, "My God! And you fell for that ex-con's babble. . . ."

"Barbara Solloway is snatched. There's no doubt about that. And she's in danger. The rest may or may not be so, but we'll straighten it out after. Right now, there's a damned dangerous hood holding the girl, and likely to get touched off any minute. That's the situation—*all* of it."

CHAPTER FOUR

The Bell

THEY raced crosstown on Thirty-fourth and pulled in with a squealing skid that ended them half in a snow-pile

at the curb, jumped out. The Marquis' dapper little figure led the way into the luxurious Grauman Hotel, straight across the huge lobby to the office over which glowed the hanging green sign: *Manager.*

He strode purposefully in without knocking.

A startled, gray-haired man in dress trousers and undershirt, with half his face covered with lather and a straight razor in one hand, opened the door of the bathroom beyond cautiously.

"Come out of it, Barnard," the Marquis snapped. "You've got a guest here—short, pudgy, fat, black hair, heavy black eyebrows, and a weak face, one pointed ear. Don't tell me you don't know him."

"Sure I know him," the other said wonderingly. "The louse has been reported a dozen times for having women in his room, but we never could catch him at it—the maid finds. . . ."

"I don't care about his love-life. What's his name and room number?"

"Hawkins—seventeen-twelve. Wait a minute. What's the beef?"

"Is he in now? The rat's a pickpocket."

"Oh," the manager said relievedly and picked up a phone, made short inquiry, hung up. "No, he's out. Will you wait till I get. . . ."

"No. Give me the master-key and you join us when you're ready."

The elevator shot them to the seventeenth floor and they stood in the alleged Hawkins-Boltby's room a minute later. It was an ordinary room and bath, and the occupant had two gladstone bags and a suitcase. Most of the contents were arranged in the bureau drawers and closets and in ten minutes searching all they had turned up was confirmation of the fact that 'Hawkins' was Boltby, that he was from San Francisco, that he had an illiterate girl in that city who wrote him letters complaining that he had walked out on her without giving her promised money.

There was nothing whatever that might bear on the kidnaping.

"Go downstairs and phone the Agency for Harry, or one of the others. Get him over here to take a plant on this room," the Marquis told McGuire. "I'll take one more look round."

Then the lid blew off. And the real, stunning ugliness that underlay even the viciousness of the kidnaping suddenly burst open—and the Marquis saw the full, bloody defi that had been flung in his teeth. He had finished his final fruitless search, was halfway out the door of the room when the phone rang.

Two long strides took him across to the instrument and he mumbled an answer into the mouthpiece.

"Arthur?" a man's voice said brightly. "That you, Arthur?"

"Yeah," the Marquis said. "Who's this?"

"Well, maybe you don't remember me, Arthur, but I'm a great friend of Gracie's. She introduced me to you one night and I was wondering. . . ."

"Gracie who?"

"Gracie who? That's a hot one! Gracie Svenson, of course. Say, I'll tell you, old boy, I just got in town and I was wondering if you could get hold of Gracie and maybe she could get a friend for me and we could do up the. . . ." The voice suddenly broke off concernedly. "Or say—maybe I'm out of line here. Maybe you and Gracie aren't going around together any more, huh?"

"Oh sure," the Marquis mumbled. "Who'd you say this was?"

"George. George Hernelius."

"Well, I'll tell you, George—suppose you come over here and we'll see. It's a hell of a time to be starting out, but we'll see."

"'Ataboy," the other said enthusiastically. "Like I said, I just got in and you—probably you don't remember this, ha-ha—but you. . . ."

THE MARQUIS' mouth had opened, closed, twice, and a scowl cut his forehead. He suddenly clamped his lips and snarled: "Wait a minute. That Irish brogue doesn't go with a Finnish name. Who the hell is this, anyhow? You, Callaghan?"

There was a silence at the other end of the wire. Then a growled: "Who is this?"

"Marty Marquis. What the hell does the Homicide Squad want with B—Hawkins?"

There was another silence. Then the Homicide detective said glumily: "I'm damned if I know. We fished this Gracie Svenson out of the river four days ago—somebody knifed her, dumped her in a snow-truck, then beat it down to the East River and was waiting when the truck came down to dump. He stood off the driver and his helper till he'd emptied the truck himself and then ducked. It didn't do him any good, because the body floated and the driver called us right away and we fished. . . ."

"What's B—Hawkins got to do with it?"

"I dunno. His name and number were one of about a hundred scrawled on the wall by the phone in the rooming-house the girl lived in. I been calling them all. . . ."

"Who is the girl?"

"Huh? Gracie Svenson. She was a waitress at Hardt's—the one on Fifth Avenue. That is, she was the last couple months, when she didn't have too much hangover to come to work. She—hey what the hell is the Broadway Squad doing in this?"

"We just got a call—anonymous," the Marquis said, "asking us to come here. Where is this Gracie Svenson now? Have they buried her?"

"No. She's still at the morgue."

"Thanks, Callaghan. If I get anything— Wait a minute. This guy that stood off the driver and his helper on that truck. Was he a pudgy little fat guy with heavy black eyebrows and. . . .?"

"God knows. It was in the middle of the snowstorm and all they could see was the big gun the guy was waving. Who is this pudgy guy?"

"Hawkins—the guy that owns this room. I'm putting a plant on the room and if he comes in, I'll notify you if you want."

"I'd appreciate it. Of course he may not have any connection at all—maybe somebody else in the house was the one was calling him—hell, the party may even have moved out months ago, for that matter. . . ."

"Yeah, sure," the Marquis interposed hastily, "That's right," and hung up.

He stood for a moment, thoughts churning in his head. A little pulse started to beat in his temple. He recalled Hamlin's description of Boltby years ago as woman-

and-liquor-crazy. Apparently he hadn't changed. And a waitress had his phone number—a waitress who had been murdered! Of course, it could be coincidence —like hell it could!

He started swiftly for the door—and the phone again began to ring, this time in short little urgent bursts. The Marquis swung back, red-faced.

This time, when he answered, it was McGuire's voice on the other end. He said hoarsely, "Come on—get down here, chief—in a hurry!" and slammed the receiver down.

WHEN the Marquis strode out of the elevator, McGuire was standing, white-faced, near the east door. Without a word, he swung and pushed out and when the Marquis emerged, he was already rounding to the driver's seat of the car. He said: "Get in—and don't ask questions."

Not till the Marquis had gotten blackly in, stared wonderingly at the redhead's taut features for ten blocks and they had come to a halt in a black little street of warehouses, did the redhead turn his hot eyes towards him. Then he asked through stiff lips: "You didn't get anything that would help get this Barbara Solloway back, did you?"

"Not exactly. Is Harry. . . .?"

"He's planted in the hotel—came in just before I called you. But if you're counting on hopping on this Boltby to crack the job, forget it. He won't help you."

"Why won't he?"

"Come here." The redhead snapped open his door, piled out into the snow. The Marquis followed suit. "Around at the back," McGuire told him.

When they stood by the luggage compartment at the rear, McGuire's flashlight suddenly spurted light downward at the lock of the compartment. "Take a look."

The Marquis' nostrils flared as he saw the dried, rust-colored stains that had dribbled out from under the closed lid. He snatched at the handle, lifted the wide, curving lid hastily till it locked into open position. A light clicked on in the compartment.

There was blood all over the compartment floor. In the middle of it, clutching his hands to his belly, was a pudgy, slack-faced little man, his little pig-eyes fishy and glazed under heavy black brows. His hat was off and his toupee-like hair was as neatly parted and oiled as if he had just come from a barber shop. One of his ears was pointed.

For three full minutes, the Marquis stood there with his temples pounding. The blond Hamlin had said the kidnaper was a killer. Killer? He was a butcher— a grim, bowelless butcher! Not for an instant now did the Marquis doubt that he had cut the waitress, Gracie Svenson, to death as well—not after a look at this.

Then the icy fear touched him for an instant—the fear that the man was insane. For there was no sanity in this.

His feverish, groping mind hastily cast up the probabilities—the possibilities. The waitress—that was an old Broadway situation. He did not even have to make an effort to see where she fitted into this nightmare. Somehow, she had come under the killer's dominance—and somehow, she had met Boltby. She—Boltby being what he was—had undoubtedly found out, in one of the pudgy little lecher's drunken moments, what he had, and relayed the information to her man. He had promptly taken steps to get control, declared himself in, seen the subtle possibilities of the snatch with Hamlin as unwilling shield— infinitely more profitable than simple blackmail of the ex-convict—and, in the end, calmly butchered both his accomplices.

That much was sane, in a way—sane, if the bloody mind of the killer felt that the sum he would reap on the kidnap justified the ruthless butchery. But why, in God's name, would be stuff the murdered body of the westerner into the car that he sent back to his victims? Obviously, he had not informed them that it was there, or Hamlin would never have offered to lend it to the Marquis. It was rashness to the point of madness. Any accidental disclosure of that body would automatically bring the police swarming into the picture. And, of all things, it would seem that police attention at this point was the last thing in the world the killer would risk. Unless—unless there was some quirk in his brain. Unless he was acting irrationally. Unless he did not really plan to seek to extort any more money from the fabulously wealthy Solloway. Unless this was his casual way of conveying that he was tossing the whole thing over, that he was not going to return the girl. . . .

The Marquis' voice was husky as he snapped: "Has he got anything on him?"

"No," the redhead said, after a minute. "He's clean. Clean and good and dead."

The Marquis swallowed. "All right. Close it up." And when the redhead had complied, "I guess we'll have to take him down to headquarters. Let's go."

McGuire did not move. Are you crazy?"

"Yeah. Come on."

"Wait a minute. God in Heaven— don't you see what you're up against? If you take him down and toss him to Homicide, the whole cat will be out of the bag. Then what do you think your chances are of getting your Barbara back—with this guy already having gone for one murder?"

The Marquis licked his lips.

"For God's sake, use your head," the redhead urged. "The minute headquarters gets this body, they can't help but squeeze out the truth. You know those clowns— they'll blunder all over the lot—make it impossible for the kidnaper to even establish contact, much less take the payoff and turn the girl loose. He'll have to duck out—and if you think he'll leave her alive when he does, you think different than I do. We've got to keep this to ourselves."

"They'll break us—both of us—if we get caught at it."

"All right. The girl's your friend, not mine. And remember—this is a Broadway job. You laid down the law in the section in no mean terms. This killer has slapped blood right in your face. If you want to go down and have the whole thing lifted out of your hands by Homicide. . . ."

"—— —— it! We can't just leave him there in the compartment!"

"Why can't we? It's cold. He'll keep —for twenty-four hours anyway. Surely this thing has to break, one way or another in twenty-four hours. If you want to give your girl friend a chance to live. . ."

It took five good minutes, before the Marquis could settle his spinning mind, before he finally said through tight jaws: "All right. This is probably our finish— both of us, but we'll go for it. But one of us will have to stay with this car every second. Can you jam that compartment

lock, so nobody can open it by mistake, or. . . ?"

"Sure. There's some cold-solder in the tool-kit. I. . . ." He ran around to the side-door, fished out hammer and solder. For a minute, there was metal racket— and then he slammed the compartment-lid down and said grimly: "Count on that Now where?"

"The morgue."

The redhead gasped. "The morgue! Are you crazy?"

"Not for this one. There's another girl down there—knifed." He tossed the details he had gleaned from the Homicide detective at the redhead, as they sped downtown.

THE MARQUIS found Gruen, Callaghan's side partner, hanging around the morgue and, as he stood looking down at the drawer in which the plump, marble-white body of Gracie Svenson, the waitress, lay, Gruen told him what they knew about her.

It wasn't much, and it wasn't new. From a small town in Pennsylvania, she had come to the city and found work in the exclusive chain of restaurants with surprising ease. Then the period of sitting at home in her room—night after night the true pitfall of New York. Then the discovery that for the price of a few beers, she could sit in a bar all evening and maybe—just maybe 'meet' some nice gent. From there on, pickups, of gradually increasing intensity—and gradually increasing dangerousness. Liquor to make her reckless, more liquor next day to drown out the shudders of the previous night. Eventually, the dropping of all inhibitions and fastidiousness, and from there to the 'wise' stage only a step.

The Homicide Squad had found a dozen men with whom she had had brief relations, but for one reason or another, none of them were concerned here. Nobody seemed to know what man had been getting her attention lately. She roomed alone and, since she had acquired the glaze of deliberate dissipation, she was aloof from here fellow-workers. It was known that she spent most evenings in one bar or another and she was known to a dozen bartenders but none had anything to suggest. Most of them claimed that she was about ripe for the hustler stage and one or two had even sounded her out. They were of the opinion that she had no regular boy-friends any longer.

Then Gruen produced the bell.

"What the hell's that?" the Marquis asked.

"She had that clutched to her belly when they found her. Funny, ain't it?"

The Marquis turned it over in small, black-gloved fingers. It was an under-size, brass bell, a miniature of an old-fashioned schoolbell. There was a tag attached to it: *Return to Salvation Army when possible.*

"Salvation Army!" the Marquis said.

"Yeah. It's one of theirs—you know, them guys they dress up as Santa Claus and stick out on street corners with a pot to collect dough in? They ring bells like these to get people's attention."

"What did they say about it?"

Gruen shrugged. "They said they had a whole outfit stole out of their warehouse —suit, pot, bell, everything. But some-body picked it up in the street and sent it back to them—all but the bell."

"They said it was stolen out of the warehouse? Not some bird wore it out and didn't come back?"

"No. It was stole."

"What the hell's the difference?" Mc-Guire asked when the Marquis had re-tailed it to him out in the blue convertible.

"Not much," the Marquis said grimly. "Not much—except that it finally turns this whole thing back where we can get at it. You damned fool—this is the break! Up to here, this crazy case needed a Philo Vance! Now—it needs the Broad-way Squad—and nobody else. If that out-fit was stolen it was stolen by some cheap grifter. Some cheap grifter that figured a new angle on panhandling. That's our meat. We're supposed to know every thief, every goniff, in this town. If we can't filter out the cheap wart who's been working this Santa Claus grift and pocket-ing the dough himself—I'll disband the Squad. There can't be more than a few of them. Wait a minute. Stop here—at this drug store. I want to phone."

He ran in to the all-night drug store and phoned the Regal Salesroom. The phone barely began to ring before it was snatched up.

The Marquis said: "This is Lieutenant Marquis. Have you heard. . . .?"

A hoarse, frightened voice that he rec-ognized as the old man, Solloway, blurted: "Yes, yes! He—he called just a little while ago. Mr. Marquis—I think—I think he's insane! He just called up and told us to go on home, that he probably wouldn't want any more money from us, that Barbara was safe and sound."

"*What!*"

"Yes. Yes! He even let me speak to her. She is safe and sound—but she sounded frightened out of her wits—as though she were repeating something he told her to say—and then it was as though the phone were snatched away from her and he came back on. He just chuckled and said, 'I have to think it over a while, but I'll probably turn her loose pretty soon,' and hung up. What—in God's name what is he doing, Mr. Marquis? Do you think he actually means not to ask for any more money? Or—or. . . ."

The Marquis swallowed hard, in order to be able to say reassuringly: "You just go home, Mr. Solloway, as he says. It's probably going to be all right. And take Mr. Hamlin with you." He hung up.

To McGuire's gasping incredulity, he bit grimly: "God only knows what's hap-pening—or what's to come next. Get down to the Agency, fast. The whole blasted Squad is going to work to turn up this penny-ante grifter."

"But—but why. . . .?"

"You blockhead! The girl must have been killed somewhere near where he had his Santa Claus pitch set up. Otherwise how would she have the bell? If we can locate him—there's just a chance he saw something—saw the killer. That *could* be the reason he ran away and left the stuff on the street! When we get hold of him, there's a one-in-three chance that we break the whole thing—and I'll teach somebody what it means to pull this in my section on Christmas. Come on, move."

CHAPTER FIVE

Santa Claws

THE amazing machinery of the Broad-way Squad went into action. Some of the twenty-two squad-men had gone home for the night. They were promptly yanked back, and the entire force set to work to milk their individual and collective networks of contacts that criss-crossed back and forth in an incredible spiderweb throughout the entire city's submerged tenth.

The little Ticket Agency on Times Square, the Squad's unofficial gathering-place became a boiler-room, its dozen phones in use every minute. As it became dawn, then early morning, then mid-morning, some of them departed silently, quickly, on unknown visits, returned without comment later, to take up the ceaseless phoning, answer in dull, short monotones incoming calls.

Tension grew. The little Agency became dense with smoke.

At ten o'clock, a silver-haired man with the face of an ascetic was explaining to the Marquis, over on the lower east side of the city at the Salvation Army's warehouse: "No, the outfit was not appropriated by one of the boys who work for us at this time of year. It simply disappeared from the warehouse during the night. A kindly-disposed citizen saw the pot standing unattended in the street last Monday morning and was good enough to phone us. We found the suit in a little shack nearby . . .

"Eh? Yes, I think I can give the address where it was found."

At eleven the Marquis and McGuire stood looking at the modest little church far over on the West Side, sunk among the stirring warehouses. "The pot stood there," the Marquis explained. "The grifter must have figured a pitch outside the church, to get people coming out." He kicked absently at the snow mound along the curbing—and suddenly looked down sharply.

"Hey!" He bent closer, as his kick, dislodging the top six-inch chunk of snow, showed mottled brown spots underneath. He hunkered quickly down and, with a stick, pushed away more shards of frozen snow.

"By God—this is the exact spot! She was killed right here—and that Department of Sanitation truck stopped just up there for the guys to get a cup of . . . The girl must have fallen on the Santa Claus bell as she went down, got it in her hand and the killer never noticed. But the —— was cool-headed enough to figure to let the snow truck get the body to the river for him, and . . . That little shack over there behind the church is where he changed his clothes. The Santa Claus guy I mean."

"Why couldn't the Santa Claus guy *be* the killer."

"Well, he could," the Marquis said. "But it doesn't make sense that a grifter that small would take on a racket this big. Come on, let's get back."

FROM nine o'clock on, he phoned the Solloway house every hour. The frantic old man, the kidnaped girl's father, grew more frantic with each passing minute—but nothing was heard from the kidnaper. The afternoon wore away, and even the Marquis began to get bloodshot eyes and strain-lines in his face. From time to time, he glanced out the window at the blue Packard, standing imperturably at the curb with its hidden cargo of murder.

As the early winter darkness settled over the section, he found himself tight-jawed, desperately assuring himself that it had to crack—that this kind of situation was, of all kinds, the one his unorthodox, murderously effective squad was solely capable of cracking. But ice began to grow in his heart as nothing but utter silence still came from the murderous devil who held the lovely little Barbara Solloway, as time passed, and passed. . . .

At four thirty, big Johnny Berthold hung up a phone and looked muddily at the Marquis. In a puzzled voice he said: "Hey, I just spoke to a certain party who says somebody *else* has been askin' around the last few days—the same question."

"What! Call him back. Tell him I'll pay a grand for the name of the guy that was asking!" But that came to nothing.

Once McGuire, himself nerve-tired and fretful, blurted in an aside to the Marquis: "This is what you get for letting down the bars to lice like Charlie Riskin. I hope you realize that."

The Marquis ground his teeth. Four o'clock slipped past, five, six—and the clawing realization that he might have thrown everything into a lead that was going to peter out began to sweat him.

A chance glance out the window and the realization that practically all the snow in the vicinity had melted away, gave him a fresh stab. He stepped quickly to the door—and felt warm air on his face. It was thawing. His reddened eyes flew to the rumble seat of the blue Packard and he licked his dry lips.

Then it broke, of course, as it had to break.

Al Hackett at a rear telephone suddenly yelled, "Screeno!" and jumped out of his seat.

As the Marquis and McGuire, a minute later rushed out with the penciled slip Hackett had handed them, the others, most of whom had ño idea of the heartbreaking tenseness of the situation began to sing: "Merry Christmas to you! Merry Christmas to you! Merry Christmas, dear teacher. . . ."

McGuire exploded as he saw the slip under the dashlight of the speeding car. "Artie Fisk! I know that little weasel. I sent him to the Island twice for the iron cure! He's a hoppy. If he knows anything, it's a cinch. . . ."

They swung up Ninth Avenue, shot through Hell's Kitchen, into the Fifties.

"Take it easy," the Marquis said. "Here! Turn here."

They shot round the corner from Ninth, slid to a stop before a row of drab, graystone-front houses, each identical with its neighbor. The Marquis was out of the car before it stopped, was halfway up the steps of the wrong house before he realized his error and ran down and up again to the doorway whose dingy numerals were on the slip in his hand. A toothless old hag, bald down the center of her head, was inside the dim-lit hallway, hanging a holly wreath in the grimy glass panel of the doorway.

She rasped: "Merry Ch—oh pshaw, a copper! Nuts."

"Where's Artie Fisk's room?"

"Third-floor rear. What's he done now?"

"Been playing Santa Claus."

The old woman rasped her throat and spat on the floor. "I told him that racket stunk," she said philosophically. "Hey—he's got a visitor right now."

"Yeah? Who?"

"Some doll from the Social Service."

The Marquis went up two flights, to the rear of the dank, dim-lighted hall, to where a door stood open eighteen inches.

". . . afraid we couldn't do that, Mr. Fisk. But bright and early tomorrow, you shall have. . . ."

A beery, pleading old voice broke in: "But please, miss—tomorrow I can't be here. Please, couldn't I have something tonight? Anything. I—miss, I'll be honest with you. I could get by. But I ain't never had a Christmas present give me in my life. That's on the level. I just wanna know how it feels."

There was a second's silence, then the hurried, choked voice of the girl said: "Why, you poor old man. I'll see that you—I'll do everything I possibly can to have your basket sent over tonight."

FOR just a second, it suppressed the Marquis' guard. For just a second, reason, sense, painfully taught cynicism gave way dizzily to a touch of mawkish, insane sentimentality that tangled, got in the way of his thinking muddily. Momentarily, he saw the old rat only as pitiful.

Raging, he banished it instantly. He was well down the hall, standing with his back turned, when the dark-uniformed, spectacled pale girl hurried out of Fisk's room and down the stairs. He swung back the minute she was below banister level, jumped for the door, caught the knob just as a key was attempting to turn in the lock, jammed it open ahead of him.

The rheumy-eyed, gray-haired warped gnome-like body of the shirt-sleeved old man went staggering backwards across the room, to slam into the opposite wall. The Marquis kicked the door closed behind him as he came in. "So, you louse. You never got a Christmas present in your life—except what you stole, eh? Stole playing Santa Claus, I mean."

The gnarled old man seemed to shrink inches. He crouched there, suspenders over his dirty underwear, his furtive little blue eyes numb on the Marquis.

"Come on," the Marquis snarled, "Spit it out. I know all about your lousy racket. And I also know what you saw last Sunday night."

The old man's Adam's apple bobbed in

his turkey neck. "Honest to God. . . ." he croaked.

"You saw that blonde babe knifed. Don't waste breath trying to tell me otherwise. Who did it? Who was the guy you saw kill her?"

The old man's hoarse voice choked: "I swear to God I dunno what you're . . . *no, don't! Please!*" He tried to dodge wildly as the Marquis jumped for him, caught him by the collar of his underwear and fairly lifted him from his feet.

The Marquis slapped him with a gloved hand, in the mouth. "Talk, you rat! I'll give you just three seconds to come out with it—then I'll beat hell out of you and send you over for another iron cure. Come on!"

The old man's hoarse voice choked: "I terror. He almost sobbed in desperation. "No, no—please, Marquis. I swear to. . . ."

The Marquis whipped a fist up and over into his face, knocked him staggering into a corner, stood over him, eyes blazing. "Well?" Then, suddenly another thought occurred to him. "Why can't you be here tomorrow? What'd you tell that jane that for? Eh? Answer me, you bag of bones. . . ." He bent over and grabbed again.

The old man almost went into hysterics of fear. "No, no," he squealed. "I—I'll tell you. Don't hit me again. . . ."

The Marquis yanked him to his feet. He was shaking like a leaf and there was almost madness of terror in his eyes. "I—yes, I was there. But I swear to God—I'd gone over by the church to take a—a smoke. I—I seen the girl fall out o' the car, seen him put her back in again, but I wasn't close enough to see who he was. I didn't wanta be. God help me if I aint telling you the truth, Marquis. I ducked my clothes and hotfooted it out o' there as fast as I could. I didn't see the guy." He swallowed so hard that it almost choked him. "But—but I think I know who it was."

"Yeah? Who?"

The old man swallowed desperately once more. "I—well I just got a message—ten minutes—five minutes ago—to blow town. I got a fifty-dollar note with it. Or else. It—it was a guy named **Charlie Riskin** sent the message. I got just one hour to get to Jersey. A—a bartender I know brought the message."

THAT should have been all there was to it—that, the swift muster, the careful closing in, and the short sharp capture of the deadly Riskin. Should have been and—by ten million miles—wasn't. The crazy soft, bathetic spot in the Marquis' armor turned it, sent the whole thing off at a tangent.

He slapped the sobbing old grifter back into the corner and said: "I guess you know enough not to talk about peeping to us. Go on—take it on the lam. Though I ought to jug you for grifting off that Social Service dame."

"I wasn't grifting! I wasn't! So help me, I—" His voice broke. "Oh—hell, you wouldn't get it if I told you. Skip it."

From the doorway, the Marquis snarled: "I suppose I should believe that gag about never getting a Christmas present, eh?"

The old man's chin came up and he blurted sobbingly: "Well, it's true! I never in my life. . . ."

"Baloney!" The Marquis slammed the door, piled down the stairs, ran back out to the car and shot grimly at McGuire: "All right—and save the wisecracks. Where does this Charlie Riskin live? Where's he staying?"

The redhead gasped. "By God! You mean he—at the Rochester apartment hotel. You mean Fisk saw *him*. . . ."

"He didn't see him, but Riskin evidently thinks he did. He just sent him a message for Artie to blow town or else—gave him an hour."

"Hey—he must be the one who was trying to locate Fisk along with us—the one Big Johnny. . . ."

"Yeah. We've got to get to him like lightning. Wait—I'll call the Agency." He turned and plunged into the corner drug store, hastily called the Agency and got Harry Derosier on the wire. "Bring three others and meet us a block south and a block west of the Rochester," he told him.

When he climbed back in the car, McGuire was twisted around, looking at the opposite corner. He sent the car shooting away even before he turned back. The Marquis followed his stare just in time to see a dark figure in a hard hat with-draw quickly around the edge of the building.

"There's the bartender that brought the message, I guess," McGuire said grimly as he whipped the car across the long block. "That surly louse, Coy. I swear I'm going to take Big Johnny and teach him a lesson when all this is over. . . ."

The Marquis almost choked as he clamped his lips shut, without saying the 'Wait a minute!' that had risen to his lips. He kept turned around, staring scowling-ly out the back window, as the redhead gunned the car across the long block. For a moment, he was absolutely foundering. He opened his mouth, closed it. Not till the long sweep had taken them to the cor-ner, till they had swung round it, did he snarl out hoarsely: "Stop a minute!"

That he would have turned aside from the blazingly urgency ordinarily, is ab-surd. It was the insane little softness, his queer perennial complex that completely deflated his grimness ever year, that tied him up in knots. And the incredible truth was that the broken old man, the pretty grifter, had somehow gotten to him with his whining about never having received a Christmas present. It was madness, fatuousness, futility—but somehow it had hold of his feverish mind like a burr. He raged at himself, cursed himself for a thousand kinds of fool, but it bore him down ruthlessly.

He said gratingly: "If that was Coy who brought him the message from Riskin, he must have seen us go in. If he figures out that Fisk stooled to us, he'll tip off Riskin and the old rat's life won't be worth a cent."

"So what? Since when do we wet-nurse rats? They take their chances."

"No, but he—" Even in the instant of fatuousness, the Marquis could not bring himself to put it into words. In-stead, he snapped open the door, said wildly, "Never mind that. You go on and meet the others. You can size up the situation and know what to do."

"Where in God's name are you going?"

"To pop that Coy in the can before he tips off Riskin. The old rat claimed he never had a Christmas present. "I'll give him one—his life. I'll be just a few min-utes behind you. Go on—get going!"

CHAPTER SIX

Nothing for Christmas

HE SWEPT the street anxiously as he swung back the block toward Ninth, but he saw no sign of the man in the bowl-er hat. That could mean that Coy was already at a phone somewhere—or would he jump to that without first bracing the old grifter to find out. . . .?

He was at least a hundred yards away when he saw the two figures—close to-gether—come quickly down the steps of the rooming house, swing for the corner of Ninth. There could be no possible doubt that the man behind was the hard-hatted Coy—and the one whom he herded in front of him was the gnarled little gnome, Fisk.

The Marquis swore crazily, broke in-stantly into a run. He snatched at his hip, filled his lungs—but the distance was too great even for a yell. He ran out into the gutter, to avoid the scattered pedestrians on the street, and the two were around the corner of Ninth before he could close up even a few yards on them. He raced on-ward, momentarily abandoning himself to extravagant worry about the worthless old grifter, though he was red-faced at the realization that he was doing it.

He burst round the corner—into the Christmas Eve crowd on Ninth Avenue—and his heart sank. Then he saw a blue-coat idling at the corner and grabbed him. "Two guys just came round the corner here—Harry Coy, the bartender and a lit-tle rat named. . . ."

"Artie Fisk. Yeah. I gave them the eye." The bluecoat craned his neck. "Look—there—down there—across the street—just getting into that cab—oops, there they go around the corner. . . ."

The Marquis charged out, fought through the crowd to get across the street. He ran a few steps, realized the futility of that and snatched open the door of another cab. "Get around that corner fast—after that Yellow ahead. Move, you imbecile!"

They spurted in pursuit, whirled round. The other hack was a block away and ducked southwards, almost in the instant that they straightened out.

"Come on," the Marquis raged, "or I'll

have your badge! Don't lose them. . . ."

The cabby took him seriously, trod down on the accelerator—and the dizzy chase went laddering down and across town. Sheer devil's luck kept the Yellow just far enough ahead so that it was impossible to do anything but hang on. They went down through Chelsea, down into Greenwich Village, the Yellow whipping around corners, always just a block or two ahead. The keyed-up cabby blurted brokenly: "—— —— it, that jobbie don't even know we're chasing him and yet he manages. . . ."

They whirled into the utterly quiet backwater of broken little Van Renesslaer Street—and the Yellow for an instant, at the curb ahead, was standing still. Two dark figures scuttled across the sidewalk, and into what seemed a garage, even as they came on, and the Yellow pulled again away from the curb.

The Marquis ground: "Go a few yards past where they got off and stop—hurry it up!"

He had just a glimpse, as they shot by, realized that the bartender had not taken the little squealer actually into the garage but that there was a door, green-painted at the side, presumably leading to apartments above.

He snapped at the cabby to wait, as he piled out, gun in one gloved hand, a set of picklocks in the other. He wasted no time in undue caution, had the door open—though silently—in seconds, and faced a long flight of steep steps to a landing.

He did not even test them, but they were solid, and his rubber-soled shoes took him up without sound to the miniature landing—and to an old-fashioned tall door that stood ajar a foot. Even as he reached it, lights went on inside the door and Coy's surly voice growled: "Go on, you stinking stoolpigeon—get in that back room—with my other guest!"

THE MARQUIS, in the very act of driving into the room, half-faltered. He was suddenly startled, questioning—and instantly silent. He slipped into the room hastily, on tiptoe, actually saw the back of the tall, wide-shouldered Coy as he stood in a doorway opposite, waving a gun at Fisk, invisible in a room behind.

"Get over against that wall," the bar-

tender snarled. "There—now stay there!"

There was just an instant when the Marquis could absorb the comfortably furnished and wine-carpeted apartment—and the tall wardrobe trunk standing open just inside the door. In that instant muddy, as he was, he moved like lightning, was crouched down behind the wardrobe trunk, out of sight of the craggy-faced Irishman, as the other turned and came back to close and bolt the door, and to throw down his hard hat on a couch.

And then with stunning suddenness, the evil little drama raced to its queer finale.

While the Marquis hesitated, trying to force understanding into his gasping brain, Coy was back at the door to the other room.

"I just had a hunch you might turn out to be a canary, you heel—and that the Marquis might catch up to you. I didn't think you could have been close enough to me to see me the other night, but I take no chances. Now you can hear me make a phone call."

There was a second's silence, as the Marquis slowly straightened, thunderstruck. Then a dial spun and, a moment later, Coy's cold, bitter voice said: "Let me speak to Mr. Hamlin. He's expecting the call. . . . Hello, Hamlin? You know who this is. All right, listen: I'm sending her back to you safe and sound. I've got her promise that you and she'll be married tonight—the old man can swing the license situation. What? What do I want? Why, nothing sweetheart. Just you be damned sure you get married tonight—that's all. And one more thing—don't expect your copper friend, Marquis, to do anything about this. He's heading like hell on the scent—only it's the wrong scent. And listen—did you find anything —a little token—in your car?"

There was a long silence, then, "No, not the picture. Something else. You didn't?" His voice was grim and puzzled. "All right, then I'll tell you what it is. Your old pal Boltby's body. He's dead, sure—killed in the middle of this little play. Get it? No? You will, chum, you will." The receiver was banged up.

To someone else, Coy said: "All right, baby. You better get this straight. Your dumb boy-friend doesn't seem to understand it yet and I don't want no mistake.

"You're going out of here without a hand laid on you. If anybody asks you —ever—what I look like, you're going to tell them I'm an Albino—red eyes, pale-blond hair. If any at time a miracle should occur and I get pinched and brought to you for identification, you're going to swear I look nothing like the guy who snatched you. And—you're going to marry that guy tonight. You're going to do all this, because the minute you miss, Mr. Hamlin burns in the electric chair.

"I'll let him do the explaining on that one, but believe this: He's my accomplice, legally, in this snatch. If for no other reason than that *he* gave the cops that Albino description of me. If anything happens, I'll have no trouble convincing them that he knew damned well different. And kidnaping is a felony and that fat rat Boltby was killed in the commission of—get it? Sure, we'll all burn together. That's right. You saw me carve him up in this very apartment, heard us arguing —and if you don't think that rap will land squarely around your boy-friend's neck, just ask him! He'll assure you it will— for reasons he may not care to disclose.

"And now, before you go, let me show you my opinion of stoolpigeons. Turn around, Artie, you stinking little squealer!"

"No, no," the old man shrilled frantically. "No—don't Harry, for God's sake. . . ."

"No, don't Harry," the Marquis said.

THE freakish, crashing end was worthy of the whole rocking nightmare. The Marquis got one quick flash of the spacious, yellow-and-periwinkle bedroom, the girl bound and gagged on one of the beds, the frantic old man with his gnarled hands aloft in one corner, Coy standing before a corner-fireplace.

For some reason, he underestimated, by a hair, the full explosive intensity of the Irishman. He could not quite change his picture of him as a surly bartender to that of slashing killer fast enough.

The craggy-faced Coy whirled, the black gun in his hand thundering flame and roar instantly. The Marquis fired, almost in the same split-second, but the murderer's bullet slammed into the middle of his thigh,

whipped one leg from under him and he slammed on his face. The freak was the Marquis' slug—it hit the killer's gun clangingly, drove it into the other's side, a red streak appeared on his craggy face, there was a sudden whine from the stone fireplace—and Artie Fisk in the opposite corner screamed, fell back in the corner, clutching his side.

The Marquis fired from the floor, as Coy leaped wildly aside, switching his gun from the numbed right hand to the left. He choked, "You son of a ——" as he fired wildly. The Marquis spun, to roll himself into the shelter of the door-jamb outside—but a throw rug at the threshold rolled under him on the polished floor, left him floundering, helpless on his back. The blazing-eyed Coy yelled, fired again and showered splinters in the Marquis' face, leaped backwards and fired again. The Marquis' shot punched out a window as he eeled frenziedly to get off his back. He couldn't. He tried to aim from there— and the last three things happened in exactly the same instant. The moaning old grifter, Fisk, suddenly pitched forward, unconscious, slamming into the back of the killer's ankles and throwing off his shot—the Marquis, firing from the incredible position let go a desperately, deliberately aimed cluster of three shots—and heavy hammering began on the door.

There was an instant of gray, stinking silence. Coy's eyes were burning holes. He stood in the center of the room, slowly lowered his gun. A little blood came from his open mouth, wandered down his chin as he fell ponderously, turning a little, and crashed to the floor.

The pounding began on the door again and the Marquis, half-sitting, was nursing his numbed leg by the time those outside got tired of yelling, "Open up! Police!" and hacked the door down with an axe, and bluecoats streamed into the apartment.

"Put up your— Who are you?" the leader roared at the Marquis. "Oh, oh— it's you, Marty. What in God's name? We were a block away in the prowler when it started being Fourth of July and . . . Good God!" as he reached the bedroom threshold.

"It's the end of a snatch," the Marquis told him. "Get to that phone and call this number and ask for Mr. Hamlin," and when the astounded sergeant had complied, "Tell him to get down here as fast as he knows how. Here—give me a hand up. Miss Barbara"—he spoke to the red-headed girl—"I know your story, so there's no use repeating it—till I say so."

"Well, hey now, Marty—wait! Where are you going?"

"To meet a guy. I'll be back in a minute. So I'm bleeding! What about it?"

H E WAS holding to a lamp-post at the corner, fifty yards away, when the cab bearing Hamlin slowed to turn. He waved him down, having stood off the attentions of the ambulance interne and the mob of uniformed men that seemed to have sprung up through the pavement around the garage-apartment.

One look at the wooden, blond youth's face—now pale as death—told him. He said grimly: "So you—" and stopped as he saw the white-haired Solloway in the cab behind him.

"It's all right," Hamlin said through tight teeth. "Mr. Solloway knows the works."

The Marquis eyed him in vague wonder. Then he said: "You figured what the racket was, eh?"

Hamlin swallowed. "Of course. He sucked me in to the kidnap, deliberately threw a murder into it, so he'd have me—with my record—nailed for a first-degree murder rap as accomplice. Then he figured to marry me to the Solloway money and dip into that, for as much as he wanted, for the rest of his life—millions, maybe. Well, I'll spike it. If you'll let me see Barbara for just a minute, I'm ready to go with you."

"Hell," the Marquis said, "that won't be necessary. Coy's dead. Miss Barbara isn't going to do any talking. You two do

the same and everything'll be all right."

"But—but good God—I'm liable as an accomplice to. . . ."

"Not unless I remember the Albino description you handed me. A hot one, eh? A few words in your mouth make you a killer or not. However, I don't seem to remember them, so—go on up and get the girl out of this mess. The only other guy who might talk has just had a painful lesson in not talking and I'll handle him. Go on—get her out of here. Merry Christmas."

He managed to hang on to the lamp post, till the pair had disappeared up the stairs through the green door and then the giddiness started to get him.

Presently he was in a hospital bed and there was bright sunshine outside the windows. The room was full of figures that presently became others of the Squad. McGuire said: "How's it, chief? Merry Christmas. Say, did we get in some licks at that Riskin when we took him. We laughed ourselves sick when we found out the joke you'd played on us—sending us on the wild-goose-chase while you grabbed all the glory."

The Marquis lay silent. "Is Coy dead?"

"Very dead. The Solloways are waiting outside, and that Hamlin, to see you when we go. They're all choked up with thinking you're a swell guy."

"See that there's some blank checks around. Did Artie Fisk come through?"

"Sure. He's two doors down the hall from you right now, with a slug in his armpit. I was just down there and the old louse was lyin' there cryin'. Can you beat that?"

"What for?"

"Claims he didn't get anything for Christmas."

The Marquis opened his mouth, closed it. "Well, send in the gelt."

As Osborne brought up his pistol, Crane threw the bottle with terrific force

Quiet Christmas Morning

By JOHNSTON McCULLEY

Patrolman Jake Osborne might have pounded pavements the rest of his life if Santa hadn't delivered a corpse to his beat!

A S HE turned off the broad avenue and went into the narrow side street, Patrolman Jake Osborne was yawning. Not because he was in need of sleep, but because the atmosphere of the district at the moment was conducive to yawns.

It was about ten in the morning on Christmas Day. Usually at this hour the avenue and side streets were teeming with feverish activity. But today it was different. The streets were almost deserted.

A few cars were drifting along at speeds that would give traffic officers no trouble. A few pedestrians trod the walks as if half asleep. Shops were closed, and most of them had shuttered windows.

Christmas Eve celebrations were over, the wild rush of buying last-minute gifts and presenting them was at an end for this year. People were indulging in the luxury of getting up late and relaxing while they contemplated the Christmas dinners most of them would enjoy later in the day.

Patrolman Jake Osborne, a middle-aged officer who had been on the Force since the age of twenty-two, was known to his superiors as an efficient policeman who took his duties seriously. His record was clean. But there was no brilliance in him. Whenever it came time to make promotions, he was never considered. He was like a piece of familiar furniture, useful and taken for granted.

Long ago, he had given up hope of being elevated in rank, unless when he grew older he was given a soft desk job at the precinct station. But he was satisfied with life.

He liked the Force. He had a wife who was a good housekeeper and an excellent cook. He had a daughter of fifteen and a namesake son of thirteen, and they were splendid kids—healthy, wholesome, polite, doing well in school. Life could be a lot worse, he thought.

His professional career had been uneventful. He cautioned roisterers at times, called an ambulance if anybody got hurt or became ill on the street, now and then arrested a quarrelsome drunk, and when he was on the night shift tried doors and at times found one unlocked and telephoned some shop owner to come down and lock up.

He had pulled gun from holster only once during all the years, and that had been to control three men he had arrested for fighting while he waited for the wagon. But he was always ready for an emergency. Religiously, he practiced at the police pistol range, and made good scores. And he worked out in the police gymnasium with as much enthusiasm as the youngsters.

WALKING slowly along the side street, Osborne came to Tony's Delicatessen, and found it open. Tony and his family lived in the rear, and Tony would open his door at any time day or night to make a sale. Several small bambinos who kicked out shoes with great regularity had something to do with that.

"Good mornin', Officer!" Tony greeted, cordially. "Merry Christmas!"

" 'Morning', Tony! Merry Christmas to you," Osborne said, as he came to a stop. "Did you have good Christmast trade?"

"Sell very much fancy grocery and wine and many turkey leg and wing. People spend this year."

"That's good! Your wife and kids well?" Osborne asked.

"All very well," Tony replied, his white teeth flashing in a smile. "Wife fat and healthy. Kids all right. I gotta present for you."

Tony stepped back into his shop and returned immediately with a package, which he handed to Osborne. The patrolman thanked him.

"Is bottle fine olives import from Italy," Tony explained. "Is also spiced orange peel and bottle good wine."

"Thanks, Tony. Let me leave the package with you until I go off duty, huh?"

"Sure!" Tony took the package back. "Will keep shop open and maybe somebody come buy. Quiet Christmas mornin'. Everybody sleep late except Officer Osborne and Tony."

"Quiet Christmas mornin' is right," Osborne agreed. "It's almost a dead morning."

That was when they heard the shots.

There were two shots ringing out on the crisp air and coming close together. The shooting seemed to have occurred near the corner, where there were some old two and three story buildings with shops on the ground floor and cheap lodgings above.

"Somebody shoot," Tony said.

Osborne already was on his way, feeling for his whistle with one hand and reaching for his holster with the other. Near the corner, there was nobody on the street. No heads popped out of windows and there were no shrill screams. The affair did not follow the usual pattern.

But Patrolman Jake Osborne knew gunfire when he heard it, and he knew there had been two shots somewhere near. One had sounded sharp and clear as if fired in the open air, and the other slightly muffled as if fired inside a building from a room where a window was partially open.

Osborne sprinted to the corner and gave a swift look around. Halfway down the block a couple of men were looking back, as if they had heard the shots. Osborne started toward them.

In one of the old buildings a door was pulled open at the top of a flight of steps leading up to the entrance. In the doorway appeared a man whose face was white. He started down the steps, clutching at his left breast, and Osborne could see blood dripping from his fingers.

Halfway down the steps, as Osborne started hurrying toward him, the man sagged and fell, to roll to the bottom and come to rest on the snow-covered walk. Osborne blew his whistle as he ran on. He knelt quickly beside the fallen man.

Then, Jake Osborne got the shock of his official life. The man dying on the walk was John Wenceley, an assistant district attorney.

Osborne knew him by sight, and his picture had been in the papers scores of times. He was known as a shrewd investigator, particularly in political matters and cases dealing with crooked corporations. His personal crusade against big-time crime had attracted nationwide attention.

John Wenceley's lips were moving, and Osborne bent and tried to catch the words. But the assistant district attorney was beyond coherent speech. His head rolled to one side, his eyes opened and became fixed. The public crusader was dead, murdered on Christmas morning, and the event would make the big headlines in the day's newspapers throughout the country.

Osborne's whistle had brought results. Windows were thrown open and heads popped out. Shrill voices asked questions. From down the street another policeman, a rookie assigned to Christmast Day duty to relieve some regular officer, came sprinting.

Some men came from across the street. Osborne looked at one he took to be calm and responsible.

"Phone Headquarters," Osborne directed. "Give the address and say Patrolman Osborne wants the homicide squad."

The man turned and crossed the street to hurry to a telephone. The rookie from the next beat ran up almost breathless.

"Take charge here," Osborne directed. "Keep everybody back until the squad arrives."

OSBORNE'S manner was calm, without the least trace of excitement. This was simply the work for which he had been trained. He could have remained beside the body of the assistant district attorney and waited and turned the case over to Homicide. But he had been taught to follow a hot trail whenever it was possible.

He got out his police Special and ran up the steps to the open door. Entering a dingy hallway, he came to an abrupt stop. A slattern of a landlady came from a room to face him. She was a fat woman who wore a dirty dress and had unkempt hair, and from her manner had celebrated Christmas Eve too well.

"What's wrong, Copper?" she asked in a hoarse voice.

"That's what I want to know. A man came out of here and dropped on the walk and died. He'd been shot. Didn't you hear any shooting in your place?"

"Heard somethin', but thought it was an auto backfirin'."

"Who occupies your rooms?"

"Riff-raff, mostly," the woman replied. "I don't know who goes or comes, and don't care as long as I get my rent."

"Hear any trouble—loud voices or quarreling or anything like that, a few minutes ago?"

"Them kind of sounds are regular around here," she replied. "It'd be funny to go through a day without hearin' loud voices and quarrelin'."

"I'll see you again later," Osborne hinted.

He had been glancing around the hallway and at the stairs leading to the floor above. The carpeting on the hall and the runner on the stairs were ragged and unbelievably dirty. But Osborne saw something that interested him—drops of blood on the stairs, showing where the dying assistant district attorney had come down from the floor above.

Osborne hurried up the stairs. Before he reached the top, a woman's shrill scream rang through the house. When he was in the upper hall, he saw doors opening and people emerging. They were in various stages of undress, most of them with bleary eyes and other evidences of a carouse.

"Where did that scream come from?" Osborne demanded.

Some of them, not relishing close association with any of the police force, darted back into their rooms and slammed their doors. One man pointed to a door on the opposite side of the hall. Osborne was looking at that door already. The blood-drop trail ran directly to it.

Gun held ready, he pounded on the door with his left fist, standing to one side so a stream of bullets fired through the thin door panel would not strike him.

"Open up!" he shouted. "This is the police!"

He got no answer. He turned the knob

with his left hand and kicked the door open. No volley came. Peering into the dingy room, he saw a man stretched face downward on the floor, a pool of blood around him, and a young woman crumpled in a corner of the room as if she had fainted there.

He heard a gasp behind him, and turned to find the landlady had followed him up the stairs.

"Tell your tenants to stay in their rooms," Osborne told her, "then come in here with me."

The landlady began shouting in a shrill voice. She followed Osborne into the room and closed the door. Osborne gripped the man on the floor by the shoulder and turned him halfway over to get a look at his face.

The landlady gave an exclamation of suprise. "Why, I know him, Copper," she said. "He's Flash Conroy, the big gambler."

Osborne knew him, too, and his history. Flash Conroy, as a young man, had been mixed in the rackets prevailing at the time. He had made and saved money, and now owned a couple of luxurious hide-away gambling houses where the take ran into thousands a night. And what was he doing here, dead on the floor of a dingy room in a cheap lodging house?

"He's dead," Osborne told the landlady. "Don't faint."

"It'd take more than one dead man to make me faint. How about the dame?"

Beckoning the landlady to follow, Osborne hurried to the young woman in the corner. He glanced at her face, felt of her pulse, raised the lid of one eye.

"Water," he told the landlady, nodding toward the old-fashioned bowl and pitcher on the wash stand in another corner of the room.

The landlady got the pitcher, waved Osborne away, and dashed water into the girl's face. The girl moaned and acted as if trying to lift her head.

"I know her," the landlady told Osborne. "Sure, I know that one! She's Smiley Crane's girl. Smiley is a small-time crook tryin' to be a big one."

"What's the girl doing here?" Osborne asked. "Whose room is this?"

"Why, it's Smiley Crane's."

The girl moaned again, and opened her eyes. Osborne nodded to the landlady, and they lifted her off the floor and propped her up in an easy chair.

"Oh . . . oh . . !" she was moaning.

"Snap out of it!" Osborne barked at her. "I've no time to lose. What happened here?"

"I—I came up to get Smiley Crane and go to breakfast with him. When I opened the door I saw . . . that man dead on the floor. I guess . . . I fainted."

Osborne looked straight at her. "What's your name?"

"Estelle Ramport. Everybody who knows Smiley knows me, too."

"Know the dead man on the floor?"

"I couldn't see his face."

"You just walked in, saw him like that, and fainted, huh?"

"That's right," she admitted. "It was terrible. It made me sick."

OSBORNE went to the door and opened it and looked out into the hall. A uniformed policeman was striding toward him.

"Homicide squad's come," he reported. "Inspector Benland was at Headquarters and came along. They're starting work in the street, where Wenceley died."

"You watch the hall," Osborne instructed. "I've got some work in here. Send the Inspector here when he comes up."

He closed the door and went back to Estelle Ramport.

"Now, young woman," he said, sternly, "you'll forget the fairy story you just told me, and tell me the truth, or I'll send you in and let you talk at Headquarters."

"What do you mean?" she demanded, with some show of indignation.

"You tried to pull a fake faint. Why?"

"What are you saying? A fake faint?"

"That's what I said. Knew it the moment I looked at you. When a person faints, the face turns almost pasty white. Your face was flushed. Your pulse was normal when I tried it. Your eye told me you hadn't fainted. You tell me the truth, and be quick about it, or in you go. How long have you been in this room?"

"Only a few minutes. I came in and saw the dead man—"

"Come in the front way?"

"Certainly."

"See a wounded man going out as you came in?"

"Why—why, no!"

"Then you didn't come in the front way a few minutes ago. I warned you not to lie to me. You stay right there a moment."

Osborne crossed to the window, which

was raised a few inches from the bottom. He tried it. It stuck a little and then could be opened. Osborne glanced at the window sill, at the roof of the adjoining building not more than six feet below the window ledge. He turned back to the girl.

"When did you see Smiley Crane last?" he demanded.

"Last night. We prowled around some, celebrating, then I went home. We had a breakfast date for this morning."

"Wasn't Crane in this room when you got here this morning?"

"No: I haven't seen him."

"Then who was it left this room through that window after you came in?"

"You're crazy!"

"Hand prints in the thick grimy dust on that window sill," Osborne pointed out. "Hand prints and footprints on the roof of the building below the window, showing where a man had jumped and lit on all fours. And he couldn't have reached up more than six feet and pulled the window down after he jumped. You tried to pull the window down all the way and it stuck. Right?"

"Why, you—you—"

"Did Smiley Crane go through that window after he'd done a little shooting around here?"

"I'm not talkin'," she said, her eyes narrowing.

"You know the dead man on the floor?"

"Everybody around here knows Flash Conroy, the big shot gambler."

"Oh, yes? A few minutes ago you told me you didn't know the dead man because you couldn't see his face. So how do you know he's Flash Conroy? You're a poor liar."

Osborne went to the door and pulled it open and called the policeman on guard there. He pointed at Estelle Ramport.

"Put the nippers on her, take her into the hall and turn her over to Homicide when they come upstairs," Osborne directed. "Tell Inspector Benland I'll explain later. Close the door after you take her out."

Osborne holstered his gun for the time being, went to the window and dropped to the roof of the adjoining building, landing on all fours as the man who had gone before him had done. He got up, drew his gun again, and followed a line of footprints in the thick greasy dust on the roof. They led around a chimney and to a trap door that stood open.

Osborne listened a moment, heard nothing, and went down a ladder to the hallway of the top floor of the building. All the doors were closed, and not a sound came from behind any of them. Greasy footprints were on the floor, and Osborne followed the trail.

DOWN the stairs to the second floor he went, and there stopped to listen again. Not a sound reached him. The light was dim in the hallway, but Osborne could see the footprints in the dust. They led to a closet, probably one that had been used for storage in better days.

Cautiously, Osborne opened the door with his left hand while his right held his pistol ready to fire. The closet was empty. But on the floor was an automatic, and a streak in the dust revealed that it had been thrown into the closet recently and had skidded halfway across to the wall.

Osborne took out a handkerchief, picked up the automatic carefully with it, wrapped the handkerchief around it to preserve fingerprints if any, and put the weapon into a pocket of his overcoat. Then he went on.

The trail led to a side stairway in the building, and down this Osborne followed it to a rear door of the next building. He knew that door. It was the rear exit of Tony's delicatessen store. On night duty, Osborne had tried that door hundreds of times to be sure it was securely locked.

It was not locked now. Possibly Tony had left it unlocked that morning when he had put out garbage for the collector. And Tony's wife and family, Osborne knew, would be at mass this Christmas morning.

Osborne opened the door cautiously and slipped inside, blinking to accustom his eyes to the semi-gloom. He could hear Tony talking and laughing with some customer in the front storeroom. He glanced around the room he had entered, a back room. And suddenly he froze. A voice had come from a corner:

"Stand still, Copper, or I'll let you have it!"

Osborne stood still, trying to judge from what spot that voice had come.

"Don't turn around! Don't move! I'm goin' out the door you just came in by, and I'll lock it on the outside. Make a bad move, and I'll shoot."

Osborne spoke. "You'll shoot with what? You left your automatic in the closet upstairs, didn't you?"

"Maybe I've got another, Copper. You

know how to find out. Just move, that's all. Only you won't live more'n a minute after findin' out."

Osborne felt the perspiration starting out on his face. He had no way of knowing whether the man behind him had another gun. He heard a move, and suddenly he dropped flat to the floor, turning his body as he did so, and brought up his police pistol.

Smiley Crane was standing against the wall near the door. He had no gun. In one hand he had an empty wine bottle, and in the other a short iron bar he had picked up somewhere in the room. Undoubtedly, he had been waiting for the customer in front to leave the shop, with the intention of slipping in, smashing Tony on the head, walking calmly out into the street and going away from the vicinity, to return later with some trumped-up alibi.

As Osborne brought up his pistol to cover him, Crane threw the bottle with terrific force. It ricocheted from Osborne's left shoulder, struck the wall and crashed, showering Osborne with broken glass. He fired, but too late. Smiley Crane had dashed past him and into the store.

Osborne got upon his feet and charged after the fleeing man.

"Stop him, Tony!" he yelled.

The customer had left the shop. Osborne rushed through the curtained doorway in time to see Smiley Crane rush upon the surprised Tony and smash him on the head with the iron bar. Then he dropped the bar, dashed through the door and into the street, and ran.

Tony was falling to the floor as Osborne ran past him.

When he rushed into the street, Crane was a quarter of a block away, running toward the avenue.

"Halt, or I'll fire!" Osborne shouted.

Smiley Crane bent forward and ran on. Osborne stopped, took careful aim, fired. Smiley Crane came to an abrupt stop, reeled, and fell back against the wall of a building, clutching his left shoulder with his right hand.

FEET pounded the frosty walk as Osborne, his breathing labored, charged down upon his man. Crane's face was white from the force of the bullet's blow. The wound was high in the left shoulder, as Osborne had wished it to be.

He pressed Crane against the wall, and handcuffs snapped.

"Come on, you rat!" Osborne growled at him. "You've done enough killin' for one day."

"I never killed anybody, I—"

"Shut up! You're under arrest and anything you say may be used against you—"

"I never killed—"

"I've got the gun you discarded, and your prints are probably on it. Ballistics will tell us whether the bullets in Flash Conroy or John Wenceley came from that automatic. We've got the nippers on that Estelle Ramport girl, too."

"She just happened to be in the room," Crane said.

"That's right interestin'," Osborne observed. "She told me she walked in and saw Flash Conroy dead, and didn't see you at all. We can make her sing."

Osborne was urging him along the street. A crowd had collected by this time, and patrolmen were busy keeping the curious ones moving.

Smiley Crane's shoulder was commencing to cause him agony. He bent his head and shuffled when he walked. Osborne gripped his right arm and made him quicken his stride.

"I tell you I didn't shoot anybody," Crane said, in low, tense tones, stopping frequently as he spoke to bite his lip because of the burning, shooting pains commencing to work in his wounded shoulder.

"Sing if you feel like it," Osborne told him. "I'll tell the Inspector what you said, and he can compare it with Estelle Ramport's story and others."

Smiley Crane decided to talk. "That assistant D. A., Wenceley," he said, "contacted Flash Conroy. Wencely was after the higher-ups in a big combine that's controllin' all the fancy gamblin' places in town—and some other towns. Flash let him know he'd talk if Wenceley would lay off him in return. Fact is, Flash wanted to get rid of the big shot and take over the job himself."

"I can understand that," Osborne said.

"They wanted to meet in secret. They picked Christmas mornin' because that'd be a good time, when people weren't stirrin' around much. They wanted a place to meet. Flash got hold of me and asked to use my room. Nobody would expect either Wenceley or Flash to be seen in a dump like that."

"Sounds reasonable," Osborne declared.

"Then Flash, who never played square in his life, got what he thought was a bright idea. He'd have Estelle there, and he'd make it look like Wenceley had gone there to meet Estelle."

"One of the oldest games in the world."

"Yeah, but it generally works. Witnesses would drop in, and Flash planned to threaten Wenceley with a scandal unless he walked the way Flash wanted him to. If that'd worked, Flash could have done as he pleased in this town, and Wenceley would lay off him."

"But it didn't work?" Osborne asked.

"I didn't like to see Estelle get mixed up in a thing like that. Anyhow, we went ahead with it. Wenceley came to the room and met Flash. I walked in with Estelle. Wencely got wise and started to leave, and Flash shot him. As he went on toward the door, Wenceley got out a gun and let Flash have it. Then he went into the hall, half dazed from his wounds I guess, and started for the stairs.

"You can guess that threw me into a panic. I had that automatic on me. Flash was dead on the door of my room. I knew the cops would be there in a few minutes, and didn't dare go out the front way. So I told Estelle to scream and pull that faintin' stunt when she knew the cops were near. And I jumped out the window and made a getaway, and she pulled the window down—"

"I know the rest, so spare your breath," Osborne said. "It can be learned easily enough if Wenceley and Flash Conroy shot each other, and your yarn and the girl's, when they wring it out of her, will explain why. And you'll go up the river, my lad, on several counts—packin' a gun for which you have no permit, helpin' work a badger game, and smashin' Tony on the head. I'm hopin' you didn't hurt him bad. If you did—!"

THEY had come to the spot where Wenceley had died. The body had been removed. Members of the homicide squad were all over the place. Osborne ushered Smiley Crane into the house, where Inspector Benland was winding up his investigation in the lower hall.

"Here's Smiley Crane, Inspector," Osborne reported. "He's told me his yarn, and it sounds good."

"Thanks, Osborne. We've made the girl sing, and we'll compare their yarns at Headquarters."

"I had to put a slug through his shoul-der. He'll have to be patched up."

"We'll handle him," Inspector Benland said. He nodded to one of his men.

"Guess I'd better get back on my beat," Osborne said. "I want to stop and see how Tony is. Crane smashed him on the head with an iron bar. That's somethin' else for him to answer for."

"He'll answer for plenty," Benland promised. "By the way, Osborne, I happen to know your record. Men like you don't make the newspapers often, but you're the backbone of the Force, the steady pavement pounders who go on year after year and keep the peace. And when an emergency comes, like this thing today, you step in and do what a policeman is supposed to do, without making any fuss."

"Thanks, Inspector," Osborne said.

"In your case, Osborne, you've been pounding the pavement for a long time. I'm right sure a man like you can be used in the precinct station. I'll recommend you be promoted to sergeant and given a desk job. That's all. Get back on your beat."

"Yes, sir."

Osborne hurried out of the house, went around the corner, and almost ran to Tony's shop. Somebody had called a doctor, and Tony was sitting in a chair breathing heavily, a bump on his head but otherwise all right. His wife and children had returned from mass, and were putting on a scene of excitement.

"Glad that rat didn't hurt you bad, Tony," Osborne told him. "I nabbed him. I'll drop in and see you later in the day. Got to get back on my beat now. I'll get my present when I come back."

He hurried to the nearest report box and explained at length to the precinct desk sergeant, who had been worrying because Osborne had missed a couple of reports. Then he returned to the avenue.

It was as deserted as it had been earlier. A few cars, a few pedestrians, that was all. Osborne stopped to chat with the man who operated a shoe shining stand on a corner in front of a barber shop.

"How's everything, Jim?" Osborne asked, after they had wished each other a "Merry Christmas."

"It's slow today, a quiet Christmas mornin'."

"Yeah," Osborne agreed. He smiled slightly as he strolled on down the street.

Regan glimpsed another man leaping toward him, and the gun slammed down on his head

MURDER ON SANTA CLAUS LANE

By WILLIAM G. BOGART

With a Blackout in Hollywood, Rookie Patrol Car Cop Johnny Regan Does Some X-Ray Work to See Through Crime!

"**B**IG BEN" Slattery was at the wheel of the police cruiser, and he steered the car deftly through the heavy traffic along Hollywood Boulevard. Johnny Regan, young and lean-looking, sat slumped in the seat beside him.

For six months now, ever since getting on the force, Regan had been riding the bus with Big Ben. Slattery was a big truck-horse of a guy, jovial and easy-going. He was well established on the Force, and he had shown Regan the ropes. They got along.

But tonight was different. For the past half hour Big Ben had been whistling "Holy Night" in an off key. Suddenly Johnny Regan blurted out:

"'It was the night before Christmas, and all through the house'... Aw, nuts!"

Big Ben looked across at him, his Irish blue eyes crinkling.

"What's the matter, kid?" he demanded. "Ain't you got that old Christmas spirit at all?"

"A fine thing it is," Regan grunted. "Tomorrow night Christmas Eve, and what do we have to do? Spend it riding around in this crate! They ought to give every cop in L. A. a night off."

"Sure," said Slattery. "And have every punk crook in town having the time of his life. I had off last year. You'll probably get off next—"

He broke off, cocked an ear as he heard the small group of young people singing on the next corner.

Slattery slowed the car, pulled toward the curb. Girls' voices were raised sweetly in a carol, and Big Ben's heavy face beamed. "Now, ain't that just swell—" he started.

"Aw," grunted Johnny Regan. "Come on." He waved his arm impatiently. "Look at things. No lights. Dimouts! Maybe even a blackout tomorrow night. And they used to call this Santa Claus Lane!"

But nothing Regan said could dim Ben Slattery's cheerfulness. Lights or no lights, he had the spirit, and he kept on humming:

Hark, the herald angels sing . . .

Their loud-speaker crackled and the voice of the dispatcher came crisply over the air:

"Car Two-nineteen, attention. An emergency call. A woman in distress. Car Two-nineteen . . ."

Johnny Regan's gray eyes brightened a trifle.

"Maybe she's a blond and needs help. Anything to relieve the monotony! Let's roll!"

TWO-NINETEEN was their car and their call. The address given by the dispatcher was not far. Ben Slattery tramped his brogan down on the gas and they were off.

Moments later they cut down the side street of small movie studios and rooming houses—Poverty Row, as it was known in the trade.

Ben Slattery flicked on the adjustable spotlight and searched house numbers. He slowed before a house half-way down the block, stopped, and pulled on the brake.

"All right, kid," he said. "Run in and see what the dame wants."

He leaned back, pushed his cap to the back of his shaggy head, and started to whistle "Holy Night" again.

Johnny Regan gave his partner a pained frown and slid out of the car. He hard-heeled up the walk, was just feeling around for the bell button when the outside door was jerked open.

"Oh, I'm so glad you're here!" a woman's voice said with relief.

She must have been waiting for him just inside the vestibule. A dim light glowed far back in the hallway, so that Regan could not get a good look at her features. But she appeared to be young, slim-built. Probably pretty.

He grinned in the half darkness.

"What's up, lady? We got a call—"

"My baby," she started, voice worried. "He's ill. I've got to get down to the corner drugstore for something and I haven't a phone."

"I guess we could run down there for you," Regan said.

"Oh, no," the woman said swiftly. "I'll have to go myself. It's a special prescription and I want to make certain that the druggist compounds it correctly. If you could just stay with Cecil a moment—"

She looked up at him, hopefully, then motioned to the open doorway behind her. Another light glowed dimly in there, a small night light of some sort. The woman turned and led the way.

"He's just fallen asleep again," she said. "If you'll just be very quiet. It will only take me a moment."

Johnny Regan saw the plainly furnished room, and the open doorway to the room beyond. The woman looked up at him again appealingly, and she wasn't bad to look at. Not bad at all.

"Just a moment, lady, until I tell my partner," Regan said, "then I'll be right back."

"Hurry," she pleaded.

He moved outside, went back to the car, was grinning when he met Ben Slattery's inquisitive eyes.

"She was," he announced.

"She was what?" Big Ben demanded.

"A blonde! Nice, too. Look, I got to mind her kid while she runs down to the corner a moment. The baby's sick, and she's got no one to leave it with."

..."What *is* this " Slattery growled. "A diaper service?"

"Now, listen," said Regan. "Only a moment, see? We've got to help her out."

A limping footstep sounded behind Johnny Regan, and he turned to recognize old Peter Kelsey, watchman at Acme Features, hobbling down the sidewalk. Pete was a nice old guy. Many a night in the quiet hours before dawn they stopped by to have a cup of coffee with him in his watchman's shack just inside the small studio grounds. Acme Features was one of the smaller Poverty Row outfits, and was located around the corner.

"THE leg bothering you again, Pete?" Regan asked with feeling, as the elderly man came limping up.

The watchman nodded. "I guess we're going to have rain for Christmas, looks like." He rubbed his thigh, smiling. "I can always tell."

From the open coupé window, Big Ben said:

"Come on, Pete. I'll give you a lift the rest of the way." He jerked his big thumb at Regan. "My partner's got to play nursemaid for a bit."

As Ben Slattery opened the door, Regan hurried back to the house. The police coupé was moving down the street as the blonde opened the front door again.

"Okay, lady," he said. "I'll wait here for you."

She nodded toward the car disappearing down the block. Regan noted that she had slipped on a light sports coat and beret.

"Isn't your partner waiting for you?" she asked.

"He's got to run an errand," Regan said truthfully. He hoped Ben would take his time, and that the blonde would be back before him. He thought it might be kind of nice talking to her for a while. She was the kind who could take your mind off Christmas, and the fact that tomorrow night you had to work.

"Be quiet now," she whispered. "Don't frighten Cecil." She hurried out then.

Johnny Regan tiptoed into the drably furnished living room, gingerly sat down on the edge of a chair. He took off his cap, then put it on again, feelish foolish. What the blazes did you do if a baby started bawling?

He started listening for the slightest sound t h a t would indicate the baby was waking up.

He found himself holding his breath, waiting. It occurred to him that it must be an awful strain to be a father. After a while he relaxed a little bit. No sound had come from the adjoining bedroom. Long quiet moments passed. Certainly the woman ought to be back.

He must have waited fifteen minutes, and was remembering that they had a box to pull shortly on another part of t h e i r beat when, disturbed now, Regan got up and tiptoed toward the bedroom. Maybe there was something wrong with the kid. Maybe it had—died!

The thought jerked him into swift action. Using his flashlight, Regan stepped to the doorway of the adjoining room, snapped the light briefly, stared around for the crib.

And he continued to stare.

The room contained a battered washstand, a portable clothes-closet, two straight-back chairs and a single metal bed. The bed was made up and covered with a cheap imitation chenille spread.

There was no crib and no baby.

"Well, I'll be a son!" Regan muttered and slammed toward t h e hall door.

What kind of a gag *was* this? Why had the blonde phoned?

In the vestibule he remembered. Phoned? What a dope he was! She had said she must run down to the druggist's because she *had* no phone. Then how in blazes had she phoned the police?

Reagan reached the sidewalk, was staring around looking for either the blonde or his partner, when he heard the shots. Two of them, flat and hard in the stillness of the long side street.

And they came from d o w n there around the corner where Big Ben had headed with old Pete Kelsey!

JOHNNY REGAN was running. It seemed he would never reach the end of the long block. He swung the corner, unloosening the flap of his holster as he ran. He saw his big partner's police coupé parked near the entrance drive of Acme Features. The door was hanging open.

Another shot sounded then, from inside the grounds of the movie company. Regan slammed through the open gates, caught the vaguest glimpse of a big form just swinging around the corner of one of the buildings. He started to raise his gun.

"It's me, kid!" his partner yelled at him. "Look out!" He waved an arm. "Over there! That back fence!"

Just as he called the warning, Big Ben jerked around in a peculiar manner. There was the crack of a shot. Regan thought, "The guy's hit!" He dashed forward, keeping close to the building wall in a low crouch.

Slattery was hit. His left arm dangled uselessly. But his big blocky features were grim as he jerked his chin toward the rear, gloomy lot.

"Fence back there," he explained tersely. "Two guys hiding. Watch it!"

"You wait here!" Regan said, and pushed past his big partner and slithered along the wall, covered by shadows of the night. He was thinking that it was his fault that Slattery was hurt. If he hadn't been such a sucker for a dame's attractive figure—

Grimly, with the .38 raised in his fist, he neared the end of the studio building, got the swift blur of a dodging form. A man was leaping toward the wire fence that enclosed the rear of the studio lot. Regan leaped out into the open and leveled the heavy weapon in his first.

A slug screamed inches from his head!

Regan threw himself down to the ground, whipped around, tried to locate source of that shot. He saw the second man going up over another section of the fence. He snapped a quick shot, looked back to see what had happened to the first fellow.

He was over the fence and gone.

Johnny Regan jerked to his feet and took out after the second man. Big Ben was running up behind him.

"I think you winged that second one, kid!" he was calling softly.

Then both of them heard the second man's feet slap the sidewalk beyond the wire fence and start running. Before Regan could even get a bead on the man, he had disappeared down a narrow alley that cut between two buildings beyond the studio lot.

Even as Johnny Regan raced toward the fence there was the sound of a car motor roaring into life. Then the motor sound was quickly fading in the distance.

Slattery drew up, swore vehemently. "Lost them!" he said.

Johnny Regan saw his friend's limply hanging arm.

"You need attention," he said. He started toward the studio building.

"Where's old Pete?" he asked abruptly. He had just remembered the watchman.

"He's all right," Ben Slattery said. His voice sounded suddenly tired. "Those two guys jumped us as we headed toward Pete's office. I shoved Pete on ahead of me inside the doorway. I might have banged his head or something. I was pretty rough about it."

JUST then, in the doorway of a small building just inside the gates, old Pete himself appeared. He seemed to limp more than usual, and he was rubbing his forehead.

"You all right, old-timer?" Slattery asked, more worried about the elderly watchman than he was about himself.

Pete nodded. "I've called the police. I guess I got a little dizzy. I banged my head on the wall when you pushed me inside the doorway." He looked at Big Ben Slattery and smiled, though he was still trembling. "Thank you for saving my life."

He reached out, touched the officer's arm gratefully, not noticing that the arm dangled strangely. Slattery involuntarily winced.

"Ben needs some attention," Regan said swiftly, and urged his friend toward the small office. At the same time, within the long block beyond the gates, police sirens were already sounding shrilly in the night.

Regan was thinking that this was a fine thing indeed. Old Pete had had to call the police, and here he, Johnny Regan, *was* the police! He had certainly bungled things in a fine way!

All because of a baby—a blond baby!

It was almost dawn when they were finally back at Headquarters and tall, alert-looking Lieutenant Anderson had checked out the men on his division. Johnny Regan and his partner, Ben Slattery, were the last ones there, remaining behind, and now the Lieutenant was saying:

"And so those crooks were apparently after some Christmas bonus money that Acme was holding on hand for various employees. It's too bad they got away."

That's the way he said it, quietly, but Regan knew what Lieutenant Anderson was thinking. A couple of patrol cops on the job and crooks had slipped right through their fingers. And all because he, Johnny Regan, had been taken in by a blonde.

Only by the slightest margin had his partner missed death. And Slattery had even risked that in order to warn Regan as he had run into the Acme grounds.

"You better take a few days leave, Slattery, until that arm is in shape," the lieutenant was saying.

The way he said it, Regan thought, was even including Slattery in a silent reprimand for letting the potential killers get away. And just recently around Headquarters they had been talking about how Slattery was in line for promotion. He deserved it. He had been some time on the force.

Lieutenant Anderson looked at Johnny Regan.

"We've checked with that rooming house," he said. "A woman rented a room there for a few days. She and her husband, the landlady said. They just moved out tonight. No forwarding address. They must have been spotting that Acme job, and the woman probably knew about that empty apartment right inside the ground floor, and worked that gag to get you and Slattery off the beat while the men pulled the job."

"Slattery's not to be blamed for this, sir," Regan blurted suddenly. "It was all my fault. I fell for that woman's story. I should have checked more closely."

"Regan probably saved my life, Lieutenant," Slattery said quickly. "If it hadn't been for him—"

THAT was like Slattery, Regan thought. Taking the blame equally. He wanted to protest, to explain that if it hadn't been for his own carelessness—

But Lieutenant Anderson finished: "So you'll have to handle that beat alone, tomorrow night, Regan. I'm too short of men to put anyone on with you, and I've promised these others that they could have Christmas Eve off."

"Yes sir," said Johnny Regan, and he and Slattery went out.

Regan had his own car parked down the street.

"I'll run you home, Ben," he said.

Both of them were pretty quiet on the ride through the early dawn, and both of them were thinking, especially Regan. This was the heck of a Christmas present to give his friend—a slug through the arm.

When Slattery climbed out, he said, grinning:

"Keep away from blondes, kid." But his face was pale. He had lost some blood.

"I'm sorry for what happen—" Regan began.

"Forget it," Slattery said.

And because there was nothing else to say, Johnny Regan drove off. He kept thinking about that blond woman, and the fact that she must be tied in with the crooks, and he was wondering how he could get a lead to the gang. . . .

He stopped around at the boarding house later that same morning. He talked to the landlady, but all she could tell was what she had told the police last night. The blond woman and her husband—"Goodness sakes, he might not even *be* her husband!"—had moved last night, leaving in a hurry, never even giving her a forwarding address for mail.

She took Regan in and showed him

the small flat where the baby was supposed to have been sleeping last night.

"Of course I didn't have the door locked," she explained. "So many people are always coming in and out to look at rooms. Why, that hussy even kept the key to my front door, and she must have known I was going out last night!"

"Yes," Regan said. "You sure can't trust some people."

He looked briefly but sharply around the small flat. He was wondering if there could be something that the blond might have left behind —some little thing that would give him a lead to the gang.

He found nothing.

Later, when he came on duty that night, his eyes burned from lack of sleep and he found himself in a tense, thoughtful mood. In the Department six months, and what a showing he had made! If he could only get a line on those crooks!

About eleven o'clock it started to rain. He recalled old Pete Kelsey's prediction last evening. He guessed he ought to stop around and see Pete a moment.

It was a dreary night. Lights were dimmed in shops. Last night he had been growling because they would have to work tonight—Christmas Eve. But it wouldn't have been so bad with jovial Ben Slattery in the car. Now it was like a hearse!

Regan steered the police coupé down the long block leading to the Acme Studio. The rain kept coming down. He was midway in the block when the blackout sirens sounded. The weird, banshee wails shivered through the dismal night.

REGAN watched to see if there were any cars moving in the block. All traffic except police and fire department cars was supposed to pull to the curb and park during an air raid warning. There had been several to date, here on the Coast.

But Regan saw no traffic moving within the block. It was deserted.

Or was it?

He was nearing the corner, driving slowly because of the suddenly blacked-out street lights, when he noted the sedan parked in gloom at the curb. He thought he detected the movement of someone behind the wheel. A girl!

Johnny Regan slowed as he passed, tried to get a closer look at the woman. Reflection of his own lighted headlamps gave him a partial glimpse of a face that was swiftly turned away from him.

Funny! He thought of that blond dame last night. He could have sworn—

A hunch told him to keep on driving, not stopping, not letting on that he had seen anyone in the car. Because he was suddenly thinking of old Pete Kelsey, and that Pete would be on duty at the Acme Studio just around the next corner. Could that woman parked there in the darkened sedan be a lookout for the gang?

Regan didn't turn at the corner. Instead, he rolled down another block, gathering speed in the darkness, cut around the square and headed back to the movie lot. Leaving the car parked in blackness in a nearby alley, he hurried toward the studio gates.

He saw an air-raid warden just disappearing down the block in the darkness. He was tempted to hail the man, then decided against it. He had pulled a boner last night. Perhaps his uneasiness now was just imagination.

He noted that old Pete had the studio entrance gates locked, as they should be. Regan moved along the fence in the utter blackout darkness, located a spot alongside one of the buildings just inside the high fence, then started climbing over. He dropped lightly to the ground inside.

Pete's office was in darkness. But that was as it should be, too. The watchman had naturally closed the blackout curtains.

Regan hurried up to the door, started to reach for the knob, then gave a start as he saw the door partway open. And no light came from inside at all!

He hurried across the threshold, had taken two or three steps when he almost stumbled headlong over the limp form lying on the floor. He dropped to his knees as he heard the man's groan in the darkness.

"Pete!"

The old man mumbled something. Regan bent close.

"It's Regan, the cop," he said. "Tell me, Pete!"

The old man's words were faint.

"They shot me—chest," he said. He coughed, and Regan didn't like the sound of that cough. "I'm done for, Regan. There's nothing you can do. But try—get them—three men—guns—"

Johnny Regan tried to prod the information out of the old man. He caught the words:

"Office—there—"

The main office, that would be it. The watchman was trying to tell him that the gunmen were in the main office of the studio, just across the lot!

"Pete!" Regan urged. "You're going to be all right. I'll be right back."

THE old fellow was trying to say something. He held to Johnny Regan's arms, and Regan heard the faint words:

"I bought lights—other Christmas tree. Thought they might let me—"

Then, suddenly, his aged body went limp in Regan's arms. The officer felt for a pulse. There was none. Old Pete was dead!

Grimly, Johnny Regan whipped to his feet, unholstered his gun and spun toward the doorway. In a way, the blackout aided him. He moved swiftly across the dark area between the buildings, positive that no one watching from the main office could spot him.

He realized that the gunmen had tried a daring scheme. Almost trapped last night, they would hardly return tonight. That's the way the police would figure. That's the way *they* figured the police would figure. And so they had come back!

Pay-day was the day after Christmas here at Acme. That bonus money was probably still in the company safe.

Regan thought these things as he moved soundlessly toward the building. In the darkness, another dark blot of darkness took form between

his eyes. The main office door—open! He approached it.

And just as he was two feet away, a man's figure appeared in that doorway. The fellow spotted the cop, dived back, kicked the door shut as he called a warning to someone within.

Johnny Regan hit the door and crashed it open before it could be locked. He fired instantly and saw a man drop, knew he was dead even before he dropped on his knees beside him.

He caught the barest glimpse of another man leaping toward him, then something slammed down on his head, the gun in the man's hand. He pitched forward, hit the floor, slid, gained his feet and whirled. His gun had fallen and someone was hurtling toward him in the gloom, now that there was no flashlight. Two forms, because he could hear the men's forced breathing.

Regan crashed into one man, and with a blur of movement knocked the fellow's gun hand aside, grasped the man's wrist, twisted until there was a gasp of pain. The weapon clattered to the floor.

The second man seized him from behind.

Regan hunched forward, tried to fling the man over his shoulders. But the fellow hung on. The patrolman twisted, slammed a fist into the man's face. He broke free, dived aside and crashed into a wall. His hand slid along the wall and touched a row of light switches. He flicked one on.

Light flooded the room. One man was leaping toward him. The other was down on the floor, searching around for his gun. Johnny Regan saw his own gun, flung himself down in a dive and clawed out for the weapon.

But the one crook had reached his own gun first.

"Don't move!" he rapped out at Regan.

The gun in the man's fist covered him steadily. Regan climbed slowly to his feet, watching the dark-haired man's heavy, menacing features.

"Get his flashlight," the man covering the cop said.

The second man behind Regan moved close, frisked the officer, and stood back.

"All right," the man with the gun snapped. "Turn off that light. Move!"

Regan edged backward toward the light switches located on the wall.

"Use that flashlight and keep it shielded!" the gunman said to his partner. "These other lights on here might bring a raft of cops!"

JOHNNY REGAN'S hand went up to the wall switches. He turned slightly to look at them. Something old Pete had said as he was dying flashed through his mind. There was a little lettered metal plate on the wall that made him remember.

He flicked the switch, found himself caught in the beam of the flashlight. The man with the gun came close to him and prodded him across the room. They moved through a doorway.

Regan saw that they had opened another door so that it shielded the office safe, which was open. The door was opened in such a way that, Johnny Regan realized, not even the light of the flashlight could ever be seen from outside.

"Aren't you going to give this guy a slug?" the man holding the flashlight demanded.

"Wait, you chump!" snapped the man who was moving toward the safe. He handed the gun over to his partner. "Wait until we're finished here," he said. "Then."

He bent down, continued rifling the drawers of the open safe. He dumped things into a sack that he had rested on the office floor. Regan was held covered by the light and the gun in the second man's hand.

He knew what was coming. The instant they were finished, and ready to scram, he got a slug. They had already murdered the watchman. A cop killing would make the rap no worse.

Regan's eyes glittered. There was nothing he could do. Nothing to do but die! If only someone—

He heard it then, the shrill whine of a police siren. The two men heard it, too, and the man bent down in front of the open safe came to his feet with a snarl.

"Douse that light!" he yelled automatically, obviously forgetting their captive.

As the light flicked out, Johnny Regan dived. He dived into the man who had been holding the gun, twisted it free of the man's frantic grasp, reversed it in his fist and fired. It was all done in a breathless instant of time.

The man screamed, swayed against Regan.

The officer shoved him aside, heard him crash down to the floor. But Johnny Regan was leaping after the other fellow, trailing the sounds of the man's thudding feet toward the front office door.

The man dived through, straight into the glare of the flashlights and the guns held by police converging on the doorway.

"He's a killer!" Regan yelled, as he saw a heavy gun barrel rap down across the escaping man's head.

That's all Regan waited to see, and then he kept running. He saw the sedan that was moving slowly past in the street outside. He fired a shot overhead and the girl at the wheel drew up in sheer horror, probably figuring the shot was fired directly at her.

Regan pulled her from behind the wheel, held her arm. She was the blonde from the rooming house.

"You and I, lady, are going to have a little talk about Cecil," Regan said grimly. "Remember?"

And as they passed through the entrance gates, rejoining the police who were gathered there, Johnny Regan looked at the two small treelike shrubs that were brightly illuminated with colored Christmas tree lights.

THE air raid warden was there too. "So I saw these lights," he was saying excitedly, "and hurried over here to complain to the night watchman, and found him in there—dead!"

"Old Pete tried to tell me as he was dying," Johnny Regan added quietly. "He said something about buying lights for his trees. Each year he used to light them up here, but this year he was worried because the dim-out rules might not allow it. He was telling Slattery and me about it one night."

"You mean, you managed to turn *on* these tree lights?" someone asked.

Regan nodded. "When they ordered me to turn off the lights inside the office, I saw the lettered plate for the switch that controlled the gate entrance lights. I took a chance that old Pete had hooked his Christmas tree lights up on that circuit. I snapped it on as I shut the other lights off."

The block warden was saying they had better get the lights off. The police were loading a wounded killer and two dead ones into a car. Regan was still holding the woman.

He pushed her toward one of the officers.

"Take care of her a moment, will you?" he said. "I want to call up Slattery and tell him I've got it all straightened out."

"You got what straightened out?"

"Blond trouble," said Johnny Regan grimly.

IN HIS ANTHOLOGY OF STORIES from *Black Mask, The Hard-Boiled Omnibus* (Simon & Schuster, 1946), Joseph T. Shaw, the magazine's former editor, sought to explain what made the *Black Mask* tales of the late '20s so different. He was certainly in a position to know; it was on his watch that the hard-boiled detective had been born.

Wrote Shaw:

> The formula or pattern emphasizes character and the problems inherent in human behavior over crime solution. In other words, in this new pattern, character conflict is the main theme; the ensuing crime, or its threat, is incidental...
>
> Such distinctive treatment comprises a hard, brittle style – which Raymond Chandler, one of its most brilliant exponents, declares belongs to everybody and to no one – a full employment of the functions of dialogue, and authenticity in characterization and action. To this may be added a very fast tempo...

By the time the pioneering editor Shaw penned those words, the great days of the hard-boiled detective could be glimpsed in America's rear-view mirror. Although there would be, and still are, notable exceptions, the golden age of hard-boiled writing lasted from the late '20s to the beginning of America's involvement in World War II. The tough, cynical stories in publications like *Dime Detective* and *Black Mask* gradually softened up after that, as a we're-all-in-this-together wartime mentality swept across the USA. The end of the global fighting saw a new outburst of teeth-gritting, gun-toting hard guys – but, as noted in the introduction, Mike Hammer was a fundamentally different character than Philip Marlowe, or even Marty Marquis.

You may notice differences of tone and approach among the stories here. And, while the tales do span a couple of decades (not counting the new Dan Turner adventure), the dissimilarities have more to do with the kinds of pulps in which they originally appeared.

"Crooked Charity" (1929), for instance, the oldest in this anthology, came from a sub-genre of magazines known to aficionados as "gang pulps," As John Locke points out in his introduction to *If She Only Had A Machine Gun* by Richard Credicott (Off-Trail Publications, 2011), publisher Harold Hersey created the gang pulps as a reflection of the times: "Prohibition had entered its twilight years, with the consequence of the law in creating new empires of racketeers and gangsters, combined with its all too obvious failure to curb alcohol consumption, the subject of considerable public discussion. Hersey's timing proved sound; the gang pulps were immediate hits."

On the other hand, 1943's "Murder on Santa Claus Lane" originally appeared in the pulp *G-Men Detective,* which had come along in the '30s (as simply *G-Men*) to capitalize on the public's fascination with J. Edgar Hoover and his FBI boys and their war against the country's criminal element, a group more or less glorified in the gang mags of an earlier time.

Regardless of the slant, however, all of these tough tales are bound together by their unlikely unfolding around the annual celebration of Christ's birth, a time for warmth and remembrance and wonder. It's in exactly that spirit that we've invited this bunch of tough guys and their blood-soaked stories to the holiday festivities.

Thanks for inviting them in.

www.ingramcontent.com/pod-product-compliance
Lightning Source LLC
Chambersburg PA
CBHW080831250626
47160CB00008B/2902